ANARC

This book is written in British English.

Copyright © 2021 by Jan Foster

Published by So Simple Published Media
First edition February 2022

Cover Design
© J. L. Wilson Designs | https://jlwilsondesigns.com

Paperback ISBN-13: 978-1-9163408-8-6
E-Book ISBN-13: 978-1-9163408-7-9

www.escapeintoatale.com

Anarchic Destiny

By Jan Foster

THE NATURAE SERIES

JAN FOSTER

CHAPTER ONE

The unannounced visitor

Chester, July 11th 1553

A tickle of the memory of his death caused Henry to squint against the evening sunlight at the stranger on the doorstep. Little else about him looked familiar, or proper, Henry thought. The old man sagged into the door frame as if he needed propping up. He hadn't even bothered to hide his bald head with a wig and yet he had banged upon the front door, so wasn't a tradesman or messenger. Henry's eyes roamed down the shabby travelling clothes, past the dust-fringed hat he held loosely in thin fingers, to boots which had seen many better days. Henry frowned, his gaze returning to the man's hairless head as he reached beyond his ever-present hunger to try to place him.

"Is Prioress... sorry, *Mistress,* Grosvenor in?" Melodious and deep, the fellow's voice jolted Henry out of his frantic scrabbling through his memories of the last thirty-some years. He shook his head silently, for words didn't come easily any more. Henry's eyes narrowed on the grey face as it fell. As if weights pulled it down, the visitor's arm dropped from the door frame, then he took a pace backwards.

After a moment of studying one another, the man said, "You look well, Fitz." His thin lips twitched up on one side. "I take it the church has been taking care of its own?"

"Where do I know you from?" Henry asked bluntly. No-one called him Fitz now. In this house, he was Henry as there were no other Henry's to be confused with. His captors wanted him to remember his namesake and father, Henry VIII. The last person to call him Fitz, short for Fitzroy, was his dearest friend, Henry Howard, who died some six years ago and whom he hadn't seen since being turned.

The man's smile dropped. "I thought you might remember me? Although you were in pain, I suppose."

Henry's lips tightened as he finally placed him. He said, quite carefully, as the memory was still forming, "I think I was trying to die at the time and the room was very dark." Henry's brows began knitting together as he considered the change since last he saw the bald man. Delirious with fever then, Henry had assumed he was one of Norfolk's priests, or perhaps a Benedictine monk.

Now robed himself in the simple dark habit - not by virtue of having taken vows but because that was all the clothing his jailers supplied him with - Henry tore his eyes away. He stared at the stone step, his skin crawling even after these many years of the pretence which had been forced upon him.

Fuzzy images of his re-birth, tainted as if he saw them through a grubby glass, seeped unwelcome into his mind. Seeing this traveller again reminded him of the subterfuge by which they brought him to Chester, instead of where his body was supposedly laid to rest surrounded by glory in Norfolk. Henry swallowed the bitterness, along with the cloying scent of fresh pine coffin which he could almost taste in the back of his throat. Having endured days of bumping blindly down the rough roads, half dead yet not alive in the locked box of a pauper, a fear of confined spaces lingered ever since. He was still trapped, a prisoner by virtue of his birth and as yet unfulfilled destiny.

"You look older," Henry said, more to fill the silence than because he intended to be rude, and the man's stare shamed him.

"And you still look like the pale-faced seventeen-year-old ginger I recall. That was the price you paid. I made no such bargain for my soul." The visitor's jaw tightened. "When will Mistress Grosvenor return? It draws late and I must speak with her before I find a place to rest."

Beyond the man's shoulder, Henry saw a brown nag, puffs of breath still gusting furiously into the air. Sweaty flanks crusted with dust showed she had been ridden hard. No wonder the monk looked exhausted.

In the passageway behind him Henry smelled his guard, Taylor, and knew he was watching. His hackles rose. Although allowed to roam the house and garden freely, Henry was not supposed to answer the door. But he had. Now, Henry's curiosity was piqued by the old monk's arrival decades afterward. "I can pass on a message to her, if you would like? Or you could wait." The man stared at him with a coolness to his brown eyes. Henry shrugged, "Or come back later."

Frowning after glancing at his horse, the traveller sighed. "Tell her, Maister Jeffries, as I was when I knew her, passed by."

Henry frowned. He could see the man was almost bursting with a need to admit something further. Nobody rides that hard without due cause. "And?"

Jeffries peered at him, wrinkling briefly as he searched Henry's stare, then he straightened himself. His jaw twitched, the tip of his tongue poking out briefly as it rolled around. The skin on Jeffries' face took on a more usual, pinker pallor, as if merely rehearsing the words in his head, then saying them revived his flagging energy. "Tell her... tell her she has lost. I could not save Edward." A glint in his eyes suggested pride, even though he spoke of the death of the King. "His soul is safe. He would not be turned - to either vampire or Catholic persuasion."

Henry frowned. Then Jeffries' broad smile proclaimed a victory which did not meet his serious eyes. "Say to her, that he named his Protestant successor, and the Council ratified it. Finally."

Henry grabbed the flaps of the Jeffries' jacket and hauled him across the threshold. Still grinning as he tumbled against the wall behind the door, Jeffries' eyes glittered with triumph.

"Who?" Henry spat out as he wheeled around to face him.

The old monk said, "Lady. Jane. Grey." Then his lips pursed, daring Henry.

Henry's hand clenched into a fist in the fabric, his knuckles touching Jeffries' chin as he held him up. Jeffries did not squirm against him, his very calmness in the face of violence surprising Henry into restraint. A gentleman did not resort to violence. A vampire might, but an inner voice of caution reminded him of a debt. Even though Henry Fitzroy had chosen the path of a revenant, he wrestled with what he considered his baser nature. As he glared at Jeffries, his logical mind made the case for releasing one of the few attendants who, he remembered more clearly now, had genuinely helped when he fell suddenly, life-threateningly, ill. His current behaviour was not chivalrous; his father would never have publicly acted with brutality, and above all, Henry still held himself against his father's regard.

Henry dropped his clutch on Jeffries, turning his head away so that he might not see the disappointment flooding his features. Much as he objected to the manner in which he found out about the death of his half-brother, he objected more to the news that Edward still refused to even acknowledge him. Although they had never met, Edward knew of Henry's continued existence in the shadows of the countryside. King Edward had, from the age of nine, ruled with the full knowledge that there was a male Tudor successor. A man who, in life at least, was groomed to take the reins in the event of Edward never having been born, or, if Edward should fail to produce his own heir.

That was his purpose, Henry had been told. The very reason he had agreed to live in perpetuity. He, Henry Fitzroy, eldest son of Henry VIII, formerly Duke of Richmond and Somerset, was destined to be a king. He had been promised the throne in the event of no legitimate male heir. Promised by highly placed Privy Counsellors, Bishops and, by implication, his father.

Henry growled, clamping his incisors together and searched the flagstones for answers. If what Jeffries reported was true, Edward, on his deathbed, had overruled even their own father's written wish for Mary to succeed to the throne. Henry had suspected that Edward's faith would put them at odds, but the Prioress assured him that matters were in hand regardless. England would not stomach a Queen when there was a male heir. Him.

But, an unknown Protestant girl had been chosen after all, and would sit as Queen instead. After all these years, all the Church's platitudes, and all of his obedience in hiding. It was for nothing. There should have been a son of Henry wearing the English crown, backed by the Catholic Church. In perpetuity.

But not now. After seventeen years of waiting, he would not be king after all.

Henry spun about on his heel and stomped down the passage. Taylor, today's guard on duty, stood silent in the dining hall doorway, his fat face passively watchful but his hand resting on the sword by his side. His head merely turned as Henry reached the pantry. With the last of his strength, he yanked on the chain looping between the latch and the metal eye on the frame. The chain broke and fell to the floorboards with a heavy chink. With the door freed, he grabbed the jug on the top shelf, dropping the weighted linen covering to the floor, then gulped the blood straight from the vessel. Although cooled since this morning's lettings, comforting red richness coursed through him. Through to his fingertips, the vitality warmed, crystallising his mind and his every sense heightened.

The smell of the meadows and medicinal herbs approached him. Henry kept staring at the shelves, flexing his fingers after replacing the empty jug. He felt a hand on his shoulder but held back his growl. Few would dare to touch him, but Jeffries clearly held no fear. The monk knew what he was, even though their plan to make Henry a vampire was not a decision which the witch had endorsed. He sagged against the pantry door, lost.

As his mind quietened, the man remained by his side - breathing in and out great whooshes of scented air over him. Not particularly enjoying the sensation of being calmed thus, Henry spat out, "You have relished bringing this news, Maister."

Jeffries met his eyes and calmly said, "It is never easy to be the one to point out how powerless someone now is, but in this situation, I am glad of it, yes. Enjoyed the telling of it..." He paused, as they both knew that there had been satisfaction in his voice when he told Henry. "There is no easy learning of this matter for one such as yourself."

"Typical of a witch."

Jeffries cocked his head. "How so? Are you that experienced with my kind that you would know?"

Henry's mouth twisted. "I know witches are as like to switch allegiances as the course of the wind slips around tree trunks. At least vampires remain steadfast to who they serve."

"And who do you serve, Master Fitzroy? Because from where I stand, you are now free to be whomever you want to be?"

Henry frowned. "Who I am, you mean?"

Jeffries nodded, raising an eyebrow at Henry. "With Norfolk imprisoned, I have few doubts that Northumberland will consolidate his powers and behead him without delay. Thus, there seems little hope that you could ever fulfil your purpose as planned, nor his."

Henry's hand tightened on the door frame. Although it was some years since his most well-connected patron had last contacted him from the Tower of London, he kept faith that some day, the Duke of Norfolk would be free and make good on his promise. For most of his teenage life, ever since Henry's godfather Wolsey had fallen out of favour, the harsh Thomas Howard had worked for both of their interests. He had been as much of a father figure to him as Henry VIII himself. Henry remembered, without remorse, that he was technically married to the Duke's daughter. 'Dying' left his wife Mary in somewhat of a limbo, he supposed. Henry was unconcerned by her fate, having only met her a few times and having never consummated their marriage, despite what appearances suggested.

"There will never again be a Catholic on the throne." Placing his hand on Henry's forearm, Jeffries said, "Perhaps it is time you accepted that fact and moved on with your very long life."

Henry swallowed down a rebuke, drew himself up tall, and pushed past him in the corridor. Only the recollection of a generosity, a kindness which Jeffries had shown both then and now, kept him from lashing out. During the fervent, whispered discussions about his soul by the procession of spiritually accomplished men traipsing through his bedchamber, only Jeffries had breathed his magic into him at precisely the point of his passing. There had been none of the ecstasy which most vampires were born of, only that knife edge of agony and relief. Jeffries' breath made that deadly transition easier, Henry knew now. The remnants of his witch strength and compassion temporarily quietening his mind as the change had overtaken him.

"I will pass your message on, Maister Jeffries," he said over his shoulder, then opened the front door. "I think you ought to get back on that nag of yours."

Jeffries bowed his head as he glided towards the threshold. He paused as he reached Henry, looking up to meet his dark gaze. "When you were turned, remember that nothing seemed quite what it was. Remember, that your eyes were cleared to what should have been an array of opportunities and possibilities. That it was only the guidance of those around you who suggested the path before you. But you were, in essence, reborn. Who you were at that point mattered not, but who you would become was placed in the hands of others." Jeffries drew in a breath, then his voice grew stern. "You now have a choice, as all men do when they are liberated. To grow into who you want to be, not what others expected you to become."

Henry's brows knitted together, and he glanced down the corridor to where the pantry door was still ajar. Jeffries squeezed his arm briefly, then bowed his head as he left. Henry considered running after him, but held himself back. He had no quarrel with Jeffries, he knew, although the healer's words struck deeper than Henry would have liked. His anger at the situation burned his gullet - not even the blood or well-meant advice calmed that.

As he closed the door behind Jeffries, Henry turned to see his vampire guard looking. Then Taylor's rotund belly started shaking with laughter. Henry watched the mocking overtake his jowls and before he could check himself, Henry lunged towards him. His hands grasped the saggy folds of Taylor's neck, his fingers squeezing the airway without mercy. Such was the speed of his attack, the guard was pushed back into the larder frame, banging the door open as his head hit the wood. Locked together, they fell in an ungainly heap. Henry sat astride his victim with thunder in his eyes.

"Laugh at me, would you?" Henry snarled as the guard's face flushed. His mouth fell open as Taylor struggled to gasp, yellowed incisors useless against the force of Henry's aggression. Chubby hands sought to grab at clamping arms, but Henry was strong, fuelled by decades of misery and captivity. Henry leant down on his grip, breaking the airway as efficiently as a hunter would its prey, then twisted Taylor's head hard around to snap the spine.

It was not enough though. The only way to be sure Taylor would not recover was to remove his head completely.

Henry leaned back and unsheathed the sword from Taylor's belt. Still sat upon him, with one hand on the hilt and the other on the blade, he positioned the metal underneath the guard's chin and pushed down. Taylor's eyes blinked rapidly as he fought to heal the severed nerves in his neck before…

The blade sliced Henry's palm but Henry no longer felt pain now, as humans did. He did not smile as the head rolled to the side once detached with a final pressure on the vertebra, but neither did he say a prayer. Like him, the vampire had given away his soul in return for immortality. Now, both of them were liberated.

The blood dripping from his wrist distracted him momentarily, and he lifted his hand high over the corpse. A thin, bright red line fell through the air onto the tunic between his legs, without pulse but running freely as poured ink. Then Henry grinned.

He was now free to be who he was - not only who he was meant to be. He licked his wound, tasting the power within his blood before the sides of the cut knitted together and sealed.

He should be both. A vampire and a king.

A king could kill on a whim. His own true father had, after all, with many who stood in his way. A king held absolute power to manipulate all around him. Choose between their life or death, as a vampire could. A vampire king with the Catholic Church behind him would rule for eternity. That vampire was him, and now he was free to step out from the shadows and take what was rightfully his.

He would be a king.

A sigh made Henry spin around on his heels, instinctively snarling. The sorrowful look in Jeffries' eyes stopped him from pouncing.

"Oh, son," the former monk said, shaking his head. "I was afraid it would come to this."

Henry's face fell.

CHAPTER TWO

Pupaetory

Naturae, July 11th 1553

Aioffe landed on the balcony to the Pupaetory, enjoying the heat of the smooth wood warmed by the summer sun on the soles of her feet. Dropping her enormous translucent wings behind her, she didn't notice the rainbow pattern on the floor as the beams of sunlight filtered through their tiny panes. Time was pressing, so she strode toward the double doors, nodding to the guards on either side, who opened them on her approach, then bowed as their Queen swept past.

The stink of young pupae assaulted her as soon as she entered the cavernous hall perched in the treetops. Small brown-winged fae turned at her presence, beaming, and the chatter level rose with excitement. The nurses quickly shushed the infants. Some, under a year old and still grubbing about on colourful mats on the floorboards, reacted only by casting their vacant eyes around, stubby beige wings awkwardly shuddering from their shoulder blades.

Pushing the thin silver crown down firmly on her head, Aioffe kept her distance from chubby hands reaching for the glittery attraction, and waved instead at the pupae as she glided through the room. She only still wore it because she had forgotten to stash it safely in her chambers before arriving. Her gaze carefully avoiding staring at the blocks lined up to one side of the sunny, bright chamber, where older pupae wobbled on the edges, preparing to jump. More than once, her presence had encouraged the youngsters to step off and launch into the open. Whilst this was often cause for much excitement, once clumsily airborne they invariably tried to grab for the enticing shiny thing on top of her long white-blond hair, or, perhaps it was simply to be nearer to her. Aioffe was never quite sure which.

At the far end, the small, faded oak doorway awaited. Aioffe fished in her pocket and pulled out a slender silver key. Calmness embraced her as she ducked and entered, latching the door behind, then leaning gratefully against the cool wood. Here, in the high growing chamber, she was alone at last. The silence was broken only by the rustle of vine leaves, gently stretching in the breeze to reach the sunlight pouring in through the ceiling windows. After a moment to centre herself, Aioffe examined the greenery surrounding her. Tall columns reached up, dressed in their finest shades of emerald, with large white cocoons suspended amongst the branches. Healthy roots just detectable at their bases, the soil around them dark and fertile.

All was well. The earthy scent of the humidity told her as much, but she loved to see the fruits of her blessings quietly developing, even in her absence. This latest crop would hang for only a few more weeks before pupaetion. Autumn would soon start to reach into the chamber and wither the vines for overwintering.

Aioffe reached inside her mind, recalling all the love and light wafting from the young fae she had just passed. Their adoring upturned faces grateful for the briefest glimpse of her, their mother. She thought about the blessing ceremony, the excitement of a community coming together for the one purpose of restoring Naturae. A sense of being whole overtook her. Then she opened her fists and allowed the thrill to pour out of her fingertips. Aioffe looked down at the roots, willing the ribbons to enter the earth and entwine with the vines.

From the tips of her fingers, she watched thin strands unfurl and leave, floating like the finest of silken threads drifting down. Slowly, whilst the rainbow skeins flowed out, she walked along the pathways between the beds. Passing the vines bearing soldiers, workers, spies, craftsmen, she reached the royal stalk at the end. In the darker corner where it grew, she paused, looking at the wispy plant. Almost immediately, the warm sensation of blessings diminished. Her fingers curled into a fist and, as she breathed out, her face sagged.

She had tried starting the blessings here before. Had even tried bringing love directly to it, yet this special vine, her family vine, refused to grow a cocoon. Now, after years of trying, of blessing, of tears of frustration shed into its roots, its pale weakness frustrated and disappointed her each time she visited, souring the joy of bestowing her blessings upon the other vines. She nevertheless persisted; there was no other way to produce an heir.

Closing her eyes, Aioffe tipped her head back and thought of Joshua. Her Prince. Her consort. Her partner in everything. She smiled as she recalled the whispered endearments between them, the smooth touch of his fingers on her, and her spirit swelled. She pictured his dark blue eyes smouldering with affection, his long blond hair like her own, and the way she felt when he held her to his chest, binding her with him forever in the embrace of his strong arms. How she loved that sense of belonging and acceptance of her truest self when he was present, that constant security he provided, even when she was at her most depleted.

She held onto the blessing pressure building inside, yet kept her fists balled until the force of love behind it became too much. Her fingers shook, wanting to open, to flow, but she held them shut until the ball of energy in her palm glowed to the point of painful. Only then, when the urge was the strongest, almost overwhelming, did she splay her fingers and allow the strands to shoot out into the roots. They fell, bright and glistening, onto the ground, then absorbed before she could blink. Always this vine was thirsty - no matter how often she blessed it, she sensed it required more. But the love she gave was all that she had to bless with, and the plant remained stubbornly a pale golden yellow.

Aioffe's eyes filled with tears as she turned away, drained. As she plodded back along the path, she glanced again at the green columns surrounding her. Most times the vinery appeared as a lush forest. Ancient twisted stalks, striking now visible as their leaves reached upwards, energised by the blessing she had bestowed. The vines yearning towards the sunlight above like their ancestors praying to the heavens. Today though, the thick linear stems curiously reminded her of bars. A cage. The thickness of the vines revealed by the rising leaves seemed threatening. An ominous chill ran up her arms although the room remained humid, and her heartbeat quickened. Fixing her sight on the door, Aioffe urged her feet to walk faster, chiding herself for being foolish. Wings beating despite forcing herself to stay grounded, although, she wasn't sure why she bothered - no-one would see her, or question her. No-one else could understand the sudden crushing fear she suffered, or why the comforting tangle had changed. Reaching the end of the chamber, Aioffe sighed as her flustered hands turned the key.

Once outside, the atmosphere of the main courtyard restored her warmth a little. But she was tired; the screams and calls of the youngest pupae hurt her ears, and the smell of bodies, sweaty from exertion, assaulted her nose. She inhaled nonetheless, telling herself she ought to be thankful for their liveliness and swept her hand over her head, smoothing her flyaway hair. After locking the door, Aioffe raised her wings and fluttered up to the walkways above rather than pick her way back through the hubbub. Here, the overhang would make her exit less obvious, and she could hopefully return to her other duties without delay.

As she flitted past the dormitories, a wail interrupted her mental listing of what she had to achieve that day. She glanced over the banister, and saw a dark-haired pupae perched on the tallest of the plinths below. His arms stretched wide, groping the air, his short wings frantically beating. As if he sensed she was watching, his face tilted upwards and Aioffe noticed his eyes screwed closed with fear. She paused, hovering just a hand span above the walkway. He was only a few feet away, but she didn't want to reach over and touch him, in case he got shocked and fell before he was ready to leap.

Aioffe checked the bottom of the plinth; a nurse waited below, beckoning encouragement to take flight. Another was already fluttering up the column. The second nurse would push him off if he didn't make the jump. Aioffe flew backwards and landed, shrinking against the wall. It was not her place to become involved; this was a necessary solo rite of passage for the young worker fae below, and the nurses were very experienced.

Eyes closed, she waited until it was over, hoping it would be quick as she had much to do. She could have carried on, but each of these young fae were born from her blessings, and she held a duty towards them and their care. Not specifically to each individual, but the

16

growing generation in general. Her stomach flopped over as she hesitated - the fear she saw in the face of the youngster was alien to her. She had always wanted to fly, stretch her wings to discover the limitless possibilities which being airborne offered. Try as she might, she could not understand the hesitancy which the workers, of all delegations, felt about flying; this age-old method seemed to be the only way to overcome it. Fly or be pushed. Aioffe breathed in sharply as she heard the screech of the pupae begin, then cut off. Her eyes flew open and she dashed to the edge to see what happened.

At the floor of the neighbouring plinth, she caught sight of the child, wildly out of control but still airborne. His wings obviously worked - as they instinctively should have - but the nurse below was lifting off herself, hands outstretched to catch his legs. As her fingers touched the edge of his loose trousers, he crashed into the plinth and fell. Aioffe watched the nurse hovering over him, murmuring words of enthusiasm and praise. The pupae's face crumpled and he began to bawl. It would take many months of practise for that youngster to master flying, and many more bruises for the workers to soothe better. Hurting, the pupae then lashed with his fists at the comforting arms of the nurses. The volume of his cries escalated to piercing, and Aioffe screwed up her eyes as if this would stop the noise.

It didn't, despite her unvoiced pleading for it to cease, so Aioffe turned, gliding along the walkway once more, conscious that if she flew quickly her escape would be more obvious. She must try to remember, find a minute for that was all it would surely take, to say a personal thank you to the patient nurse. Maybe she could find her at the ceremony, acknowledge her kind care then. As instantly as she speculated, she knew it was unlikely she would find an occasion to. Her attention had to be on the ceremony as a whole, not with individuals. Yet that nurse - she didn't even know her name - was but one of many who spent their days caring for the next generations of fae. Day in and day out. What a task that must be.

She blinked quickly, frustrated with herself for not even having time to be polite. Not having the courage to intervene. But there were too many now for her to get personally involved with individuals. There was no small amount of relief also - that she didn't have to perform the thankless job of raising the pupae herself. The realisation that supporting the new generation was time-consuming and perhaps tedious work was not new, but the trapped sensation earlier, coupled with her desire to run from the youngster, caused her to pause at the door. She owed it to herself to acknowledge this realisation properly.

She truly *didn't* have the time for individual pupae. Time for everyone and everything. The attendants were doing a more than adequate job. Her role here was to create new life. This was only one aspect of her duties as Queen, and it was exhausting enough. Although she and Joshua had discussed the heir situation, there was no getting around the problem that she was too busy with all the other elements of ruling to get involved with the upbringing of pupae. Even her own heir. She understood now why she herself had spent scant time with her mother while growing up. To admit this much to herself came as a relief, and, with the acceptance of it, strangely lighter. Unburdened.

As she left the Pupaetory, she saw Uffer waiting on the far edge of the landing balcony. He wore his official red sash but his robes looked muddied and crumpled. As he turned to face her, Aioffe frowned, mirroring the concerned expression on his face. He fidgeted with his hands, and her heart skipped a beat. "What's wrong?" Aioffe said, rushing towards him.

Uffer looked over her shoulder, checking the guards were out of earshot, then he whispered, "It's your brother Lyrus, our Queen. They've found him."

Aioffe's eyes flared. "Where?"

"In the excavations of the old Beneath."

Aioffe realised he was dusting off mud rather than wringing his hands through nerves. She laid her slim hand on his arm to still him. "Is he...?" Her eyebrow raised as their eyes met.

Uffer nodded, although his expression remained guarded. "Weak, but yes, alive."

Aioffe exhaled, a long and forced breath. Looking down at the boards of the platform, she remembered the time Uffer had first brought her here, to show her the decay which had overtaken Naturae. He did not enjoy being the bearer of bad news, and once again, here he was, informing her of a threat to her Queendom. She glanced into his eyes, acknowledging his fear. She squeezed his forearm, although it was scant comfort to her friend.

"I suppose I should see him," she said. Swallowing back her concerns, she took a section of her hair in her hands and began to wind it around the rest of her locks. Once she had gathered the loose strands into a long bunch behind her, she felt better. She adjusted her crown so it sat unmistakably high on her head. All the more prepared to confront her brother.

Back from the dead.

Aioffe's heart sank. "Where is he now?"

Uffer pointed down, his lips tightened. Aioffe peered over the balcony, then her hands flew to her mouth. At the base of the huge trunk which supported this corner of the Pupaetory, a crowd of workers clustered, hovering. Their wings sent clouds of black peat dust into the air obscuring her view, yet she could make out a dark grey lump on the brown earth. Her advisor Thane, still wearing his leather gloves, glanced up and caught her eye. His eyes darted away again as he barked a command to the others.

As the fae dispersed, Aioffe flew down, unable to lift her eyes from the crumpled body in the clearing. The grey was Lyrus's armour, dented and squashed into an unrecognisable shape. Twisted limbs had been splayed like a broken spider as the workers attempted to remove the plate pieces, now that he was clear of the dangerous hole they must have found him in.

Aioffe landed and went to his side. Her brother's head, matted hair plastered about his face, lay unmoving on the earth. His face looked skeletal, muddied skin stretched thinly over his pointed features and dirt darkly crusted around his mouth and nostrils. As she leaned over him, his head revolved towards her. There was no mistaking his sneer.

"About time, sister," he rasped.

CHAPTER THREE

Nothing to take

Chester

Jeffries extended his hand to Henry, averting his eyes from the headless body in the centre of the pool of blood. "Now you will have the Church to answer to. How long before the household returns? I thought she kept you with a goodly supply of blood from the lettings?"

Henry's mouth dropped, and he gazed at his palm where the evidence of his actions was still faintly visible. "Why did you come back?" His voice sounded childlike and Henry felt a too-human remorse rush up in the man's presence.

Jeffries shrugged. "I realised you did not make any attempt to try and argue for your faith, or for your Church."

"So?" Henry raised his eyebrow. What had faith to do with what he had done? Someone with a conscience would not have just killed a man. Henry told himself to have no shame at that moment. He was a vampire, and now a free vampire. There was no need to pretend he had a conscience anymore. He pushed his remorse away and stared at Jeffries insolently.

Jeffries said, "Having spent many years hiding how I felt about the Catholic faith myself, then living in the light of the true church under King Edward, I began to wonder as I rode, whether you were harbouring any doubts yourself? Whether you too were looking to reject the idolatry and pointless rituals, and step forward into the path of righteousness. Of course, I could only discuss this with you without the presence of the former Prioress, so I came back to speak with you before she returned." Jeffries glanced at the guard's body before saying, "Although I see that my suggestion of your new freedom had some immediate impact on your sensibilities."

Scowling, Henry pushed himself up from the floor and met the old man's eyes in a glare. "If you have come to convert me, you have wasted your time."

"How so?" Jeffries said.

"I lost my faith as soon as I was turned." Henry spat. "It's abundantly clear that no faith reconciles dying with what I am. Or you! I did not go to Heaven, or Hell, or Purgatory. I gave up my soul in return for living forever. No amount of hours in furtive Masses since have persuaded me that there is any truth in what I have heard preached for so long. Catholic practices serve only to provide vampires with sufficient foodstuff. It's only for gullible human fools who can be enthralled to forget what they are - food. But that does not mean that your Protestant faith is any different. Mark me, all faiths are just a means to an end."

Jeffries looked grave. "Is that what you truly believe, my boy? That all faith is just about feeding? Taking without giving?"

"You can call it what you will - feeding the soul, feeding my kind, we all take something from it, whichever language you preach in."

Jeffries put his hand on Henry's arm. His cool fingers did nothing to chill the heat within. "After all these years, I can understand why you must have questioned your faith. I might not have agreed with the choices you made, or were persuaded into, but if I had thought you would give up on the Lord entirely… I am sorry. I believed I was doing God's work when I helped you. Regardless, I thought you would be safe amongst those who believed in you - whatever destiny they had in mind, or whichever religion they were."

Henry said, "The only thing I believe in now is that the power of *a church* is as absolute as it always was." As he spoke, Henry realised what he had to do. The only question remained, which church was the more powerful now? Which would support his claim? He looked at Jeffries, considering how embedded he might be with the Church of

England, with the Protestant movement itself.

Tilting his head towards the body on the floor, Henry said, "I will not stay here now. The freedom you spoke of means I can now choose who I align myself with, does it not? If your faith is as willing to harbour witches as mine was to feed vampires, perhaps we should discuss my allegiance."

Jeffries flared his eyes. "If you think any church would condone what you have done and absolve you of it, you are mistaken. You know the rules, feeding is allowed. Killing is not."

"But," Henry took Jeffries' arm and gripped it tightly, "I am willing to repent for my sin." The side of his mouth turned up and he leaned into the monk. "I am open to being reborn..." Deliberately, his eyes glazed as he met the monk's brown depths, Henry slowly dropped his eyelids once, twice, blinking the power of his desire into the short distance between them. He'd seen Taylor do it with many a tradesman, but this was his first time attempting the vampire power himself.

Jeffries' face relaxed as he breathed out. Henry inhaled the stale exhalation, tasting in it the pollen from the meadows he had ridden past, the ale he drank from an inn on the way, and the purity of the monk's belief in his God. Henry smiled. "I think it would be the perfect time for us to travel to meet your friends. The ones who support you the most with your endeavours." Jeffries nodded slowly. "And perhaps," Henry said, "you can tell me more about your..."

He stopped, realising that there was a glint in Jeffries' eyes which hadn't been there before.

"Oh, do go on," Jeffries said, as a smile played around his lips. "I was so enjoying your thrall, I quite forgot what we were talking about?"

Henry dropped his hands and frowned.

"Something about repenting for your sins, wasn't it?" Jeffries continued, "although until today, I doubt there have been that many. All the same, I would prefer you to save your methods of persuasion for a more susceptible kind of person. It doesn't work on us creatures you see, or did they not tell you that?"

Henry swallowed, his lips tightened with frustration. Seventeen years a prisoner, he ought to have known that there was more strategy to being a vampire than the constant requirement for blood and only blood. He felt a fool. A different approach would be required.

"I apologise. It was clumsy of me to assume." He sighed, then looked at the latticed ceiling of the hallway. "I should have learned that." He turned to face Jeffries again, his pale face the picture of remorse and innocence. "She kept me here with no outside contact, you know. No-one to talk to, nothing to do but count the hours until the next Mass in the cellar." He chuckled hollowly. "The garden is perfection itself, every blade straight, every leaf green and tidy. I have read the Bible five hundred and seventy-three times, and I cannot remember the last time I sat on a horse, or played a lute. You thought you were saving me, but I have been reduced to a child by these people."

Henry kicked the legs of the dead guard. "I'm not one to complain, but all I have had fed to me is the blood of innocents, and a diet of sunshine, holy orders and vague promises to keep me in check. Hidden. So that when the time came, I might re-emerge and take my throne." He looked at Jeffries through his lashes. "And now you tell me that will never happen." Henry took Jeffries' hand, "And I thank you for telling me the truth, Maister. For I would never have known it; they would never have told me." He shrugged. "For all I know, the inconvenience of harbouring me might have pushed them to even more extreme punishment."

Jeffries squeezed Henry's hand back. "I am glad we are of the same mind. The truth has an ability to set one free, once you have found it."

"Or heard it," Henry said wryly. "Perhaps there is more truth to your Church than mine."

Jeffries smiled, then glanced at the door. "What time did you say Mistress Grosvenor would return?"

Henry blanched. "I have not yet heard the old Vesper bells, but she will return for that. I must away." He pushed past Jeffries and plucked his cape and cap from the peg. "I'm sorry, but I just can't give her your message now. You can wait here, if you want?" He glanced at the body, "And blame me for that. I can't care any more. You are right, I ought to be free."

Then Henry paused, raising his eyebrow as if this were a perfectly ordinary question and there was no particular urgency to his actions, and asked, "What is she like? This Lady Jane Grey?"

Jeffries' mouth twitched into a slight smile. "A godly and pious pawn. Her father has married her to a Dudley and together they convinced the Council she will be biddable enough to do their work until she has a Tudor son." He sighed, glancing at Henry. "Edward liked her well enough though. She is studious like him. And, he had little other Protestant choices except her mother, who might have been less obedient and is far past childbearing age. The crown would have eventually passed to Jane anyway, so I hear her mother stepped aside."

"Will she be a good Queen?" Henry said.

"Not as good a Queen as you would have made a King," Jeffries admitted. "You were born to it, tutored for it in a way she never was. But, she is the right Queen for this country, I have no doubt. Also the right Queen to carry out Edward's vision for the Church."

Henry bit back his retort, turning his face as he opened the front door. Ahead, the patchwork fields dipped towards the river Dee. Jutting up in the left of his field of vision, the water tower turret stood proud and alone into the skyline. The silence was broken by the seagulls which had flown up-river, squalling as they wheeled around scavenging for scraps. Looking out at the peaceful rural vista, he laid down the daily burden he bore, relinquished his constant window-ledge watch for a boat to glide downriver and take him away from his prison. He nodded, as if bidding farewell to the familiar view, and stepped over the threshold. Lifting his head, he took a deep breath and marched down past the flowerbeds, towards his freedom.

On the pathway through the front garden, the tired mare nibbled more of the grass below the stone wall. Henry's pace faltered, and he absently patted the horse's neck. He waited, seemingly just breathing in the summer air. It was stiflingly hot, even the grey tail hairs flicking the flies away from the horse's sweaty rump clumped together damply. Finally, he heard the click of the latch and the sound of Jeffries' boots on the flagstones. As the old man untied the reins from the gate, Henry smiled weakly and allowed tears to collect in his eyes. "Fare-thee-well then," he said, deliberately allowing a waver to enter his voice before he bowed shortly. As he straightened, Henry let his gaze linger on the saddlebags before stepping away.

Jeffries caught his arm. "You leave with nothing? No clothes for the winter, no baggage?"

Henry blinked, clearing his eyes before he thrust his chin forward.

"I have nothing to bring. Once, I was the Duke of Richmond and Somerset, and I now have nothing. Am nothing." He took a deep breath and looked at Jeffries with an earnest gaze. "I have had no need of money, or title, and scant clothing or chattel to carry. Pray for me, Maister, and maybe your Lord will provide."

Jeffries nodded sagely. "Indeed, you can carry nothing of your life into a life after death, I suppose." He pursed his lips, waiting for the question from Henry.

"Where were you heading, anyway?" Henry asked, looking down at the ground.

"North. I have work to complete in Scotland," Jeffries said. "I don't suppose you have a horse yourself?"

Henry smiled and looked up at him with a hopeful glint in his eye. "No, but I am - I *was* - excellent at riding double."

Jeffries snorted as he looped the reins over the mare's neck. "You may walk alongside me a while. If you wish, we can wander around the walls, past Bridgegate to the wharf, and you can see about finding transport there? I will fund a room for you this night, if no ships leave this late in the day. Just to get you on your way, you understand?"

Bells pealed from the cathedral higher in the town, swiftly followed by others from within the castle walls. The watch would change soon and there was no better time to leave. Henry smiled and set off down the road toward the river, trusting in Jeffries to follow.

CHAPTER FOUR
The Council

Naturae

Whilst checking the concealing mist level, a desperate messenger fae had found Joshua, requesting his presence most urgently at the citadel. Despite flying the several miles back as quickly as he could, he fretted he would be late. By the time Joshua reached the High Hall, the hastily called Council meeting was already in session. A worker fae crowd gathered to watch the proceedings, so his flustered entry was hardly unnoticed. He paused by a trunk-seat, to straighten his attire after his rush from the far edges of Naturae island. Now, on top of being damp from the droplets of the cloud, he was sweaty and ill-prepared for whatever lay ahead. Joshua caught his breath in the humid atmosphere of the vaulted-ceilinged hub of their community and sent a brief prayer upward to calm himself. Already, he sensed the tension within the vast chamber, although tempered by silent respect from the observers as their representatives deliberated.

Present around the wide oval table which he had helped to craft were his Queen and wife, Aioffe; her closest confidante and advisor, Uffer or Lord Anaxis, as he was formally titled, who now oversaw the running of the Palace instead of the Beneath; Overseer Thane, the acknowledged spokesperson of the entire community of worker fae; the aging Captain of the Guard and fifteen worker representatives from across designations. None of the Nobles were there, which suggested to Joshua this matter did not concern the wider realm but Naturae island specifically. Had it been a full session, Joshua hoped that he would have been given proper advance notice of the meeting, but, he was only the Prince and had no formal responsibilities within Naturae. This session was thus urgent, but not disastrous. But he could be wrong, he realised; the debate, as he slid onto his seat, was decidedly more combative than usual.

He dropped his wings and tilted his head slightly to acknowledge Aioffe next to him. She flicked a grateful glance his way, her elbows resting on the table and her chin in her hands as the Council argued. He slipped his hand to her knee and squeezed it, and she smiled without turning her attention from the conversation. The smile didn't reach her eyes. Instead, he saw they were a darkened blue and filled with worry.

"He needs to be kept away from us all, for our own safety!" Uffer said. His fists stopped just short of pounding the polished wooden surface.

Thane sided with him. "Lyrus is of the old order. It's too much of a risk to have him around." His head shook, causing tiny particles of mud to spray into the air. Down one cheek, a dark smudge still decorated his weather-beaten face.

"We should have left him buried," a worker representative said, shaking his head. "I wish we'd never dug him out." Thane nodded sagely, his mouth downcast.

Joshua leant over to Aioffe and whispered, "What did I miss?"

In a trembling voice, she muttered, "Lyrus was pulled out of the remains of the Beneath this morning. Alive."

Joshua gasped, "Still alive? After seventeen years?" He leaned back as he tried to imagine what it must have been like to be buried underground for such a long time, unable to die in the suffocating darkness.

"Barely, but yes." She turned her attention to the conversation. "I would appreciate hearing the opinion of the Captain of the Guard, please? Before we can come to a consensus about what should be done with him."

The Captain nodded curtly; the grey hairs turning silvery on his head as they caught the light streaming through the windows, which only added to his gravitas. "My Queen, it would be remiss of me not to point out that I have a conflict of interest. Lyrus was my predecessor. He was, regardless of his actions, an outstanding soldier. He taught myself, indeed, all of our older army, everything. For that, we have a debt of responsibility towards him. A duty of care, you might say. But," he sighed, "I also fear that rehabilitation into our ranks, *were* he to recover sufficiently in a physical sense, risks his opinions, his manner and style, corrupting our new generation of soldiers."

"So where does that leave us?" Thane interrupted. "What are my workers to do with him? I won't tolerate him spreading discord."

Shrugging, the Captain said, "We no longer have a Beneath in which to hold him whilst we wait out his recovery and ascertain the threat level he poses. And, he was the most senior of all Guards - Captain as I am now. He should be accorded the respect he is owed." The loyal officer then glared through his tufty grey eyebrows at Thane.

"He will surely need medical attention for many months," Uffer interjected. "Perhaps if Lyrus were to be placed in one of the palace rooms, under strict guard, until such a time as we can determine where his allegiances lie?"

Joshua thought this sounded like a typically sensible suggestion from his friend, and nodded. All the while, he kept a gentle hand on Aioffe's knee for support. His other fist clenched and unclenched in his lap. Two previous encounters with Lyrus had both resulted in differing traumatic outcomes. He held Lyrus fully responsible for kidnapping Aioffe and dragging her away from him, then leaving her captive in the Beneath, thinking he was dead.

Joshua glanced across the table, pondering the changes which had happened since then. The re-building of Naturae and establishment of Aioffe's new Queendom had taken precedence, and their community grew closer as well as in numbers. No-one had missed Lyrus, and there had been no need for the Beneath; that entire area had been forgotten about - until they needed the space. Joshua knew they were excavating around there to build new ground level outbuildings to house their growing numbers of livestock, but he hadn't anticipated they would dig so deep as to discover what lay in the Beneath.

He glanced at Aioffe again, seeing the tension in the way she held her slim body. This must be a shock for her, although she focussed on the conversation as if it were just another matter within her

Queensland. He worried about the conflicted emotions she surely felt - this was her brother they were discussing, even if there had been little love between them.

If Lyrus was alive, what did that mean for them? Joshua's tongue ran over the gap in his jaw, left by the tooth Lyrus had extracted while torturing him for information, just minutes before the Beneath had collapsed in an earthquake. As this happened some seventeen years ago, Joshua had tried to bury the memories and his guilt. At the time, it had seemed perfectly reasonable for himself and Spenser to tie up and leave his enemy in the Beneath whilst they rescued Nemis and Fairfax, but now?

At some point, he would have to see Lyrus. Face the brother-in-law whom Joshua had thought was dead. Joshua could not have known, and frankly wouldn't have cared at the time, that Naturae would be almost uprooted with the violent shaking. He guessed Lyrus would hold him responsible, but to his mind, his imprisonment underground still didn't make them even. Whatever pain Joshua had endured, Lyrus had caused far greater emotional agony for his wife, and that was unforgivable.

Aioffe stared straight ahead, trying to ignore the glowers which were being exchanged around the table. "I would like a Council consensus on where he is to be housed whilst he recovers." Her mouth tightened. "We do not have medical facilities and whomever we assign to his care must be able to withstand his 'methods' of persuasion."

The Captain splayed his hands on the table, reaching forwards towards his Queen. His eyes grew earnest, as he said, "Many of us remember the way he would manipulate minds. Your Highness, I still think it wisest if he is placed directly under our care. He, being of royal blood, will doubtless recover very quickly with the Lifeforce we can provide. But his injuries sound severe. The Lifeforce will restore his essence and speed healing, but without correctly positioning of his bones and wings, he would be left a cripple. Although we fae are not healers, we could send for the one who knows our ways, to ensure he makes a full recovery." He glanced at Joshua, "I believe you know of one such person, our Prince?"

Joshua's lips pursed. One of the few fae to have been severely injured - several times - and his life saved whilst in the human world, only a tiny part of him empathised with Lyrus's future, doubtless painful, journey back to health. Joshua's own recovery, after being slashed and squashed by Lyrus, would not have been possible without the very man the Captain referred to - Maister Jeffries. A witch and heretic. A man Joshua had no option but to trust, only to have been used and betrayed. He nodded briefly, pushing away doubts about whether he wanted to be in contact with the monk again, to be deliberated upon when he had a moment with Aioffe. Until he knew her thoughts on the matter, he did not want to commit to anything.

"We can't allow unknown others, even if they are healers, into Naturae." Simeon, one of the worker representatives, cried out. Around the table, Joshua noted many of the other workers shared his concern. "We don't need outsiders. The risk is too great they will talk about us."

"There is also the Treaty to bear in mind," the Captain said. "Remember, only fae are allowed onto Naturae. Any visitors would have to be certain their stay here goes unnoticed."

"We go into their world when we like." Thane weighed in, "It is only by the bounty which our Queen has bestowed on our city that we have sufficient resources, sufficient strength, to learn from humans ourselves. Do not forget that."

Joshua smiled - Thane had proved over the years to be more open to mixing with the wider realm than Aioffe and he had ever expected.

Another representative, Oldy Elizae, known for her dislike of humans or indeed anything not fae, but well respected in the worker community, said, "Why couldn't we ask a healer what they would do, without bringing them here? But then, I suppose it's difficult to explain what we are without actually seeing the problem." Her voice tailed off, realising she was not particularly helping.

Aioffe nodded her head slightly, and Oldy Elizae smiled once more, grateful to have had the chance to be heard. Aioffe said, "I understand your fears, and yes, there is always a danger of exposure when we try to involve ourselves in the human world. But," and her eyes flicked over to Joshua, "We do know there are healers experienced with fae there, and even if we cannot find the one who healed my husband, we should think about how to find an alternative. Where is Lyrus now?"

"Outside." Thane grumbled, "Shouting still, hissing his poison."

"With no guards? We must protect our Queen! Who knows what he will do now he's out," Uffer said, frowning at the Captain. "And that means protecting her from the likes of Lyrus as well as foreign intervention. He should be kept apart from everyone until he has healed sufficiently to answer for his actions." The voices around the table began to rise again.

"Lyrus cannot be expected to justify what happened before when he was under the orders of the former Queen." The Captain grew defensive - understandably, Joshua realised. He likewise had served under her rule yet was respected here as if he had not also perpetrated the unkind methods the old Queen used to get what she wanted. "He should not need a guard. Lyrus is not a threat to anyone and remains a sworn Queen's Guard."

Thane raised his voice, "Doesn't need a guard? He was the cruelest of soldiers, the most wicked of any aside from Queen Lana, and the most scornful of those who were not his equal. I am not convinced he has any place in Naturae at all. Lyrus should be kept completely away from everyone. He has had years to plot what he would do when eventually discovered. Keeping him apart from us is the safest course of action. Isolate him under heavy guard somewhere else on the island. I don't want the workers at risk. If Lyrus recovers, he will be strong, and there is no guarantee he will reform his behaviour and attitude to suit our current, more inclusive, circumstances. Our Queen has the full support of our workers, our army, and this Council - her security is paramount and he cannot be trusted."

Joshua glanced at Aioffe, wondering how strange it must be to have your safety discussed as if you were not even present. There were too many differing opinions to make sense of, and he could see the tiredness in her eyes. He squeezed her knee again, but then Aioffe stood. Joshua's heart swelled with pride.

"I do not wish to make a final decision about his future here without your full agreement on the matter." She said, "All I know is, right now, my brother is lying in a clearing, surrounded by people staring at him and he can barely move. He is in pain, and certainly starving after so many years buried. Uffer, please ensure that he is assisted to feed from a small live animal. I know my brother - the urge to take Lifeforce will overwhelm him, and to deny him that risks him attacking any fae who happens to be close by. You will remember how fast he can be, even if injured. I doubt anyone would be able to fight off a crazed frenzy-feed from a maniac like him. Better to give him as much as he needs to heal from our supplies."

The Captain said, "My Queen, then it would surely be safer for us all if he were to be placed in a chamber, rather than out in the open."

"I agree," Aioffe said, "There are many guardable side chambers which we could place him in for now. Rotate the soldiers outside but keep them close, Captain, and make sure they understand the potential threat he poses. We cannot afford for them to be swayed by his former authority over your army." She smiled at the officer, "I know you will be cautious to keep us all protected." She turned to Uffer, "As Lyrus will be kept within the Household, I can rely on you to ensure he is fed."

Joshua said, "I recommend rabbits, Lord Anaxis. Small enough to sustain but will not provide much energy for significant or aggressive movement." He looked at Aioffe to confirm. "We will need to first discover Jeffries' whereabouts."

Aioffe rolled her eyes. "That will be impossible with the few spies we have and such a large realm to cover." She shook her head, glanced at the lowering evening light streaming in through the windows, and frowned. "I must take my leave, I have much to attend to."

"Shall I assist, my love?" Joshua asked, standing as well.

Aioffe's lips lifted, but the smile did not reach her eyes. "No, I know you have other matters to oversee. These are not affairs which I need you for."

Joshua nodded and looked down at the table. He swallowed, then his eyes followed her as she flew out of the room. He turned back to the Council and saw most of them gathering their personal items and making ready to depart. Uffer engaged in conversation with some of the worker representatives about which rabbit enclosures to use. Thane met his gaze though, and they descended the few steps from the raised dais side by side. As they pushed through the cluster, Joshua heard the worker's whispered shock. No doubt gossip about what had happened would travel quickly, leaving each to make their own minds up about the implications of the return of a known enemy of their beloved Queen.

Where the crowd thinned out, Thane, in his deep, authoritative tone which he only used when speaking in an official capacity, said, "Our Queen must be encouraged to proceed with the plans for the Ceremony. You know the workers are looking forward to welcoming this third generation into their ranks. The rite of passage it represents for our young must not be forgotten in the upheaval. I look to you, Prince Joshua, to ensure that this distraction does not take away Queen Aioffe's focus."

Joshua caught his regretful glance as they passed one of the smaller gathering areas to the side; neither of them had much time these days to sit and converse about their development plans as they had done in the early years of Naturae's re-greening. Thane was the informally recognised leader of the worker fae, and Joshua felt honoured to work by his side, sharing ideas as they created and grew the citadel. The level of trust and mutual respect between them well established, so much so that Thane was not overstepping, however formally he had asked his favour.

"I will discuss it with her, of course. I cannot see any reason why we would not continue, despite the upheaval. Have we any sight of Ambassador Spenser and Nemis yet?" What a time for them to return, Joshua thought.

Thane shook his head. "I have had a watch close to the jetty as you requested, nothing as yet."

"There is time still," Joshua said. "Nemis may know where Jeffries has ended up as well."

Thane stopped and glanced at Joshua, lowering his voice to say, "Are you sure you want to bring him here? It is well known what Lyrus did to you, and I realise how you feel about Jeffries." He raised an eyebrow at his friend.

Meeting his eyes, Joshua said nothing, but his mouth tightened. "We have little choice in the matter. Lyrus is my wife's brother. He is 'royal' as a result and that might be all that matters."

CHAPTER FIVE

Reunion

The moss-wick candles provided scant light on the jetty where Joshua waited. He did not need their glow to see through the dark sky; they were placed simply to highlight the target. In the dead of night, the slap of the waves against the wooden poles ticking the time away towards dawn. He hovered close to the shore, scanning the stars above as they shone over the water. Finally, just as he began to lose hope, through the mist he glimpsed a flutter. A small boat, pulled by a fae rather than its patchwork sail, slipped through the grey wall and he darted forward.

"Ho!" Joshua shouted, and his heart sped up as he heard "Ho!" echo back. Flying quickly, Joshua reached his arms wide. Spenser grinned as they embraced mid-air, clapping hands to shoulders in greeting. He looked exhausted, Joshua thought, as he grabbed the ropes behind his friend and pulled to share the burden. Joshua glanced down at the deck of the vessel below and his grin widened when he saw Nemis stirring below. Raising her eyes and blinking, she waved when her sight cleared enough to recognise him. Then she turned, shaking awake a bundle lying next to her.

"Nearly there!" Joshua called down. The bundle emerged from the blankets, sat up and shook its head. Joshua's heart sank. There should have been more heads appearing, older ones, but it looked like just one child had accompanied his friends on their voyage. Moving together, the two fae began to pull the ropes back, past the mast, to slow the boat approaching the shore. Joshua felt the strain in his hands as Spenser leaned against his harness, his thin but long wings beating against the yank of the tide. Joshua pivoted to match Spenser's angle and hauled despite the pain.

With a thud, the keel nudged the jetty, and Joshua flew down to catch the end of the rope Nemis prepared to throw. He landed and caught the painter, looping it around a thick upright stump to secure it. Nemis walked the few yards to the back of the boat and dropped the anchor stone in. As she turned, Joshua noticed the slump to her shoulders. He jumped onto the deck and embraced her before she could even say hello. Nemis sagged into him as she felt his strong arms around her. He breathed in the wild, witchy scent of flowers and sea-salt in her hair, briefly closing his eyes and raising a prayer of gratitude for her safe passage to their shores. Joshua reached up and pulled down the shawl she wore looped around her face. Nemis brought her head from his embrace and gazed at him, her pale blue eyes scanned his face, checking he was still the same. A smile played on her mouth, as she said, "Tis good to be freed from my cover, and good to be here."

Joshua said, "And you are, as always, welcome to be free here, my friend. Free as the wind which brought you. And your husband, of course." Nemis shook her long dreadlocks, tipped her face to the moon and giggled. For a moment, Joshua glimpsed the young yet wise girl, who had guided him here on another, more disastrous voyage years ago. A fully grown, cunning woman now, the century of difference in age slipped away and they embraced with the strength of teenagers.

Spenser landed on the small jetty and dropped his wings. "It is certainly smoother to sail in this weather, and my aging bones are grateful for it." He joked - although the flight had taxed him, he was still in the prime of his eternal life and they all knew it. Joshua had no idea how old exactly Spenser was, but he suspected the age difference between Nemis and her fae husband was well over a millennium, perhaps closer to two.

"When did you leave Anglesey?" Joshua asked.

"Three days ago." Spenser began unbuckling himself from the straps attached to the pulling rope. "We could have done with higher winds during the daylight; the long day means a shorter night to fly in though. But Nemis knew we would make it in time." He looked indulgently at her, but she was busy folding the blankets away.

"The mid-summer ceremony is always both a blessing and a curse," Joshua chuckled. "But I am relieved that you all made it this year." Picking up one of the candles, he peered down at the boxes and baskets on deck, then at the child leaning against the side of the boat, watching him with wide eyes. "And you bring your family as well. What's your name?" Joshua crouched to the lad's eye line, held the candle up and smiled.

"Mark," Nemis said. "He doesn't speak much yet." She looked apologetic, and Joshua saw her pull back slightly and turn into Spenser, ostensibly helping release him from the ties to the ship.

"He'll be six next month," Spenser said. As the straps fell to the deck, he bent down and reached out his hand to the boy, "Come now, this is our friend, Prince Joshua." Spenser flapped his wings, and pointed at Joshua, "He is a fae, like me. I said there would be more like us, with wings of all kinds. And here we are, in Naturae, where we can fly freely. I can carry you still, and we can soar amongst the birds. We will walk on the beaches here and be safe. You might even see a seal, or dolphins!" Spenser smiled and beckoned to Mark, "Stand up now, and let's get on land again."

The boy looked at Nemis, who nodded encouragement as she picked up her skirts then held her hand out towards him. Mark shook his head, curled himself into a ball and wrapped his arms around his ankles. His curls shook as he buried his head, refusing to look at anyone. Then, no-one said anything as the boy began to rock from side to side, banging his knuckles to the wood as he tilted one way then the other. Nemis sighed, then reached over to stroke his hair. Spenser gathered their belongings and shot a glance of resignation at Joshua.

"Let me help," Joshua said, setting the candle by Nemis and Mark, then picking up a large basket with one hand and a leather sack in the other. He looked back as he stepped off the boat with one long stride. "Shall I wait for you?"

"Better we meet you there," Nemis said. "We could be a while, but I know the way."

Her eyes met Spenser's and Joshua recognised the lingering glance between them. He felt a pang of longing for Aioffe; when was the last time they had shared such a look? He was not jealous - rather, relieved that his friend's marriage was still so strong and intimate after so many years. Even though his own joining had been far longer, lately he had begun to wonder if their circumstances would ever allow them to connect in the way that he used to with Aioffe. Would they ever share the upbringing of a child of their own, he wondered? He knew the issue of an heir weighed on Aioffe, and, if he was honest, seeing the young pupae growing up made him wish all the more for a family they could truly call their own as well.

Joshua forced a smile on his face. "Of course you do - I asked Uffer to prepare your Ambassadorial room as usual. I believe he has even finally mastered a pigeon pie in your honour!" Joshua winked at Nemis and she smiled wanly back.

Spenser and Joshua took to the air, awkwardly carrying their burdens, and flew inland before speaking further. Once they had passed the top of the shoreline and entered the thick forests, Joshua slowed. Spenser shot ahead then paused, turning to see why Joshua lagged.

"Old friend," Joshua said. "I am so glad to see you."

Spenser raised his eyebrow, "What ails you, mon ami? Trouble in the treetops?"

Joshua's eyes darkened. "Lyrus. He's been found."

Spenser's other eyebrow joined his forehead. "But, when the tunnels collapsed…"

"Yes, I know. We assumed he died there. But he lived. Lives still."

"Ah."

"Yes." Joshua drew in a deep breath, saying, "It has caused quite the upset."

"And the Queen? How does she feel about her brother's return?"

Joshua shrugged. "We have not had time to discuss it, but I know she is conflicted."

"Does she know it was us who left him trapped down there?"

Joshua shook his head.

"Then perhaps, it is better to tell her, no?"

Gnawing on his lip, Joshua could see the wisdom in Spenser's suggestion, and knew that Lyrus would likely have no hesitation in naming his executioner as soon as he laid eyes on him. Yet a part of him could not bear for Aioffe to think any less of him, especially right now, when she felt so distant. He had pushed the urge to confess to her down, deep within himself for so many years, it was almost as if he had forgotten about it. But he hadn't, and a prickling guilt had risen, crawling over him like a rash since that afternoon's revelation.

Spenser could see the dilemma playing across his friend's face so he placed a comforting hand on Joshua's arm. "Have you told anyone?"

Joshua knew he meant in a confessional, as he was still minded towards Catholic traditions, and shook his head. Afraid always that once he started to talk about his life as a fae, everything would come tumbling out and he would be judged. He flew slowly onwards, through the gaps between the trees, avoiding looking at Spenser as he wrestled to get his feelings in check.

"My Prince," Spenser caught up with him to say, "I am happy to take the blame for this, if that is what you desire. There is no love lost between Lyrus and myself. We have known each other, danced around each other, for centuries. But, know this - there should be no secrets between man and wife. There is also none between a man and his God, even if one has not expressly said as much out loud."

"I know," Joshua said. The words sounded hollow, even to himself. "But it was I who left him there. Trapped."

Spenser smiled and met Joshua's eyes. "I know you are a papist at heart. You should embrace the advantages your faith has afforded you to unburden your soul and cleanse yourself of the sins which you have committed." He looked away, then said, "Many do not have that opportunity for relief."

Joshua glanced at Spenser as they approached the clearing below the Pupaetory. "You carry burdens of your own?"

"Nothing more than I deserve," Spenser said. "And nothing which a priest could help with." He raised his eyebrows at Joshua and shrugged. No-one knew better the difficulties of hiding their difference amongst humans than Joshua and Aioffe, and, with Nemis being a witch, he understood the additional pressure and suspicion which the family no doubt endured.

Spenser landed and turned towards the low wooden shacks where the livestock were temporarily housed. "May I?"

Joshua dropped beside him and rested the baskets on the dried earth. "Of course," he said, unlatching the gate, then ducking inside the shelter. Moments later, he re-emerged with a brace of small rabbits held by their necks.

"Here," Joshua thrust one of them towards Spenser. "You'll need to replenish after that flight, I'd imagine. We have goats also, and sheep, but they are being kept for the ceremony tomorrow. Not that they provide much of a chase of course, but we've struggled to keep deer on the island, and the boar aren't reproducing enough yet to be hunted."

Within moments, the rabbit had been reduced to a shrivelled sack of bones and fur. Spenser tossed it into the crate next to the wall and held out his hand for another. "Am I the last Noble to arrive?" Spenser asked, glancing into the nearly full crate of desiccated corpses.

Before Joshua could confirm, Spenser delicately bit into the nape of the second rabbit as if it were a fine wine presented to him in a goblet. Joshua nodded, then stepped back on his heels and surveyed his friend as he drank the Lifeforce in strong gulps.

The jaunty dark yellow doublet and smooth hose he wore were of the finest materials Joshua had seen in a long time; Aioffe would doubtless ask where it came from when she saw it. The sleeves were baggy but not as excessive as he had seen in England, with deep slashes circling the bicep, displayed beneath a golden hued fabric. It was the colour synonymous with Spenser's European ancestors, as much as silver was associated with the Queendom of Naturae. Around wide shoulders, keeping his neck warm, he had fastened a small lynx fur collar. His shoes were rounded at the toe, rather than the square shape, which had been the fashion the last time Joshua had been amongst wealthy humans.

"The last you may be, but also the most welcome, and the most fashionable." Joshua bowed with a flourish and a smile.

Spenser's mouth twitched at the teasing. He finished his meal, licked his lips delicately and said, "I may not be a Prince, but I, at least, know how to present as one."

Joshua looked down at his comfortable trousers and loose tan shirt and felt like the poor relation. He had no need for fancy clothing, no need of disguise these days. Although he owned smarter attire for occasions, such as the embroidered tunic he would wear for the ceremony tomorrow, he had little desire to truss himself up like Spenser and was grateful he had no requirement to.

"How is Nemis?" Joshua asked.

"Tired," Spenser said. "As am I." Spenser raised his eyes to the balcony to their right, the main landing platform to the Palace.

"Should I go back for her?" Joshua asked, concerned again for the woman he loved as a sister.

Spenser shook his head. "She will come when she has calmed Mark. He is... a challenging child." His lips tightened, and his head dipped with his eyes. "It has not been an easy few years."

Joshua wished he could say something to ease the pain which flashed across Spenser's face. "Are you sure I cannot help?"

"Bring the basket and box up. She will be along soon enough. Sometimes it can take a few hours to get his head in a more amenable state. Better to let her bring the boy into a new situation, on her own, in the dawn light. My wonderful wife manages him far better than I ever could - the patience of a saint, you might say. They will be safe on the Wanderer. We can collect anything she can't carry in the morning."

Joshua glanced back towards the forest, then picked up their belongings. "I hope it's not too chaotic before the ceremony," he said. "You know how Uffer likes it orderly." Spenser laughed as they ascended to the balcony, but Joshua caught him looking down the pathway also, his dark eyes weary despite the Lifeforce.

CHAPTER SIX

A fitful prophecy

When Aioffe arose the next morning, nudging Joshua as she clambered out of their bed, preparations had already been underway for some hours. Dressing in a simple light blue shift dress, Aioffe then flew down the long corridors and outside to see the progress. Dozens of fae fluttered around the open space in between tall trees which formed the foundations to the Palace. A sweet scent of phlox, geranium and lavender wafted about as clusters of brown winged people tied garlands onto ivy vines looped about and up the trunks. These flowers had been grown especially for the occasion in a small garden area adjacent to the sacred trees, Ash and Elm. Now swept clear of debris but with tools and wood scattered about, the clearing beneath the Landing Platform and all the way through to the Pupaetory was taking shape for the formal initiation ceremony. Peering over the balcony edge, Aioffe smiled as she spotted Uffer and Thane with their heads together, absorbed in coordinating arrangements. Carpenters banged planks onto a modest stage close to them. The air itself was thick with the hum of wings and anticipation.

As she stood on the landing platform outside the Palace and gazed around, she breathed in the hopes and excitement already emanating from the community. To her, the unseen ribbons which floated up, the merest tendrils of Lifeforce, were the sweetest and most refreshing. The vortex which would focus the ceremony later that day, where belief was the substance, was like the main course of an ethereal Lifeforce feast. But the blessing-gathering ritual which was just one aspect of today's unique plans. The joyous strands which she inhaled now were efficiently satisfying her hunger, and her vivid blue eyes glittered as the fae's energy coursed through her. Turning, she reached her hand out to Joshua, emerging from the double doors of the Atrium. He ran his fingers through his jaw-length blond hair, then over his face, waking up in the bright sunlight.

He grinned, grasping her hand so that he too could taste the power of the crowd as she did. Where their skin touched, it tingled, and he squeezed her fingers as he gazed over their homeland with her.

"All the planning is finally coming to fruition," Joshua said. This day had been seventeen years in the making, and all of Naturae expected to be entertained, enthralled and their achievements celebrated.

Aioffe broke away from his gaze and looked over at the clearing again. "I just want everything to go well. This is a first for everyone." For Lyrus also, this would be the first time he could witness her in the role of Queen. She wondered how he was recovering, and, whether he ought to be invited to be a part of the proceedings. Gnawing on her lip as her eyes followed a pair of worker fae adjusting a colourful vine, the question played on her mind with no satisfactory resolution. She felt Joshua shift slightly. He would, of course, have an opinion on the matter yet she remained torn. There was no easy solution. No consensus amongst the Council. Aioffe knew she ought to just make a decision and order it, but there were so many considerations she wanted to be mindful of. She glanced up at Joshua, trying to push away all thoughts of her brother away and enjoy the moment.

"We all know our roles, don't worry," he said. "And Ambassador Spenser and Nemis arrived, finally, so I can fill them in on what to expect."

Aioffe turned back to him and squeezed his hand gently before dropping it. "I will go, I want to meet their children anyway."

"Child," Joshua said, a bleak look appearing on his face.

Aioffe's eyes flared. "Oh no! What happened to the others?"

Joshua shrugged. "I didn't like to ask." He looked at the wooden balcony floor, blinking furiously. "They were tired. Their boy, Mark, was unsettled by the arrival, or the journey possibly. I didn't want to get him further worked up by throwing plans at them before they even landed. I may be wrong, but I imagine Spenser would have said if they had left any other children in the care of someone else, instead of bringing them."

Aioffe touched his forearm, turning to leave. Joshua kept her hand on his arm though, his warm fingers clasping hers. She looked at their hands, confused, then glanced up at him. The earnest, loving expression he wore made her feel guilty somehow. She asked, "What is it, my love?"

He blinked, saying in an oddly gruff voice, "I am so proud of you. All of this," he swept his arm around, "is because of you."

Aioffe took a step back. "It's not only my work," she said. "Everyone has to come together to make it happen."

Joshua nodded, glancing over her shoulder to see the Captain of the Guard approaching from the Palace doorway.

"Good morning your Highnesses!" The Captain called over. He bowed as he reached them. "Are you ready to inspect the recruits?" The beam which accompanied this invitation told of his pride in this moment, at being able to make such an offer.

Aioffe glanced at Joshua. "Could you? I have to visit Nemis and then get changed." She turned to the officer, "I would like to see them for the first time in their new armour, on display. I think they would feel more 'presented' that way, as well."

"I think that would be most proper, our Queen." His head swivelled to face Joshua. "Although I know you have seen the armour before, our Prince, it is quite something spectacular when worn." He nodded, almost to himself, then said, "The designs you created for the army are... appropriate."

Not hiding his grin, Joshua gestured to the air and the Captain led the way. Joshua rolled his eyes, then tipped an imaginary hat at Aioffe. After he lifted off with a wave, she dashed into the Atrium. He would enjoy seeing the results of his labour, she consoled herself, surprised she hadn't thought of suggesting it before.

She flew down the hallways, avoiding all eye contact and thus conversation, as workers scurried about polishing the woodwork to a deep shine. Although Nemis had only visited a few times over the years since they had met, her husband, and Naturae's longest serving European Ambassador, called in more frequently, several times a year, and generally updated them on how she fared. But, he had not mentioned anything about the loss of his family. Aioffe blinked away her own tears which rose as she thought of it - their offspring only babes when they had last all stayed on these shores. Her heart ached for them; the children should have been nearly adults by now.

Or, the thought struck her - had she simply been too busy to make time for her friend and ask? She swallowed her frustration with herself; she ought to have known, ought to have asked. As she reached the Ambassadorial Quarters, she slowed, landing outside Spenser and Nemis's designated chambers at the far end. The rooms were part of the recently built extension to the Palace, and designed with Nemis in mind. They were double height, as most Noble's quarters were, but with an additional turret that afforded the occupant a higher view across the forest and towards the sea. A space to relax in, just for Nemis - Joshua had been insistent at their planning, and, as Queen, she had been happy to agree to his design for their friends. Nemis was a se'er witch and found peace when she was able to gaze out upon an expanse of nature before her. On previous visits, Nemis had also used the turret to create her restorative concoctions, which Aioffe found she had great need of.

Outside their carved doorway, she tapped gently but firmly, and stood back. While she was waiting, Aioffe smoothed her hair down, twisting it into a long rope to the side of her neck. Hearing no footsteps approaching, she bent forward and knocked again, a little louder, but kept her head close to the wood. Inside, thought she heard bumping. The scuffle of feet on floorboards? Aioffe's mouth tightened. She turned the handle and pushed.

The first thing she noticed as she poked her head around was the triangular shape of a child's shift. The waist-high figure stood with his back to her, his legs apart and arms outstretched to either side. Curls on his shoulder-length brown hair shook as he tossed his head from side to side vigorously, moaning like an animal in pain. Aioffe approached slowly.

"Nemis!" She cried out as she saw what lay at his feet.

"Do not worry," Spenser said, gently supporting her face, which was terrifyingly pale with her mouth agape. Nemis's long hair writhed over the floor as her body shook with a fit. Kneeling and bent over her, Spenser didn't look up as he said, "Please, pass me that bag. On the side, the one with the red ribbon fastening."

For all his calmness, his shoulders were tight around his neck. "Is it a vision?" Aioffe said, grabbing the sack as requested.

"Yes," Spenser replied. Then, he acknowledged the lad, who had now ceased shivering and moaning and was frozen, horror twisting his small face. "Mark, she will be fine. Fear not."

The boy let out a fearful howl. Aioffe glanced at Spenser, unsure of what to do. The child quivered still, his hands so wildly shaking she wondered at whether they might jerk off at the wrists. "Should I...?" She said, flicking her eyes between Mark and the door.

"No," Spenser said, torn between comforting his son and preventing his wife from injury. "He will hopefully stop when Nemis comes back to us. There is a brown bottle in there." He nodded at the bag. "Black cork stopper and an orange tie around its neck. Jeffries made it for when these fits occur."

Aioffe rummaged, pulling out scarves, wooden toys and trinkets as she felt right to the bottom. "Could it be in a pocket?" She asked, her hands coming up with nothing from the pouch to match his description.

Nemis shrieked, "He comes! The dark heir, he comes!" Aioffe jumped, startled. Even Spenser leant away from the screech.

Spenser recovered quickly and glanced over at the bag again, frowning. "I'm sure she packed it in there. But maybe, yes, there is a pocket at the back, near the strap."

Aioffe felt the leather, one hand in and the other outside. Nothing. She shook her head. Reluctantly compelled to look at Mark, her eyes roamed over his shift. There were pockets in the ankle-length outfit, she saw, bulging and bumpy but hidden, such as a lady might have in her gowns. There was little time for diplomacy, but Spenser had already seen the direction of her gaze.

"Mark?" He said, frowning.

The boy did not respond. "Mark?" Aioffe said gently, "Do you know where Mama's medicine is?"

The child stood stock still and ceased shaking. His eyes did not move from his mother, but Aioffe thought he was perhaps leaning slightly to the right, away from them. She turned to Spenser, unwilling to approach the upset boy. "Let me take Nemis. I think you need to give your son some support."

Spenser's eyes briefly closed, then he shuffled, holding Nemis's still tortured head up from his knees so that Aioffe might slide in and replace him. Once they had switched, Aioffe looked down at her friend's slack face and whispered, "I am here, my friend. We hear you. You are safe with us."

Aioffe stroked Nemis's forehead despite it bucking underneath her ministrations, then frowned. There was more she should try. Reaching into herself, she tried to push compassionate and loving thoughts down, through her fingertips and into Nemis. Her intention to comfort was interrupted by her own rising bewilderment at the predicament. Aioffe's frustration rose - even after spending a century living amongst humans, she simply had no experience of other-worldly, or other creature, conditions like as this. Fae were never ill as they healed themselves, and Naturae was ill-equipped to cope with someone so poorly.

As Spenser shuffled across the floor to his son, still on his knees so he was the same height, Aioffe scrunched up her face, focussing until she felt the blessings unfurl from her fingertips. But, distracted by a childish whimper, she glanced over to Mark, touching his energy as well. It was crumpled, as if parchment strips had been folded over time and time again, yet never entirely straightened. His ribbons zigzagged around his head, whizzing and darting with no discernible pattern or direction. The child's Lifeforce, she knew, would never be quite true and pure. It was daemonic, she understood, destined to be peculiar all of his life. Instinctively, she tried to pull it towards her, absorb it, but it resisted. The ribbons kept dashing away to resume their frantic dance.

Aioffe's heart sank, for she had never encountered quite such a twisted tendril, all pathetic and frayed, in her lifetime. She looked down again at Nemis and understood the tiredness in the deep-set wrinkles on her forehead. This child would always be a worry, always be a challenge. Always be different. And that posed a very particular problem for a witch and a fae to keep hidden.

Her blessing was not enough, nor would ever be sufficient, to heal this family. She felt quite powerless to assist. As her eyes filled with tears, to her shame, gratitude nudged its way into her mind. It crept in, then demanded her mental acknowledgement - she would never, could never, have to deal with a child that took so much time, such considerable energy.

Spenser retrieved the bottle from Mark's pockets and reached over towards Nemis whilst still holding his son's limp hand. "A few drops into her mouth," he instructed. Aioffe's hands shook but she breathed to calm herself, before dripping the strong-scented herby liquid between Nemis's lips.

It took a few heartbeats but the tension in the room seemed to ease as soon as the convulsions stopped. "Tis a miracle cure!" Aioffe exclaimed, smiling briefly at Spenser and Mark. She searched Nemis's face for a sign that she was coming back to awareness.

"It may take a while," Spenser said. "She is often very drowsy after." He squeezed Mark's hand, saying, "Let's get Mama on the bed to rest, eh?"

It surprised Aioffe to see Mark remain completely devoid of expression. Did he not care for his mother at all? Although the shaking had stopped, he gazed ahead with a vacant stare. Spenser tried to drag him with him as he stood, but the child remained as a statue. Aioffe watched as Spenser glanced away, then dropped Mark's hand with a sigh. He bent and gathered Nemis's limp body in his arms. Spenser clutched her close as he walked to the bed. Aioffe turned aside, touched by his care, as he tenderly whispered endearments into her ear.

After setting her down, he pulled knitted blanket over his wife. Aioffe then took Spenser's hand in hers. Centuries of friendship between them distilled into this quiet moment of support standing watch over their beloved patient. As they all held their breath watching for a change, finally, Nemis's breathing settled to a regular pace. Her face relaxed as if she were in the deepest of slumbers once she was on her back again. Unwilling to just leave but satisfied the danger had passed, Aioffe sat on the side of the bed whilst Spenser wordlessly returned to Mark.

As she stroked her friend's hand, now returning to a pinkish colour, she glanced over at Spenser. A new appreciation for him grew - although she knew him to be a loving husband and a well-connected Ambassador, there was an unexpected gentleness about him, and, she saw now, a sorrow. The formal, fancy clothes he wore hid it well, she thought, but she saw it in his actions as he brought a jerkin over to Mark and attempted to push the child's arms through it, soothing endearments and reassurances. Aioffe's hand flew to her mouth, then she looked down at her dress in horror.

"I must go! I have to get changed!" Aioffe glanced back at Nemis. "Will she recover in time for the ceremony, do you think?"

Spenser shrugged, "I will stay and take care of her until she awakes."

"I was supposed to tell you both what to do," Aioffe said. "Uffer and Thane have all these plans for where people are expected to stand during the ceremony." She chewed on her lip and stood up, smoothing her dress. "Although, I don't suppose it matters terribly as no-one has planned such an event in such a long time, and never had to include a witch or daemon."

"Maybe she should only observe, then?" Spenser arched his eyebrow. "There is Mark to consider anyway, and he cannot really be expected to participate."

Aioffe moved towards the door, asking, "Could a nursemaid look after him?"

Spenser shook his head. "Nemis is the only one who can reach him, especially if he takes a peculiar turn." He peeked over to the lump in bed and sighed.

"What did she mean? A dark heir?" Aioffe asked after a moment.

Spenser did not meet her steady gaze. "I do not know. She says it quite regularly these last few weeks." Then, he raised his head, despair in his eyes. "The visions are happening more frequently, more violently as well. Which is why I had to bring her here, regardless of..." He glanced at Mark, "the danger."

Aioffe nodded. They both knew that daemon blood was particularly alluring to fae, but Aioffe now understood the desperation which Spenser must have had about Nemis's condition. To move an innocent child, a vulnerable one, into the increasingly populous and confident Naturae, was a risk he would have wrestled with. "I will speak to the Council and make sure that he is given protection. That you all are."

Spenser smiled. "Thank you, my Queen." Aioffe, opening the door then stopping herself, looked over to Mark. Although his back was turned to her still, she said in as light and friendly a voice as she could muster, "Goodbye Mark, I will see you later. I do hope you enjoy the celebration - there will be lots of colourful things, and music to dance to." She winked at Spenser, hoping he would be able to cosset the boy into a better mood, before leaving.

CHAPTER SEVEN
Hunting

Chester

Henry made only scant enquiries at the riverside, leaving just sufficient time for Jeffries to dawdle out of sight before he hurried after him. If the monk had been significant enough to be present at both his death and Edwards', then, the more he thought about it, the more important it was to ingratiate himself with him. Travelling together could also provide him with some much needed information about the current political situation, so he resolved to go wherever Jeffries was heading. For the time being. Trusting him was another matter entirely.

"Wait!!" Henry raced to the plodding figure ahead of him, smiling to himself. No-one who had been in such haste earlier to impart the news of Edward's death only trudged along now. This monk had an agenda, and it most likely now concerned himself. Henry was becoming more certain of it.

Jeffries paused and looked over his shoulder. Raising an eyebrow, he said, "I confess, I was not convinced you would be able to secure passage at this late hour, unless you were willing to wait until the morn."

"May I join you after all?" Henry asked. "If the offer of a room for the night is still available. I would appreciate some time to think on recent events."

Jeffries turned back to the road ahead. "If you must."

They fell into step together on the dusty track, the horse in between them. Jeffries picked up his pace. After a few miles, Henry, being of similar height to his companion, was surprised to find himself struggling to stay abreast of the older man. Weakened after so long without exercise, and despite his recent meal, he found himself bewildered by his lack of stamina. Henry's discomfort grew as the sun began to drop towards the horizon and the temperature dipped. The chill intruded upon his silent musing. He had to put aside all planning for the next step in his new life, to simply focus on his next stride.

Jeffries, noticing his laboured breathing, pointed ahead. "There is a decent inn a few miles up. We should reach before sundown if you can keep up."

"I'll be fine, old man," Henry couldn't resist. "It is only the result of years of low rations which holds me back." His lips spread into a lopsided smile. "I am free now though, as you say, to make my own way. Feed for myself."

Jeffries nodded, then looked at him with a stern expression. "I have a bow you may borrow. I would prefer you to prey on animals over humans whilst you're in my company."

Henry's eyes flared - he had always had his blood supplied to him. Jeffries continued, "It is not a large inn and any absence would be noted. Any enthralling would equally stand out. Even if you were to get privacy, it would be difficult for you to feed openly. There is no need to draw attention to ourselves. You should be able to slip out during the night to hunt. I'm sure the techniques of using weaponry will return to you quickly. You used to be quite adept, if rumours were true."

Ignoring the compliment, a thrill ran through Henry. Did the monk mean Henry should hunt an animal for himself to drink? He recalled that feeling of conquest, superiority, when one brings down a live animal.

Jeffries' suggestion led to another revelation - a more surprising one. Why didn't he yearn for satiation from a human, as most vampires did? But then, he had never drunk directly from a human either. Perhaps it was a case of what you didn't know, you didn't crave? Henry was suddenly conscious he lacked suitable practise on living beings, human or animal.

As they walked, his eyes scanned the hedgerows to the side of the road with all his senses tuned for animals. Finding nothing, Henry considered that it might be easier to remedy his lack of experience with drinking from people in a town. He smiled to himself - the thrill of the potential hunt remained, yet the prospect of embracing his truest nature was definitely as enticing. Most particularly, the freedom to learn the vampire methods of persuasion. Enthralling was a skill which Mistress Grosvenor hadn't deemed necessary for him to master, and subsequently she had only mentioned it in her brief 'How to be a vampire' education. There was no hurry though. He could play along with Jeffries' request, for now, and savour the anticipation a while longer. Time was, after all, on his side.

Peering over the horse, he saw that strapped underneath one of the packs was indeed an old, but serviceable, bow and quiver of arrows. "Not much good to you there, if you are set upon," Henry remarked.

Jeffries gazed ahead, confidence and experience exuding from him. "I have never yet been attacked whilst on my travels. I have found peaceable talking usually resolves most hostilities."

Eyes narrowing, Henry looked away at the fielded landscape around them rather than argue. When he had travelled the realm as a boy, it had been amongst a large retinue, for safety and to protect his almost-royal personage. Even then, he had witnessed bickering and arguments break out between the party, which made journeys uncomfortable. He thought back to those few occasions when it had been just himself and Henry Howard, his best and most beloved of friends, when they had traversed the country with only a few servants lagging behind with a cart full of belongings. He swallowed away the pang of loneliness, wishing Henry were here now, instead of Jeffries. How this walk would then hold the promise of fun, rather than the role-playing he was currently burdened by. How Henry would have sweet-talked anyone with a stable to get them both astride horses, such was his impatience.

Up ahead, a wisp of smoke rose into the cooling summer air. Jeffries picked up the pace. "Not far now," he encouraged Henry. "I, for one, will be glad of a rest this night." Jeffries glanced over at him, a twinkle of jest in his voice as he said, "Tis a shame you cannot partake of their most excellent meat pie."

Henry stiffly replied, "After seventeen years, I have all but forgotten the taste of human food." He hadn't, and it still rankled.

Inside the warm traveller's inn, the unfamiliar smells of body odour and yeasty hops reminded Henry of his own strangeness. Grateful for his dark habit, as it obscured the droplets of blood he knew were there, hiding his nature amongst the fibres, although he recognised his unruly long ginger hair was at odds with the costume. There were only a few other patrons, mostly travelling traders and two husbandmen, hunched over a small ale, but Henry felt uneasy nonetheless as their eyes flicked over to examine the newcomers.

Jeffries made no attempt to introduce Henry to the bar-keep, who welcomed him like an old friend. Having secured beds in the back room whilst Henry stood looking awkwardly at the floor, Jeffries settled himself on a bench and glanced around. "Go and check the horse is well stabled," he suggested, probably louder than was necessary. His eyes flicked to the door again, before he lowered his voice. "Dusk falls shortly and you will find a suitable wooded area to the west, I'm sure."

Henry nodded, then bent down to retrieve the long leather pouch and quiver propped against Jeffries' saddle bags. His stomach clenched with anger at being dismissed but, simultaneously, excitement at the opportunity to hunt once more.

Once outside the fenced square enclosing the inn's land from the surrounding countryside, Henry set off away from the road. Crossing fields with increasing speed, the exhilaration of freedom, coupled with the realisation that his legs were running at an extraordinary pace covering the ground, almost made Henry want to shout. As he ran, he glanced from side to side, in case a labourer was herding livestock and might glimpse his movement, but he realised he was moving so fast, one blink and he'd be past.

Energised by his release, Henry was slightly disappointed to reach the small copse, then beyond it, a wall of trees signalling a larger expanse of woodland. He slowed, heart barely thudding despite the exercise. His breath calmed as he circled the cluster of willows, elegantly drooping tendrils in the stream. The waterway marked the boundary between the tenanted farmland, waving with ripening barley, and the woods. As he jumped over the cascade with a long stride, he briefly wondered whose animals he would be poaching.

Henry entered the woodland where there was no path and little undergrowth to impede intruders. The passing trunks thickened as he crept deeper in, pushing aside low branches, which sprung back to absorb into the stillness. Henry paused after a hundred feet and lifted his nose, sniffing.

Before he went further, he needed to ready the bow, currently just a straight pole in the pouch slung across his shoulder. Unwinding the leather stay holding the flap at the top shut, he pulled out the tapered wood and ran his hands over it. Not the full sized longbow which he was more used to practising with - the weapon of the soldier and noble - this shorter shafted tool was more practical for travel. He turned the bowstave over, checking for weakness or cracks. The smooth yew was pliant and warmed to his touch even though he knew himself to be cold-blooded. Henry rubbed his thumb over the heartwood centre; the familiar gesture for luck soothed him and for a moment he felt human - Fitz once more, about to enjoy his daily target practise.

As he unwound the hemp bowstring, his eyes scanned the spaces between trees and his ears filtered the rustles of the leaves for telltale sounds of beasts moving around. He leant down on the bow, bending it so that he could loop the sinew into the horn nook at the top. The wood flexed evenly, and as he raised it to test the draw, Henry smiled. This bow was a fine balance of weight and spring - although probably only English yew, the supple sapwood facing the forest in front of him still flexed without hesitation, but held the promise of sufficient power for the range and accuracy to be suitable for this environment. Then, he pulled out a goose-feathered arrow from the quiver before slinging the pack behind himself again. He would only need one arrow, even after so much missed practise, his vampire sight and speed would more than make up for inaccuracies.

Standing still with only the gentle rustle of leaves for company, he waited, balanced evenly on both feet. Henry held the arrow resting neatly on top of his thumb, three fingers ready to pull back the bowstring with speed. Time seemed to slow as he scanned the darkening area around him. This was not the noisy, dog-chasing, exhilarating hunt he had been used to, but in that moment, it was the right way for him to hunt. With patience, his prey would eventually come to him. The stillness of the forest suited Henry, focussing his mind and calming his soul.

The snap of a twig behind him was his reward. Whirling around, a doe ambled towards the stream and he let loose the arrow before it could take another step away. His aim was true. The deer fell without crying out, its body hitting the earth with a deadened thump. Henry rushed over to its side, his eyes gleaming in the dusky light filtering through the leaves. Before the doe pulled a last instinctive breath, even though its brain was already dead from the arrow jutting through its eye, Henry knelt by her side. Placing a hand on the warm chest, he bent over his prize. Pointed incisors punctured the neck exactly where he'd seen the pulse of its last heartbeat and he drank.

Flush with success and sated, Henry walked back across the fields without any particular haste. The fresh night air brought a refreshing coolness from the humid day, and with it, he savoured his liberty. The crickets had ceased chirping, and birds their roosting calls, and he watched the skies and hedgerows ahead for the awakening of the nocturnal creatures. Midsummer, the sky darkened sufficiently for him to observe the myriad of stars overhead, widened pupils marvelled at the pinpricks of white light dotting the cloudless expanse.

His acute hearing picked up the sounds from within the inn long before his physical approach - the grunts of punches being thrown and clatter of stools falling. Wary of the fight tumbling out into the yard, Henry quickened his pace. When he opened the heavy wooden door, his eyes darted to where he had last seen Jeffries, on the bench to the side. He was not immediately obvious. Henry paused, looking past the flying elbows and kicking legs of the tussle destroying the furniture around the bar.

"And you're a damned papist also!" Henry wheeled around to the voice beside him, and then swiftly ducked as a fist swung towards his head. Henry's hand shot up and grasped the man's arm. As he rose back up, swivelling his grip, he twisted the limb. The man gasped as he was spun about and pinned by his own arm being pulled behind him. Henry yanked the arm up, forcing the trader to bend down with the deadlock.

"I am no papist," Henry hissed. He jerked the arm for emphasis and was satisfied to hear a gasp of pain. "And you will mind your manners when you do not know of whom you accuse." With more force than was probably necessary, Henry pushed the man away and he fell, sprawling, to the straw covered floor. Leaving his assailant to roll around clutching his twisted wrist, Henry turned back to the fracas.

Before wading in his eyes narrowed, assessing the measure of the likely sides in the dispute. There were seven men, mostly labourers and the two husbandmen he noticed before. The fight appeared to have gone out of half of them, and they stood now on the sidelines, panting and holding hands to bruised or bleeding cheeks. The smell of the fresh blood would have been intoxicating to Henry had he not just completely drained a deer. It was alluring nonetheless. He glanced again for Jeffries, trying to ignore the jeering from the sidelines. God only knew where the barkeep had disappeared to.

"Princess Mary will rise against this outrage," a labourer spat out. "You show him, Ned!"

"Makes no difference," one of the husbandmen snarled back. "And you should go to Hell for suggesting she challenges a god-given right for a monarch to choose their successor." The fellow jabbed his finger. For a moment it seemed as though their fight was about to rise again, when Henry saw Jeffries slip out of the shadows and place a calming hand on the man's shoulder.

"Good fellows, this is not your fight to have," Jeffries said. The man turned at the intrusion and raised his other fist to take a swing. Without thinking, Henry dashed around the fisticuffs in the middle of the room and grabbed the husbandman's arm before it connected with Jeffries' chin. The man's eyes flared, finding himself trapped. Henry frowned.

As he brought his grip down, his head drew in close. Henry gazed down into the man's brown eyes and calmed his breath. "I think," he said, maintaining his steady look as he blinked slowly, "this has all been an overreaction and we ought instead to let our betters make such decisions in the best interests of the people. Wouldn't you agree?"

He kept contact with the fellow's eyes and poured his will into the gaze between them.

The man recoiled, his body resisting the intrusion of the eye-embrace. Henry grabbed his chin, forcing a maintenance of their gaze. He blinked again, and reiterated, "This is not your fight to have."

Henry could feel Jeffries watching him, but he did not let go of the man's arm or jaw until he sensed there was an acceptance of his suggestion. It had happened in the briefest of moments, but the shift in the husbandman occurred as Henry felt the tension in the limb relax.

There was no time to celebrate this milestone though. Henry turned to the scuffle at his back, still grunting, ducking and throwing punches behind him. And completely unaware of what had just occurred.

Without hesitation, Henry placed himself in the midst of the three and held out his arms. A farmer, bulky and stinking of dung, snarled and leant back as if to throw his weight behind yet another punch. Lunging, the man seemed to assume that the outstretched arm would collapse with the force of his own movement. But he was mistaken. Henry simply moved his arm so that the thrust would result in the base of his hand hitting the centre of the man's chest. This left Henry ample time to dodge the other swinging fist.

Lying winded from meeting the iron rod of Henry's arm, the other two looked at each other with shock. Henry's mouth twitched into a half smile.

"Gentlefolk," Henry admonished. "This is no way to spoil a glorious midsummer evening." His head dropped slightly so that he looked at them both with the mesmerising gaze he now felt more confident using. He leaned forwards, his hands catching their arms with the slightest of touches. "A change of monarch will have no impact on whether it's a good harvest or no. On whether your families will eat." Henry smiled, and blinked. "Surely it is better that we simply respect and love our Queen, or King, as we know they love us all regardless. They do not dictate who we labour alongside, after all. Only that we labour in their name and the Lord's."

The men nodded, then one turned to the other and said, "He's right, it doesn't matter who brings in the harvest, as long as it's brought in." The man on the floor grunted and sat up. He was still struggling to draw breath, so Henry dropped his gaze and crouched down. As he supported him getting up, he caught the fellow's eye, saying, "Let's get you to a stool now." He blinked. "This scuffle is just a difference of opinion, nothing more, and not worth taking before the Parish."

The man nodded. From behind, Jeffries approached and helped pull the injured farmhand into a stagger over to a table. Henry righted a stool and held it whilst the fat dolt sank onto it, nursing his now swollen jaw.

"Tis an awful pain," the farmer complained, still short of breath, chubby hands circling his broad chest.

"I have a tincture I can give you to help with that," Jeffries said soothingly, then he crouched over and took hold of his jaw. Henry watched as he appeared to examine the bruised and swollen chin whilst breathing steadily into the man's half open mouth. Within seconds, the healer's magic eased the mesmerised man and breathing came easier to him.

Henry turned back to look around the rest of the crowd, similarly nursing their wounds. Heads shook as the confusion of what had happened seemed to pervade. No-one noticed Jeffries magic, Henry noted. And no-one seemed inclined to continue the fight, indeed, perhaps they had forgotten why the fight had broken out in the first place. By disrupting the support of some of them, the remainder retreated and gave up. It was an interesting lesson, the calculating part of himself logged.

And, incongruous though his habit may be, he himself was just... ordinary. No-one glanced at him with any sort of suspicion now, Henry realised. Another subject. Just a boy in a bar, picking up the pieces after a scuffle had broken out. He moved around the room, righting stools and mugs, his mind distracted. It was as if he were invisible, he thought, frowning. He had never been in a position where people didn't know who he was, and had to act as if he were a mere commoner. Even as a prisoner in Chester, the very fact that he was guarded and waited upon reaffirmed that he was different. Special.

Henry sat down on a chair in the corner, watching through hooded eyes. Was this what the rest of his eternal life was going to be like? Being a nobody? The thought made the blood in his veins run cold and he knew he would be awake long into the night considering it.

CHAPTER EIGHT

On ceremony

Naturae

Joshua took Aioffe's hand and together they glided through the double doors, out of the Atrium and onto the landing platform. He glanced at her, his breath catching in his throat as he saw how the sunbeams glittered on her white-blonde hair, almost outshining the delicate crown she wore. The sense of occasion lit her from within, her skin positively glowed with anticipation. She was truly a Queen, Joshua thought, as their wings rose up behind them, shimmering like the silver threads of the delicately embroidered trees embellishing her green silk dress.

Attired in formal black robes himself, his huge dark wings beat in synchrony with hers as they ascended as one to a hover above the balcony. In the clearing before them, spaced out in a wide arc, the stubby wings of the worker fae formed a curtain. No more the drab tans and beige of their everyday attire; today, all wore their finest shades in all the colours of the rainbow. The sheer volume of fae before him caught his breath. The entire community living on the island, as well as the Nobles from the wider realm across England, Scotland and Wales, had come to honour this ceremony. As hundreds of wings buzzed, the breeze they generated wafted loose hair into clouds around eager faces.

As the royal couple descended to the ground, so too did the swarm. Joshua and Aioffe touched down on the platform, where the Queen's Guard stood arranged in rows before them. Their armour polished and dazzling white in the sun - an effect which required precise positioning and timing. Joshua couldn't help but beam himself, knowing also what was to come. Letting go of Aioffe's hand, Joshua stood to the side as she walked slowly along the line. He watched as she acknowledged each of the several dozen elder soldiers, most of whom were now greying and weaker, but still proud to be there. Some had even fought in their last fae war, the Sation wars, against the vampires, and survived to tell the tale.

As Aioffe reached the Captain of the Guard at the far end of the line, he bowed then took her hand. Together, they turned and faced the crowd, sweeping their arms in circles around the ground and air, for the masses to acknowledge the fallen fae of old, now delivered to ashes on the winds.

Thane stepped forward, resplendent in new, deep red and purple robes embroidered down his back with all the colours symbolising the workers' designations. He motioned for the crowd to arise. Taking to the air once more, it took a few minutes for the audience to arrange themselves into a steeply sided amphitheatre. Joshua flew over the stage and waited at the back as he'd been instructed to, next to Uffer. The protocol for having a Prince in Naturae, when none could remember one being present before at such a formal ceremony, had been the subject of considerable debate. Joshua hadn't wished to cause any more upset, when the question of Lyrus was still very much unresolved as well.

Thane turned to Aioffe., "Your Highness, the Council and I present for your inspection and acceptance the newest members of our community. May they serve all of us diligently and with the honour and *faeth* with which you have bestowed upon us." He dipped his head slightly and then took his position by Aioffe's side.

From within the crowd, all members of the Council and the Nobles flew forward and formed a circle above the cleared ground below. Joining hands, they rotated slowly through the air, around and around. Joshua admired the coordination of the halo canopy, but could not spot Spenser within it. He forced his face to remain respectful, and not frown. Where was he though?

From either side of the platform, a procession of young worker fae entered, each wearing newly sewn robes and bearing tokens of their status. Joshua looked then, not at the individuals, many of whom he already knew, but at the proud faces of their carers in the crowd. These fae, the first generation born of Aioffe's blessings, were known as 'The Alice's'. They all were named by the letter A, in honour of the human child who had been an unfortunate victim of Lyrus when he captured Aioffe in Beesworth. Although her death had been the last brutal act against humans recorded of late, the return of Aioffe to Naturae had brought about the change, the revitalisation, which the community needed.

Today the Alices, aged sixteen, were considered to have reached adulthood, ready to be accepted into the community as fully fledged workers. It was a celebratory day for all - those who had nurtured and trained this unique generation, and for those who had made it possible in the first place after nearly 500 years of no new pupae being created at all.

Joshua held back his tears of pride. Aioffe stood at the centre of the platform watching, her back held stiff to resist the overwhelming emotion of the moment. From somewhere in the crowd, a clapping rippled through the wall of fae, the sounds blended into a beat, swelling in volume as the Alices processed. As the line stopped before Aioffe, under the Council flying above, she stepped down from the stage.

As she then walked from one end of the line, welcoming each individual fae with her hands on their shoulders and a brief word of congratulation, Joshua breathed easier. Having been acknowledged, the worker fae then turned and, usually with a massive smile on their face, flew up to join their family in the wall of wings. In this manner, crafts folk, carers, household, farmers, all grown from their designated vines, accepted their 'Alice' as one of their own vine family.

As the last worker fae rose to join their group, the crowd gave a collective sigh. Some dabbed at their eyes, while the newcomers were jostled and accommodated into the wall of wings.

Aioffe turned, beaming with tears in her own eyes as she flew towards Joshua on the platform. He smiled, escorting her to the ancient silver throne which had been brought down from the High Hall. He then stood to her side, his back straight like the ornate chair, and gazed out over the crowd. Aioffe arranged her skirts neatly as a drum beat its announcement. They exchanged a knowing glance; she was ready for his surprise.

Joshua stepped forwards and waited for the Captain of the Guard to join them on the other side of the throne.

"Our Queen," he announced. "It is with the greatest of honour that I present the next generation of soldiers to protect your realm."

He turned to the Captain, who stared stonily ahead at the crowd. "En - ter," the Captain shouted.

The crowd's eyes turned to the landing platform above them, where a line of soldier fae balanced, on tip toes on the balustrade. Although there were only twenty of them, lithe and shining with rose-silver armour plates, each face was focussed. In their hands, they wielded slim swords, pointing up to the sky. A nod from the Captain began the sequence which they had rehearsed over the last few months as a part of their training.

Whirling acrobatically around, the soldiers formed two groups, taking to the air to form a spiral. The coil began to spin, advancing on the ground with a speed that drew gasps of fear and amazement from the crowd. In the spiral's core, their brown wings blurred; the nimble fae twisting, spinning flashing blades through the air. The spiral zoomed close to the edges of the crowd, then up and above them, hovering for a heartbeat before plunging down to the clearing floor once more. Flying only feet above the earth, the solders maintained their formation, advancing towards the wooden dais like a lethal rolling log.

When they reached the edge of the stage, they dropped out of the air. As soon as their feet touched earth, their bodies springing into an attack stance. Slashing swords stilled, and they reached behind their backs to unhook slim, triangular metal shields. The troupe flashed the metalwork proudly at their audience, showing off the detailed handiwork by Joshua and other fae.

Joshua's heart sped - impressive though the coil had been, his main input had been the design and creation of their new weapons and their use. The shields were burnished iron, black and toughened to withstand the impact of bullets and arrows. Narrowing to a fine point at the end, they could also be driven into the ground to provide a temporary wall or create an enclosure. Twin dips at the top, sharply edged all around, making the shield itself a formidable blade which would slash a deep wound when correctly wielded.

Stern of face and focused, the soldiers then marched back, forming two lines facing each other. A strictly choreographed routine of balletic battle followed. Each individual fae was allowed their moment of glory in demonstrating their prowess with a weapon, or whirling movement, but there was no doubt that the Alices from the soldier vine were working as one unit. Joshua could see the glances between them as the sequence unfolded, each knew their role and timing, but it was only co-ordination as a group which kept them all alive in the frenzy.

The crowd began to clap - at first a smatter rippling across the clearing, then a noisy encouragement with whoops and shouts. Joshua glanced at Aioffe, staring at the spectacle wide-eyed in awe, oblivious to the growing cheers. But then, her gaze jerked away and her mouth fell open.

His eyes followed the direction of hers, to the landing balcony above. A child's scream pierced the air, cutting through the hubbub. Joshua and Aioffe stood; their wings instinctively flaring behind them.

Mark wobbled at the top of the old steps leading down from the landing platform. His arms wheeling as he teetered on the edge. The cause of his backwards retreat into danger wasn't visible from their seats, but Joshua and Aioffe dashed towards him. As the crowd's heads turned to watch the unfolding drama above, Spenser appeared, lunging for his son's arm.

Joshua reached the balcony first, in time to see Spenser pulling Mark away from the edge. The boy grabbed at Spenser's hair, his face white with terror. Nemis rushed towards them, one arm stretched towards her family, the other pushed behind as if to warn off the threat. Glancing at the double doors, Joshua's heart faltered.

Lyrus. A twisted sneer accompanied the warped arm which grasped towards Mark. Hunched over, his broken body propped by a rudimentary crutch, the former Queen's Guard was a pathetic sight. Gaunt, pale skin stretched skeletally over his face; pointy features protruding in a nightmarish vision. Through lank blond hair, dirty and loose in rats tails, his dark gaze met Joshua's. The sneer turned into a frown. He wavered, his body sagging into the vast door frame and he seemed to diminish. As Joshua glared, Lyrus withered further when he looked beyond Joshua, to Aioffe, noticing her crown and formal attire.

"Lyrus! Why are you out of bed?" Aioffe demanded, advancing on her brother.

In a weak voice, Lyrus answered, "I was only trying to protect the Queendom from intruders." He then snarled and ducked slightly as if struggling to bow. "Your Highness." His tone verged on sarcasm, stopping her short.

Joining her side, Joshua's glare narrowed at Lyrus and his mouth tightened. He said, "You do not need to see him now. I will make sure he is returned to his chambers."

She flashed her blue eyes at him. "He should have been guarded."

Joshua's gaze slid back to the crowd, looking for the soldiers who were supposed to have been at Lyrus's door. Already airborne, the community had naturally gathered, eager to discover what had stopped their show and so distracted their Queen. Their whispers reached his ears and his heart sank.

Lyrus, perhaps sensing he had misjudged the situation, forced a conciliatory look onto his face. "I hope, even in my weakened state, I can still be of service to Naturae."

Everyone on the balcony watched as he attempted to straighten his bent body. He shuffled his wonky legs together, bandaged and wincing with the effort. Lyrus then raised his head, jutting his chin out. "I would never knowingly miss a ceremony." His eyes flicked to Joshua, then returned to Aioffe as the crowd fell silent. He waited, and some pride in his former position filtered into his visage, bearing him up against what Joshua surmised would be agony.

Aioffe, breathing heavily to control her fury and hesitant at first, then took a step closer to him. "Brother, things are not as they were with our mother." She swallowed, then said, "You have awoken into a new Naturae. A revived one. A place where all are equal, and welcome." Her eyes flicked towards Nemis and Mark. "Be they fae, witch, or daemon. All life here is precious." She smiled at the boy, still clinging to his father, and her tone softened. "All are sacred and will be protected."

Lyrus's lips tightened briefly, then he forced a nod. "Understood. Your Highness."

"And that includes you," Aioffe continued. "We would welcome you back to us, if you will agree to abide by our rules."

Although not quite imperious, her command left little choice in the matter. Aioffe usually ruled by consensus but that did not diminish the orders which she alone imparted - it enforced them. She looked at the crowd for their support and acknowledged their approval by steadily turning back to face her brother.

Lyrus dipped his head and kept it there, staring at the planks. Aioffe, with Joshua half a step behind her, approached him. Only when she touched her brother's withered hand did Lyrus look up at her. With apparent honesty in his eyes, he said, "I do."

Joshua stood beside her shoulder - ever ready to defend Aioffe, and ever alert to the possibility that Lyrus might yet rally. He had not forgotten the cruelness with which Lyrus had tortured him before the earthquake in the tunnels. He could not forget the agony of the beating he endured when Aioffe had been torn away from him, or that he had been responsible for Alice's death. Having now seen Lyrus, broken of body but still alive with spirit, the fear of him receded, and he drew himself upright. His jaw clenched; he was more than a match for the experienced soldier he suspected, and would never again be in a powerless position against his old foe. But trust him?

Never.

CHAPTER NINE

Observing from the sidelines

Joshua touched Aioffe's arm, breaking her gaze from Lyrus. "I will escort him back to his chamber. Until you have decided on his role here, perhaps that is best?"

Aioffe's head spun around, taking in the crowd who had gathered, hovering beyond the rails of the landing platform and watching her intently. Although the throb of many wings filled the air, they both heard the whispers of dissatisfaction. Their cherished ceremony had been rudely interrupted, a snub to the community, and Lyrus was only partially to blame. Not for the first time, he saw Aioffe's face drop, but there was little comfort he could offer.

"Yes, please." With reluctance, Aioffe turned away from Lyrus and rose into the air. She forced a smile onto her face and opened her arms in a gesture of welcome. "Let us return now to the ground," she said to the audience. "I believe there is some music to enjoy, and I know you all wish to spend some time relaxing with our newly welcomed fae."

Thane flew forward, his rich purple ceremonial robe bright amongst the green of the leafy trees. "Fae of Naturae, you have all worked long and hard to bring us to this momentous day. Now it is time to celebrate!" He raised a fist and cheers erupted. Within moments, the throng had dispersed to their homes to settle their new family members and prepare for the festivities after.

Joshua and Aioffe looked over at Spenser and his family, still huddled protectively around Mark. The boy clung to Nemis's skirts, and Spenser hovered a foot above the surface, awkwardly bent over mid-air to hold Mark's other hand. Joshua didn't want to drag Spenser away to help with Lyrus, although he could have used the moral support. He sensed his friend would not want to leave his little family just yet. Joshua's lips tightened as he clamped his hand firmly on Lyrus's arm.

Lyrus's dark eyes narrowed as Joshua began pulling him away. His face contorted at the physical reminder that he was not quite a free fae yet. But then, Lyrus turned to Aioffe and called over to her hovering back in a calm voice, "I would be grateful for the rest, sister. I hope you enjoy the rest of the celebrations. I see..." He paused, waiting for her to turn and look at him. Aioffe's face was masked in stone, as Lyrus's gaze then flicked around the clearing and over the repaired entrance atrium before he continued. "Much of your particular talent has gone into restoring the Queendom." He nodded, almost to himself. "You should be proud to have achieved what our dear mother could not."

Joshua watched as a flash of regret swept over Aioffe's features. Yet, she said nothing. A slight tilt of her head was the only goodbye she gave before flying off the landing platform. Joshua yanked Lyrus around as he arose from the floor. There was no harm in reminding his torturer that he was in fighting-fit health, he thought, as he flapped towards the palace dragging Lyrus along behind him.

*****

Having locked Lyrus in his chamber, Joshua returned to the celebration in the clearing. The atmosphere had brightened considerably, with a small group of fae strumming and banging an assortment of instruments in the shadow of the landing platform. Some more familiar to him - pipes and lutes - whilst others were entirely the creation of the fae. One looked to be some sort of percussion arrangement - stretched animal hides of varying shapes, sizes and colours patch-worked onto a large upright frame. Two fae darted acrobatically around, thumping the smaller panels with hands and feet, to produce a subtle yet lyrical background beat. To Joshua's ears, the noise they collectively produced was only vaguely reminiscent of the harmonious twanging and whistling which he would have called music in the human world.

After listening for a few minutes, Joshua concluded he couldn't identify any individual tunes. Rather, the lilting melody, whilst not unpleasant, was unfamiliar in both tone and cadence. It spoke of a musical heritage alien to him, yet somehow felt ancient and mystical. True Fae, rather than the hybrid he was, might have understood the rhythms, but not he. Reminded of his difference and perturbed, Joshua moved away from the noise.

As he looked around the clearing, the music seemed to elicit a response as the community whirled and giggled together. Joshua's heart lifted as he watched the smiles upon the faces of both younger and elder fae, enjoying the afternoon sunlight and each other's company. He strolled about, inhaling slightly. Emitting from them without their realising it were the stands of Lifeforce which he, and especially Aioffe, craved as their sustenance. Warmth spread through him and he enjoyed its relaxing sensation. Joshua grinned and searched for Aioffe.

His eyes fell upon a group of the Alices lurking on the edge of the clearing, who he didn't know at all as well as the young soldier fae. Their brown robes were embroidered with the silver eye, showing they were from the spy vines. As he approached, he studied their faces. Although they were smiling, something about their uniform, fixed expression didn't quite convince. "Not dancing?" He called out as he joined them. Only two of them turned to him with a genuine welcome as he sat with them on the cluster of logs.

"Not a tune I'm familiar with," Joshua said, hoping one of them could enlighten him. "I'm more of a church hymn man myself."

The young fae next to him chuckled, glancing around at the others. "Perhaps you should be singing those to us then."

In physical appearance, they were about the same age as he, Joshua reminded himself. He thought back to how it felt to be that gangly of limb and socially awkward. Outwardly his aging had ceased from that late teenage point when he had been turned, but he still sometimes felt as youthful today as then, regardless of the development of his mind and experience. All worker fae would gradually slip into older age, but over centuries, not millennia like Aioffe and he. An Alice's life was just beginning; it lay in front of them, waiting to be discovered. Experienced. Of all the fae here, the spies had yet to enjoy the thrill of duplicity and discovery – as they were bred to. Had they failed to excite them sufficiently about it during the ceremony, if not before?

"How's the training going?" Joshua realised he had no idea who was leading the group, either in a pastoral or professional sense. He then inwardly grimaced, as he thought about his hours of tinkering with armour, rather than really supporting Aioffe with their young. He ought to know. Guilt pulled at him but he kept his face friendly and approachable as always.

"It isn't," the boy next to him said. "We thought that someone would be helping teach us by now, but…" He shrugged.

Joshua frowned. "Who is supposed to be looking after your training?"

"Issam," the only female fae sat there said. "But he is… very old. Doesn't pay us much attention."

"Old? Experienced though, I'm sure." Joshua tried to remember which of the elders Issam was. Certainly, he wasn't one of the Council, which was surprising in itself. Most of the fae who carried responsibility for others were. "Where is he now? I'd like to talk to him about his plans. Maybe I can help. I'm fairly well versed in how things work with humans, even if I haven't been amongst them for a while."

Everyone on Naturae knew his story by now - the human who became fae because of Aioffe's love for him. The Catholic who had been left with no Church after the reforms of Henry VIII's reign. And now, he was their Queen's consort, her Prince, and the only one with huge black wings. He ought to be the bridge between the two races, Joshua thought. And yet most of the time he felt like neither, although after so many years, Naturae was home. But what did he know about diplomacy? Or spying?

"I think Issam's retired for the day now," the fae next to him said quietly. "He said before that he wasn't much one for celebrations. That spies should keep to the sidelines so they can watch and report."

"And what have you seen?" Joshua asked, curious about how they would surmise the occasion.

The group glanced nervously amongst themselves, saying nothing.

Joshua stared at each in turn, feeling them withdraw from his gaze. He hadn't intended to frighten them, but, it appeared either they were afeared of revealing something remiss, or they genuinely had not seen anything of note. "It's surely allowed to practise your craft on your own people," he reassured them. "How else are you supposed to gain the skills you need?"

The girl fae shifted and turned to look at the crowd, still whirling around and chatting in the clearing. Joshua also glanced over at the celebrations, his thoughts returning to Aioffe, but still he couldn't spot her amongst the throngs. She was close though - he could feel her with his mind. The sensation of that lightest of mental touch, silvery-grey calmness, reassured him and the sides of his mouth lifted.

"I saw Issam talking to Lord Uffer earlier," one of the youngsters said hesitantly. "They looked deep in discussion, then Uffer stood up and walked off abruptly."

Joshua glanced sideways at the boy, then nodded thoughtfully. "What else?"

"A lot of people were busy finding their pupae after the incident on the balcony." The girl shrugged as she spoke. "I know my vine-family were quick to locate me but then they told me to go and be with my friends, then went off in a huddle with others. The upset with that human boy and Lyrus was all they wanted to talk about. But, it's not our place to question, is it? Could be something, could be nothing." Her brown eyes were guarded when they met his.

Joshua's gaze flicked back to the crowd, studying the faces of those still dancing with new concentration. Was her inference correct, he wondered? The smiles and gaiety did seem a little forced now that he observed them. Thane was circulating, diving in and out of groups, laughing too loudly and slapping backs as if he was the life behind the party. As subtly as he could, Joshua inhaled again. Something about the ethereal Lifeforce he ingested now was conflicted.

With a sinking heart, he recognised the tinge which affected their auras. There was a question within it, which hadn't been there before. A questioning of belief he uniquely understood. It could only be the effect of Lyrus's return. For the fae of Naturae's faith in Aioffe and in what they were collectively achieving had previously been unshakable since that first gathering seventeen years ago. But, Lyrus's future here was not something he felt he could constructively influence; that decision lay with the Council, and Aioffe.

He stood and brushed his legs down. With a friendly smile as he turned to the gathered spies, he said, "Keep watching, and learning. And try to relax. This is your day to celebrate." The grin broadened, but even as the words left his mouth he knew it wasn't adequate. He needed to do more. Raising his hand to them as he loped away, Joshua set off to find Spenser, although he thought he guessed the answer to his question already. The Ambassador had enough to cope with right now. Suggesting he ought to have input into spy training was probably too much to ask for, yet he had to try.

CHAPTER TEN

Exposure

Naturae, 14th July, 1553

"Your Majesty," Spenser said, inclining his head towards Aioffe, "this matter should concern you, indeed, us all, very greatly."

Aioffe shook her head, "I think I understand your conundrum, Ambassador Spenser, but we cannot worry about what is happening over in Europe when there is so much work to do rebuilding Naturae."

Around the table, heads nodded support of her statement. Yet her friend's shoulders drooped with tiredness and his chin had set in that determined way. Aioffe's lips pursed as she considered him for a long moment. "Explain again, perhaps in simpler terms, why you are so worried?"

Spenser sighed, and looked at the fae assembled. Although Naturae was usually friendly, accepting of himself as the foreigner who brought them news of other realms and had married a witch, Aioffe understood that there had always been an alienation between his people and hers. This fact no doubt frustrated him. Naturae was so insulated, protected from the influences of other species, she understood how closed-minded it was at times.

"Although we have all had to find other ways to sate our needs," Spenser said, his hands wafting in the air, as if to illustrate his words. "And Naturae has discovered the unique power of its Queen," he nodded deferentially at Aioffe. "The same cannot be said of fae communities across the water. They heavily rely on spiritual worship to pull the ethereal Lifeforce. Then, you must account for the spread of the Protestant faith across our realms. As a result, numbers in many churches are in decline. The humans are conflicted - pulled apart by what their monarchs tell them to believe, what they want to believe, and who else believes. Whilst the fervour for Calvinism, and other such reformist worship has rejuvenated the attendance at religious services in some areas, ever fewer truly worship under the old traditions. They call them the pagan ways, and like here, they are outlawed. But, worse, believers are punished. Vilified. We fae risk becoming obsolete, our ways forgotten about. I cannot put it simpler than that."

Aioffe felt Joshua's hand on her knee and glanced down. Their eyes met and she saw that he was also conflicted. It hadn't been long since Naturae had been under similar threat, but their isolationist solution relied entirely upon her ability to draw Lifeforce from fae, as well as humans, to bestow her blessings. As far as she knew, Aioffe was unique amongst Fae Queens in this regard. The realm was reviving, but it was at huge personal cost to Aioffe and most around the table knew it.

"There is more," Spenser continued, looking now at Joshua. "The Catholic Church which, as you may know, is heavily infiltrated with vampires, grows more militant in its intent. Their desire to dominate the belief landscape partly, I believe, in response to these growing threats from other strands of Christianity, has made them aggressive. In Spain and Prussia, Catholic Prince Bishops steadily hunt down creatures. Most especially witches, but not limited to them, under the guise of branding all of us demons. Unnatural. They are now burning those they catch without trial, or dunking them until they die as proof of their unnatural state." He shook his head. "This is a purge by any other name. By the vampires, against all creatures, being fought in the name of purification. But it is a battle which spreads and will become a war involving Naturae humans if we do not prepare."

A gasp arose from the end of the table where the worker representatives sat.

"Those who are lucky enough to face a trial, such that it is, in these vampire inquisitions, are almost always found guilty of something."

Spenser warned. "You can be certain that clothing would be removed - I hear they strip the accused with witnesses to examine them for marks."

Aioffe sighed. "It is only a matter of time before they expose a fae then." Having lived amongst humans for a century, she and Joshua understood well the lies and pretense it took to remain undiscovered, and there had been some narrow escapes.

Spenser nodded. "That is our greatest fear. I know, on some occasions if revealed, we have been able to explain away our distinction and pose as angelic beings. But I have grave concerns, your Majesty, that with the investigations which people are being subjected to as a part of determining whether someone is possessed, or working with the Devil, or whatever branding they put upon a person to vilify them, a fae's wings would be documented. It is only a matter of time before one of us is caught by a human rather than a vampire, and our race is exposed. Our physical difference is so great, we know the humans would view us as ungodly. An abomination."

Uffer spoke, quietly but with the authority and respect he had earned. "We must stop all visits off the island, your Majesty. The threat of exposure seems too great." He shook his head. "Hunting creatures... those who are different in any way. We should not risk more lives, especially untrained ones. No workers should leave Naturae, at all."

A murmur of agreement rippled through the room. Aioffe's lips tightened, "I take your advice on board, Lord Uffer, but cutting off all outside contact with the humans equally poses a risk. We must maintain a sense of what is happening in our wider realm."

A voice from the side of the High Hall called out, "Then we ready ourselves! Every fae, worker, solider, spy, or noble, we train to defend themselves against these foes."

The Captain of the Guard's eyebrows shot up, then he frowned as Lyrus hobbled towards those seated around the table on the dais. Yet again, his guards had been evaded, or persuaded to look away. As he paused at the bottom of the steps, propped on two crutches, the difficulty in mounting the slight rise seemed a step too much. Aioffe stood, and beckoned for a pair of soldier fae at the back of the Hall, to approach. Between them, they hauled their broken former Captain up the stairs as the Council watched in silence. Panting heavily from the exertion, Lyrus eased into a chair vacated by Simeon, one of the older generation of worker representatives.

Those around the table adjusted themselves in their seats, and Aioffe could sense some discomfort, and some deference as well, at having Lyrus join them at the meeting. Yet she could not dismiss his idea entirely, nor his many centuries of experience as her mother's advisor.

"Captain," she asked, "what do you say of my brother's suggestion?"

The Captain of the Guard sighed deeply, half-glowering at Lyrus. "Your Majesty, we are already spread too thin. Even though there are but few of the new generation of soldier fae joining our ranks, I am struggling to train them to their true capability. Those who joined us at the ceremony yesterday have really only learned their basic manoeuvres. It will take time and effort to get them fully prepared for battle or to protect our realm as well as it ought to be." He glanced at Lyrus. "I don't have the capacity to take on more commitments from worker fae not born to wield a weapon." He looked apologetically at Aioffe. "I'm sorry."

"I thank you for your honesty, Captain." Aioffe said.

"Majesty," Thane's deep voice rumbled. "Even if the workers were to be trained in self defence, it is not their way. Our way. It is not what they were pupated for. Physically I am unsure if they would be able to fight even half as well as a solider, or have the courage of one. Especially as their age advances."

"Nor does it solve the issue really," said Joshua.

Lyrus silkily suggested, "Then we delay until we are more prepared. We send the Church the witches they desire. Let the vampires stay busy with them, whilst we prepare." His lips twisted into a grimace, before he raised a thin white hand to point. "If the Sation wars taught us anything, it is that vampires go to any lengths to protect their blood supply. They are not interested in our blood after all, just those of humans. To survive, human blood must be kept pure. That is why they are hunting down witches and daemons. Given the chance though, they would destroy us. Pact or no pact. Vampires do not change. You have no option but to fight." He jabbed in the air as his eyes darted across the room to measure his support.

Aioffe looked around the table, meeting frightened eyes. Except for

Lyrus, whose hooded gaze now stared back at her with a depth of conviction. Holding the contact for a moment, she was sure his eyelids narrowed slightly, but then the side of his mouth tweaked up and he gave a slight incline to his head.

Aioffe blinked, not sure if she had imagined it, or misread his expression entirely. She turned instead to Spenser. "There is much to contemplate in what you have told us, Ambassador. And I thank you for making the situation clearer so that we might all deliberate on the best way forward."

She placed her hands on the table and stood again. "We will convene later and consider our response." Aioffe noticed that the worker representatives were quick to remove themselves from her brother's proximity as soon as she had issued the invitation to leave. She walked around the table, and by the time she reached him, the platform had cleared except for Joshua who remained seated, glaring at Lyrus.

Aioffe sighed. Now was not the moment to mediate the way through their past battles, although she knew at some point Joshua would have to confront Lyrus and make peace with him for her kidnapping. In her heart, it was a confrontation she dreaded, for it would not end well for one of them and would only lead to heartache.

"Sister," Lyrus said, as she approached. "I hope you do not mind that I joined you?"

"Not at all," Aioffe said tightly. "I hope you can see how we work together in Naturae."

Lyrus's smile was too slight, yet Aioffe thought perhaps genuine. "Indeed, it is a novel approach."

"It works for us all," Joshua said forcefully. "Queen Aioffe is, of course, our ruler, but everyone's voice is heard."

Lyrus's eyes glinted as he stared back at Joshua. "It is not possible for everyone to be equal, when there is clearly a disparity. An anomaly."

Aioffe pulled her shoulders back; her wings started to rise. "I do not know what you mean, *brother*. Everyone is equal here, I have told you that."

Shifting his stance, Lyrus held up his withered, pale hand. "I meant nothing by it, *sister*." He struggled to keep the sneer from his voice. "It was merely an observation that your court appears now to embrace all forms of creature as you said. And yet, not all creatures *are* equal. As Queen, you know this, for are you not extraordinary yourself amongst fae?"

Aioffe gritted her teeth. "All creatures, fae, witches and humans are equal, Lyrus. We may be different, there are even differences between fae, but we are all powerful in our own way. We all have a right to be heard."

"Of course," Lyrus said, then he looked at his twisted fingers. "Except... for myself. Perhaps I am too... damaged. Too influenced by my pain, too infirm to be considered relevant here."

Aioffe couldn't help it - she stared at his mangled limbs and felt sorry for him. He looked up at her, and she couldn't miss the pain in his eyes. He slowly tried to twist around in his seat, making sure that she saw the flash of agony cross his face which accompanied the movement. Although she knew he was deliberate in showing her his misery, it did not diminish the fact that he hurt still. A shadow of the dynamic and controlled fae he used to be.

She glanced up the table towards Joshua, who had been watching the whole time. Briefly his lips tightened, then he turned away, his fists clenched as he strode from the dais. "It is possible that another creature can help with your suffering," she said. "Bear that in mind as you consider your future in Naturae."

Leaving him on the chair, Aioffe flew down the High Hall and joined Joshua as he reached the doors. Landing lightly, he held open the door for her and followed her out.

"My love," he said, as they walked across the inner atrium. "He should not be trusted."

"I know," she replied. "But what am I to do with him?"

Joshua took her hand in his and squeezed it gently. "You will find a way, I am sure. Perhaps he could assist somehow."

She paused and looked up at him. "I worry that he would be too influential with pupae, or," her voice lowered, "too persuasive with the older ones to return to the way it used to be. He is a war-monger, as bad as any human king. You know it was him who decorated the soldier's training room, with those images glorifying war. I worry he thinks he can be that mastermind. That hero. There shouldn't have to be a war. But what if there is? What if it's coming whether we want it or not?"

"Then the solution is to keep him apart from everyone." Joshua said in a clipped manner. "It can be arranged."

"But, given what we may face, isn't that a waste of his experience? He used to be my mother's Captain of the Guard, overseeing elite training."

"He is not really able to do much in the state he is in right now. This notion of training all worker fae - I can see it has merit, for what else have nobility done for centuries but order their tenants to fight for their King and country when required? But, it is somewhat far-fetched to expect our small community to raise arms we don't have for a fight they don't know about. As for training them, Lyrus cannot support the Captain when he can barely move."

Aioffe shook her head. "Then he must be helped to get well again. I thought I should visit Nemis and see if she can make something which would ease his pain. When he recovers more, then we can form a decision. I can make a decision. Oh, I don't know any more, there is just so much happening."

Joshua sighed. "There is still the possibility we could send for Jeffries, if Nemis is unable to assist."

Aioffe mulled the idea as they walked down the hallway towards the Ambassadorial quarters to visit their friends. Knowing well that Joshua held mixed feelings about the monk who had helped him to heal, yet had also used him as a cover for his own purposes, she was beginning to feel overwhelmed by the fresh problems presenting themselves this week.

Joshua knocked on the door, and within moments, Spenser opened it. Before they could enter, a terrible scream filled the corridor and Aioffe watched in horror as Spenser's tired eyes flared. His body swivelled around in response, and his hand reached back into the room.

"Nemis, no!"

CHAPTER ELEVEN
Unruly attraction

Preston, 14th July 1553

Late afternoon brought Henry and Jeffries into the town of Preston. They had ridden hard for miles after their overnight stop at an inn north of Warrington and both were relieved to see the river Ribble ahead. As they rounded the base of Castle Hill, Henry noticed the mound where the old Penwortham Castle had stood and remembered the last time he had been here.

As a child of only six or thereabouts, he had asked his guardians if he could run around the ruins. He'd been restrained by his godfather, Cardinal Wolsey, who said it was not befitting the Warden of the Marches to play when he was supposed to be impressing the might of his father upon the unruly northerners. Henry recalled feeling as bad tempered as a Scot that night, sulking with the servants when they tried to change him into yet another outfit for yet another dinner when he was tired. They had called him 'a petulant' and said, because he was all amort, he'd better stop whining, lest it further dampen his spirits. That he ought instead to try to enjoy travelling through the land which he would possibly rule over one day, before they reached his new home of Hutton Castle. There had always been a caveat attached - 'until the true Queen gives His Majesty a proper heir' - as if his own mother were deficient. He could not remember the last occasion he had seen her, so Henry imagined she must have been lacking in more than just position, in a manner of speaking.

His father had saved him, seen something in him even as a babe, Henry mused. The concept of ruling a kingdom seemed remote in early childhood, but the older he grew, the more his father hinted at it. It was one of those things people said without really imagining he, a bastard boy, would come so close to it, irrespective of how many titles he was granted in readiness. Henry studied the river instead, hoping the babbling water would soothe the anger which rose, unbidden, amidst the tranquil surroundings. Their hollow platitudes and flattery had turned out to be just that. Hollow.

"I must secure the boat for tomorrow," Jeffries turned in his saddle interrupting Henry's memories. "And you should decide how far you intend to accompany me." He raised an eyebrow.

Henry nodded but said nothing. They had talked little these last few days. Jeffries had kept their pace north through the countryside swift, having secured new horses for them both from the inn at Fordham. Conversation was thus restricted to when they slowed to rest the horses. Henrys' thighs and rear pretended they ached from the barrel-like width of the brown gelding he rode - some kind of cross-breed cart horse which farted continuously and had an uncomfortable gait when cantering. The truth was, he was grateful that he didn't feel pain any more, otherwise he would have definitely given up riding. Several times today alone, he had contemplated simply killing the beast, then running on ahead of Jeffries, rather than suffer the ill-tempered, lazy mount a moment longer. A grudging admiration for his elder companion's fitness grew.

Reaching the other side of the narrow bridge, they dismounted, and Henry followed Jeffries along the muddy track next to the embankment. Although the river was miles from the sea and few seagulls circled above, it was still deep enough to carry larger, sea-worthy ships. Small barges and wherries passed them, heading upriver, even this close to the end of the day, ferrying passengers and cargo inland. When they reached the cluster of jetties and single story wharf houses, Jeffries stopped and handed Henry his reins. "Wait here, and keep a close eye on my bags."

Sailors, red-faced from ale rather than the battering of waves, lolled outside a warehouse watching the comings and goings. They didn't react to their arrival, but Henry was aware that he had been noticed. Monks were less common than they used to be, and his height alone made him stand out. "I'd sooner take the horses into town and find some better grazing," Henry said.

Jeffries pointed to a road snaking to the right, lined with a terrace of low stone houses with thatched roofs. "If you follow past the forge and Church Street, you'll reach some common land. We'll need to locate somewhere appropriate for you to feed, and me to rest for the night. It will be cheaper on the outskirts." He turned away, saying, "I'll catch you up."

The words faltered from his mouth as a scruffy, ginger-haired gentleman approached, then laughed. Henry frowned as he watched Jeffries' back stiffen.

"Well, I didn't expect to cross your path again!" The man's voice was as jaunty as the hat he wore, with an enormous red plume sticking out. "Where are you headed this time, Maister Jeffries?"

"Thomas Fairfax." The way Jeffries said it verged on spitting, Henry thought, almost like a schoolmaster scalding an errant whipping boy.

"The very same," Fairfax replied and stuck out his hand. Jeffries made no move to shake it. Henry drew a little closer, and saw, despite Jeffries' intentional slight, the freckled face break into a broad grin. He had brilliant white teeth and a friendly twinkle beamed from wide, bright green eyes. Henry judged him to be in his mid-thirties, and his attire, although slightly askew, suggested he prospered in life.

Fairfax lent back on his heel instead, spread his arms lightly and bowed. As he stood upright again, Jeffries glanced back towards Henry, his face sinking as their eyes met. With a sigh, Jeffries flapped his hand down by way of introduction, as if Henry were no more than a servant. "My travelling companion, Henry."

"Henry...?"

"Just Henry," Jeffries admonished. "As you will be just Thomas." A steely glare reminded Henry that this was a monk well versed in keeping secrets.

Fairfax's grin dropped. "As you wish, Maister." He took off his hat and smoothed his hair down. It seemed an oddly insecure gesture to Henry. For certain, Jeffries was not pleased to bump into him.

"How fares William? And his father, my Laird James Kircaldy?" Jeffries asked cordially.

Fairfax's face lit up and the grin returned. For Henry, drawn closer to him now, it was as if a candle sparked spontaneously to light a darkened room, and he could not tear his eyes from drinking in the sight of him.

"William is well; in France still, I believe. And Kircaldy, alas, he is recovering, slowly, after his release. The French cells took it out of him. He spends much time now writing missives. Furiously." Fairfax's wide lips widened as the warmth of his gaze slid to Henry. "Not my thing, as you know, Maister. Not my thing at all."

Jeffries sniffed and started to walk towards the docks again. "I wish the family well. Please pass on my regards, should you see them, of course. I am sure news of Edward's successor will be of consolation, once it reaches them. I head to Scotland myself, as it happens. The west though."

Henry's eyes narrowed. Now he understood why Jeffries was interested in a ship.

"What do you mean?" Fairfax said. "I have heard that Dudley marches nearly a thousand men to Suffolk, to see Mary."

Jeffries' head shot up. "Lady Mary?"

Fairfax nodded. "She has claimed she is Queen."

Henry looked at the track, his mind tumbling over the possibilities. His half sister, who had been in Kensington Palace also when he died, was staunchly Catholic. Petite yet firm willed, Henry had no doubt that she would be able to command support for her claim. Especially over the relatively unknown girl, who Jeffries had been so pleased to champion as Queen. But Mary, although irritatingly pious, had been kind to him when he fell ill. She had sent constant messages, consoling him that his immortal soul featured in her daily prayers. And she did pray. A lot. Not that it had done him much good in the end.

He raised his head to see Jeffries' lips tighten briefly, then forcing them to relax. Jeffries hadn't taken his eyes from Fairfax, and the man was squirming under his scrutiny.

Jeffries drew in a long breath, then said, "Thank you for the news, Master Fairfax. I will bid you farewell, and leave you to your travels." Glancing to Henry, Jeffries said, "I'll see you later," then he began striding towards the river. Henry was certain he heard cursing carried on the breeze.

Fairfax shrugged, turning to Henry. "Join me for an ale? You look in need of one." He jerked his head towards Henry's horse. "Especially if you've been on that fat lump all day."

Henry grinned; the man's energy was infectious and reminded him of his friend Henry Howard. Then he remembered and looked away. "I'd join you, but I need to…"

Did he? Did he *need* to find grazing for the horses? Henry looked down that path at Jeffries' retreating back. "You are welcome to join me if you are walking my way, but I'm not that thirsty for ale," he said.

"Suit yourself," Fairfax shrugged. "I haven't any particular plans for the next few hours anyway." They exchanged a glance, and Henry felt the touch of warmth, an invitation of sorts, creep into his being. He yanked on the reins and turned the horses around. He could almost imagine that Fairfax's eyes were on his rear as he moved forward.

"Where are you heading next, then?" Henry asked as Fairfax appeared by his side, walking in step with him along the track.

Fairfax's head tilted towards him. "Where are *you* headed?"

The invitation was clear, yet Henry wasn't sure of anything right now. His skin prickled with anticipation, such that he hadn't felt since being with Henry Howard years ago. He couldn't have explained, if asked, how drawn he was to this strange man whom he had only just met, only that he was eager to find out more about him. Choosing not to respond, he looked ahead instead and swallowed.

Next to him, he noticed Fairfax's jaw slid to one side a little, as if trying to restrain another smile. Henry realised he too, was gritting his teeth in an attempt to keep his face neutral. He inhaled and tried to relax as he breathed out. Glancing sideways, he caught Fairfax looking steadily at him again.

They reached the fork in the road where, to their left ran Church street, but ahead lay the common grazing land as promised. Although Fairfax gazed pointedly at the overhanging sign proclaiming the King's Head Inn, he remained by Henry's side. Realising that Fairfax was studying his profile as they trudged along the incline out of town, Henry averted his face and searched the rolling countryside in the distance.

As they approached a modest orchard, Fairfax glanced back before saying as if musing to himself, "A lad your age, not wanting a small ale. A monk's habit. Pale skin and red hair. And King Henry's profile."

Henry stiffened, glancing sideways at his companion; Fairfax was gazing straight ahead with only a dimple in his cheek to suggest his expression. Then Fairfax turned and studied him brazenly.

They stopped and the silence between them grew uncomfortable. Henry said nothing but was reassured by the acceptance he saw on Fairfax's face. He blinked, expecting some form of judgement, but Fairfax just smiled with a gentleness which caused Henry's palms to sweat.

"Mere coincidence," Henry said, without taking his eyes off Fairfax. He blinked, then said, "That you should think someone like myself bears any resemblance to the late King is flattering, and I thank you for it. But it is just the light, and you are tired." As he spoke, he tried to believe it and pass on that belief. He blinked again, hoping it would be sufficient, but Fairfax's mouth had already split into a grin.

"That's the missing piece to the puzzle of you!" Fairfax said, then laughed. "I always wondered how an apparently fine and healthy boy, a man, should suddenly take ill and die."

Henry took a step back. "It happens."

"Was it very horrible?" Fairfax asked.

"Why do you care?"

Fairfax shrugged, "I just heard it was either a wondrous, godly experience - dying and being reborn as a vampire, or, it was terribly painful."

Henry snorted. "A godly experience it most certainly was not."

"Hmm, painful then." Fairfax's teasing look made light of the cataclysmic change to Henry's being, and Henry found he too felt lighter about it.

"Horrendous."

"Dreadful?"

"Unbelievably terrible." Henry nodded, yet a smile was creeping onto his face.

Fairfax tutted, "Awful thing to happen to a chap." He took a breath in, glanced at Henry again and said, raising his eyebrows, "But not the *worst.*"

Henry thought about this for a moment. "No," he said. "The worst is that I had little choice in the matter."

"Ah," Fairfax said. "That would be an issue, I can see. But, still, it's not the worst thing I've seen." His tone turned jovial. "You could have grown wings, for example. I've heard of that. Or, actually died instead." He tilted his head to one side, "Or even, I suppose, lived and had to watch how many step-mothers your father married!"

Henry laughed, "And how many was that in the end?" Although he joked, keener than ever to establish a rapport with the one person who had brought some laughter into his life in years, Henry suppressed his annoyance that Fairfax mocked his father. His father had been a great man, a great King. The best of fathers. The worst of husbands, admittedly, but that didn't detract from his success as a ruler in Henry's eyes.

"Just the six, I believe," Fairfax laughed, oblivious to Henry's discomfort. "And only Edward to show for it all."

"And Mary and Elizabeth."

"Yes, but they are women, and don't count here."

Henry was silent then.

Perhaps realising he had pushed it too far, Fairfax touched Henry's arm. "You know I speak the truth. Even if Mary takes the crown, she will have to rule with a man for this country to accept her."

Henry let the horses have their heads to graze. He leant against the flank of his and said, "There was a fight, two nights ago, where we were staying. It wasn't about the fact that Mary and Lady Grey are women. I think whomever becomes Queen will have more of a battle about which religion they enforce, than their gender."

Fairfax raised his eyebrows, "And you, still here in the shadows. I wonder that you haven't been pushed forward. Some miracle touted around, about being hidden all these years. If you were to stand beside Mary…"

Henry shook his head. "Sadly, although ruling was my intended path, my advocates have left me behind. If it wasn't for Edward's birth after I passed, there might have been an opportunity. But, as it was, he lived long enough to lock up my guardian."

Fairfax nodded, "Norfolk. I hear he still 'lives' in the Tower. Just about." Henry's face looked bleak. Seeing this, Fairfax asked again, "So what are you going to do now, then?"

Henry shrugged. "What can I do? Jeffries has pointed out that I am free to choose, and yet you recognised me."

"Only because I have been in a great many alehouses, collected a lot of books and paintings and," Fairfax paused, "been to Court a few times. I've a good memory for faces, is all."

"Still, I cannot be who I am."

"Then you should be whomever you choose," Fairfax said, gleefully. "I am." He made a mock bow, then struck a pose with his chin up and his hands resting on his hips. "Meet Thomas Fairfax, landowner and gentleman." He removed his hat, his body shrunk as he rolled his shoulders forward, tilting his mouth down into a grumpy, pinched line. "Or Tommy Fair, hostler and gambler." Then he stood straight again and peered down his nose. "Or Timothy of Flanders, rake and voyager par excellence." He winked and leered, waggling his right eyebrow up and down.

Henry's mouth fell open; it had been like watching a player to see how Fairfax had changed his entire persona with just subtle alterations to how he held himself. He felt an overwhelming rush of attraction and almost reached out to touch his arm.

Seeing his hand drop, Fairfax smirked. "I know," he said, wriggling his eyebrows again and thoroughly enjoying the admiration. "I can teach you too?"

Henry shook his head, "I'm not one for disguises." He slapped at his habit, "I can't even pass for a monk."

"That's because you don't believe you are one," Fairfax said knowledgeably. "But you could convince people otherwise." He raised an arched eyebrow.

Henry let out a burst of laughter. "But not you, and not Jeffries."

"That's because we are... different."

"And I am poorly practised."

"No," Fairfax said, and took Henry's fingers. "I've seen others like you do it, the bewitching, persuasive look. It just won't work on creatures."

"Creatures?"

"Witches, vampires, daemons, or fae."

"Fae?" Henry had no idea what he was talking about. And demons? They were, according to the Bible, something to be afeared of.

"You'd do well to stay clear of daemons," Jeffries said from behind them. "In my experience, they always lead to trouble." The growl in his voice made them both jump.

"So you say, Maister. But don't forget who aided you when you needed a ride," Fairfax said, dropping Henry's hand. "And whose blood you no doubt used to prolong dear Edwards' life, so that he might write a will which favoured your choice of successor." Fairfax sniffed, then winked at Henry.

Jeffries had the grace to look away. "I suppose you have your uses."

Fairfax turned his palms up, "If you need to refill your bottle, you only have to say, Maister."

"And you would charge me a hefty bag of coins again, I suppose."

Fairfax shrugged, "Someone has to keep the crew fed and cloth on my back." He gestured at Henry, slightly abashed now. "Or, perhaps, that is why you have a vampire travelling with you?"

Henry began to understand that Fairfax was not at all what his open face appeared to be, and felt a pang of disappointment. Had he imagined that there was something between them? He gritted his teeth and glared at Jeffries, who responded by rolling his eyes.

"No," Jeffries said. "Henry travels with me for now because he chooses to, not because I have need of him." Glancing at Henry, he laid his challenge down, then picked up the drooping reins of his horse and put his foot in the stirrup. "At this moment, calm heads are needed, and Henry has demonstrated admirable capacity to make the right choices."

Henry swallowed and guarded his eyes as he turned to Fairfax. "It was a pleasure to meet you." He gathered his reins, lifted his cassock, and prepared to mount.

Fairfax lent over and patted his arm. "Henry," he said, "Thomas Fairfax, when I am he, lives at Denton Hall, in Yorkshire. If you are passing, be sure to stop and see my library."

Henry nodded, then with a smooth jump, swung his leg over the rotund mare. The smile he flashed Fairfax as they trotted off with was touched with regret.

CHAPTER TWELVE

Two requests

Naturae

Joshua pushed the door fully open and rushed into the dimly lit chamber. Spenser froze, staring at Nemis. Her head tipped to the ceiling as her awful shriek pierced the room, yet her eyes were vacant and glazed. The scream ended as Joshua approached, just in time to catch Nemis as she collapsed, swooning into his arms.

Joshua glanced at Spenser and Aioffe as he hauled her body up, onto the covers. He then noticed Mark, motionless and wide-eyed as his mother was yet again, yanked from his side by her visions.

Seeing her begin to convulse, Spenser left the doorway and dashed over to the bags on the shelves. Aioffe, closing the door behind her, went straight to Nemis's head. Crooning, she stroked her forehead as Joshua arranged her legs on the bed, lightly holding them down as they began to shake.

"It'll be over soon, Mark," Spenser called over. His hands shook slightly as he approached with the little brown bottle. Gently, Aioffe held open Nemis's mouth and he dropped a little of the liquid onto her tongue.

"How many fits has she had?" Joshua asked Spenser whilst they waited for the medicine to take effect.

"Today?"

Joshua met Spenser's eyes and his heart skipped a beat. He looked back at Nemis, then shook his head. "We need Jeffries."

Spenser's mouth tightened. "There are not many doses left." He grimaced as he replaced the cork.

Aioffe said, "Does anyone know where he is?"

Spenser's head shook. Swallowing, Joshua suggested, "We could send kestrels?"

"We only have a few," Aioffe said. "And he could be anywhere."

Sighing with frustration, Spenser pointed out, "Without information as to his last whereabouts, they might never return."

"We need to narrow the search." Aioffe said. "Perhaps the nobles know?"

"It is worth a try," Spenser said, "but they would not keep their eye on a single witch who, as we know, travels around a lot."

"Fairfax..." Nemis whispered. Everyone turned to her with relief. She smiled weakly, but stayed resting.

The knot in Joshua's stomach began to ease. He sighed, "I suppose he might help. At least he is embedded within the circles which Jeffries moves. Or moved."

Aioffe stroked Nemis's head. "You are amazing, dear friend."

Nemis said faintly, "Knows the way here too."

"Wouldn't Fairfax be just as difficult to find?" Spenser asked.

Joshua grinned. "Not exactly. Just follow the trail of chaos in his wake. Look for the trouble and he'll be at the heart of it."

Even Aioffe giggled, although it was faintly hollow. Their daemon friend was well known for inadvertently causing upset, but somehow always managed to wriggle away from it unscathed. The only time he had been on Naturae, Fairfax had accidentally killed Aioffe's mother, forcing her to step up and rule. But, he had also sailed Joshua here, so he would always have Joshua's gratitude.

"He isn't usually far from his ship," Nemis said. "Narrows the search."

Joshua walked around the bed, sitting then at a desk under the wide-open window. "So the kestrels need only scour the coastline. Assuming he's not voyaged off somewhere." He tore a strip of paper from the sheet on the desk and picked up the quill. He paused, tapped the feather to his lips, then began scribbling.

Spenser helped Nemis sit up in the bed whilst Aioffe passed her a cup of water. Mark, who they had all almost forgotten in the urgency of the fit, burst into tears. Joshua immediately replaced the quill in the inkwell and went over to the lad.

"It's alright," he said, taking one of the boys' hands as he knelt in front of him. "See, your Mama is fine now."

Spenser smiled reassuringly and patted the cover next to Nemis. Joshua glanced over to see Aioffe's fingers twitching, as if she were feeling the surrounding energy. Her face fell and she stepped back from the bed as Mark was guided towards his mother by Spenser. The little family clung to one another.

Catching Aioffe's eye, Joshua smiled, but then she turned away. Perhaps it was the fear on her face, which he assumed she didn't want their friends to see. Perplexed, he returned to the note. His soul ached that she would feel such empathy for the boy, but she had pulled back from joining in with consoling him, as if she couldn't bear another burden. Joshua, helpless for a moment, looked down at his writing.

Ought it to be in code, he wondered? In case someone other than Fairfax intercepted the message. He turned the notion over in his mind, thinking about the skills which Fairfax had with duplicity and spycraft. Another idea took shape, so he scribbled a second note.

"Nemis," Aioffe said, "When you are recovered, I wonder if we may talk about my brother?"

"What about him?" Nemis sounded cautious. She clutched at Mark's thin shoulders and the boy returned by reaching around her ribs even more.

Aioffe glanced towards the entrance to the turret, where Nemis had sometimes brewed a restorative potion for her. Joshua suspected they were a special blends of herbs, possibly no more than any other cunning woman would have concocted, but Aioffe had always said she felt better after taking some when she was particularly tired from blessing. Nemis usually deferred to other witches she knew of, or Jeffries, as being proper healers where there were more significant injuries. Joshua wondered now, in the light of the fear he read in Spenser earlier, whether this was to do with maintaining their reputation and trying to stay hidden.

"He is in a lot of pain. I fear that he will never regain full use of his limbs. Even if," and Aioffe gestured at Joshua, "we can find Jeffries and bring him here to treat you, and do something to help Lyrus, I wondered if there was some tincture you could make for him in the meantime?"

Nemis looked at Spenser, who tightened his grip on her shoulders. "I'm not sure I can," she said. "I'm not sure I would either."

Aioffe nodded. They all knew that Lyrus had tortured Joshua, and Nemis viewed Joshua as the brother she never had. Nemis would be rightfully afraid of Lyrus, and she hadn't even been present at the Council meeting where he suggested offering up witches to the Catholic Church. Spenser would doubtless have told her though, especially as Lyrus had already attacked Mark just days earlier. Nemis had no reason to want to help Lyrus, which they all understood.

Joshua said, "We will protect you, Nemis, and your family. You know this." He turned to Aioffe, who was pacing the floor. "And I will take responsibility for ensuring Lyrus cannot move around the palace unguarded."

"Until such a time as we know his intentions," Aioffe said. She walked towards the bed again. "I would so appreciate anything you can do to help. But, only when you feel strong enough."

Nemis frowned then glanced at Mark's head nestling in her armpit, before saying, "What if, Lyrus is the dark heir? I couldn't make out a face in my visions, but…"

Aioffe's eyes widened.

"I don't see how he can be," Spenser said, his eyebrows knitting together. "He is male, and only a Queen can rule. A soldier fae more than he is a royal. How can he be an heir?"

Joshua stood and crossed the room to his wife. "I'm sure he isn't," he said, and touched his hands to her arms. "You are the rightful heir to Naturae."

"But I have no heir to follow me, should anything happen," Aioffe whispered. She looked at Joshua's feet, planted solidly in front of her. He placed his fingers gently under her chin and lifted it so she met his eyes.

"My love, we have plenty of time to worry about that."

"And other pressing concerns to manage," Spenser added.

Joshua felt Aioffe pull back and look beyond him, to Nemis. He turned and saw the troubled expression on her face.

"What is it?" Aioffe said, "Was there something else in your visions?"

Long dreadlocks fell over Nemis's brow as she dropped her head. Joshua and Aioffe went to her side.

"Tell us, friend, what has upset you so?" Joshua said. Spenser pulled her into his shoulder, rubbing her neck absently. Nemis sniffed and leaned into her husband's embrace. Joshua's protective urge rose again, along with a flash of regret. Although he understood Aioffe's desire to help her brother, it should not be at the cost of putting Nemis and her family at risk. With the witch hunts on the continent, the pressure on the family, especially her, to hide must have increased tenfold. Naturae ought to be a safe place for them all, and yet they could not feel comfortable with Lyrus around. Joshua urged, "Please, let us worry about Lyrus. He should not be your concern."

Spenser looked at them both, and said, "I don't think this is entirely to do with Lyrus, is it?" He dropped a kiss on Nemis's hair, and she burrowed deeper into his warmth. Joshua, not knowing what he could do to ease her suffering, stood instead.

Aioffe knelt on the bed and took Nemis's hand. "Let us know what we can do to help, dear friend. Whenever you are ready to share what ails you, we will be here." She turned to Spenser, "Why don't you take Mark to see the seals? Let her rest a while with me."

Spenser nodded, squeezing his wife briefly then slid off the bed.

Joshua noticed Nemis's cheeks were wet with silent tears. Spenser scooped his son up onto his hip, grabbing his cape and opening the door. As they left, Joshua finished his notes and rolled them tightly into a scroll. Then, he smiled at his wife and friend, huddled on the bed. "I am but a call away," he said, dropping a kiss on both of their heads.

Aioffe looked at him gratefully and his heart leapt. For once, he thought he was doing the right thing, however minor a gesture it may be. He hoped it was the right thing, at least. As he closed the door behind himself, Joshua twirled the scraps tighter together. He would find time soon to talk to his wife about his second request of Fairfax.

CHAPTER THIRTEEN
Opportunity

Preston, 15th July 1553

As a glum-faced Jeffries and Henry neared the docks at dawn, it was with some surprise that they heard a kerfuffle. Jeffries paused, then glanced uneasily at Henry before continuing down the road, towards the noise. Passing barrels left ready for salting fish later, Henry identified Fairfax's grunts coming from the end of the embankment aboard a small sailing vessel harboured there. A scuffle was taking place on the deck - all Henry could see was the occasional burst of a red feather as boots thudded on the planks.

"Bobolyne! He never learns." Jeffries mumbled his insult, then looked upriver, towards the largest of the boats moored there. "That's ours. Best get these packs stowed quickly. The Captain wants to catch the tide."

Henry's lips tightened as he watched the incident, instead of doing Jeffries' bidding. Two men were now dragging Fairfax down a gangplank and he wrestled against their every move. At the end of the jetty, an officious-looking man, wearing dark robes and a square pointed hat, waited for their prisoner to be brought to him. Henry's mouth dropped, as he recognised one of the men holding Fairfax's arm as having been in furtive conversation with Jeffries last night. Afterwards, Jeffries had brushed off his query as merely a request for news of a local friend.

"What did you do?" Henry demanded.

A small smile played on Jeffries' mouth. "It is nothing," he said. "What becomes of Master Fairfax is of no concern to you. His kind will always get into trouble of one sort or another." Jeffries had been in a foul mood since their arrival in Preston and their discovery of Mary's rise to the throne. Frowning, Henry ran out of patience with him. He dropped Jeffries' bag on the path side and stalked off towards Fairfax.

"Henry!" Fairfax cried out as he noticed him striding past the stretch of jetties which formed the harbour. "Tell them!"

"Tell them what?" Henry called back.

"The gloves for his daughter were a gift from you, not a promise from me. *Will* you tell him?"

Fairfax's eyes looked desperate, a vivid green in a sea of freckles. His dishevelled hair needed slicking down, but hands were clamped around his wrists. Fairfax dug his heels into the struts of the gangplank, making the precarious gap between boat and jetty all the more dangerous as he resisted their yanks forward like an unwilling goat being hauled onto a cart.

Henry immediately understood the request and approached the gentleman in charge, pulling his cape around him as if he could hide his attire. "My good sir," he said in a clipped accent. The man turned his face to him obligingly. Ignoring the weasel-like set to his stern expression, Henry smiled, without bearing his teeth, and leaned closer. "I would be most obliged if you would reconsider. You see, as my friend here says, it was I who proffered the gloves... There has been a misunderstanding."

A tall man dressed in a monk's habit looming over a small, well-dressed gentleman would have looked peculiar to some, and the suggestion of tokens being exchanged might have seemed far fetched, but Henry blinked slowly into the official's gaze. He continued, "I meant for them merely to be a token of my regard, not mistaken for something more significant than that." He blinked again; the man stared back as if Henry were the singular, most fascinating person in the world.

"Certainly not a proposal of marriage!" Fairfax called out, having stumbled down onto the jetty with the prospect of freedom at hand.

"Most certainly not a token to be misconstrued as anything other than respectful towards your daughter." Henry said quietly.

The man nodded. "My daughter... who are you?" The weasel face relaxed and seemed almost benign.

"Your daughter's honour and virtue is not something which I, or you, should question." Henry said, pouring his will into his gaze, and then blinking slowly once again. "This has been a disproportionate reaction to a simple, well-meant gift. That man is entirely innocent of any wrongdoing. As am I," he added.

The gentleman nodded slightly. Henry put his hand on the man's arm. "Now, let us all return to our day, as I am sure you have much to attend to. There is no need to delay us any further. You should order your men to get back to their work instead, so you can return to your business."

In his peripheral vision, Henry caught Fairfax jerking his arm from the clutches of the two men on either side of him. He noticed a sealed letter sticking out from the edge of the man's coat pocket. "You must make haste with that missive after all."

"Yes," the gentleman said, his eyes still not wavering from Henry's as he spoke. "Rogers and Smith, go back to the stables and fetch me my horse. I must carry on with my visits."

Henry blinked slowly again, then stepped back. "It was such a pleasure to meet you, sir. I do hope that you will pass on my best regards, and well wishes for her future prospects, to your daughter. I would not wish for us to keep you from your business any longer."

"Yes, yes," the gentleman muttered, patting down his jacket as if he had lost something. His hands grasped the corner of the folded paper. "I must..." He turned, then glanced back, manners prevailing. "I bid you farewell, sir," he said, before scurrying down the road.

His men looked at each other in confusion, then shrugged. "Sorry," one of them mumbled at Fairfax, who waved his hands as if it had been of no matter, then they ambled after their master. Once out of earshot, Henry turned to Fairfax and beamed.

"I told you it would work on normals," Fairfax said. "Thanks for coming to my rescue."

Henry was slightly taken aback by Fairfax's cavalier approach to the imminent danger he has just been in. It looked very much like he'd been about to be hauled in and forced to make good on a promise to a maid, yet he had shrugged off the dalliance and the threat as if it was nothing. Henry looked back up the docks towards the ship which Jeffries waited beside. "I'm happy I could help."

Fairfax's eyes lowered. "It wasn't by chance that I was waiting on my boat this morning."

"Oh?"

"I need Jeffries. Needed to catch him before he sailed." Fairfax's eyes glinted, "And it's always good to see you, of course." Fairfax clapped his hand on Henry's arm. "Thanks again for getting me out of a spot." He winked. "I knew you were the right man for it. Some day I'll have to make a chaste woman honest, but not today. Or last night," he laughed. "I should stick to..." Then his eyes darted away, almost shyly, from Henry, and a flush rose to his cheeks.

The energy now fizzing from him reached Henry's nose and his skin prickled again. Henry resisted his urge to touch Fairfax, just to see what would happen, and turned instead to look towards the boat Jeffries had pointed out. Against the rising sunlight, Henry saw Jeffries was aboard, watching them from the prow of the twin masted trading ship.

Fairfax took off, "Must dash!" He called back, "Before the Maister leaves without my message!"

Henry followed, catching up easily. Fairfax shot him a grin as they rushed up the road. Henry felt as if somehow, he would always be caught in the tailwind of his whirling daemonic energy. It made him wonder what adventures they could have together. And he realised, he wanted that also, for the thrill of it.

"Maister!" Fairfax called, "Come down!"

"Not likely." Jeffries' tone was final. "Henry, we sail imminently. Come aboard if you come at all."

"I had a kestrel at dawn," Fairfax shouted.

Jeffries froze.

Fairfax wouldn't give up that easily. "From Joshua! Do you remember...?"

Jeffries frowned. "What did he say?"

"I cannot shout that up to you," Fairfax said. "Bring your bags."

Henry watched as Jeffries' lips tightened, yet he turned and disappeared. A few moments later, he reappeared at the side of the ship and gestured for a crewman to push out the gangplank again. He had no bags with him, Henry noticed.

"I will not entertain any of your foolishness," Jeffries said as he stepped down to jetty. "Now tell me what the note said."

Fairfax plucked a small scroll from his breeches pocket, pulled it open, then slid out a second scroll rolled up within the first and thrust it towards Jeffries. The outer note he stuffed back in his pocket.

As Jeffries unrolled the tiny paper and squinted, Henry glanced at Fairfax whilst he waited. That same energy, a gleeful expectancy, exuded from him, and once again, Henry felt a pull towards him.

Jeffries reached into his pocket and pulled out a wood-rimmed monocle, which he then used to study the lettering. His shoulders drooped, and he crumpled the note into his palm. "I assume you have seen this?" He asked. As Fairfax nodded and restrained his broad grin, he turned and retreated back into the ship.

"He's got to come," Fairfax whispered, absent-mindedly.

Henry's eyes widened. "Come where?"

Fairfax's response surprised him. "To the Queendom of Naturae." Then he frowned, "But you cannot."

Henry's brows knitted together. "Why not? Where is it?"

Before Fairfax could answer, Jeffries plodded down the gangplank. Henry reached out to help take his bags, but Jeffries clutched onto them and turned slightly away.

"This is where we part company," Jeffries said, looking at Henry.

"But…"

"I have been forced to," Jeffries broke off, glaring at Fairfax, "alter my travel plans." He shook his head. "You may not join us."

Fairfax looked at the ground, then back up at Henry. His lips clamped together and a look of regret appeared in his eyes. "Unfortunately," he said.

"I don't understand," Henry said. "Why can't I go with you?"

"Why would you want to?" Jeffries grumbled. "When your new world is out there? Go. Enjoy your freedom."

Henry glanced at the ship on which Jeffries had arranged passage for them both on. It didn't matter now. Jeffries had been the one who wanted to go to Scotland, not him. What was so compelling that the monk would drop his other commitments so quickly, he wondered? No-one saw Henry's eyes narrow as he thought of his own plan. He wasn't ready to give up yet. He needed more time with Jeffries.

Fairfax bent over to take one of the saddle packs. Shooting him a pleading glance, Henry said, "Perhaps I could ask you to take me with you some of the way? Just to get me further on my journey." Fairfax instantly beamed at him.

"No," Jeffries said firmly.

"It's my ship," Fairfax said. "We can make a stop to drop him off up the coast." His grin widened. Henry immediately felt the tingle of his anticipation and his own rose once more.

Jeffries shook his head, glaring at Fairfax. "It is bad enough that I must come with you," his voice lowered, "but I will not risk a vampire in your proximity."

Fairfax held Henry's gaze, then winked. "I am sure I can handle myself," he said. "Henry's strength will help us to get there faster as well."

"Only when he has been fed sufficiently," Jeffries growled.

"And I will, of course, only hunt animals." Henry pointed at the bow slung across Jeffries' back. "I could bring you fresh supplies."

Jeffries snorted before turning towards the embankment. "Do not say I haven't given you fair warning, Thomas. Henry is, to all intents and purposes, a new turning. I cannot protect you should he find you as alluring as other creatures do." He set off down the track. "I am surprised you are as keen to return yourself. It is not a place I relish going to, I confess. But, I am compelled, and this may yet," Jeffries glanced at Henry with some reproach, "provide me with the opportunity to discuss your crisis of faith, so…"

Henry and Fairfax fell into step with each other again as they followed Jeffries to Fairfax's ship. It took Henry a great deal of restraint to keep the skip from his feet as he kept catching Fairfax's mischievous glance.

CHAPTER FOURTEEN

Unburden

Naturae

In the quiet of the Ambassadorial chambers, Nemis clutched at Aioffe's hand. Letting her friend's silent sobs flow out of her, Aioffe crooned a comforting song which seemed to ease her friend's mind. The lyrics spoke of love and loss; Aioffe wasn't sure what brought it to her mind, but the tune had reached her in times of sorrow, and it sprang to her lips here and now.

"We will keep you safe," Aioffe whispered when she finished, although she began to have doubts about for how long. As the day deepened into afternoon, Nemis relaxed her hold on her fingers.

"I know you will try," Nemis said, and more tears threatened. "It's just being here, without the constant watching. Allowing me to feel. To breathe. And now, Lyrus. But then, nowhere is ever really safe, is it? There's always something to worry about."

"Would you like a drink?" Aioffe asked, getting up from the bed and thinking about how she needed to get back to her duties now her friend seemed to have calmed down.

Nemis shook her head. "No, I would prefer to go for a stroll. There are some plants I will need and they are at their most potent if plucked in the half light."

Aioffe smiled, "I will have a basket fetched for you. Do you want some company? I can see if Joshua is back yet, or Spenser?"

Turning her dark, puffy eyes to Aioffe, Nemis reached for her friend's arm. "I would rather speak with you. I think it is time we both talked of what is on our minds."

Aioffe looked at her fingers. "I have some things..."

"I know - which you must attend to." Nemis pulled Aioffe's hand back in hers. "But you must also attend to your mind, Aioffe. If not to quieten it, at least to give it a voice. I know I am not the only one who needs to unburden."

Aioffe felt her fingers tingle, uncertain if it was something in Nemis's growing aura, or the need to unfurl the blessings niggling. Perhaps Nemis was right. Talking might help. Aioffe could feel a pressure mounting in the long, indecisive silence between them. Her wings drifted up behind her, half-heartedly as if preempting a fight but without certainty. But Nemis was her trusted friend. There was no purpose in running now. She was simply offering her ears to one who maybe had need of them. Feeling foolish as there was no threat, Aioffe stood back, nodding her assent, then waited whilst Nemis clambered off the bed. They smiled shyly at each other, witch and fae. Creature to creature. Women. Mothers. Wives.

Wrapping a shawl around her shoulders, Nemis then pocketed a sheathed tiny sickle, a small empty jar, and some roughly sewn hemp bags. Instead of heading back towards the central atrium, Nemis led as if she had always lived there, down the ladder from the turret. Aioffe flew by her side the entire way down, still watchful in case her friend might lack the strength to hold on to the rungs. Once safely on the ground, Aioffe took her arm and they ambled across the clearing through the forest.

"Which way?" Aioffe said as they reached the sacred trees, Ash and Elm. Nemis sniffed the air with her eyes closed. She turned, her feet making dips in the dry earth beneath, and walked about the trunks. Aioffe waited in silence, her nose filled with the many scents of the flora around them but unsure of which in particular Nemis had in mind to gather.

"That all rather depends," Nemis said. In the half-light, Aioffe could see the guard on her friend's face.

"Depends on what?"

"Whether you feel you need to heal Lyrus."

"Or?" Aioffe frowned.

"Or Naturae?"

Aioffe froze. "What do you mean?"

Nemis sighed, "I know I talk in riddles when I'm having a vision, but I'm trying to be clear about what it is you are asking me to do?"

Her frown deepened as Aioffe said, "Lyrus, of course." She touched the rough bark of Ash, warm to her touch and pulsing with the Lifeforce with which she had infused it with so many years ago as a part of the regeneration of Naturae. "There's nothing wrong with Naturae."

Nemis looked at her through veiled eyelashes, and her mouth tightened.

"Nothing that time won't cure," Aioffe went on. "More blessings, of course." A comforting yet tangy scent caught Aioffe's nose, one which she didn't recognise, and she rose a few inches off the ground, turning towards it. "It's more the time, actually." Aioffe said absently. "I never seem to have enough of it these days."

Nemis followed her. "Time for what?"

Aioffe sighed as she fluttered slowly through the tree-trunks. "Time for anything. It seems like it's always one thing after another. Thane needs this, the pupae want that, the Council wants this matter looking at and deciding upon."

Aioffe stopped and turned to Nemis, her eyes flaring as she cocked her head to one side. "Except they don't decide. Before we all seemed to be pulling together; now we can't even determine where to keep Lyrus. Or what to do about him. Or anything, despite my best intentions. We talk around in circles most of the time." She sighed. "And there are so many pupae to bless; each wants to feel special. Ought to feel special." Aioffe looked at her hands then, and felt grateful Nemis couldn't see the pain in her eyes.

In a small voice, she admitted, "And to me, they are just more people to consider. All special because they are new fae, who will go on to give back to the community, I know. And yet, no-one is special. No-one individual. So many little ones." She glanced up at Nemis, and was surprised to see tears brimming in her eyes once again.

"Oh Aioffe," Nemis said, and her voice cracked. "All these children, and I have but one left."

Aioffe's stomach dropped. "Nemis, I.... How thoughtless of me. I am so sorry."

Nemis blinked away the tears. "It's all right. How were you to know?"

"Joshua said he was expecting there to be a larger brood of children you would bring with you. Then, when it was just Mark, I thought maybe you had left the others with someone... I am too clumsy. I'm sorry."

"No, they were lost." Nemis's lips wobbled as she leant against a tree. Aioffe rubbed her arms, still too ashamed to look her friend in the eye. Such matters were difficult to speak of, even though loss was a part of every family's burden. As a cunning woman, Aioffe knew Nemis would have witnessed far more children die than most, yet to lose your own was entirely different. Common, but painful none the less. Aioffe had no experience of losing a child. She found she couldn't even imagine it, so great was her fear to envisage such a devastation. She searched the woodland floor, reaching for the right words to comfort her friend, and failed.

"What happened to them?" Aioffe asked, as Nemis's silence seemed to invite her to say something. Anything.

Nemis shrugged slightly, "Childhood fever for Robert and Emily. The sweating sickness claimed one in the womb. Nearly took me also, but Spenser saved me." She looked at the nettles growing at the base of the tree, and almost as if to take the greater pain away, rubbed at the leaves as she talked. Aioffe winced but understood that Nemis needed to say what was most pressing in her heart, irrespective of the anguish it was causing her to talk of it.

A gentle breeze caught the stalks and after a minute cooling her face in it, Nemis said unfalteringly, "Every babe since then I have lost. There's only Mark left, and he is troubled also, but by what I cannot say." She glanced at Aioffe, "I think he is a version of Fairfax, of his kind somehow. Because of his tendencies, we have to keep him hidden. I cannot go out, or leave him alone." She shook her head. "Only when Spenser is home can I have some kind of freedom. But, even in Anglesey, they watch. The Church. The village. They know I'm not... normal. So I must behave impeccably. Attend church, house calls to make a few pennies, and interact as if there is nothing different about my episodes at all. Just an occasional illness. But there is. I fear going out in public in case a vision overtakes me. Mark sees it, it must be affecting him. Even Spenser knows the visions concern his realm not mine." She sniffed and started to twist her hands together to ease the remnants of the stings.

"Mark is a complicated child, I know," Aioffe said. "I have felt the confusion in him. And it's not just the daemon side."

Nemis nodded, "I wouldn't be without him, but he does take extra loving, that's certain."

Aioffe bent down and breathed onto a dock leaf sprouting in the shadows. Seeing it ripple with her magic, she picked it and crumpled it into a ball, before passing it to Nemis.

"At least he is truly yours," Aioffe said hollowly.

"Ours." Nemis looked at Aioffe and touched her hand.

Although Aioffe's lips tugged up to the side, she knew it wasn't reaching her eyes.

"And what of Spenser?" She asked, not sure if she wanted to know the answer. "What does he do to help?"

Nemis's eyes brightened; her love for her husband glowed as she said, "I feel so blessed with him by my side." But then, her face dropped and she followed with, "*When* he is by my side."

Aioffe looked down. "I'm sorry," she said. "I didn't realise. I'll tell him he doesn't need to be here so often, if it helps."

"It's not Naturae. It's all the courts in Europe." Nemis sighed. "I think there's something going on that's keeping him there."

"Not another?"

Nemis smiled gently, "No, I'm fairly certain it's not that. For all his gadding about and gaudiness, he loves me. But he just can't talk to me about the fae there, or to them about me. I know that. He has to keep our lives separate." She peeked at Aioffe, shrugged, then looked down. "We know it's only here that we can be together, or on Anglesey, deep in the wilds."

"It's a foolish rule." Aioffe huffed. "Has he said nothing about what's happening?"

Nemis shook her bowed head. "Only that he insists on me being on guard at all times, to be careful what I say or do. For protection as I'm so obviously 'different.' And to, above all else, follow the laws on the religion of the time, even if it is not what we believe, I must appear to be god-fearing and true. Never give anyone cause to suspect us of anything other."

"And the visions, don't they give you warning of trouble?"

Nemis glanced at Aioffe, her eyes wide. After a moment, she said thoughtfully, "These latest visions are too disjointed. Brief, sudden. Grey." She looked through the trees, to where wisps of the mist had begun to creep closer, shrouding the island ever-thicker as the evening drew in. "Then, I'm wading through the darkness. And I can't see the way out, or even the way ahead."

Aioffe put her hand on her friend's arm again. "That sounds dreadful. Scary."

Nemis shivered at the recollection. "What's worse is that they are silent. Sometimes, I hear things through it. The haze. But lately, it's been deadened, as if I am deaf as well as blind."

"Don't you hear yourself crying out?" Aioffe asked.

Nemis blinked. "Mute also, then," she said. "I don't know how to explain it better, except that I am all alone, with the wall of grey all around me, and I just know, I can't interpret how, but I just know, that there is something coming. Something dark and wrong. I don't understand what it means." She shrugged. "No faces, figures, or anything. I feel utterly disconnected."

"The sooner we talk to this Maister Jeffries, the better, I think." Aioffe picked up the basket, not knowing what else to offer as help. For all of her own magic, a witch's visions were mysterious and rare. "Maybe Spenser will be able to tell us what else you have cried out, apart from the dark heir coming. I can also search the Scriptaerie, just in case the recording scrolls or reports from Nobles might mention something which might assist."

Although when she would find the time, Aioffe didn't know. The Scriptaerie was the central repository of millennia of Naturae's history, a vast library where one could spend a lifetime reading and still not know everything. Aioffe suspected there was scant solid information about witches, despite them existing nearly as long as faekind, but she wanted to show her support.

Nemis pushed herself from the trunk she had been leant against, and nodded. "Thank you." She walked on a little way into the woodland, sniffing the air. She crouched down, delicately cutting bunches of herbs as they passed them on the pathway.

Aioffe inhaled deeply as they strolled, the soothing salty tang of the seaweed drying on the beachhead calming them both with companionable silence. Unburdened, but still unresolved.

CHAPTER FIFTEEN
Not smooth sailing

North Atlantic Ocean, off the coast of Scotland

By the third day of sailing, Henry and Fairfax had established a routine. As Captain and navigator, Fairfax spent most of daylight steering with the whipstaff at the stern, with Henry lounging against the side of the low aft castle, sometimes helping him haul the long pole across when they tacked into the wind. Their hours were filled by chess, cards, or Fairfax tutoring Henry in the finer points of accents from around the country. Colourful language he should pepper his speech with, and the very latest in bawdy jokes he ought to repeat when in fine company. And a great deal more which he shouldn't. The debate about which was appropriate, and which not, was Henry's contribution. The youthful eight-man crew of the caravel - short, skinny boys indistinguishable bar their different coloured neckerchiefs holding back their unkempt hair - giggled occasionally at Fairfax's entertainment, but kept themselves generally apart from the guests on board.

From his viewpoint, Henry enjoyed watching the crew's camaraderie as they nimbly clambered up the two masts to hoist the triangular lateen sails which enabled their swift progress regardless of the direction of the wind. It reminded him of jousting practise where dares meant dicing with death. Less enjoyable to watch, much less participate in, were maintenance tasks, such as, swabbing the deck, oiling the sails, or re-caulking the above-water sides of the ship to ensure it was watertight. Henry hadn't bothered to venture much below deck the entire sunny voyage thus far; Fairfax having warned him that the cargo space was very low, full of barrels for a client, and refusing to be drawn into the nature of what was inside them.

Jeffries had marked himself out a comfortable seating and sleeping area on the far deck. Within an hour of being on board, he bade one of the boys to fetch him hay from the humid quarters below. He then oversaw the arrangement of the strands loosely into a nest-bed between two of the small cannons. Their eldest passenger proceeded, once nestled, to scowl at anyone who approached him, except for if food was offered, which he readily accepted, gobbled, then promptly dozed back off again. Using Henry's cape to keep the prickly stalks trapped into place, his exhaustion after the hectic travelling became apparent as he alternated between reading and nodding off as time was scored by the hourglass attached to the aft castle stairs.

Each watch, roughly four hours, was punctuated by Fairfax walking down the boat, casually shouting 'Turn' just as he passed Jeffries, arousing him from his slumbers with a jump. Then, with a stern expression on his face as if his shout had been purely coincidental, Fairfax marched past the nest, heeled boots slamming noisily on the wood, ostensibly to check the crew's tasks were being performed to exacting standards, thus preventing Jeffries from immediately returning to his dreams.

It was, Henry thought, as if Fairfax felt obligated to prove to Jeffries how tightly run his ship was. He could not deny he relished their shared glances and hidden chuckles when Jeffries jolted so violently at times, losing his eyeglass amongst the hay in the process. The resulting glare did nothing to deter Fairfax; if anything, it goaded him to shout louder the next watch.

Weak from lack of sustenance, Henry barely noticed when first the winds fell. The crew enjoyed strict rations consisting of a half-gallon of beer, a half-pound of biscuit, a sliver of butter and a generous three salted herrings, distributed twice a day, but Henry's particular needs had not been catered for or considered in the haste of their departure. The lads had stopped questioning why Henry didn't eat after the first day, gratefully sharing out his portion between themselves. There were few luxuries on board, although Fairfax kept a stash of strawberry jam which he would sneak a slop of when he thought no-one was looking. Rations or sweet treats weren't much use to Henry, though.

Wary of upsetting the balance on the ship, knowing there were no livestock currently aboard bar the treasured hens, he had decided to wait out the journey hungry but without argument. Even though both Fairfax and Jeffries knew of his requirements, and he had offered to hunt if they would only put into land, Fairfax had yet to head into a harbour. Every time they passed a port, there seemed to be good reason to sail on, run with the winds whilst they had them and maintain a steady progress north. But then, as they gradually lost momentum in the water, with the sun beating down upon them, Henry began to consider how he could use his methods of persuasion on perhaps just one of the boys.

Mid morning, a lull left them only drifting in the calm water. The sails lay flat and unfilled. Across the sea, the jagged rocks marking the northern tip of Scotland sat tantalisingly close, yet too far away to row towards. Fairfax had decreed it was too hot to get the oars out, and, confident the wind would pick up shortly, he ordered the watch to rest. With nothing to do, the crew gave up on playing cards and opted instead to doze under the cloudless blue sky around the edges of the deck, trying to grab what little shade there was. Fairfax tied the whipstaff securely, then curled up in the corner of the aft castle, a smile on his face as he napped.

Opposite, facing so he could see the horizon through the hole behind the rudder shaft like a framed picture, Henry kept watch. Not needing to sleep himself, he was content to let them all doze rather than rouse them, only to have to row in the baking sunshine.

After he flipped the hourglass for the third time in silence, his nose wrinkled as the acrid smell of pitch wafted up as it dried out in the sunlight, mingled with the inevitable smells of sweat and rancid food. His tongue, swollen with thirst, began to ache and Henry could think of nothing else but the cloying richness of blood to ease it. While all around him slept, he closed his eyes and tried to plot a way off the ship and onto the shore and back. Without being discovered.

In his weakened state, it took Henry a moment to react as his nostrils picked up a different, dangerous smell. He jerked himself from the boat side and stood, shaking as he scoured the deck below. Halfway down he saw the culprit - wisps of smoke rising tentatively into the air! Henry ran down the steps, towards the hay chair upon which Jeffries was dead to the world.

"Fire!" He cried, but just as the words left his mouth, he stopped. The tiny flames whooshed up, catching the fresh pitch and oil on the deck. Within seconds, the blaze had streaked along the border of the boat.

"Get up!" Henry shouted, "Fire!"

Groggily at first, the confused faces of the crew quickly turned to horror. Before Henry could move to stop him, a lad lurched to his feet, in his panic kicking over the bucket of oily pitch by his feet. Spreading onto the deck, it ignited with terrifying speed. A great flash of orange warmth grew as the slick spread. Henry darted around the flames towards Jeffries, worrying that he would be too late.

Reaching him after only a few quick strides, Henry saw the hay and woollen cape were smouldering, only kept from being fully aflame by the residue of sweat and lack of air from the old man's back. Jeffries' terrified expression told Henry it wouldn't be long before the nest caught though. His gaunt limbs flailed against the nest as he attempted to lever himself up and out of harm's way. As Henry appeared in front of him, Jeffries glanced up. Henry stuck out his arm with a face of fury, grabbing Jeffries' lapels with the other and hauled him upright.

"Thank you," Jeffries panted out, stepping quickly away before turning to assess the damage.

Henry caught the glint of the wooden monocle amongst the hay and knew what had started the fire. He pushed Jeffries towards the mast. There would be a time for recriminations later. "Get the buckets filled," Henry said, his dark eyes absorbing the chaos around the deck.

On the aft deck, Fairfax seemed frozen, clutching the rail as he watched his crew flail about. His face pale with fright, his hair sticking up in all directions. Shaking his head with annoyance, Henry strode across the full deck and pulled leather buckets from their hooks on the central mast. He thrust them into the hands of two boys, then ran over to the side of the ship where the blaze had not yet spread. The drop of ten feet to the sea below had not deterred a crewman from already jumping straight over, the threat of fire seemingly outweighing any concerns over the danger of such a leap. The lad yelped, waving and sinking in the calm sea several yards away from the steep side.

"Grab a pigskin," Henry shouted over his shoulder, yanking on a coiled rope and tying a bucket to the end. Keeping his eye on the boy, still bobbing around in the flat water, he tossed the pail down and let the cable run through his hands. Jerking it so it filled, Henry hoisted the bucket back up. Behind him, a crewman dithered, waiting with his container. He nodded gratefully when Henry splashed his seawater into his awaiting vessel then scampered off to pour it over the flames.

"Tie another, or this will take too long." Jeffries said, a voice of calm when others around him were scared. He thrust forward a lad to take Henry's place, dipping and hauling the water, and turned away to find another coil of rope. Henry looked around, realising the monk was correct. The fire had already spread along the entire side of the full deck, picking up pace as it burned through dry tinder en route.

Henry glanced over to where Fairfax had last been seen, his eyes widening as he realised the mizzenmast sail on the aft castle was flapping. The wind had risen finally, only not enough to propel them anywhere. Just enough to fan the fire into spreading. Then his gaze dropped to the stairs down, searching still for where their Captain, who ought to be commanding proceedings, might have gone. The oil-filled smoke thickened to a billowing fog; even he struggled to see through it. But, his gaze followed the straight lines of the ship, hunting for familiar protruding corners to keep his bearings. The hatch to the quarters underneath the aft deck was closed. Blinking, Henry peered closer. The storage cupboard door next to it was hanging ajar!

Henry felt his heart drop into his stomach. Fairfax had been at great pains to boast about his precious supply of gunpowder. Despite having joked about how paltry the small deck artillery would be were they ever to come up against the might of one of the kings galleons, Henry knew the explosive held enough incendiary potential to blow this ship to pieces - were the flames to reach the cupboard.

"Jeffries! The gunpowder!" Jeffries turned to where Henry pointed and his mouth dropped. Cursing, the old man dashed across the deck, picking his way around pools of flames. Mentally urging him to move faster but knowing it would achieve nothing to nag, Henry cast his eyes around. Of the crew of eight, half were unaccounted for. Where were they? And where was Fairfax?

"You, you and you," Henry pointed at the three lads closest to him.

They turned and stared at him vacantly, frightened yet desperate for someone to tell them what to do. "Form a chain and get those fires doused." One of the boys held the pigskin he'd requested, which Henry grabbed, inflated, then quickly tied off before tossing it down to the seaman in the water below.

"Hold that, and fill the buckets!" Henry's confident order startled the lad below, whose head momentarily turned towards him, before slipping under the wave. "Can't he swim?" Henry grumbled under his breath.

Freckle-face beside him shrugged, saying "I tried to teach him, but…"

When the head reappeared, Henry shouted over, "Paddle, like a dog. You can make it!" Motioning with his arms, he watched only until the boy's arms grasped the air-filled bladder, then darted to the storage cupboard to help Jeffries.

The keg which Jeffries had hauled out was short and squat, a little over a foot tall and just under a foot wide. It looked light enough to carry, although rolling the wooden barrel was clearly out of the question across a deck on fire. Frowning as he wondered why Jeffries hadn't yet moved the gunpowder away, Henry glanced over Jeffries' frozen shoulder. On the shelves, floor, and hanging in a net slung across the ceiling of the cupboard, more kegs awaited, wedged in together.

The tiny room was chaotically rammed. A massive explosion in a cupboard, in the middle of the deck. Henry shook his head in dismay. Removing one piece in the jigsaw could dislodge another, allowing the barrels to tumble out, roll all over the deck… to disaster. Yet leaving them packed together would blow the entire ship to pieces from the inside.

Catching Henry's eye, Jeffries muttered, "That dotepol Fairfax, I should have known he'd hoard."

Henry knew then there was little hope. Even with every hand helping, they would not get all the kegs tossed into the water before a blaze reached them. He looked across the deck and his face fell. Although the three crewmen he had instructed were valiantly sloshing seawater onto the flames licking the boards, the fire had now taken hold of the dry wooden rails of the small forecastle.

From beneath him, he heard the scraping sounds of larger barrels being rolled, and knew where Fairfax was. If the cargo could be brought up, Henry suspected that it would contain highly flammable, alcoholic liquid. But, the hatch in the centre of the deck was surrounded by flames. Staying there, Fairfax, and whomever he had helping him down in the hold, were trapped in what would likely become their tomb.

Despite all the surrounding noise, Henry's mind quietened. He breathed in the oily smoke, the panic, and the burnt pitch. As he exhaled, there was a moment when he considered jumping off the ship himself. A strong swimmer, he was confident in his own abilities to reach the shore, even though he was already running on reserves of energy. But as soon as the thought crossed his mind, he pushed it away.

His eyes narrowed; a leader of men does not abandon them in the heat of battle. A king does not turn aside from difficult decisions.

And a vampire does not let mortals go to waste when he is hungry.

CHAPTER SIXTEEN
Jump!

"Get that sail down!" Henry waved at the billowing square mainsail. His authoritative tone drew the crew on deck to a stop, and one by one, they all looked up at the huge pole.

"You and you, with the red scarf," Henry shouted. "Get up the mast and bring it down, rolling it. Unfasten the whole sail, completely off, but don't tie the roll together."

Henry pulled Jeffries away from the cupboard, not roughly but firmly enough to indicate he had a method to his madness. He pushed the door shut tight, then pulled off his heavy woollen tunic. "Drench this," he said, "And put it at the base of the door." Jeffries nodded as Henry strode to the side of the ship where the lines with buckets still attached hung.

Peering over, he saw that the boy below had followed orders after all, and was clinging to the pigskin life-buoy with one arm and using the other to tip the bucket so it filled with seawater entirely. Henry yanked up the rope and handed the pail to the lad who still stood next to him at the railing, uncertainty on his freckled face. "Get your shirt off and soak it. Spread it over the hatch, then tip the rest of the water over your clothes and the deck," Henry ordered. "We need to give them as much time as we can."

Casting his eyes around, Henry began assessing the best place to position the mainsail for their strongest chance of success. He glanced over at the mast, reassured to see the nimble fingers of the two lads already at work. He tossed another bucket down back and went in search of more. By the time he returned, the freckled boy was back.

The two climbers descended, grunting as they then dragged the rolled up sail towards Henry. "Line it down the deck," Henry said, tossing a bucket of water over the planks in the centre, dousing momentarily the oily flames which crept inward. The boys panted through the smoke as they hauled the fat worm of a sail around, until they were perilously close to the flickers at the forecastle steps. The enormous sail stretched along the length of the deck, but in haste to consume new fuel, the flames licked towards the greasy stretch.

"One of you is going to have to stay there," Henry ordered as the boy at the far edge of the roll recoiled from the heat. Henry tossed a bucket of water over him, the splashes also temporarily dousing the flames behind him. "Find the top ties in the middle and hold on to them. You too, at the other end." Uncertainty was subjugated by a glare from Henry and the red scarfed lad bent down again. The other crewman ran down the deck and began to rummage, pulling out the thin rope ties before he too would be on the receiving end of Henry's dark stare.

Sensing the return of the helpful lad, Henry smiled as he saw the downcast look on his face. "There will be ale a-plenty, and probably more besides, if we get out of this, don't worry. Now, pour water over yourself. Make sure you are good and soaked."

He turned to the crew and addressed them, aware that behind them the fire would continue spreading as soon as their dousing ceased. Confidence in his plan must outweigh any doubts they may have about him not being their commander.

"What I ask of you all now will require bravery, more than that which you've already shown yourselves to possess. Captain Fairfax told me he had the best crew, and I believe him. Show me your strength and endurance now. Red 'kerchief and you," Henry pointed at the two boys nervously holding the ends of the rolled sail. "The finest riggers I've met. Well done for working so quickly, but it's not over yet. Your task is to hold those ropes. Do not let them slide, no matter how much it jerks. My friend here, and I, are going to take these corners and run through the fire."

Henry paused, gazing down at Freckle-face next to him. Although the boy's eyebrows were high into his forehead with terror, Henry touched his arm and met his eyes. "I will heal you," he said, and blinked slowly. "You can do this, I promise. Just do as I say."

He looked over at the far side of the ship and pointed. "Taking a corner each, we will run with the sail, then jump over. Once the sail is spread behind us, we will let go, leaving it hanging over the side." Henry turned back to address the boys at either end of the sail, beckoning for Jeffries to step forward as well. "As soon as we are overboard, you two, and Maister Jeffries, must lie down, arms up, and roll yourselves over the top of it. Be quick. Roll all the way across the deck, flattening it down."

"What?" Red scarf piped up, horrified.

"Be sure to quash the flames quickly with your weight," Henry added.

"The sail ought to be thick enough," Jeffries added, seeing the wisdom in Henry's plan. He nodded, meeting nervous young glances with his mature reassurance.

"Ready?" Henry looked at the freckled boy as he walked over to pick up the corner nearest the forecastle. Realising that Henry planned to take the side which had higher flames licking across the deck, the lad's head dipped almost imperceptibly. Pale but resolute, the youngster picked up the edge of the sail and wrapped the tie-rope around his hands. He shot a miserable glance at the lad bearing the inner rolled tie and received a slap on the shoulder in return.

"On three..." Henry lifted the corner above his head, and counted.

They ran. The heavy sail dragged initially, catching against the deck, but then the two lads holding the ends of the roll had the good sense to lean back, lifting the bulk slightly to ease its unfurling. The breeze which was earlier their enemy dipped under the fabric as it opened, billowing as it filled with warm air.

Henry reached the boat side first, his longer strides covering the deck in a matter of seconds despite not running with vampire speed for the sake of keeping the unfurling even. Pausing to look for his companion, he yelled, "Come on!"

Even though Henry stood where the flames licked highest, the heat didn't hurt. Henry's linen undershirt caught fire whilst he waited for the boy to clamber up, smouldering also, onto the wooden edge of the boat.

Henry spotted the boy's terrified expression, stared hard into his eyes and blinked once before he ordered, "Jump!"

CHAPTER SEVENTEEN
Confusion in the deep

The dangerous leap from the high sided ship into the sea may have started with the best of intentions. In that moment between hitting the water and pulling the sailcloth in after him, when he tried to turn towards the side, Henry rapidly became disorientated by the shock of cold sea against his burning skin. Numbness spread as he sank, bubbling, beneath. He kicked as he sank, then his feet entangled with the edge of the sail.

Deep underwater, the fabric softened and trapped him, pulling Henry deeper in his confusion. He tried to stiffen, thinking to allow his mind time to process which way up he was. But his joints screamed a complaint as his long limbs rejected his mental order to cease, lashing traitorously instead against their constraint. Despite the sensation of panic as he sank, Henry forced himself to bring his hands together, to where the ties wrapped around his palms and fingers. Regardless of his feet, still tangled in the edges of the sail, he would be unable to dive or surface if he was nevertheless attached to the sinking fabric.

The last air in his lungs had bubbled out before he finished unwinding the straps. Never having been submerged as a vampire, and not especially, he thought, needing the air itself, he remained uncertain as to the effects of inhaling water. It wasn't a risk he was willing to take. Reaching down, wrenching at the sail caught around his ankles, Henry focused his blurry eyes on freeing himself.

Once liberated, the sailcloth billowed underwater, a wall of white with a life of its own. Glimpsing which way the now dispersed bubbles rose, he flapped his feet and turned himself upright, using gentle motions rather than the large kicks of moments earlier. His fingers traced the smoothness of the sailcloth as he propelled himself towards the surface.

Rising quickly, when his forehead pushed the oiliness of the sail, Henry understood he was caught between it and the boat. The heavy fabric pinned him underneath, but his feet automatically pumped the water. He dropped his hands to hip height, propelling, pushing himself higher despite the weight bearing down. Face surfacing finally, Henry drew in a spluttered breath.

Then Henry dived, deep enough below the line of the sail, allowing the oiled cloth to follow his wake whilst he swam out from under. When he surfaced again, shaking the hair from his face, he swivelled to look at the ship. Treading water, he grinned. The square sail almost completely obscured the boat as it hung over the side; an off white beacon to the shore. Although the air around still held the smell and taste of doused soot, no flames licked up from the deck. But nor was there the cheer of a crew hanging over the edge to congratulate him on a plan well enacted.

His smile dropped when he scanned across the waves, over to where the boy ought to have been. Because the fabric completely and squarely covered the side of the vessel, he assumed that meant Freckle-face had successfully kept the line of their leap and not, as he had, ended up between sail and ship. But, as he spun, treading water, no bobbing head appeared in the water. Henry looked again at the sail cloth and realised that there was a pull to the far side of it. Weight was still attached, yanking it ever further down, off the deck.

Before Henry could react, the sail slipped further from the low railing above.

"Hold it!" Shouts reached his ears. Without thinking further, Henry dived, his long legs twisting to turn him towards the rear end of the ship. His body warmed with the motion as it slipped through the stillness. Henry squinted through the salty water, only needing the off-whiteness of the sail drawn ever downwards as a guide. Hauling himself deeper with his hands, he searched below.

He reached the hem, tracing down beyond where the hazy sunlight could reach. Then, his fingers touched something more solid than the pliant fabric. He kicked down, reaching through the shadowy depths with waving arms. There, again, he felt the softness of flesh. This time, he gripped. Drawing himself alongside the body, he dragged it into his chest. With his other arm, he felt around to where he guessed the ties had remained wrapped around the Freckle-face's wrist. The boy's head lolled almost intimately on his neck. Henry glanced around - the water was clouded red. A large gash on his forehead, the culprit.

Henry kicked up, realising it was futile to waste time trying to untangle the ties. As they drew closer to the surface, he had to push his legs even harder. The weight of the boy and sail were no match for the drive which propelled Henry upwards. When they broke above the surface, Henry carried on kicking. Lying on his back, he hauled the boy further up his chest so he bore his weight despite his own head being submerged with every rippling wave.

He switched grip, putting his hand underneath the lad's chin. With his head tilted up to receive the air the boy needed, even if he wasn't as yet drawing it in, Henry spluttered as a ripple washed over his face. Then he bellowed, "Rope!"

As his legs chopped circles beneath them both, Henry snorted out sea water from his nose whilst he waited for a response. The smell of the iron from his blood when Henry breathed into clear nostrils encouraged him. Although Freckle-face was not breathing, his fingers and senses told him there was still a heartbeat, however occasional, as his wound still bled. He pushed the thought of licking the blood away from his mind, remembering with some regret that he had made a promise to heal this boy. He would stand by that oath even though the temptation was almost overwhelming.

"Rope!" Henry shouted again, then twisted in the water to get closer to the ship's side. He kept dipping below, the combined weight of the slipping sail and inert body pushing him under, despite his legs waggling away. When he next looked up, his eyes slid towards the small stern castle, where, against the sunlight, he could make out the dark outlines of figures leaning over.

A spray hit his forehead and Henry grunted. With his free arm, searching once again. Finding nothing, he was forced to haul the boy higher on his chest so that he could be more upright himself to spot the cable. There! He scissored his legs to push over to find the end was already sinking slowly into the water. Only distantly could he make out the shouts from above.

Once he had wrapped the rope twice under the boy's arms and around the chest, there was only just enough slack to loop and tie it. Henry's fingers, stiff from manipulating thick, sodden cord, had lost all feeling in them, and his arm muscles jerkily objected to the additional strain of holding the dead weight above water.

Finally, Henry tilted his head back and shouted, "Pull!" By then, his movements had brought them closer to the side; the shaded waves slapping loudly against the hull like incessant background chatter. He felt the yank of the Freckle-face's body leave his arms. Looking up as he released him, for the first time, he realised just how far below the deck railing he was. The rise of the ship loomed above, its vast shadow deepest under the bulging side. He blinked, thinking how close he had been to being dragged under, should the vessel have been moving at any speed. How reckless, in retrospect, to have jumped overboard. Freckles hadn't been as fortunate as he and must have hit some part of the ship underwater with the force of landing, hard enough to have knocked himself unconscious. But, under the circumstances, he wondered if he could have done anything differently?

Shaking his head as the line tightened, dangling bare feet nearly hitting him in his face, Henry decided no. His plan may have seemed foolhardy, but he'd quenched the fire thus saving the ship. Failure to do this would have cost everyone their lives, whether the vessel had gone down in flames or been blown apart. Better one life lost, than all of them.

Fairfax leaned over and shouted down, "Another rope coming down for you!" He disappeared again, a coil then splashing down next to Henry. As he pivoted in the water, watching the slow, jerky progress of Freckles being hauled up, Henry remembered the earlier jumper.

He looked at the rope, deciding.

"Throw it to the other side," he called, as Fairfax's gingery mop reappeared. "There's a lad there needs help."

Henry tipped onto his back and swam around the stern, keeping an eye on Freckles' ascent. By the time he had reached the wide stern, hands had reached down to grab the dangling torso by the arms. Just before Henry kicked out of sight, Freckle's legs twitched; Henry smiled, hoping that was a good sign. But as for the other lad, would he find a body?

CHAPTER EIGHTEEN
Purpose

The boy safely bobbed in the water some fifty feet away from the side of the boat. A weary smile spread across his sunburnt cheeks as Henry swam towards him. He didn't appear to have the strength to do more, looking distinctly pale against the tan of the pig bladder his cheek and shoulder rested upon. Under the other arm, a leather bucket, come loose from its tether, had been upended so it held air as a float. Seawater had evaporated from his lips, leaving white traces in the cracks.

"Did they forget about you?" Henry joked as he reached him. By the scruff of his shirt, Henry started dragging him closer to the ship. "I think the fire is out now. You'd be welcome back."

"Not sure about that," Fairfax called over, and another rope splashed close to Henry in the water. "Cowards aren't what's needed at sea."

Henry glared up at his friend and frowned. "That's alright for you to say. Where were you when the crew needed some direction? Pretty cowardly move - looking after your own best interests rather than fixing the problem."

Fairfax shrugged. "I knew they'd be fine. And so would you."

Henry scowled, not sure how to react to the blasé retort. Did Fairfax simply not care about his crew or was it a sign of trust that someone, himself, would step up and co-ordinate dousing the fire? No-one else had seemed to have the slightest idea on what to do, and that infuriated him. And yet, irresponsible though Fairfax was, he was not uncaring. Were Henry not to have been on board, would the daemon have made a different choice, maybe? He wondered perhaps if Fairfax meant for Henry to rise to the danger. A test of his character?

"Get this crewman aboard," Henry ordered. "And make sure someone has fastened the other rope. I'll climb up myself."

Henry pulled on the bladder supported arm of the tired lad and drew underneath the dangling line. He helped him manoeuvre the rope underneath his shoulders, tying it before glaring up at Fairfax. The boy gazed vacantly at him - too exhausted to help much with the rescue.

As Henry scaled the side of the ship, his discontent grew. It was one thing to see what Henry was made of, quite another to have done it under such risky circumstances. By the time he clambered on to the deck, he was furious. Fairfax was still bent over the railing as two crewmen pulled up the rope. Henry gritted his teeth, watching as Fairfax tried, then floundered with grasping the youngster's shoulder to haul him up. Henry covered the space between them in only a few strides, leaning over the rails himself. With one smooth heft, he hoisted the lad up and dropped him to the planks. The boy belched loudly.

Fairfax's head whipped around, his face flooding with joy at the sight of Henry. Henry gripped the daemon's loose, dry clothing, spinning on his toes and shoved him against the balustrade.

"What..." Fairfax managed to splutter out before the backs of his calves hit the rails. Henry stepped forwards and straightened his arms, pushing Fairfax's torso out over the sea. Fairfax's arms flailed, frantically reaching for something solid to grab hold of.

"This is for risking the lives of everyone here," Henry spat, his eyes narrowed and blazing. Then, to the sounds of laughter around him, Henry leaned forward and let go.

Fairfax's back hit the water with a tremendous splash. As he sank, Henry froze. The thought that he had made a terrible mistake flashed into his mind, remembering his own confusion when he had crashed into the cold depths at speed. The white foam left as the only remnants of Fairfax dispersed as quickly as Henry's rage. His eyes widened as he watched the wash below, a lump forming in his throat. Henry's hands tightened on the railing, as a seagull blithely landed on now calm ripples and shook its head.

Fairfax… he'd only been trying to help Henry become the man that he was. Because he cared. Because he believed in Henry. Because he loved him? The revelation smacked him about his face and his heart dropped into his boots.

The crew fell silent; he could sense their stares on him. Henry was just about to lift his leg over when fresh bubbles burst to the surface. The seagull squawked - panic, or perhaps it was relish - Henry wasn't sure.

Fairfax's head emerged and immediately tilted back to breathe. Pushing his long wet hair from his forehead, he began to laugh. Henry looked over his shoulder, as the crew and Jeffries burst into relieved guffaws as well. Henry's mouth twitched, then he too chuckled under his breath as more gulls descended, splashing Fairfax with fluttering wings as they investigated a potential food source.

Enjoying the camaraderie of the company as much as the back-slaps which then rained upon him, Henry looked out over the calm sea. His amusement waned. Against a rushing of their heartbeats which filled his ears, all of their vocal noise faded. He drew in the air, and closed his eyes. Despite their attention and accolade, he was still an outsider, and suddenly, ravenous again. The proximity of the crewmen, their sooty smells and yes, the welcome scent of blood, reminded him that he was not one of them. Not mortal.

More than mortal, perhaps. A king amongst mortals.

He liked it, he decided, nodding as he gazed over the water. It reaffirmed his inner belief that he was destined to greatness. Unproven until now, these men had relied upon him and he had delivered them to safety. They accepted his orders even though they knew not what he was. Or, what he wanted from them.

His eyes slid back to the pair who had held the sail ties on deck, their arms clasped around each other. Such a human response to relief. A part of him wished he could be like that again. Open. Yet he was not ordinary and never would be. Were they to know his truest nature, he perceived they would be repulsed. Fearful. The thought nagged at him, ruining his elation.

"We should leave him there," Freckle-face said, holding a rag to his forehead and still looking pale and wobbly.

"Ha!" Jeffries' deep chuckle joined the higher pitched shouts of amusement. After glimpsing over the side then he paused, eyes twinkling as he pointed out, "I happily would, but he's the only one who knows the way!"

Fresh laughter surrounded Henry, and, for a brief moment, he forgot about how different he was. He looked down at Fairfax, splashing with pure abandon and roaring with amusement and relief. Their eyes met, and Henry knew he wouldn't be able to push Fairfax away so easily again. Just looking at him, surrounded by a flock of seagulls poking his clothes to be sure they weren't edible and revelling in the aftermath of the chaos, made Henry feel somehow more accepted. More whole. Feel more of everything, he realised. Fairfax's actions had made him step up and act as a man would. A leader of men. A hero perhaps. A genuine smile stretched across his face, flooding his being with the warmth of love, and yes, gratitude. Fairfax stopped splashing abruptly, his grin and sparkling eyes for Henry alone.

"Leave me here if you want," Fairfax shouted back as the laughter died down. "But you know I'd find you, and your measly lives wouldn't be worth living then." Grinning his most infectious smile, he shook a fist at the crew, who again fell about laughing. Although he was too far away for the crew to hear, Fairfax gazed directly at him. Henry distinctly heard the words meant only for his ears. "For you are truly living now."

Henry reached over and flicked a rope towards Fairfax. "Get up here," he called. "The very least you could do is donate your fancy pants to mend holes in the sail."

"But what would you wear then?" Fairfax joked back. "Talk about religious - your cassock is definitely the wrong kind of holy now."

Henry looked down at himself and laughed. "Perhaps it's time for a conversion," he said, well aware that Jeffries stood next to him. The former monk raised an eyebrow and turned away. Still grinning, Henry hauled Fairfax aboard.

CHAPTER NINETEEN

Confluence

Naturae, 20th July 1553

"Aioffe?" Joshua called through the door to their chamber. "Are you in here?"

"Just coming," she said, straightening her crown as she stood before a highly polished silver oval on the wall. She turned, asking, "Am I late?"

Joshua shook his head and smiled. "Even if you were, they would wait." He held out his hands and approached her. "You look beautiful, as always, my love."

A lock of hair fell over Aioffe's face as she looked down. He squeezed her fingers gently. "What's wrong?"

Aioffe shrugged, and she pulled away to push the strand into place again. Their eyes met briefly in the reflection before she turned back to him.

"Aioffe, please tell me. Let me help?"

She blinked before replying in a quiet voice, "This will be the first blessing ceremony since Lyrus..."

"You don't need to worry about him, my love. What can he do?"

"It's not what he could do," she said. "This is the first time he has seen our version of Lifeforce gathering."

"So?" Joshua frowned.

"So, I can't help but wonder what he will make of it? Compared to what my mother used to do."

"It is a completely different situation. There's no comparison. Of course, I never saw what she did. Did you?"

Aioffe shook her head. "By the time I grew old enough to have asked, those ceremonies to collect Lifeforce at the sacred stones had ceased. I only found out about them when I returned after, well, after we met. Believers in our ancient practices had already died out. I wonder if that is why my mother could never heal Naturae the way I can. Even if her heart hadn't been broken, and her mind along with it, the change in human faith was too great. And now, centuries later, no-one believes in the power of faeth. No humans would attend the rites. If Spenser is right, hardly any of them worship fae as they used to in Europe either."

Joshua took her hand, and they walked towards the door. Pausing before they left their chambers, Aioffe glanced up at him. "I do wonder if it's why I cannot grow an heir?"

He frowned. "I thought your mother told you it was the essence of a person, and love and pain, which caused you and Lyrus to grow?"

Aioffe shrugged. "That's what she inferred in our last conversation. But, I can't believe that is all it took. We have tried love, and loving, there. Tried sacrificing our blood into the earth. Prayers even. I have cried so many tears over the vines. What more can I do? All I know is that when I was cocooned, the old gathering ceremonies were still happening. Maybe it was a different kind of Lifeforce she used? But," she sighed, "There is no way to bring back the past. The old ways cannot be revived. It's impossible. Especially now with the strength of the Christian faith. I can't even get a small group of fae to agree on anything. Convincing humans to believe in faeth whilst remaining hidden is inconceivable."

It was all she could do not to stamp her foot, for that would be petulant and not befitting a Queen. So she scowled instead.

Squeezing her hand, Joshua said nothing, but his helpless expression told her that he had no other ideas. Whilst she was grateful for his silent support, it made little difference to the problems Naturae faced.

"My love," he said, "For now, just focus on this moment, this

Lifeforce gathering." He smiled gently, saying, "I have faeth in you, and faith that the answer will appear when it is meant to."

Aioffe looked into his eyes, wishing she believed that as well. Breaking away from their gaze, she walked before him down the corridor to the assembled fae outside.

*****

"There's the mist!" Fairfax shouted, excitement in his voice. "Henry, make ready to drop the sail."

Henry glanced ahead at the wall of grey, absorbing the expanse reaching into the sky, and wondered about what lay beyond the slight shimmer of it in the sunlight. Any other sailor would have immediately begun to turn the ship around, but Fairfax grinned and leant on the tiller, pulling his hat firmly down on his head. Sitting high in the water, the ship leaned as it swung about, directly towards the danger. Henry grasped the rope to drop the sail, but the reassurance he sought felt damp already. Having moved swiftly over the calm waters just moments earlier, the wind dropped like it had been sucked clear.

The vessel slowed as if its timbers were reluctant to continue forward. Or the thick fog was pushing them back. Henry wasn't sure which. Yet they glided on with only the faintest breeze propelling them towards the ominous entity in their path.

As the forecastle slipped into obscurity, Jeffries groaned as he hauled himself out of this re-made nest mid-ship. "I suppose you'll need my help also," he grumbled. Both Fairfax and Jeffries, without consultation, had abandoned the rest of the crew in a little village on the island of Sanday. This subterfuge had been much to the boys' disgust until Fairfax offloaded a barrel from the hold into their wake, for them to swim out and retrieve for entertainment and by way of payment for their lodgings. Never thinking he would miss their chatter, now Henry suddenly longed to hear anything other than the creaking of the timbers, as ominous fog swelled before them. Henry suddenly had an inkling that he might have made a mistake convincing Fairfax to let him stay aboard. But he had been very, very convincing... and it was too late to jump ship now.

As Jeffries stood up, the solidity of the mass encroached further, looming above the sail. Seeming to curl over, eating the vessel and its three occupants, Henry gasped as a chill touched him. Before the grey entirely enveloped them, he glimpsed Jeffries' arm clutching the mainmast. Henry tried to draw in a breath, but found his mouth instead gaping open and closed like a trout. The mist filled his throat and he dared not swallow or inhale for fear of what might happen if he absorbed it. Deep within his ears, he heard a high pitched tingle, rushing through his head as dark, icy dread attempted to invade his every sense and overtake him. Henry yearned to gulp, clear the blockage inside, but compelled his mind to refuse its own request. He shivered.

The sensation of dread grew to being almost unbearable when, without warning, sunlight filtered through from the prow. Within seconds, a dazzling whiteness surrounded him, lighting up the droplets of the mist with a painful brilliance. Henry's eyes widened as, around him, then burst a rainbow of shimmering haze, and he forgot that he wanted to resist the invasion.

He blinked, and within moments the mist had dissipated. Henry couldn't help but feel he had been judged, and found worthy. Clear waters lay ahead, the sunshine dappling on the dips of the waves.

Fairfax coughed, then shouted, "Drop it now, Henry!"

Henry looked over, wondering what would have happened if one should fail the mist's icy judgement, and saw Jeffries had already uncoupled himself from the mast. The old man's face glistened with droplets but underneath his skin was tinged with grey; his movements slow as he untied the line on the other side of the ship.

"Ready?" Jeffries snapped, wiping his arm across his forehead. Henry set to and unwound the rope from its cleat. Together they hauled the sail up as Fairfax adjusted the caravel's course. Ahead, tall trees poked into the skyline, their lush lower branches a spiky fringe over a narrow beach.

*****

Thane and Uffer led the fae into the air, spiralling around the clearing in a wide circle at first. In the centre of what would become the vortex, Aioffe and Joshua stood calmly waiting. Even though it wasn't necessary for Joshua to stay with her, and sometimes he joined in the flock of fae swooping up and chanting, today he decided that being on the ground watching was a sensible precaution. Finally, the soldier fae circled up, a glistening ribbon of strength twirling outside, protecting the inverted cone.

Glancing up to the landing balcony, Joshua half expected to see Lyrus. From where he stood, though, nobody was visible at the balustrade at all. His earlier confidence that his brother-in-law wouldn't interfere wavered, and now he regretted suggesting to Nemis that she could watch from there if she wished. At least, Joshua thought, Mark would be kept away altogether, for his own safety. The boy had been taken seal-spotting on the opposite side of the island by a kindly Pupaetory nurse, as Nemis had reluctantly conceded the lengthy blessing ceremony would be too overwhelming for him.

And yet… Joshua's gaze slid down the stairs, then over the expanse, checking. All the plans he had made to try and circumvent potential hazards could still go awry.

Lyrus, smouldering with disbelief and fury, remained in his designated position after all, slouched on a stool at the base of a massive, palace supporting trunk to the side. Despite his relief at seeing him where he ought to be, Joshua's lips pinched together. A guard stood behind him, although the armoured young fae's attention raptly followed the mesmerising spectacle, and not the dangerous fae in front of him.

Joshua watched Lyrus twitching, wriggling about in his seat. To his admittedly untrained eyes, the potions Nemis had brewed appeared to be having an effect. Lyrus's movements seemed less painful in that they were smoother, more fluid, even though his wings were still broken and hung virtually useless behind his crooked back. In the cool of the shade, he hunched his body up as if poised to spring; gaunt features tight as he muttered no doubt bitter words to himself. Joshua struggled to determine whether his obvious dissatisfaction was due to his physical limitations, or being closely guarded. Maybe it was the blissful yet focussed fae spinning around him, overlooking him as a part of the wider community.

As the chanting increased in volume, Aioffe splayed her fingers and her head tilted slightly back. Joshua moved lightly away, not wanting to intrude on the silken threads which, he assumed, only he and she could see, weaving towards her. Moving to the outside of the circle, his gaze lingered on the spinning swarm, awestruck as always by their vibrant beauty.

Spenser was not amongst them. Joshua wondered whether perhaps Nemis had been taken by another of her visions, and he briefly worried for her. If her husband was with her, at least she would be safe, he reasoned. But Lyrus's distemper still irked; as the ceremony was entering its most powerful vortex phase, Joshua decided to move closer to him. Just in case.

He glanced back at Aioffe, who was lost in the moment and fluidly weaving around to capture the Lifeforce. Joshua parted his lips, inhaling just enough to sense the spirit of the crowd. A rush of energy flooded through him, causing him to smile as he appreciated the curve of his wife's waist through the figure hugging robe she wore. Perhaps Nemis and Spenser were using this precious time alone more fruitfully than watching the ceremony, he wondered. He hoped so, the more he thought about it.

*****

"Look! A boat!" Mark pointed over the calm waters. He took off towards the shoreline before the nurse could grab him. She dithered, not knowing what to do, but all of her instincts suggested she should take her charge away from the potential danger. But the boy had already splashed into the shallows, waving madly at the approaching vessel.

"Mark!" The nurse shouted, and took to the air. Just as she reached him, he stumbled, seaweed catching around his ankles as he waded further into the sea. Dragging her eyes from the looming shadow of the boat, she screeched as the boy rolled, spluttering, in the waters.

Mark splashed about, then let out a loud wail of pain. The nurse dropped next to him and hauled on his arm, trying to help him upright. His hand thrashed through the foamy wave with another cry. A large gash in the palm pulsated with bright red blood! The child wrestled against her, pulling at his limb so that she would release. As she resisted, Mark planted his feet in the loose sand underneath, and snarled at her.

Shocked by his sudden change in demeanour, the nurse's fingers flew open. Mark fell backwards, clutching his hand to his chest. His entire body folded into itself protectively and he balled up in the wetness. As she watched the ripples breaking against his shaking back, Mark moaned and started to rock. The nurse's mind wheeled with indecision. With panic. This child, so unlike any other she had ever worked with - what was it about him? He was almost an animal. The noises - spluttering against the relentless seawater - deepened, guttural and haunting.

Within moments, a darkness moved across the sky and sea, engulfing them. She froze as the sands shifted underneath her feet, accompanied by a loud creak.

"Is he hurt?" A voice reached through her terror from above, and the nurse's head shot towards it. The ship cast a long shadow from its beached position just a few yards away. She gazed up the high bulging sides, her eyes growing wide with horror.

Another voice called out, "He is bleeding. I would get him out of the salt-water. It'll surely sting." Something in its deep tone chilled the nurse. Another dark head appeared next to the other, their silhouetted features indistinguishable against the sunlight behind them.

A rope ladder clattered down the wood, the bottom of it not quite touching the shallows in which the boat rested. The sight jolted the nurse into action and she dashed over to the balled up boy. Hearing the sounds of heavy feet walking down the deck, she bent down to Mark and whispered, "You must come away, Mark. It is not safe here." She glanced back - already, long legs dropped over to find the rungs. In desperation, she reached out and touched his shuddering shoulder, but he didn't respond. Entrusted to her care, yet unsure of what to do, the nursemaid shook him fiercely. Anything to garner some reaction to her presence at least.

Mark turned his face, looking not at her but beyond, to where the unmistakable thudding of boot toes against boat heralded an invasion of sorts. He screwed his eyes up and curled further into himself, completely ignoring the wave which broke over his head. "Please, come away," she pleaded. Her hands grasped his coat and she tried pulling him out of the water. Her wings beating furiously with the effort, but it was as if Mark had become a rock, embedded in the sand. How could such a small child weigh so much?

From the corner of her eye, a black robe approached, splashing through the shallows. The nurse yanked harder, positioning her own body between Mark and the darkness. Then, pale hands grasped Mark's legs and pulled. With a squelch, the boy was free of the cloying sand. She gasped as Mark was dragged away from her.

She wheeled around, but there was a human blocking her escape, grinning with green eyes and open palms to pause her. "Don't worry," he said. "Henry will sort him out."

The nurse's eyes narrowed as she hesitated. The freckle-faced man looked familiar. She frowned, trying to place where she might have seen him before in her limited experience off the island. Why was he here? How was he here? Why had the mist not deterred them?

She sniffed, sensing a wildness about him which she didn't recognise as entirely human. A wildness not unlike...

Mark's scream filled the air. His arms rigid against his torso as he was dragged out of the foam. The nurse instinctively flew up, reaching for him. Then, as suddenly as it had started, the shriek stopped.

The man in a cassock bent over the child, rubbing his hand against Mark's wrist. With his head so dangerously close, dark hair obscured the boy's face so she couldn't see his probably terrified expression. The speed at which the dark robed one had moved! In only that short space of time between her studying the not-so-strange stranger and becoming airborne the nurse knew - this intruder was not human.

She froze, mid-air, then decided. Propelling herself high, as fast as possible, the fae acted purely on fear.

A warning must be given.

Naturae was being invaded. The poor child, it's first victim, she thought.

CHAPTER TWENTY

Conception

"What was that?" Nemis said, sleepily. Her eyes blinked at the afternoon sunlight streaming in through their chamber's open windows, hazy with pollen. The monotonous chanting and buzzing drifted in on the breeze, so regular and low they had otherwise tuned it out for the past hour.

Spenser nuzzled her shoulder. The brief screaming noise would sound louder to his ears than it would to Nemis's, but he only said, "Maybe a part of the ceremony?" His voice lilted up at the end, as if he wasn't convinced either.

Nemis's brow furrowed. "Sounded a little like Mark, but," she twisted into his embrace, "it stopped too quickly for me to be certain."

"I'm sure he's fine," Spenser said, although he didn't look at her. Dropping a kiss on her neck, he stretched and swung his legs over the edge of the bed. He shifted, studying her, then raised an eyebrow. "We should catch at least some of the ceremony. Contribute a little of our very loving Lifeforce to the collective. Although, you are making it very tempting to just stay tucked away here."

A slow, lazy smile spread over her face and she moved her fingers down to rest on her stomach. She muttered a heartfelt wish and prayer, then sighed reluctantly. "I suppose we ought to make an appearance," she said.

Spenser stood and held out a hand to help her up. "I'll go on ahead and check on Mark. I'm sure it is nothing untoward, fear not." His reassurance and care touched Nemis as deeply as the love which they had just shared. "Take your time getting robed and ready. The ritual has a while yet."

After swiftly pulling on his clothing, he dropped a peck to her head and left their quarters before Nemis had even finished drawing her dreadlocks through the head-hole in her greying petticoat. She glanced at her dreaded stays. With its laces half pulled out and lying like spider-legs across the floor, she decided to allow herself to breathe today. Instead, she chose a wraparound robe of Aioffe's design, prettily embroidered with thistles and heather along the hems. The silky fabric called to her skin, still tingling and sensitive after their earlier exertions.

*****

In the clearing, the vortex was reaching its maximum revolution when Joshua felt an urgent tug on his arm. He looked up to see the Pupaetory nurse who was supposed to be looking after Mark, now flustered, red-faced and alone.

"Where's Mark?" He demanded.

"Taken!"

"What? By whom?"

The nurse pointed back toward the forest, panting. "Invaders!" Her flaring eyelids told him she believed this, and feared it as much as anyone would.

The hairs on Joshua's neck rose. Immediately, his gaze shot to the circling fae, searching for but not spotting the Captain. He jumped into the air and spurred himself higher. "Do not worry," he shouted down to her. "We are well defended." Wheeling around the outside of the vortex, as he approached the rim. Having still not spotting the Captain, he pivoted over the uppermost fae, then dived to the ground. In the centre, swaying with her arms outstretched, Aioffe barely noticed him arrive.

He touched her shoulder, feeling the jolt of the powerful, hypnotising Lifeforce rippling through her transmitting into his own body. The shock of it jerked him, but he kept his grip, pushed his mind into hers and, after only a moment, Aioffe's face turned to him.

"My love?" Forcing his voice to remain calm in spite of the upsetting news he had to relay, he said, "The nurse who was with Mark on the beach tells me we have been invaded!"

Aioffe smiled dreamily. "It is not an invasion," she said. "I have felt their Lifeforce. Greet them. Fairfax. Others…"

Joshua sighed with relief. It was short lived - his heart sank as he realised that Fairfax and Mark were akin, but not alike enough for the poor boy not to be terrified. He did not know how Mark would react to 'others' either. He flapped up as quickly as he could.

As he reached beyond the highest circling fae, he glanced down into the shadows of the palace. Lyrus's eyes met his; a slight jutting of his chin in response suggested he had noticed. Something unexpected was happening. Cursing to himself for alerting him, Joshua realised he didn't have time to worry about him now though - from the edge of his vision, he caught the motion of Spenser taking off from the landing platform. A deep frown darkened his face. Joshua flew over to divert him from Lyrus, and interrupting the ceremony.

"It's Fairfax," he called out as soon as he was near enough for Spenser to hear him. "I think Mark is with them."

Spencer wheeled around to face him, confusion and consternation in his eyes. "Where are they? I thought I heard him scream, but I didn't want to worry Nemis. We must send out a search party. This is Fairfax we are talking about. You know what happens with him."

"I doubt Mark will come to much harm as long as we are quick. Let us hope Jeffries is with him; he will calm Nemis's nerves I'm sure." He glanced down, spotting the nurse already flitting around the whirlwind; he hoped she was simply doing her duty by contributing to the ceremony. Had he done enough to assuage her fears, he wondered?

Spenser nodded. "They won't get far if Mark is being awkward. He's not used to strangers."

"Has he ever met another daemon?" Joshua asked as they flew over the treetops towards the shoreline.

Spenser shook his head. "Not to my knowledge. I wonder if they know a kindred when they meet?"

Joshua flapped higher, Spenser following. Reaching the centre of the island, they darted around high in the sky, hawkish vision searching the shores for signs of a landing. Spenser shouted to Joshua as he began to dive south east. A large, unfamiliar vessel was beached almost exactly where he had suggested Mark go seal-spotting! Joshua circled into an eye-watering drop to catch up.

"See? All healed." Henry rotated Mark's clean palm back towards him and smiled gently. His lips were closed, partly because he didn't want to alarm the boy with his incisors, and partly because his tongue was still relishing the spicy warmth of the unusual blood he had just licked away. The wound had bound beautifully under the touch of his own blood, and Henry fleetingly regretted the speed with which he used his tongue to clean the redness away. The sight of the pulsing red was clearly distressing the young lad though, so he held no regrets about his actions overall.

Mark sat up, staring alternately in wonder at the robed man kneeling in front of him and his hand, which had stopped hurting. Their eyes met, and Henry's head tilted slightly, in recognition of the unspoken gratitude he saw. But then, Henry's vision swam. He drew in a breath, which felt surprisingly difficult to do. As the boy seemed to be holding himself now, Henry dropped his palm to the sand. His fingers curled into the grit as he focussed on trying to inhale.

His eyes flickered around, catching sight of familiar boots to his left. Henry felt himself reeling, dizzy as if he was seasick, and the strength drained out of him and he crumpled onto the sand. The last question in his mind before it closed completely was of the blood. Both his yearning for more after such a long time without, and, of the revulsion as his body rejected it.

Joshua and Spenser landed simultaneously a few feet away from the four people on the sands. "Mark," Spenser cried out, running towards his son. Everyone except a black cassocked man lying on the beach spun around, their otherwise silent arrival making them jump. Joshua couldn't help but grin when he saw Fairfax, older but probably no wiser, standing once again on Naturae's shores with a bedraggled feather protruding from his hat. The look on Jeffries' face was more guarded, but Joshua put aside their past history and grabbed both of their forearms in greeting.

"Welcome!" Joshua glanced down at the pale-faced figure, inert on the sand. "Who's that?"

"That is Henry," Jeffries solemnly introduced. "He is, I should warn you, a relatively young vampire who has yet to learn that drinking daemon blood is very bad." Fairfax rolled his eyes but Joshua saw the concern in his gaze when it swept down to rest on the body.

"Will he recover?" Joshua asked. Not because he was particularly concerned about the death of a single vampire, but his cassock suggested that he remained true to the Catholic church. His arrival was suddenly more complex than anyone could have imagined, and already Joshua's mind whirled with the implications.

His head peeking over his father's shoulder, Mark piped up, "Wha's wrong wiv' him?" Spenser swivelled, glancing finally at Henry and the colour drained from his face. Meeting Joshua's eyes with a warning, he stood up. "Nothing for you to worry about, son," he said, then his lips tightened. "But we shall go and find Mama now, don't you think?" With a brisk nod at Joshua and Fairfax, he gathered Mark into his arms and flew up.

Frowning at Jeffries, Fairfax asked, "He will recover, won't he? I'd give you my blood for free if you would take care of him?"

Jeffries chuckled. "After how he saved my skin? I owe him anyway." Sighing as he bent over Henry, Joshua saw a gentleness to how his former companion turned Henry's face up.

As Jeffries breathed into the vampires' open mouth, not touching it but close enough for the magical life-giving breath to enter, Fairfax gasped. "That really is a trick I need to learn," the daemon said, only slightly envious. He knelt and took Henry's hand in his own. In that singular action, Joshua realised that this vampire meant a great deal to both of them. And potentially something else entirely to Spenser.

Joshua's eyebrows knitted together as Henry's lanky body stirred. As his head sought Fairfax, Joshua had the distinct impression that he had seen the man before. Although deathly pale, there was a familiarity about the cast of his face and the auburn hair, already slightly curling as it tugged free of the sand. What trouble had Fairfax brought to their shores, he wondered?

CHAPTER TWENTY-ONE
Fallout

Henry leant on Fairfax's shoulders for most of the way along the winding pathway through the forest. He found he couldn't take his eyes off the black translucent wings which laid neatly down the back of the person in front of him. 'Master Joshua Meadows,' Jeffries had called him, Henry thought, but the memory of it was hazy. Although groggy of mind and with a terrible stomachache, his senses were recovering through the exercise. Perhaps it was the after-effect from his infusion of Jeffries' witchy breath, but under the shady tree canopy Henry felt bombarded by the smells and noise of the woodland all around. He could even taste the pollen, musty in its release, from the dogwood and shrubs which lurked in dappled hollows.

Truly, it was as if he had awakened in another world - not just because of the peculiar mist through which they had traversed, but because he was also in the presence of at least one, if not many more, creatures which appeared as human as he, yet clearly flew like birds. What else could they do, he wondered? He shook his head, wishing the fug would clear so he could properly assess the situation he found himself in. A little sup of blood would help, he thought, licking his lips. But he wasn't hopeful of a jug being presented to him any time soon, and frankly, after what he had just endured after the boy, he wouldn't trust it anyway. Just when he was beginning to feel more relaxed with his own vampire self, and, with a new understanding of the true nature of witches rather than the fables he had been fed as a youth, he was faced with another race of creature entirely. Once again, the sensation of being alone, the only one like himself, nudged into his consciousness.

Glancing sideways at Fairfax, he noticed how comfortable he appeared. Without fear, he walked tall as if her knew where he was going and would be safe. Henry took heart from this judgement. There was no reason to presume that the fae would pose a threat to him either. If they could accept Fairfax, then why not himself? As if he understood the internal dilemma Henry had just resolved, Fairfax turned to him and grinned. Henry's lips rose also as he met his clear green eyes.

"Wait until you meet Queen Aioffe," Fairfax said, nodding to the dark appendages waving in front of them. "If you think Joshua's wings are big, hers are something else."

"I'm looking forward to it," Henry replied. The spark of energy from their exchange gave Henry strength, and he shifted his weight so he was bearing himself fully as they walked. It felt somehow important that he present himself as being independent of Fairfax. He walked shoulder to shoulder with him though. There was no harm in taking comfort from his proximity just yet.

The pathway ahead twisted, opening into a small clearing in which stood two enormous trees. Amongst the branches, Henry's attention was diverted by a number of bunched feathers, colourful ribbons, and other such tokens. He had never seen a pair of trees quite this tall and wide before, but he understood they held a significance to this race purely because of their embellishment. Once, when travelling through Derbyshire, someone in his retinue had pointed out a garlanded tree. Tatty scraps of fabric fluttered from the branches, some also nailed around the trunk in a similar fashion. Henry had been told later that the gully through which they walked, forged by sacred waters, was deemed mystical by the old religions. The willows which remained were thus adorned with wishes, even though, to that day, people were not supposed to wish, but pray instead and deny the existence of any other forces which would influence their lives. Although that didn't stop them wishing, Father James had grumbled. Pagan prayers had no place in a Christian country. Henry had never understood that viewpoint, for what was a prayer but a wish with an address?

Whilst wondering if this ancient land was still pagan, raised voices reached him from ahead. He faltered, glancing again at Fairfax. Jeffries looked back, directly at Henry, with a grim expression.

"Wait here," Joshua said, before loping through the shadowed pathway leading from the clearing.

As he disappeared from view, they fell silent. Henry pulled himself straight and brushed down his holey cassock. Even though, as they walked, the wet edges had dried, some sand still remained. Fairfax, dishevelled as usual, tugged on his tunic also. Catching Henry's eyes, they both bit back a giggle. Peering down his nose at them in warning, Jeffries sniffed and arranged himself with his legs slightly parted and satchel slung behind with his hands. It seemed as if he also felt the need to present himself, although as what, Henry wasn't entirely sure. The former Maister's face looked dead ahead, tightly guarded, with only a betraying tick on his sunken cheek.

"I never asked, have you been here before?" Henry raised an eyebrow at Jeffries while they waited. From the note he had received back in Preston, Henry had the perhaps mistaken impression the old man knew about this place, but seeing his forced expression now, he realised that they had all placed their faith in Fairfax to bring them here, without input from Jeffries at all.

"I have not," Jeffries replied, still staring straight ahead. "Although I am familiar with faekind, this is my first time visiting their homeland. I almost travelled here before, with Joshua, whom I presume is now the Queen's consort."

They fell quiet, each fiddling with their clothing in an attempt to smarten themselves after their unorthodox landing. Henry took the opportunity to quieten his mind, resolving to take each new piece of information he learned with pragmatism. Thoughts of blood, rich and relaxing, intruded constantly though. The minutes began to drag by with only soft cooing of birds to listen to. Unable to stand still for that long, Fairfax gave up and wandered over to the trees. Henry joined him examining the strips, hoping to find out what he could about these new people as much as to stay by his friends' side.

They were thus unprepared for the flashes of silver which announced that their delay was over. Henry's eyes widened as a troop of boots landed with a thump next to him, sending a cloud of dust into the air.

*****

"There is simply no protocol for this, your Majesty." Uffer glared at Joshua as he ran into the wide central clearing, before his barely contained frustration returned to Aioffe. "You should have told us to expect visitors."

Aioffe's expression had lost the dreamy quality which the ceremony had provoked. Her hands clenched as she met Joshua's eyes with a silent plea for his support. He immediately went to her side before facing the assorted Elders and Council members which had gathered underneath the landing balcony. All around, a jumble of agitated fae were flitting about the clearing, no longer circling, but muttering or standing in clusters, shooting glances towards their leader.

Joshua stared hard at Uffer, who blinked then looked down. "Your Queen is under no obligation to share every detail of her plans. However, there is nothing to fear," he said, raising his voice and hoping his calming manner would touch all of the concerned gathering before him. "You all know of Fairfax the daemon - he was here before, when Aioffe ascended to the throne and stayed whilst we rebuilt a vessel for him to leave in. He has brought Jeffries, a healer of fae, who we discussed in Council when Lyrus was found."

"That is all who landed?" The Captain's gruff wariness reminded Joshua about the strange vampire. "My Queen..." he thankfully didn't wait for a response before growling with indignation. "I was led to believe this was an invasion. The guards are already airborne and searching."

Aioffe closed her eyes and sighed. "Captain, whilst I appreciate your swift response to the potential threat, next time, please ensure you have cleared it with me before you instruct the soldiers to take to the air weapon-ready."

The Captain had the grace to bow his head. She turned to Joshua, saying, "Where are they now?"

"Waiting by the sacred trees," he smiled as if to relieve but his lips were tighter than usual. He kept his gaze firmly held to hers, so she would know there was a 'but' hidden behind them.

Aioffe nodded. "Then I will go and greet our guests. Uffer, please accompany me so that we may organise their lodgings." She gestured to the Captain. "Stand down and order your men away. I will be quite safe. They were invited here at my request." She strode ahead. Joshua ignored the grumbled whispers of concern for Naturae's borders from the Elders and followed, catching her hand.

Passing through the crowded clearing, Joshua raised his hand to various fae, attempting to reassure them. A glance at Aioffe confirmed she also was pretending to make light of the unusual ending to the ceremony, by smiling graciously as if this were a simple leave-taking. But it was a lie, her grip on his fingers bordered on painful. He quickened their pace, knowing Uffer trailed, glowering most likely, close behind them.

Once they reached the bushes which gave way to the narrow path, Joshua paused, unable to put it off any longer. "My love, there is another person arrived with Fairfax and Jeffries." His look darted to Uffer as he lent in. "A vampire."

Aioffe's eyes flared. Uffer's mouth fell open. "That cannot be!"

"I understand," Joshua said. "The Treaty document after the Sation Wars no doubt states something about vampires not being allowed on fae territory. But, he is here now. Just one man. He, I think, healed Mark but suffered some sort of malady afterwards. Jeffries has done what he can but all the same..." Joshua shrugged. Having seen their reaction, he contemplated if he should have insisted on guards to accompany them. He didn't know much about vampires, but he had heard rumour of their supposed speed, which could pose a threat to Aioffe.

After sighing quietly, Aioffe said, "Then we have no choice but to welcome him in the spirit of peace as set out by the Treaty, and hope that he will respect that."

"He may not know of the Treaty," Joshua pointed out, his apprehension growing. "Jeffries said he was a young vampire."

"So they still make vampires then?" Aioffe said, raising her eyebrow as if he would know the answer. "I was under the impression that since the Sation Wars, the creation of new vampires was heavily discouraged, for fear that their bloodline would become weakened and their eternal lifespan shortened."

The implications of their increase in numbers caused Joshua to consider afresh the comments Spenser had made regarding Catholic response to the Protestant faith. His eyes met hers, and he wondered if she was thinking the same.

"Vampires are not to be trusted!" Uffer's greying head shook and he almost spat his next words. "I may not have seen much of the Sation Wars, but what I saw of them was enough."

Aioffe turned to Uffer and frowned. "There have been centuries of peace since then, Uffer. What are you saying?"

Uffer sniffed. "Vampires used all manner of tactics back then. The Queen's Guard was formed specifically to protect the royal line from all possible attempts on her life. During wartime, I was instructed that vampires are deceitful in their every action. They have a power over humans to bend them to their will. Enact their bidding." He shook his head. "Many fae were lost, picked off individually by mortals in their thrall before they even got to a battlefield."

"Are you talking about assassinations?" Joshua tried to keep the incredulity from his voice, but failed. Aioffe gasped, her fingers shooting up to her crown as she swung to look at Joshua with fearful eyes.

With one hand already reaching to reassure her, Joshua clenched his teeth and breathed out through his nostrils. Always, Uffer was quick to imply the worst-case scenario. Forgetting that only moments earlier, he himself had been considering whether they ought to have been accompanied by guards, Joshua wanted to say something to dispel this concern, yet discovered he couldn't find the right words. He knew what Fairfax was, and how duplicitous Jeffries could be. The trio faltered midway down the path, each silent and considering the likelihood of danger ahead.

CHAPTER TWENTY–TWO

Time

The sound of marching feet broke their reverie. Aioffe heard it first, twirling around so she could see down the pathway. Her wings rose and, in response, Joshua and Uffer joined her, hovering slightly above ground as they waited.

A trio of armour-clad soldiers appeared in the distance, abreast of each other but with nervous faces. Their spears pointed forwards, splayed and catching the low branches as they progressed down the narrow track. Behind them, a formation of flying guards held their weapons directed inward, encircling three figures walking steadily through the undergrowth.

Aioffe wanted to tell them this show of force was unnecessary, but after Uffer's caution, she hesitated. Her eyes narrowed as they swept over the approaching prisoners. Fairfax grinned back at her, yet still she wasn't reassured. The tall, bald man she surmised would be Maister Jeffries, although he wasn't wearing a monk's robe as she had assumed he would be, but ordinary clothes. Their eyes met and Aioffe immediately understood that the witch was no threat. His thoughtful expression held a depth of compassion which she sensed in her core was both complex yet well intended. Whilst she didn't trust him, as she knew Joshua held reservations still about his intentions, she touched the witch within him, and knew he was strong and pure of intent.

Wearing a black cassock so she assumed he was of Catholic faith, her judgement of the vampire was impeded by the fact that he kept his head low. She held her palm up. "Stop. I would speak with them before you progress."

The middle guard nodded curtly, then gestured for the others to stand to the side so she could approach. Warily keeping their spears pointed at their prisoners, the fae above remained hovering. Aioffe smiled at them, admitting to herself their vigilance was a comfort.

Joshua and Uffer stayed glued to either side of her as she steadily paced forwards. The vampire dropped to his knee, head still bowed. She decided it was best to ignore him and instead held out her hands in greeting to Fairfax.

"Welcome back, Master Fairfax," she said, after which he swooped down with an extravagant bow.

"Your Majesty." Fairfax, still low, remembered his hat and whipped it off. The damp feather sprayed her feet with flecks of mist droplets. Aioffe's lips rose a little; there was something very endearing about this clumsy daemon-man. Although, as she inhaled, she was reminded of the necessity to keep his alluring Lifeforce away from all but the most well fed of fae. He peeked up at her, all guileless green eyes sparkling with excitement. Aioffe dipped her head in a silent acceptance, then turned to Jeffries.

In closer proximity, she felt her earlier impression reaffirmed as he bowed to her. Not the extravagant, courtly manoeuvre which Fairfax effected, but an efficient and respectful acknowledgement of her position. "You must be Maister Jeffries," Aioffe said. "Thank you for answering our request for assistance. We are grateful that you are safely on these shores, and so soon. It must have been a short voyage to have brought you here only days after we sent out the kestrels."

A scowl flickered briefly across Jeffries' face as he glanced at Fairfax, then he said, "I confess, that swiftness has more to do with the fortuitous winds and a happenstance meeting, your Majesty."

Behind her, Joshua subdued his quiet snort of amusement. Aioffe guessed the monk was not entirely happy with the manner of him being brought to Naturae, but there were no other ways to reach the remote island without wings.

Jeffries continued, "But, even were this not to have been the case, I would, of course, have been at your service regardless."

"You will no doubt be pleased to know that your friend Nemis is with us on Naturae," she said.

Jeffries cocked his chin, but a smile threatened. "That is news most welcome."

Aioffe glanced back at Uffer then said, "We will find quarters for you close to hers, for she is also in need of your expertise. As for the other case, the injured fae requiring your healing abilities, he must remain housed on the other side of the palace. I am sorry for the distance which this will mean you travel between patients, but, it is for the best."

She turned to Henry, still hunched over his knee. Fairfax jumped in with, "Your Majesty, may I present, Henry."

Aioffe arched her eyebrow and waited.

"Get up Henry," Fairfax whispered.

Still with his head bowed, Henry smoothly stood, then clasped his hands before him. In the heartbeat of silence which followed, he slowly lifted his face just enough that she would see it, but not that she could make eye contact with him.

"You may be aware, Henry, that your presence here breaks an ancient treaty between our people."

Henry's dark gaze flew up to meet her icy cool one.

Her chin jutted out as she felt the jolt of their different races collide.

"I was unaware of this, your Majesty."

She frowned, noticing then that his voice did not shake in her presence. Were he to have been faced with the entire community on Naturae with all due ceremony and presentation, she considered even then, this vampire might hold his nerve when faced with a ruler. Relieved that they had such a minimal audience for this meeting, Aioffe considered perhaps this would provide her with an opportunity to read this vampire more clearly, rather than if he were simultaneously being examined by hundreds of prejudiced fae.

Henry straightened, moistening his lips. Something of a noble bearing entered his voice as he stated, "If my presence here is in any way unwelcome, I humbly beg your forgiveness. I will, if you wish it, henceforth leave your shores rather than cause you any diplomatic concerns." He paused then glanced at Fairfax, who squirmed nervously, before looking directly once more at Aioffe. "It is not my place to question or bring into jeopardy any agreement which was made before my creation. I swear to you, Queen of the Fae, I will abide by your realm's rules. I am what I am, that cannot be helped, but this is your land."

Aioffe was aware that everyone was now staring at her, awaiting her verdict. She considered that she ought to put forward the situation to the Council for their agreement, however, feeling the heat of Henry's gaze, the pressure to take an immediate decision was strangely empowering. Her eyes flicked to her husband standing steadfastly beside her, and she knew he would protect and support her whatever she decided. She regretted not discussing this issue with him as soon as it arose, for he would have preferred to prepare a thorough plan to account for all eventualities which having such a guest on Naturae inferred. The Council would probably also want a containment strategy in place, however, reaching consensus was another matter. Look what had happened when Lyrus reappeared, and that situation was still unresolved.

Yet, Henry's steady stare, although not insolent in any regard, implied that the judgement about his fate here was entirely down to her. His deference to her position of authority, the absolute conviction in his voice that he would abide by her ruling even if the consequences were not to his liking, emboldened her.

Aioffe looked away, thinking about mistakes she had made before when judging someone's intentions. Knowing she was slow to trust as a result, her caution had been justified in the past. In her gut, she felt this was one such instance. Trust needed to be earned. Just as Uffer, Thane, Nemis, Fairfax and, of course, Joshua, had proved they could be trusted in their steadfast support of her over the last few decades. But trust a vampire? That would surely take more time.

The silence from everyone waiting for her response weighed on her. Behind her, she felt the warmth of Joshua move closer and she realised - she did not need to trust Henry, only to tolerate this visit with him without incident. The answer was there before her. She and Joshua had co-existed in the same places in England as vampires, so she knew it could be done. There was no threat of attraction between their races; Fairfax was more of a risk in that respect. Moreover, she was now ruling Naturae. It was right that only she should make the decision on what to do with the vampire. She didn't have to protect him, just ensure that no damage came to him or her people.

"Henry, I know you will understand that, for your own safety, you must be escorted for the duration of your stay on Naturae. This is not because you are a vampire, but because you are new and one of a kind here. Fae, like vampires, have long memories. I would not wish for any harm to befall you in answer to crimes which your fellow creatures perpetrated against our race centuries ago. Be warned however, this is not England, but a fae realm. You represent the face of those who harmed our kin. In this regard, it is perhaps better that you make it obvious in your actions towards us that you are from a new age. A more enlightened one."

As Uffer had positioned himself behind her shoulder while she spoke, Aioffe could only imagine the glare on his face, warning the vampire to heed her words. She watched as the implications of what she said sunk in, then he nodded.

As she turned to leave, Aioffe extended her wings to their fullest, flapping them gracefully before gliding off.

CHAPTER TWENTY-THREE

Spies like us

28th July 1553

Within days, Naturae appeared, on the surface at least, to absorb its visitors into the realm. This was, Joshua acknowledged, due in no small part to Uffer's determination that their lives not be entirely up-ended by the arrival of a vampire into their midst. After consultation with the Captain, Henry was largely kept to his designated chambers and brought livestock on a daily basis to feed upon. This reduced the demand for guards, eliminating the need for him to hunt as well as protecting him from curious stares.

Once a day he was escorted to see Fairfax wherever the daemon could be found as a poorly concealed attempt to normalise his existence on the island. Jeffries busied himself with brewing potions in the turret with Nemis, whilst Fairfax wandered between his ship and the workshop, keeping himself away from the community by focusing upon repairs.

Predictably, the Council were divided on what to do about their guests and much else besides. Aioffe patiently listened to their concerns, telling Joshua afterwards that she grew ever weary of their maturing methods of garnering support for their points of view. Attendance in the High Hall during daily Council sessions was increasing, in numbers and noise. It pained Joshua that Aioffe usually retreated from everyone, including himself, after these discussions, preferring to spend more and more time alone with the vines.

Aioffe sent her apologies that day - pupaetion was imminent, and she was needed elsewhere. Joshua knew it was also because her patience was wearing thin - the very prospect of juggling egos filled her with dread, tiring her before she even sat through the sessions. In her absence, the Council members that morning re-opened the question of their reaction to the threat overseas. Bustling in late, and failing to conceal his anxiety adequately, Ambassador Spenser announced he had just received a kestrel, which brought news of the capture of one of his human contacts within Spain, and a concern that their torturing would reveal the names of other heretics he associated with. Fears about inquisitorial methods perpetrated on the continent caused emotions to run riot around the great table. A second kestrel, a bold one which screeched an echoing introduction to the vaulted room, arrived during the meeting. This messenger carried stern orders demanding the Ambassador return to Europe forthwith.

After calming the bird, Spenser requested a firm decision on Naturae's plans so that he may reassure the other realms that an adequate response was in place. Seeing the debate then flounder in the absence of a consensus, Joshua, growing in frustration himself, resolved to do something practical to influence the Elders into an agreement about such matters now and in the future. It struck him that his initial instinct regarding on-the-ground knowledge was the solution, but, for that to happen, he required expert advice. Tired of feeling overlooked, and not one to raise his voice where it wasn't wanted, he was spurred into taking the matter into his own hands with an urgency that hadn't been present before. Leaving them still muttering vague ideas, Joshua set out to find Fairfax.

Flying over the heads of two soldier fae sitting in the shade at the top of the shore, he located Fairfax in the hull of his ship. Stripped to the waist, the daemon was covered in sweat and pitch as he heaved barrels out of the way to make watertight the beached vessel, from the inside as well as out. The sunshine evaporated the vapours of the foul smelling tar, making Joshua's eyes sting.

"I need to ask a favour of you, old friend," Joshua called down through the hatch.

"Name it! Or better yet, come down and help. Then we can talk."

As his eyes still stung, Joshua replied, "Thanks, but my wings are black enough as it is without you splashing pitch on them. Come up and cool off."

Fairfax's ginger mop appeared through the hole, followed by Henry's slightly darker straggled tresses. They were both grinning madly. Joshua suspected ship repairs weren't the only activity that had been shared whilst he had been sat wasting his time listening to arguments. He was almost envious.

Once Henry and Fairfax had clambered down the side, then liberally taken a bath in the shallows, they used the sand to scrub the grime from their faces. Joshua lay on the beach, watching the pair frolic openly as they rinsed off in the sea. Glad that his friend had found happiness, he tried to remember the last time he and Aioffe had danced in the sky, but couldn't recall. This only firmed his resolve to find a solution to the problems which beset Naturae, if only so that they might have time for such pleasant interludes once again.

"Clean and vaguely presentable," Fairfax shouted as he strode towards Joshua, then rattled his head like a dog. Henry laughed as the spray hit him, and he playfully shoved Fairfax away.

"That's a matter for debate," Joshua said, tasting the waves of Lifeforce emanating from Fairfax. He remembered not to inhale, but glanced instead at their bare chests. "I trust you will be fully clothed by the time we return to the palace?"

"Absolutely," Henry said. He jerked his head towards his stern-faced escorts at the top of the beach. "They are worse than nursemaids; tidying up after me, ensuring I'm dressed appropriately, making sure I'm where I'm meant to be at the right time to avoid, well, everyone."

"Ah, but at least you blend in a little more now, unlike in that ridiculous cassock," Fairfax joked. "Apart from the lack of wings, of course." Being of similar height, Joshua had loaned Henry some of his long shirts and loose trousers to wear, both of which were much appreciated by the vampire in the heat of the late summer. Henry had laced closed the wing holes.

Joshua glanced at Henry, and decided that if he was that intimate with Fairfax the chances were he knew something of his friend's lifestyle. He got straight to the point. "I need your help with our spies."

Fairfax's eyebrows rose. "Your spies?"

Joshua nodded. "Yes, Naturae's. Aioffe's first pupaetion. They need training."

Seeing Fairfax's eyes slide over to Henry, whose mouth simply twitched up on one side, Joshua felt relieved that he hadn't put his foot in it with his friend after all.

"Who is supposed to be doing it?" Fairfax sounded sceptical.

"An old spymaster, the last of his generation, called Issam. However, it has been many decades since he finished 'working' and I fear he is, shall we say, not a natural tutor."

Henry raised his eyebrow. "How old is he?"

Shrugging, Joshua hazarded a guess based purely on Uffer's age, as he didn't know Issam well at all. "Probably over seven hundred, which is quite advanced for a worker fae."

"I see the problem." Fairfax pursed his lips. "Techniques and times have moved on since then, I imagine."

Joshua pushed himself to a stand. "Is that a yes, then? I have a few ideas which I'll write down, topics to cover which sprung to my mind. I'm sure you can add to it. I don't know how long you will be here for but anything would help."

Henry grinned at Fairfax. "Sounds like fun. Maybe I can pick up some tips from Tommy Fair or Timothy of Flanders."

Fairfax rolled his eyes, then crouched on his toes, leaning on Henry's shoulder to straighten. Joshua became aware that Fairfax was now, in human terms, almost middle-aged. Not that you would have known it from the way he danced across the sand towards his ship again. "Just getting some equipment," he called back. Henry chuckled without taking his eyes from him.

"Quite the character," Joshua said.

Henry nodded, but then his dark eyes turned and bored into Joshua. "I could perhaps be of some use to you as well. I used to move in courtly circles myself."

It fell into place for Joshua. The familiar profile, seen countless times on crown and shilling coins or inn signage. The name, although so many were called Henry in honour of the monarch. The gingery-red hair. But how could it be?

Seeing the cloud cross Joshua's face, Henry grinned. "But perhaps you knew of my father?"

Joshua felt winded for a moment. It had been seventeen years since he had last set foot in England. Henry VIII, he knew from Spenser, had died some years ago, leaving his legitimate son Edward on the throne. So, who was the teenager before him? A bastard, perhaps? Joshua frowned, trying to recall what he had heard of court gossip.

Henry watched him wrestle for a moment, then said quietly, "I am Henry Fitzroy, Duke of Richmond and Somerset, bastard son of Henry the Eighth. By birthright, I should be Henry the Ninth, but now…" Henry glanced at Fairfax, "I have been set free. I beg you…" Henry's expression grew earnest as he requested, "Do not make the mistake of thinking I would not stop the tongue of any man, fae, or witch who exposes me before I am ready to be shackled once more."

A disquiet grew over Joshua as he stared at Henry. The vampire held his gaze and blinked, and Joshua felt a calmness spread through him. There was no question in Joshua's mind now; he would not tell anyone of the bastard prince who became a vampire. It was as if the thought had never occurred to him, an omission of a memory that was once there. Joshua found himself shaking his head slowly. No question. Nothing to say.

As he turned to walk back up the beach, Joshua's head cleared sufficiently enough for him to ask himself what had just happened. And worse, there was a nagging feeling somewhere in his mind that there was a threat. Was it to his life if he talked about the vampire? But what was there to talk about? He was just a vampire, just Henry. He shook his head as if that would dispel the cold greyness which clouded his vision, and walked on.

CHAPTER TWENTY-FOUR
Dissent in the ranks

Henry left Fairfax with his rapt pupils and walked across the clearing to the Palace. Behind him trailed his two guards, who, as weeks passed, had become less vigilant about watching his every move. Perhaps, Henry reflected, they didn't believe in the rumours about vampire speed. Knowing he could dash to the edge of the island before they could even raise their wings pleased him.

A casual stroll towards the palace invigorated him after the closeness of the falling-down shack in which the trainee spies gathered, deep in the forest. With no sense of urgency they ambled along, Henry enjoying the lead in the walk through the warm afternoon air. The clang of hammers on metal and the smell of charcoal from the forge. The chitter-chatter of worker fae sloshing laundry by the stream. He smiled, and almost automatically whispered a prayer of gratitude. Stopping himself, he frowned. For all of his discussions with Jeffries, and protestations to priests, he didn't really believe there was a god any more. So why had he fallen back into old habits?

As he climbed the stairs to the landing balcony, Henry snorted. Although he felt at home here, at peace, he knew he was the only one in charge of his destiny, not a higher being. But, religion was the currency by which a person gained power, and so he would have to continue the disguise. It was funny how merely discussing religious matters, as he had just been doing with the trainees alongside Jeffries,

155

had brought the lifestyle, the rituals, back to him. The church, completely absent here, was not missed. He understood that they believed in something - each other and their Queen, but the fae did not even appear to be concerned about their afterlife. Certainly not in the way that it preoccupied and guided humans. Henry knew there was no glorious afterlife for him either. So what did it matter what he did in the present?

His lip curled as he thought of the fervour with which he used to pray. For a good hunting pony. A mother who was present. Respect from his father. For forgiveness for his sins with Henry Howard. What a waste of time. Now, he understood there was no right or wrong religion. It was a prop which pacified or incentivised people. A tool to be manipulated, as other vampires did. He just needed to work out how best to use this superior knowledge for his purposes.

The inner atrium, cool and airy, was a welcome relief to Henry so he dallied there waiting for his guards to catch him up. Then, after a brief discussion, they permitted him to enter the High Hall as a trio, as long as he kept his distance from other people. Towards the far end where the Council session was already in full swing, Henry and his guards took a seat at the side of the huge chamber, on a comfortable bench surrounding a massive trunk-pillar. His view was hampered by the many attending fae, standing, muttering in clusters whilst the discussion went on. It irked him immediately that the chattering onlookers would not quieten, to listen to the proceedings, but, he had no authority here to demand their silence. It did not prevent him from tuning his ears to the debate raging on the platform at the end of the hall. With half an ear on them, and half on his guards who whispered their names to him, it took only minutes before Henry identified a voice to a rank, as displayed by colourful official robes and sashes.

Prince Joshua, whom he knew already, was talking about the developments with the spy instruction, although he was cut off by grumbling from the Captain (of the fae army), who wanted some of their time to deliver hand to hand combat training, and then by Thane (leader of the worker fae), who had been asking for space for an archery range and wanted their schooling area moved. His labourers' work involved a clearing to be created in the forest and the old shack in the middle was scheduled to be torn down. Henry whole-heartedly approved of this idea - every Englishman was required by the laws of the land to train weekly with a bow, and if the male spy fae wished to blend in, they would have to display competence with the weapon, even if they still looked like teenagers. Also, he wanted to practise, and was looking forward to showing them his skills.

The argument began to turn ugly, as Uffer, who Henry already understood oversaw the household, seemed concerned at the deforestation which the range would require. Habitats they were working so hard to restock with deer (poached from Scotland and smuggled here with some difficulty) could be destroyed.

Debate then broke out about to how that space could likewise be used for weapons training by the Captain, an idea which didn't appear to convince the leader of the fae army. Henry couldn't fathom why, as so much could be learned about the art of ambush, a surprise attack from the woods. He remembered stories of battles, such as Agincourt, where concealed troops in woodlands rushing the enemy had been the winning strategy.

What the fae were preparing for, in terms of a war, he also didn't quite understand. His own experience of real conflict was non existent, despite his former rank and privilege, although he knew his father had seen combat since his turning. Also, there were so few fae soldiers, especially compared to the numbers a human army could muster - how could they hope to be effective in a battle situation, he wondered? Perhaps he should watch their practises, Henry decided. Wings ought to give them some advantage, but how did they capitalise on this unique attribute?

The Captain, however, gathered support from some of the soldiers in the audience, who expressed their displeasure at the suggestion of practicing outside with calls of "What's wrong with the Training Hall?" and "Why change what works already?" Nodding his agreement before turning back to the table, the old warrior seemed reluctant to embrace the opportunity Thane proposed.

Henry chuckled to himself - the fae could be easily defeated with gunpowder-powered weaponry anyway, and he hadn't seen any evidence of that here on Naturae. They were a backward realm in that regard and it didn't appear as if anyone wanted to drive forward the changes they would need to survive were they to be exposed. The shambles of the meeting strongly suggested, even if they had the knowledge, no-one would be able to decide on what to do with it.

Calling for the conversation to move along, Joshua raised his voice, citing that he needed to get back to schooling and must finish his presentation without further digression. He then outlined much of what Henry already knew, listing the subject areas and who was delivering the training. All for the purpose of getting them ready to go out and work as they were meant to, for Naturae. Henry was flattered by the Prince's acknowledgement of his own lessons in courtly behaviour and protocol, languages and sports. Even more so by his glowing praise of Henry's aptitude for devising codes and ciphers. It made Joshua's own contributions to exercises in handwriting and forgery seem unimportant, when those involved in the teaching knew that these were vital elements in successfully passing on information.

Noticing some discomfort when Joshua outlined Fairfax's subjects of concealment, costume and sleight of hand, Henry was even more surprised by the crowd's response to Jeffries' religious instruction. For once, the voices of dissent seemed unified - these 'new' religions had no place in fae culture. Heads were shaking, fists clenched, demanding these lessons be stopped. Yet, around the table, the Elders remained silent. Henry felt moved to stand and make the point that the church dominated the lives of all folk in England, when the flamboyant fae who had been on the beach when he arrive, the one he knew as the daemon boy's father, shouted.

"Have you understood nothing?"

The hall fell silent. Spenser glared around the table. "Just because you do not perceive a value in their religion, or carry about old scars from the Sation Wars, does not mean that human faith is irrelevant."

Henry felt like cheering. Here was a man who spoke sense!

"The differences in their religious beliefs is costing lives, and will further cost many more. And that's not just amongst humans. Whilst you have been bickering here, a Catholic Queen has taken the throne in England. If you think this is irrelevant, I have warned you before, it is only a matter of time before fae lives are lost as well. The Catholic Church, along with the vampires, will not hesitate to give her their full backing."

Spenser whirled around to face Queen Aioffe, his ornate cape glittering with gold embroidery. "Your Majesty, I must leave for the continent." From this viewpoint, Henry watched Aioffe's face fall. "Mary's emergence as the victor in the battle for England's throne has far-reaching implications for our realms there, who will no doubt feel that it tips the balance of power back into Catholic hands." Spenser turned and warned the Council, "You would be wise to decide how best to respond to this yourselves. Whilst Scotland is ostensibly ruled by Mary Queen of Scots, an eleven-year-old girl in France and likely to marry another catholic monarch, make no mistake - there are dissenters on your borders also, even between Mary's regent and parliament. The Dauphin's witch mother will influence her every move, indeed more so when she marries. There is chaos coming, and, I fear, Naturae is woefully ill-prepared."

Henry held his breath, waiting for Aioffe to say something to salvage the situation. Instead, she pushed back her chair, and with her chin jutted out, she walked calmly from the platform, took to the air and flew over the heads of the assembled crowd. His eyes returned to the dais to see Joshua hurrying after her, followed by Spenser stalking through the crowds. Henry allowed himself a tiny smile. Fairfax would have enjoyed this moment also, he thought, knowing how much his friend and lover revelled in drama.

As he stood and joined the chattering clusters now bustling out from the Hall, Henry started to process the news the European fae had imparted.

Mary, his own half sister, had claimed the throne of England completely. He briefly wondered if Jeffries knew, and could not resist a tiny smile. It didn't change matters for him personally - after all, he still wasn't on the throne, but he considered what opportunity this news presented him with.

Mary was weak, like Aioffe. Mary had always leant on the Church, on prayer for guidance. And, she was a human. Malleable. Enthrallable. Doubtless, some priest was already whispering in her ear. That could be him, Henry realised. The lessons which he had witnessed, the skills he had picked up from the spy training. That could be him.

Walking quickly through the corridors to his chamber to await his daily meal, Henry's chest tightened in anticipation. A doorway was opening up for him. A moment when, serendipitously, he could take what was rightfully his.

A throne.

The idea spurred him on, so much so that he almost missed the royal couple arguing in the hallway leading to the Ambassadorial quarters. He slowed, ducked his head, and avoided eye contact. He paused, tucked into a doorway.

"I have too many other matters to attend to," he heard the Queen say, her tone impatient.

"I understand that, my love," Joshua pleaded. "All I am asking for is that you consider it."

"Spenser will do what he must," Aioffe sighed. "I don't understand why you are so bothered if he stays or leaves."

There was a pause before Joshua said, "I thought you wanted Lyrus cured and put to good use. Yet, if Spenser goes, the burden of protecting Nemis and her son from him will fall to me whilst we still do not know his true intentions. This takes me away from all the other matters, important ones, for Naturae's future."

"Why wouldn't Nemis go with him, and Mark?"

"Because she is unwell every morning, Jeffries tells me. She should not travel. He is concerned, and I am as well. She needs our help, my love. Can we really not spare a few guards?"

Aioffe's voice rose. "I cannot be responsible for the well being of everyone on this island! Asking the Captain to release more fae from their patrols, their training - it is too much. Nemis, much as she means to me, probably should leave with her husband."

Henry heard Joshua's sharp intake of breath. "These are our friends," Joshua said. "It is not like you to brush off their safety like this. Not when you know the threats they face on the mainland, let alone the continent."

His guards, having found him lurking in the passage, poked him forwards. Henry's eyes narrowed, but he walked on. Aioffe and Joshua must have caught their movement as they flitted the other way, their argument paused.

As he reached his chamber door, he rested his hand on the latch, then turned to the usual young servant fae waiting in the hallway. He whispered to her, "Who is Lyrus?"

Henry saw the glance between them all. He raised an eyebrow when no-one volunteered an answer. Then one of the soldiers pushed open his door and stood back. "Your meal will be with you shortly."

After a lingering glance at their discomfort, Henry tipped his head, accepting they would not willingly answer, and entered his room. He would have to ask Fairfax or Jeffries instead, as he was not easily able to interact with anyone else. Henry suspected the affable Prince Joshua would similarly not respond to his request, although he could be persuaded of course…

No matter, it could wait.

CHAPTER TWENTY-FIVE

Hatching

19th August, 1553

Aioffe sat next to the roots of the withered royal vine, sobbing. Whilst grateful for the solitude, her barren family plant was not a comforting witness to her unattractive heaving. She tried not to think back to when she last cried this heavily, during that awful moment when she had questioned her very existence in the depths of the Beneath, many years ago. Then, as she contemplated starving herself so that she might fade into the earth itself, the prospect of ending her life had seemed very reasonable. Now though, the heavy weight of the decisions she was supposed to make regarding the future of Naturae, for the good of its people, made her feel as if she had been utterly selfish at the time. Shallow even.

How was she meant to make sense of this quandary, Aioffe asked herself. She might have been born to the ruling line, but that didn't equip her with the fortitude, or maybe foresight, to carry out decisions which affected her race, did it? Having never wanted the crown, she bitterly regretted ever accepting it. The never-ending responsibility for the well-being of others. The creation of all future fae. The burden of administration to ensure that correct tallies and representation was made of all things relating to Naturae. Accounts even! She was certain her mother had happily avoided all matters to do with trade and coin with her isolationist stance, but Aioffe had encouraged connection with the human world, and for that, one needed to master economics as well. In hindsight, she wondered if her mother's position had been the right one after all.

And as for the Council, she sniffed and squeezed her eyes closed, if only to prevent them rolling. There were too many dissenting voices for her to guide down a path to a consensus. Her utopian vision of collaborative working was a mess. They were supposed to support her with ruling, but now the battles took up more of her time than it saved. More often than not, the daily meetings descended into barely lucid arguments. The Elders had now become so entrenched in their positions that any deviation from them risked their factions haranguing them outside of the High Hall.

Bickering had become the main currency within Naturae. Asking the community to believe in her seemed futile. She couldn't even believe in herself any more. It was only a matter of time before the blessing ceremonies became so fractured by their differences of opinion, they wouldn't work. And then what? Even Spenser was abandoning her. Aioffe balled herself up, shaking her head in her knees. The thin silver circlet perched on her hair slipped, and she did nothing to straighten it.

Trying hard to get a grip on herself, Aioffe shoved her worries to the back of her mind. As the tears eventually slowed and her shoulders dropped, she dug around in the pockets of her tunic for a kerchief. Pulling out the hastily stuffed linen, she opened it out and prepared to blow. She froze as she looked at the tan square, then bit her lip. There, in the corner, was a little heart motif which she had sewn into most of Joshua's clothing and accessories when they had lived in England. The sight of it now, a reminder of all that had gone before to reach this point, made her spirit sink.

It was so abundantly clear to her now that Joshua was meant to be a father. She saw how he took even the most awkward child, Mark, under his wing and nurtured him. And yet, she had no time for children, her royal duties made sure of that. She had failed him. She had failed everyone in Naturae, it seemed. No matter what they tried, she could not produce a child for him to love. An heir for Naturae. Even today, their argument held the undertones of his dissatisfaction with her, she was sure. As a Queen, she lacked. As a wife, she also lacked. Aioffe sighed again, feeling the shudder in her ribs push up against her with the ragged breath.

Breaking the silence in the Vine Room, Aioffe heard a creak, then an almost imperceptible tearing. She looked up as the smell of maturing intensified. A muted thud as a cocoon dropped from its vine. Standing up in haste, barely straightening her skirts, Aioffe then dashed down between the beds. She pushed the leaves aside as she went, searching for the cocoon.

There, by an ordinary worker vine, a head-sized oval cocoon had rolled back towards the wall. Aioffe smiled, gathering her skirt so she could reach in to pull it towards herself. An early one! As she touched its light brown coloured outer layer, she could feel the limbs of the wriggling pupae inside. The knobs of its joints strained against the hardened exterior, cracking it. Aioffe held the cocoon in her arms, wondering if she should call for a nurse. But then, a tiny fist punched through, pink and smooth. Carefully using her nails, she picked away the flap of shell, exposing a larger hole through which an arm could fully extrude. The pupae's shoulder cracked the cocoon, so she poked her finger into the gap and pushed up through the seam, between the silken interior and the damp flesh of the sac membrane.

Sitting on the ground, Aioffe determined which way up the pupae faced, and placed the cocoon safely between her propped up thighs. Then, crooning tender words of encouragement, she helped the youngling push aside the covering, peeling off the clingy sac from its skin. The tiny head tilted back and a bud-like mouth opened. The pupae's first cry took her by surprise, more of a yowl than a lusty bawl, which faded as quickly as it had sounded. Still, the pupae did not open its eyes to see its mother. With gentle thumbs, she swept over its face, hoping the touch would stimulate this most innate of actions. But the pupae steadfastly refused to open its eyes to the world.

This moment should have been full of joy, Aioffe thought. A new fae ought to be cause for celebration, a fresh life to be led. A future full of promise and hope. As she gently placed the pupae, still protected by the shell of the cocoon, back on the earthen bed, Aioffe realised what the nagging hole within her was. The one from which all the fears and indecisiveness stemmed from.

She felt as if there was no future, because she had no heir to pass on what she worked so hard to create. The newly hatched pupae let out a thin wail - which sounded alien, uncomfortable even, to her, serving only to reaffirm that whilst she technically was its mother, the pupae was not for her. Its destiny was to join the swarm, not lead. It would be welcomed by the worker community as one of their own and thrive there, but it was not unique as her heir needed to be. Not a rare bloom. She needed a child of her own; nothing else would do.

Whilst this was not news to her, for some reason Aioffe acknowledged the issue of an heir was not selfish vanity, but necessary for the entire future of Naturae to be secured. If she could not lead them as Queen because she was, underneath it all, unable to see that future, then she was left with no alternative but to focus on that problem. To the exclusion of all other matters. Suddenly, nothing else was as important as solving this puzzle. It was no longer a question of 'it would be a good idea to have an heir' but now a necessity, for any future for Naturae. Any future for herself.

Glancing around, the vines which she occasionally viewed as bars of a cage, now she could see were merely plants. Built for survival. Created to provide, bearing fruit in the cycle of life. She touched one of the leaves, stroking its veins. These were the channels - taking the light of Naturae and feeding it into the fruits, the cocoons. Aioffe tipped her head back, feeling the last rays of sunshine from the day bathe her face with warmth.

Then, thinking afresh about the ingredients which a vine needed, she considered again why her royal vine still withered even though it had blessings and light. If she were a gardener, a tender of plants, what would she prescribe to prompt a better harvest? Aioffe wondered about the orchards which bore the autumn bounty of fruit. When a previously fruit-bearing tree withers, grafting it with a strong sapling gives it strength.

She glanced back at the royal vine in the corner, golden still but droopy-leaved and cocoon-less. That had been her mother's vine. The same stalk she had been pupated from. Perhaps, she needed to nurture her own vine? If she couldn't make the vine which she had been grown upon bear a cocoon, then she needed to find another one to graft to it. For strength. Like her own love Joshua, who she had created from mixing royal fae Lifeforce with human. Her powers to create were strongest when mixed together; maybe, the royal vine needed to be mixed also?

Aioffe frowned as the thought took shape. But, it had to be with another royal vine, not one of the worker ones, for they were too green. A royal vine grew yellow. The worker vines were too, well, different. It needed to be of similar stock. Instinctively, she knew that too much of a hybrid simply wouldn't graft - the vines themselves were just too specific. Is this even possible, she wondered? And where would one get a new royal vine from?

She rolled her eyes, cross with herself for not having seen the possibility before. They had royal vines in Europe, surely. Her mother had always been concerned about being replaced by a European Princess, so they must have. Aioffe gathered her skirts and ran - time was short - a nurse for the pupae was needed, and Spenser was about to leave!

CHAPTER TWENTY-SIX

Flighty

"I have to fly to Europe!" Aioffe said, closing the door behind her. Her face was blotchy and puffy, and Joshua knew she'd been crying. Yet, for the first time in a while, he saw a light of hope and excitement shining through her.

"Why?" He frowned, then a worried note entered his voice. "It's dangerous. You heard what Spenser said."

She shook her head, "I realise, but you of all people know I can pass for a human. I must. It's the only way." She crossed the room and pulled out a travel bag.

"The only way for what?" Joshua's confusion meant he couldn't keep the tone of desperation rising in his question. He put the quill down and stood from the desk.

"To grow an heir," she tossed over her shoulder. She opened one of her chests and began rummaging.

As if that answered anything, Joshua thought. "I still don't understand."

Aioffe looked up at him, and her eyebrows knitted together. Her hands fell still as she spoke earnestly. "That's what I, what *we*, need. The royal vine needs an infusion of royal fae strength to it. It must be that. Everything else we've tried so far has failed. It's just got to be too much. I have to do something different."

"Not for want of attempt." He didn't mean to be grumpy, but he was. All he had done lately had been to try to relieve her burdens, so they could spend more time together and she would be happier. She didn't appear to appreciate any of his efforts at all. Instead, she was looking at him with a curious defiance.

"So I'm going to find one. In a European vine room," she announced, as if that were the end of the matter. She returned to pulling clothes out of the chest, furiously tossing discarded items to the floor. "Has Spenser left yet? I must reach their vines before they wilt for the winter. I need him to show me where to go, who to speak to."

Joshua looked away. He hadn't agreed to this. Didn't agree with this idea. Felt with every bone of his being that it was a bad plan. He could lose her again. He blinked back the tear he felt lurking, and with a sneaking glance back at her excited face, all of a sudden realised he would lose her if he didn't let her leave. That was what it came down to - losing her voluntarily or trapping her with him. To be miserable. Which would eventually lead to one of them leaving. And he knew he was the superfluous one to Naturae.

Worse, she didn't even ask him to go with her. With his shoulders sagging, he walked slowly over to their door.

"Joshua!"

He turned, but she was still glaring at him. He recognised her stance; at any moment, the usual Aioffe would stamp her foot.

"Don't walk away from me. Please."

His fingers found the embroidered heart she had sewn into the lining of his jacket and picked at a loose thread, while he considered whether there was anything more for them to tell each other. "I don't know what you want me to say, Aioffe."

As he said the words, a rush of annoyance over her lack of appreciation for him and everything he had done, swept over him. Asking her to stay, or take him with her, seemed futile. She didn't need him. Perhaps she didn't even love him any more. She seemed to have flipped again, changed her mind to being so determined, so focused on getting an heir, instead of what he thought they wanted for Naturae. For them. He was used to her lightening fast changes of mood, and too used to her pulling away from him now.

"Say, you agree." She paused, but he wasn't sure why she wanted his consent now. She had already made up her mind, and his own was blank as to reasons why she shouldn't go. It seemed like this idea of travelling hundreds of miles away from Naturae - from him - was the only thing which had brought light into her being. Bought joy to her. Hope and urgency lit up her face, rather than concern for his feelings on her idea. A hope he was nothing to do with. The thought winded him.

Aioffe pushed herself up and paced around. "I have to go now. The cocoons are ripe. The pupaetion has just begun, so the vines need no more blessings for a while."

He couldn't take his eyes from her, drinking her in as if this were the last time he would see her.

Rather than noticing though, she gazed out of the window, perhaps already plotting her route away. Ticking off on her fingers as she said, "Spenser is going anyway, so I can travel with him. Lyrus is healing and doesn't appear to be causing the trouble we were worried about, after all. There's enough of that happening with the Council, but that isn't going to change in my absence either. You will be here anyway if it does get out of hand. And, if I don't go now while the days are long enough, the vines will wither for winter."

It sounded to Joshua like she was compiling a list of reasons why now was the only time she could leave. He nodded. Under pressure and without warning of this, he could think of no reasons to stay, right now, to counter the extensive itemisation of the burdens she bore. None of which he had been able to help with. All of which he could see why she needed a break from.

Across the wide room, their eyes met. Blocking his mind so that she wouldn't touch his hurt, Joshua felt his bottom lip waver. Before she could notice, he tightened his mouth, then replied with the only neutral thing he could find to say. "I'll find Spenser now. Tell him you will be his travelling companion."

Aioffe blinked as if she were expecting him to say something else. Joshua turned and left.

*****

Joshua rubbed his hand over his face, feeling the bristles of his two-day beard catch on his delicate fingers. The action did nothing to ease the dull ache in his chest, which he knew would only grow heavier with each passing day Aioffe was absent. Rolling his shoulders back, he straightened himself before knocking on the Spenser and Nemis's door. What he had to ask of his friend put him in a difficult position, exposed his own weakness in being unable to protect or keep his own wife.

"Just the man!" Spenser's narrow smile suggested he had shrugged off his earlier grouch, but not entirely. He ushered Joshua in. "I was just saying to Nemis that it would be terribly rude of us to sail off without saying goodbye."

Joshua glanced around at the bundles and boxes strewn about their chamber, and his heart sank. Of course, Nemis would never leave Spenser if she could help it. "I thought you were still ailing," Joshua said to her. "I should have realised you would all be leaving together."

Spenser's lips tightened. "We decided it was for the best."

Nemis resumed stuffing nightshirts into a bag, her head bowed. The scene in their bedroom was not unlike the chamber he had just left - clothing, shoes and other essential travel items strewn everywhere. Spenser then confirmed what Joshua already suspected, although he saw the fear flashing across his face. "Even though Jeffries has made her stronger medicine, the visions have increased. Every night, since the last blessing ceremony, my poor Nemis has been in turmoil with nightmares."

"I'm not able to leave these chambers at all," she said sadly, absently folding a nightshirt and placing it into a basket. "There's something here preventing me. I just can't. I used to feel so free on Naturae, but now..." She shrugged. "So I have to leave."

Even though she kept avoiding his gaze, Joshua noticed the dark circles under her eyes. His jaw clenched as he considered the burdens his friend bore without complaint. "I wish it were different," he said after a long pause, during which two more shirts were added to the pile. "I always wished you to find peace here, but I understand."

"Besides," Nemis said, turning to him finally, her lips lifting as she cradled her flat stomach. "A little maritime discomfort for a few days won't hurt. I'll just have to void my morning stomach over the side, instead of into a bowl. Apart from the nightmares, I'm not ill. Just pregnant." She shrugged.

Without hesitation, Joshua broke into a wide smile. "I am so pleased for you!" He darted over to give his brave friend a hug, meeting

Spenser's proud but still guarded eyes over her shoulder. "I, ah, am truly delighted for you both, for you all." He looked around for their surviving child. "Where is Mark? Does he know?"

"Not yet," Nemis said. "Not until I feel it quicken. So, don't tell anyone, please."

Joshua tapped his finger to the side of his nose and grinned again. Pulling back from the joyful embrace, he remembered why he had come. Then, he took a breath in as he straightened his shirt before laying out his request.

"I come, not just to say goodbye, but to ask something of you. Of you both, I suppose. Aioffe has decided on her future." He paused and looked at Spenser warily. "She has decided she needs to go to Europe. With you. Quickly."

Spenser's eyebrows shot up. "But, her place is here?"

Joshua nodded. "It is what she wants - needs to - do. Something about a vine room, she said. She needs you to guide her." He held his gaze on Spenser and tried to keep his voice as steady. Everything in him ached to collapse just verbalising his wife's wish to leave him. "I am to remain here. So, I need you to swear on everything you hold sacred, to protect her."

Nemis could not see the desperation which Joshua could not hide from his friend. She patted another shirt into the bag, saying, "Mark and I were going to travel with him, so we could all stay together. We can't fly."

Silently Spenser acknowledged what Joshua was asking of him, then he turned to his wife and took her hand. "I confess, I still don't feel comfortable about you travelling with me, or alone again at home on Anglesey. Not with...." He glanced at her stomach. Nemis smiled but it was crooked. Joshua sensed there was something he was not a party to, but politeness held him back.

"There's nowhere else for me to go but home, though," Nemis said. The folding resumed. "I know there are no healers there, but maybe it will be fine. A normal birth." She didn't sound convinced.

"And if it isn't?" Spenser said.

Nemis swallowed. She pulled out a blue shift dress, laying it on the floor to straighten it. As she flipped the fabric back, revealing embroidery which Joshua recognised as Aioffe's handiwork, her hand shot to her mouth, fingers pushing against her lips to stop them from trembling.

"Is it the lack of healers which concerns you?" Joshua asked. He crouched down by her side and placed his hand on her shoulder. "I'm sure we could find a cunning woman to attend to you, when the time comes."

Husband and wife glanced at each other. "It might require a very specific skill set," Spenser said, then looked at Joshua's wings pointedly.

Joshua's eyes flared. "How do you know?"

Nemis shrugged, and too casually said, "I've seen it."

That Nemis would have prophetic visions was not new to Joshua. After all, she had claimed to have already known his face and his purpose when they first met, seventeen years ago. She knew all about his missing wife and how to get to Naturae when she'd never even been here before. All from her visions. Thinking about what they were implying, it sort of made sense to him that she would know if something in her body was different to a usual human, or witch, baby. After all, the father was a fae. Joshua beamed at them both, realising that there was still hope for Aioffe and he to bear a winged child, if a witch and a fae could produce one.

Spenser's expression did not match Joshua's. His brow had darkened, and his posture straightened. Then he said, "I know what we decided, Nemis, but now is not the time for adventure. For risk. It is too much for me to take on the responsibility for three, nay, four lives by dragging you all with me across the continent. Even if Aioffe pulled the boat alongside me, there would still be the slow passage over land to contend with, and she is not known for her patience."

He slumped onto the corner of the bed, shaking his head. "I just don't see how I can keep all of you safe, yet travel quickly. Nor can I be sure you will be safe in Anglesey, my dear. I cannot be in two places at the same time." Joshua crossed the room and put his hand on his friend's shoulder, noticing the fabric over his hunched back strained across the wings beneath. He didn't think he had ever seen the usually suave and in-control Ambassador so low before. The blame was partly his, yet Joshua had little choice but to ask him this request.

"Let me help, dear friend," Joshua said. "I will take care of Nemis. She is as close to family as I have. Under my personal protection on Naturae, and away from the gossiping fishwives on Anglesey. Jeffries is here if there are requirements for tonics or any other sort of healing. I know Mark is happy here - thriving even. Then, when you return, you can decide together where to locate for the new arrival. You won't be gone long, surely, to finish your business on the continent?"

He turned to Nemis, hoping to see her support for his idea. She chewed her lip whilst they all considered his proposition, then said, "Yet I remain a prisoner in these chambers."

"Explain to me how," Joshua said. "Do you not feel safe here? No-one would harm you."

Nemis paled visibly and reached for her husband. He hauled her slight weight up and pulled her onto his knee. Wrapping her arms around him, she turned her head into his shoulder so it faced Joshua. In a quiet voice, she said, "It's more of the sensation, a grey and dark loathing. I cannot step out from the door without it overwhelming me. Perhaps it's more of an anticipation of darkness, than an actual threat."

She took Spenser's hand in hers and met his eyes. "But I do not want to add more concern to your burden, husband. I cannot. Much as though I want you by my side in all things, I understand your role is to move back and forth between the realms. If you are always worrying about me, I would only be more worried myself. You have told me how much times are changing - and I know how often my behaviour, and Mark's, exposes our family to the culture of fear which will prevail." She shifted on the bed so that they could look each other in the face. "At least here, we would be safe from that sort of concern."

Spenser looked forlornly down at her. Unspoken sadness passed between them, a silent acknowledgement of their dilemma. Joshua sympathised, shifting his weight between his feet and trying with all he had not to think about his own separation. The parting between himself and Aioffe was, and would continue to be, gut-wrenching. He wasn't even close to accepting it yet; his devoted friends were at least attempting to separate by mutual consent. Fleetingly, he thought of rushing out to try and repair the damage with his wife, but shunted the idea out of his mind for now. There was too much pain there to consider it fully at this moment.

Spenser shook his head, saying, "There are no ideal options for us, my dear. Together or apart, here or on the continent, or even at home on Anglesey." He snorted. "I feel like I am standing on a stone finger with three mistresses atop the crumbling cliff edge shouting at me."

He glanced at Joshua, flaring his eyelids in horror. "Not that Aioffe would ever be my mistress, of course, but you understand my divided loyalties."

"A man of many loyalties you may be," Joshua said, the side of his mouth lifting to dimple his cheek. "But a truer, braver friend I shall never have. I trust you with my wife, as much as I hope you would trust me to protect and care for yours. As for the European mistress, I know her not. Yet, she barks at you by kestrel and has several times demanded your return. Your loyalty to her is bought by coin and vine-right, and delivered dutifully over centuries. I would hate to see those ties severed for want of worrying about your family, when I can provide for them until you return."

At this, both Spenser and Nemis nodded.

"We fly at first light then," Spenser said, looking deep into his wife's eyes. "Tell Aioffe to be ready."

"I will," Joshua said as his heart flopped over in his chest then sank, tightening his stomach with pain; Aioffe leaving him was becoming a reality. He hoped enabling her to go was the right choice. He prayed this action would allow her to return freely to him.

CHAPTER TWENTY-SEVEN

Spies

16th September 1553

"They are ready to fly out into the world," Fairfax insisted. "There's nothing more I can teach them." He watched, fatherlike, over the tired and dishevelled trainee spies, who after the long flight were now trudging up the sands before them.

The mission had been a success, Joshua supposed, since all were safely returned and had been able to survive for two nights off Naturae. Some looked hungrier than others, but all had apparently survived the trip undetected in their human garb. It remained to be seen how valuable their information was, specifically any evidence of the rising wave of Protestantism in Scotland which the spies had been tasked to gather, but anything was a start.

It was a subject which both Fairfax and Henry had suggested, but of lesser interest to Joshua. Longer periods of time embedding themselves within a community would hopefully yield more accurate assessments of potential threats to Naturae. From his own experience, Joshua knew that it took a certain skill to identify with whom it might be useful to ingratiate oneself with, so that an opportunity would not be missed. If nothing else, their first mission would have taught them lessons about blending in and returning on time, as they had all arrived from their designated areas at roughly the correct hour.

Joshua gazed out to the sea, the choppy waves in the distance a grey-green under the September skies. He sighed, knowing Fairfax was right in his assessment of their fledgling tribe, yet he worried still about letting go of his young protégés. Teaching them had provided a welcome distraction from the tense Council meetings of late, not to mention his heartache. Rather than follow the spies homeward, Joshua and Fairfax walked along the shoreline instead, but then his friend paused. Lost in his thoughts, and only realising after a few paces he was alone, Joshua swivelled his head back.

"I have to leave Naturae also," Fairfax said. For once, his eyes appeared cautious, hesitant to impart this news. "It's been a pleasant interlude, but Henry and I have business we must attend to. And, I've run out of jam."

Joshua snorted. "And Jeffries?"

Fairfax mumbled, "He's been wanting to go for a while, actually."

Why he should feel a sense of abandonment whacking him when the Maister had barely spoken to him lately was a mystery to Joshua, but it smacked him in the gut regardless.

Fairfax did an odd snort. "I'm not sure which is the worse idea - Jeffries on a boat with me and Henry, or him staying here moping about, when he clearly loathes that creature he's treating."

Joshua could well understand his hatred. The pain of resetting Lyrus's limbs, which had required several fae to hold him down whilst Jeffries re-broke them only to reset, had been minor recompense for torturing Joshua in the past. Unfortunately, his brother-in-law's temper had not healed as well as his reshaped physique. Neither had his voracious appetite abated. But, out of deference to Aioffe and the Captain, his increased mobility meant restrictions upon him were relaxed, enabling him to observe more of the rebuilding of Naturae. Joshua always knew when he was present, lurking in corners silently, as the workers close by would suddenly become more industrious. Whilst occasionally their respect for Lyrus irked Joshua, he much preferred a peaceful existence within the worker community. The very last thing he needed right now was any more battle lines being drawn; the continued disagreement amongst their representation in Council was wearing enough.

"You have done well to teach them as much as you have, my friend. I, and all of Naturae, thank you for all you have done." Joshua turned back and walked over to put his hand on Fairfax's shoulder. "I would value your, and Henry's, thoughts on where we should station them to best supply us with information, before you leave."

Fairfax's green eyes sparkled. Not just with the compliment, for these were rare in his line of work, but because he had, for once, planned for this request. "Henry thought you might ask for that," he grinned. "He's also desperate to get off the island." Fairfax's nose wrinkled. "The food supply weakens him, he says."

Joshua's eyes narrowed, and he couldn't help but grit his teeth at the ingratitude. The vampire had been well kept with fresh blood to hand, even if it was all animal in origin. Fae survived on far less, and Joshua wouldn't be sorry to have the drain on their resources leave. There was something about Henry which sat uncomfortably with him. A sense that he was being judged, and found wanting as a Prince.

"You will have to be more careful on the mainland with Henry around," Joshua warned. "Whatever is between you draws attention to you both, and that is dangerous for a man in your line of work."

Shrugging the caution off, Fairfax grinned. "Henry has ways of placating people. Besides," Fairfax winked, "He could be very good for my trade. Knows the right sort of person."

Joshua sniffed. He was forced to acknowledge that Henry's classes in etiquette, current church practises, and who was who in the English realm were an eye opener to him. As well as being delivered in a style which commanded respect, they were vital lessons, required by any fae to blend in. Even though he had been, as Henry put it, 'held captive by the Catholics', the vampire had lived within a large town and seen first hand the substantial changes which were imposed upon the English.

Joshua himself had, over the years, visited small coastal towns in Scotland for trading purposes, being not more than a day's flight there and back, for him. From these infrequent trips, Joshua had gleaned scant understanding of the dissolution of the monasteries. This process had barely started when Joshua and Aioffe last lived amongst humans, but he could not have foreseen the devastation of these great centres of learning, medicine and prayer that Henry VIII had authorised. When Joshua had asked Henry why the destruction had been necessary, Henry had explained that war against the French cost money, of which the monastic establishments held an impressive quantity.

England, under the reformer Edward VII, then completely altered the church service, destroying sacred images, forbidding the burning of candles, processions and many of the cherished holy days. Perhaps the most surprising aspect of the protestant obliteration of Joshua's cherished faith was the ability for clergy to take wives, or dissolve a marriage partnership. After this disclosure, Joshua felt the dual aspects of marriage no longer being a sacrament was possible cause for much relief for many people.

Naturae's closest country, Scotland, appeared less affected by the reforms sweeping the continent currently, even though it was 'ruled' by an absent Queen who apparently remained a Catholic. Joshua felt decidedly more comfortable at the thought of travelling in the Gaelic-speaking country, as the system of clans and the wildness of the terrain seemed more of an appropriate reflection of Naturae and its people.

As he walked slowly away, contemplating the implications and realising he needed to come up with a plan, Fairfax caught up with him. Keeping pace whilst Joshua mulled over the implications of Fairfax's announcement, the bounce to the daemon's step returned.

To release the spy fae into the realm was a step towards achieving his own goals, Joshua knew. His immediate concern revolved around the issue of blending in for a longer period of time. Talking now in their native Gaelic with Fairfax, Joshua was able to switch into English or Latin with ease. He worried the same could not be said of the spies, though, despite their inherent talent for concealment and language. Joshua remained disappointed by the conversational ability they displayed, but, he reassured himself, there was nothing like being in the midst of a human conversation for the nuances of tone and inflection, body language and situation to help with quickly grasping the finer detail of what was being said.

His silence and meandering pace must have suggested to Fairfax that Joshua still needed convincing, for he said confidently, "I think it's very much a time for them to sink or swim. Issam would probably say the same, if only he was able to observe them in action. No-one is ever perfect, and there will always be a danger of exposure, but… well, it's your decision." Fairfax glanced up at Joshua. "Unless you want to put it to the Council?"

Joshua grimaced. For once though, he felt as if it were his decision. No-one on the Council - no-one else entirely it seemed, aside from his non-winged friends - had shown much interest in what he thought they saw as a vanity project. Few could raise their heads above their own interests in Naturae to see the bigger impact a successful spy network could have on their overall security. And, Aioffe was not here to say either way. He drew in a deep breath to counter the sudden pain which appeared whenever he thought of her, then sighed.

There had been no kestrels. No word from her at all since she left with Spenser a full moon cycle ago. The fractured feeling within his marriage not even papered over as Aioffe hurriedly packed through the night, issuing vague suggestions to a succession of Council members who knocked on their door as they found out about her imminent departure. Joshua's silent frustration and hurt descended into a simmering anger with Aioffe as her failure to adequately plan for her absence became evermore apparent. With tempers barely restrained as they snapped at each other about inconsequential gripes, the dawn departure drew ever-closer; neither one had retreated from their stance by the time her bag was packed.

Even as the two families gathered on the sand for their separation in the hazy red morning light, he had felt them broken. He said nothing to her of the tiny silver arrowhead he had placed inside her pack, hoping that it would someday be discovered by her and she would know he always would protect her, no matter how awkward matters were between them at this moment. As the waves had lapped their feet, neither was able to say soothing or loving words of comfort and support to each other.

Mark, during the awkwardness and packing, had become nearly hysterical faced with the disappointment of his father leaving. The poor child had to be dragged from his father's arms. Joshua felt obliged to help restrain him - more to prevent him dashing into the sea in pursuit of the pair in flight than because he wanted to prise a child from its parent. This had created an awkwardness when Aioffe attempted to give him a parting kiss – which, to Joshua, felt forced upon them by the close embrace shared by Nemis and Spenser. When Mark then lashed out with his fists into Joshua's tender regions, the moment was lost.

Nemis, advancing in her pregnancy now yet still confined to the Ambassadorial Quarters, had done her best these last few days, reassuring him that her husband frequently did not keep her updated with his activities, and would just show up when they were completed and he was ready to be a husband and father again. But who knew when that would be?

There was just the slimmest of chances, Joshua realised, that a spy could learn if something untoward, something peculiar like a winged person, had been discovered, and such information then shared to the English. It was a chance he had to take, in the absence of any other intelligence on Aioffe's whereabouts.

"Let's go back and look at your plans." Joshua turned towards the top of the beach and began plodding through the shifting, drier sand. "I'll have to match the spies with the Nobles for those regions anyway, which means, I'll need Lyrus's help." He glowered down at the seaweed-crusted pebbles as they approached, his tension rising at the very prospect.

Little else made him feel as much of an oddity than his inability to understand faelore, their written word. Worker fae, such as Thane, Uffer, and the other worker representatives on the Council, couldn't read or write. Aioffe had mentioned when she showed him the library of Naturae called the Scriptaerie, only a royal or an ancient Noble had been taught it. However, the few Nobles there were in the realm had already departed back to their regions, fed up with the bickering. Plans for the realm had included a better education for the worker fae, in faelore and history, but there were always more pressing needs to attend to and the Council had failed to agree on how such a school might be run, or who would receive lessons first.

Joshua had taught the spy fae how to scrawl messages or copy letters using a basic cipher devised by Fairfax, to be translated into English, but he had not managed to learn faelore beyond a few symbols. There were only a few Nobles still alive and most did not live in Naturae full time, but hidden away in their lands. Annoyingly, only Lyrus was available and sufficiently educated to decipher the ancient texts that detailed which Noble oversaw which lands, and thus could be responsible for spy fae in that location.

Not for the first time, Joshua pushed down his frustration at just how much Aioffe had abandoned him, and Naturae.

CHAPTER TWENTY-EIGHT
Crunch time

Finding Lyrus proved easier than Joshua anticipated. As soon as Fairfax and he emerged into the clearing below the main palace, a cackle drifted over to them from beneath the landing platform. In the air, soldiers whirled in a mock fight, their faces tense with concentration. A duelling pair had become entangled and were wrestling as they fell to free their wings, clothes, and weapons. From a distance, they watched Lyrus's face contort briefly with frustration as his short bark of a laugh was replaced by "Useless" and a sneer.

Fairfax raised a querying eyebrow to Joshua, grinned briefly yet apologetically, and then scurried up the steps, leaving Joshua to approach his nemesis alone. The Captain, standing beside a seated Lyrus, glanced up as he approached. The old fae's expression barely masked the disappointment at his trainees' failure.

"It is fortunate you have no battles as yet, Captain," Lyrus said, still staring at the young fae disentangling themselves. "For these young fools would not last five minutes against a well-trained army." Lyrus's eyes slid towards Joshua and narrowed. "But then, the *Prince* here is determined to find ways to avoid confrontation, by the gathering of information, to avert it. Your fledgling army may still have time to prepare. A futile effort, but then," Lyrus failed to keep the contempt out of his voice as he said, "What can you expect from a half-breed but ill -conceived ideas."

Joshua's lips tightened before he could form a thin smile. "Precisely what I wanted to talk to you about, Lyrus. If the Captain can spare you, that is?"

Over Lyrus's head, the Captain shot Joshua a grateful look. "Whilst your input is always appreciated, Lord Lyrus, the trainees are shortly required for their rotation on the watch. Should I fetch some workers to assist you with relocating?"

"That will not be necessary - I am perfectly capable of walking and climbing. It will not be long before I am fully restored and can provide a practical demonstration to your soldiers of how training should be done." Although the words were polite, more polite than Joshua expected of Lyrus, their tone was chilling in superiority. Lyrus stood, straightened his back, and jutted his chin out as he looked up to meet Joshua's eyes.

Deciding the Captain was wise enough to pick his own fights, Joshua pressed on with his request. "I would like you to accompany me to the Scriptaerie."

Lyrus snorted. "Why? What use are papers to a half-breed like you?" A gloat appeared in his sneer as Joshua smarted from the insult. He tipped his head backward, understanding as his calculating mind ran through the differences between them. "Which is why you need me." He took a smug breath in then exhaled, looked down his nose before turning his back to Joshua and smoothly walked towards the stairs.

The Captain touched Joshua's arm briefly, as he strode past into the clearing, as if to apologise for the slight. After a tight smile, Joshua lifted his wings and flew straight up. As he waited for Lyrus at the top of the stairs, he tapped his fingers against his thighs.

By the time Lyrus reached the landing platform itself, he must have fully absorbed the power which his knowledge gave him over Joshua. "I do wonder that you have not needed my help before."

Joshua kept his gaze on the double doors; to show Lyrus his anger now would not help matters.

"After all," Lyrus continued conversationally, "with your wife absent, and the Council leaderless, your position here is tenuous."

Holding the door open for Lyrus, Joshua refused to grace him with any acknowledgement of the truth in what he said. His teeth began to ache from clenching them together so tightly though.

"And, it's not as if you have anything special to offer to Naturae now, is it? Tinkering with metal is hardly a unique skill, and you needed your *friends* to train the spies because you are too witless to know what is happening in the wider realm." Lyrus kept pace with Joshua, proving that he was well mended thanks to Jeffries' efforts.

"But of course," he continued as they walked past the trunk in the inner atrium, "you aren't really one of them any more either, are you?"

Joshua wrestled with why Lyrus was trying to goad him into a fight. He resolved to ignore it and focus on achieving his own aims. Except...

"I wonder if my dear sister will even return," Lyrus said slyly. "She always had a unique rapport with the Ambassador. Those European fae.... They are alluring, there is no doubt. Such an ancient history. It would be hard to see how our Queen could resist the temptation. Oh that's right. She didn't."

Trying to shut his nasal tone from his mind, Joshua stomped grimly on down the corridor. Just get what you need, he reminded himself, his gaze bouncing from side to side, looking for the correct door which would lead to the Scriptaerie. Ignore that his mind boiled, regretting that he had ever thought to ask for Lyrus's help.

"They say, that once you have lost the love of a fae Queen, you are doomed to live your eternal life in misery."

Joshua's arm shot out before his brain could temper the reflex. Grabbing Lyrus by the throat, he wheeled around and pushed the fae against the hallway wall. In a technique which Lyrus himself had used on him, Joshua took to the air to add the force of his large black wings to the pressure on his airway.

Lyrus's eyes bulged yet still the twist on his lips did not falter. Hissing out, "Did you ever think you could last an eternity with one such as she?"

Joshua blinked, his jaw aching from keeping it shut in the face of such offense. The urge to be rid of his tormentor almost overrode his sensibilities. Rare to rise to anger, a part of Joshua was surprised that the red mist of violence had washed over him so quickly. Yet he knew, in part, it was a vent for all the frustrations of late. His fingers tightened as the vision of Aioffe, laughing and full of light amongst faceless glittering fae, flashed into his mind.

"You know nothing," Joshua said, trying his best to keep his speech even.

"You will never be a royal, you know," Lyrus stuttered out as Joshua pushed deeper into his grip.

A hand rested firmly on Joshua's shoulder, then Henry's calm voice entered his gathering storm. "And yet he has married one, and behaves as a leader ought."

Joshua's head whipped around. Henry's grasp on him gentled as their gazes met. But then, before the full force of his suggestion could take effect in Joshua, Henry's attention turned to Lyrus. Dark eyes hardened on the smaller, weaker fae pinned against the wall.

"You could learn much from your Prince. He may not have been born to the role, but there is more to being a ruler than birthright."

Joshua's eyes flared. Of all people, he would have supposed Henry would side with Lyrus on the issue of birthright to rule, yet here he was, facing down Lyrus, born of the royal vine.

Lyrus hissed. "Vampire!" Pushing against Joshua's clamp, fury reddened his face; pointed teeth made to snap at Henry. A surge of energy seemed to fill the space between them. Joshua reacted swiftly by beating his wings to reapply the pressure holding Lyrus to the wall.

Henry stepped back, eyelids lowering over solemn eyes as he dropped his hand from Joshua's shoulder. "Do you wish me to leave, Joshua?"

"I think that might be wise," Joshua said after a heartbeat of thinking. As if to make the point that he was the dominant fae here, he pushed Lyrus higher up the wood, raising him off the floor. Too late, he realised the mistake in this as Lyrus pushed his feet against the panelling. The balance of weight shifted. Lyrus shoved against Joshua's arms with the full force of rejuvenated limbs. A leg snapped up. Lyrus twisted his torso into the wall and turned, shooting his foot back out again. It landed squarely to Joshua's stomach, punching him away.

Joshua, already airborne, flew backwards. Aware that his wings were too large to be of much use in the narrow corridor except for flying through it, he absorbed the punch, pivoted upside down and over mid air. Catching his foot against the opposite wall, he rebounded and rushed at Lyrus. But instead of reaching for Lyrus's upper body, Joshua dove down, aiming for ankles as Lyrus jumped back up.

The speedy tackle brought Lyrus crashing to the floor. As Lyrus tumbled over, onto him, Joshua felt skeletal fingers grabbing at the wing-joints on his shoulders. Joshua wrenched his shoulders backward, quickly pushed his arms up and grasped Lyrus's armpits. His fingers found the hollow hook just as his feet planted themselves ready. With a grunt, Joshua flung the slighter fae back over his head and to the ground once more.

Before he could reach Lyrus's feet, Henry had moved - crouching, holding Lyrus's shoulders to the floorboards. Joshua bent down and held Lyrus's legs before he snarled in his face. "I asked for your help, not your insults. Nor your insinuations that my wife would leave me. Now I see that it was pointless to even try to support your return to Naturae. You should leave, your assistance is no longer required."

"I will not leave my home," Lyrus spat back. "It is you, and your so-called friends, who are the intruders. Go back to wherever you came from. You seem blind to the fact that you are the unwelcome ones here."

Lyrus relaxed into the floor, implying that his statement was the final word. Joshua knew the fight had not left him, just been controlled for now. As Henry and Joshua's eyes met, "No-one needs you here," Lyrus interrupted, almost amiably. "Without *her*, you are simply a curiosity. An anomaly. A bastard."

The words cut into Joshua's mind, a piece to the puzzle he didn't know he had been trying to solve. Lyrus might, after all, be right. Before Henry could see the quandary which would undoubtedly spread over his expression, Joshua looked away. He was the oddity. He was not necessary to Naturae.

"Bastards have their place," Henry jumped in. "And if what I have heard is to be believed, as much royal blood runs through you, Joshua, as anyone. Do not listen to *him*."

Lyrus's face twisted into a smile. "Where you come from, vampire, no doubt that missing piece of paper is significant. To be a natural son is something to be ashamed of, perhaps, although very common. But here, this half-breed is a freak. All true fae are pupated from their defined vines; there can be no such thing as a bastard. I am pupaeted from the royal vine. There is no changing the purity of my bloodline."

Joshua kept silent - to reveal that Aioffe's plan was to make a hybrid version of the royal vine would no doubt provoke even more upset, if purity and lineage was such an issue for all faekind. The very last person who should find this out was Lyrus.

Leaning back, Joshua considered again what Lyrus said. Before he could stop it, a niggling question rose in his mind. Was he the reason Aioffe couldn't grow an heir? Was his peculiar make up, a mix of both human and fae, so impure that their love was not the right sort of love? Tainted?

He stood and gazed vacantly at the wooden panels stretching along the hallway. All the way into the distance, they ran in a true line. Regular and straight, without knots or blemish. Was she, in fact, better off without his kinks? Joshua's breath in was sharp, drawing Henry's attention away from Lyrus. Before he could exhale, Henry was in front of Joshua.

"Never think that you are less because you are half," he said quietly.

Joshua's blue eyes flicked to meet Henry's darkness, and for once, Joshua felt a kinship with him.

"Except you are," Lyrus snarled. With a scramble, Lyrus got up and Joshua caught a last glimpse of his sneer before he was gone, running down the hallway towards the High Hall.

Joshua finally exhaled, collapsing against the wall.

He had to go. Lyrus was right. There was no place for him here.

He was the one holding Naturae back now. He was the one who should leave.

CHAPTER TWENTY-NINE

River rescue

Bavaria, 23rd September 1553

Aioffe had a new-found appreciation for the Ambassador family line. Spensers' shorter dark brown wings, although longer than a worker's, were clearly built for endurance and distance. Huge and colourful by comparison, hers were easily capable of a day's flight even at speed, however the constant travel - pausing only to feed voraciously, then flying again all through the night- left her appendages aching as the miles increased. She had never needed much sleep; fae used their bed time as resting hours in a meditative state. Yet, more than anything now, she craved lying motionless for more than the hour or so Spencer permitted them each day. As the weeks progressed, it was her good humour, rather than his, which sank into anxious, silent and exhausted dread.

"Tonight, there should be another spectacle in the sky. The last of the summer storms approaches." Spenser called over to her, yet Aioffe could already taste the singe of electricity building in the atmosphere. It had been a humid season on the continent; more than once, their night flying had been above lowered grey clouds illuminated by streaks of lightning beneath. "Except we will be up here, I suppose," she replied. "Panting through it as usual."

"Better to avoid the gale. The air would still feel thin, were you on the ground," Spenser advised companionably. They rose once again, above yet another range of mountains. Aioffe had been quite intrigued by the first ones, asking to stop so that she could experience the forests atop the snow capped Alps of France. By this stage in the day though, when the sun was in descent, she was more interested in the tiny villages, clinging to the sides of foothills which held the promise of her next meal. "You will find the humans less satisfying," Spenser warned. "I have always believed the two factors are related."

"Are we close to the court yet?" Aioffe asked, hoping the answer would be 'not far now'. Niggling concerns about finding his nomadic people had been plaguing her the entire journey.

Spenser shot her a toothy smile and raised his eyebrow. "That rather depends." He pointed to a mountain in the distance. "That is the Tyrol border where I last left them. It is possible they are still there." A mid-air nonchalant shrug followed. "But they could equally have moved to fresh grounds."

Aioffe frowned. "Then how would you know where to find them?"

"They leave a message for those seeking them, if you know how to look."

The prospect of playing hide and seek did not cheer Aioffe up and she rolled her eyes at his enigmatic answer. But today, he noticed the exhaustion on her face and reached into his deep pocket. He pulled out a tiny globe with what looked like a thick bronze stick poking straight up behind it. They hovered, catching their breath for a minute whilst he fanned out the sticks into struts, until it formed a semi circle with the engraved map hinged in the centre. Miniature moveable rings with notches for measuring could slide around the globe. Along each of the sticks, Aioffe noticed minute indentations - faelore on some, others with sporadic dots along them. Upon closer examination, each dot was in fact a star shape.

"My personal astrolabe," he said. "If they have disappeared from where they were based, somewhere close by someone will have marked their intended latitude and the day on which they fled, so I can calculate where they have gone. The position of the stars and the date today is therefore all I need to keep a track of, in order to know in which direction they can be found." He fiddled with the gadget, applying its setting before passing it over. "Don't touch the rings now, that's where we are."

Aioffe cradled it in her hands, caressing the warm, slightly worn metal. What a work of engineering this instrument was. How Joshua would have loved it, she thought, recalling with a smile his fascination with the nautical instruments which Fairfax used to navigate. This object though, was a completely new level of miniature complexity, which she doubted many could operate without years of learning and instruction. A beautiful and unique piece of artistry with a clear purpose. Just the maps alone were far beyond anything humans had created; the advantage an aerial view and keen eyesight afforded. "Can you teach me how to use it?"

Spenser winced. "It is for the more mathematically minded," he said carefully. "I could try. Your skills, my Queen, lie more to the artistic and the intuitive. I thought that you might appreciate the beauty of it though."

"It is more for Joshua than myself," Aioffe said. "I find I have little need to navigate with an instrument such as this. He would understand the workmanship in it, as well as find use for such an item for travel. His internal compass is not as reliable as, well, mine."

Spenser nodded. "Your capacity to stay a course in a specific direction is remarkable. It is a rare ability to hold a line intuitively. Even your father, whom I believe you said was a human from the North, would have used a special 'sunstone' to navigate their ships with. This treasure, devised by those of the east not the west, is how we far- travelling fae know which course to take when all options are open. In the air, anywhere is possible."

"Thank you for showing me." She smiled and handed it back to him. Tilting her body back to horizontal, she flew ahead, blinking her eyes against the ache appearing in her chest at the reminder of her left behind lover. Without realising, Aioffe slowed.

Spenser caught her up, then as he touched her arm lightly, his tone was serious. "What did the Ambassador say when a horse walked into Court?" She frowned in his direction, unsure whether this was some peculiar custom of these fae which she ought to know about.

"Why the long face?" Spenser tumbled over mid air, laughing at his own joke. Aioffe grimaced and rolled her eyes. How had she never noticed how poor his humour was before? On a daily basis, he poked fun - making jokes about anything and everything in an attempt to entertain her through the long hours of flying. She wondered whether his more relaxed demeanour, displayed the closer he drew to his home people, proved that Spenser was an entirely different person the further away he got from his responsibilities to herself, and his wife and child. But she could not have been more incorrect, as he grabbed her hand with new focus, diving down suddenly.

Aioffe's eyes widened, scanning the landscape below as they dropped like birds of prey honing in on a mouse, but could see nothing in particular to alarm. Her long blonde plait pulled loose from its pins, streaking behind as her vision narrowed in on a gap in the dense forest covering the side of the mountain. Slicing through at the base of the peak, she saw glimpses of a wide gorge, white with rapids. Spenser turned his head back and shouted through the wind, "The Royal barge! Below us!"

Looking harder, ahead to where the river entered a valley, Aioffe could not see anything out of the ordinary. Many times they had followed the course of a tributary, snaking between mountains, with occasional boats meandering along, but here, she saw nothing which suggested the pomp and pageantry which she associated with a flotilla. She pulled against his hand to slow him. "Whatever you've seen, better we present in a less bedraggled and frantic state, surely?"

His mouth tugged up at the corner and they swooped up again. When he flapped more sedately next to her and averted his eyes, Aioffe adjusted her gown to its proper position on her slim frame beneath her front-strapped bag and smoothed her plait over her cape. In a nod to her preparations, drifting down but upright, Spenser smartened his jacket. After a look of gratitude from Aioffe, Spenser then held his bent arm out, awaiting her slim hand. Horror swept across her face, then her heart quickened - not just from the impending introductions, but the sudden realisation that she was unadorned as well as unannounced. She freed the straps at the top of the leather sack and rummaged inside. Locating her silver crown, as soon as she placed it on her head, her nerves dissipated. Drawing in a deep breath as they gracefully descended, Aioffe finally dropped her eyes to see what spectacle lay below.

"I think she's grounded!" Spenser pointed, his voice serious. Finally, Aioffe saw what he had spotted from such a great distance. Further up river, ropes of varying lengths linked a flotilla of small rafts, camouflaged by leaves and greenery so that they would appear from the water to be floating bushes. What could only have been noticed from above were flashes of silver structures within the bushy cladding, glinting as they caught the sunlight whilst they bobbed along. A linking chain had become entangled in the jutting stones where rapids narrowed and frothed. The rafts at the back clumped together, jostling for access between two wide, flat rocks where presumably a bridge had once stood, now collapsed.

Worker fae, with mottled grey and brown wings, fluttered across the water like enormous dragonflies, attempting to free the trapped rafts from each other and their unfortunate anchors. The river, at this point, flowed fast and noisy. As they approached, Aioffe picked out their panicked voices, whispering muddled commands in Latin.

Her eyes widened as she examined the convoy. Bushy exteriors with inner fortifications were further hiding within them large wooden barrels. Inside each, a familiar fae pupaetion vine twisted around the tall silver cage, their distinctive leaves obscuring brown, fluffy cocoons. As the vessels lurched, banging against the rocks, Aioffe's heart sank as she watched them precariously dangle, almost bashing the solid metal hoops. It was only a matter of time before one connected and a life would be lost before it was even begun.

One of the rafts in the middle, which had been cut free entirely to allow it through the bridge stones, was now crashing along a swiftly flowing section of water. Aioffe drew in her breath sharply, realising that carnage was about to occur to this floating Vine Room. Ahead, and oblivious, two red faced worker fae battled to hold on to short ropes, which slowed the separated chain of bobbing bushes at the head of the procession. As the current pushed the flotilla onwards, these front four rafts were in danger of running aground where the river widened into a rippling bed of pebbles.

"Oh! Stop that one!" She shouted, pointing at a solo raft, picking up pace as it headed straight for the trapped barges. Without thinking, she spoke her native English. Spenser understood however, and they dashed across to the lone bush. His arms disappeared as he shoved them through the camouflaging branches, flapping hard as the river propelled the heavy craft onwards. Aioffe, realising that his efforts were merely a temporary stay, darted to the riverside. She landed, running as soon as her feet touched ground, over to a nearby pine tree.

Its trunk was covered in wide-leafed ivy. Placing her hands on the creepers, Aioffe closed her eyes, pushing her will into the stems.

The vines began to grow at an extraordinary pace, reaching, weaving in the air across the eddying current. Aioffe opened her eyes, guiding them into twirling together as they stretched out, still growing, to form a thicker rope which drifted towards Spenser. As they reached his reddened face, he released one of his arms and grabbed it, twisting the still expanding, entwined ivy onto the interior metal structure. Once satisfied the raft was anchored so it would drift no further, Aioffe turned and dashed back to the water's side.

"Fools! There is water coming in!" A nasally voice shouted. Aioffe looked down-river, her eyes flaring. The airborne worker fae stopped as one and turned in the direction of the raft at the front. It was the largest craft, lurching from side to side in the current, grounded at the front in the shallower waters where the river widened. The two fae guiding the convoy had been unsuccessful with steering as it caught in the smaller, pointed rocks to the riverside. The base structure was breaking apart, leaving splinters bobbing around the hull. Perhaps there was already a hole? At the screech, these two workers dropped their cables and darted away, leaving the vessel to lurch from side to stoney side unguided, continually battered by the rafts behind caught up in the eddy.

Aioffe chewed on her lip as she thought. Although a creeper rope could steady the craft temporarily, the rate at which the wood was disintegrating suggested an onward journey was unlikely. The more she considered its unusual structure, the more she realised that this was more boat-shaped than the flatter, square rafts upon which the bushes sat. There was distantly a curvature to the low sides, narrowing to a point at both ends. This also meant it wobbled quite a bit more between the rocks, lifting as it smashed its pathway down-river.

A loud crack prompted a frustrated screech which echoed around the steep-sided gorge.

There was no alternative, Aioffe realised. The only way to salvage the lead craft from which the voice had emanated was to lift it clear of the torrid shallows, and over to greater depths, or better yet, land, so repairs could be made. She turned back to the ivy and started to grow even more creepers. "Spenser," she shouted, "I need a knife!"

Cape flowing around him, he appeared by her shoulder and

immediately grasped the purpose of the web of woven ivy she was laying out on the ground. Aioffe was creating two large creeper hoops, sufficient to catch a stern or prow in, from which each had two longer vines twirling away. They'd both seen lifeboats secured in a similar fashion to the side of a galleon when they left the shores of England, which could then be raised or lowered over the ship's side, as required. A central pair of vines linked the two circles to provide additional support underneath the vessel. "Twist some extra in," he said, "for they will need to be thicker for our cargo." Flashing his friend an appreciative smile as he handed her his knife, Spenser flew back out, over the river.

"Over here!" His authoritative command brought six of the workers flying down stream to their aid.

"You would leave me to die, you ungrateful low-downs! Disgraceful!" The shrill voice demanded attention, but Aioffe ignored it and focussed on cutting and checking her knots on the sling design.

"Two to each rope," Aioffe said, switching herself to Latin so she would be understood when the fae approached. "These loop over the front half of the barge, and these," she gestured to the far pair of ropes, "secure the rear. We fly over the prow first, then draw them underneath to hook the other circle over the back. Spenser and I will lash the two lines together above the boat with this." She held up a shorter piece as long as both her arms. "Like wrapping a parcel." The fae glanced at each other, but before they had time to object, Spenser flew down and grasped the front creeper-twists and shoved them at the closest workers.

"Work together," he suggested, returning to retrieve the back fastenings. The fae hovered at first, tentative about the arrangement, so Aioffe grabbed the trailing middle creepers and they followed her lead across the ripples beneath.

"Imbeciles! What *are* you doing out there?" The bellow from below them caused an instinctive jerk away from the angry bush. Aioffe persisted, yanking on the rope-vines so the rescuers had little choice but to return to their formation. Drawing closer, she narrowed her eyes, peeking through the leaves of the camouflage bushes. Movement inside outlined a bulging, golden-clad woman, sat cross-legged in the middle of the boat. Pudgy hands glittering with jewellery waved manically up and down as if they would balance her mass whilst the craft was buffeted by the current, tipping one way, then the other as it rebounded from stones with no control at all. Long, thin green wings, reminiscent of Aioffe's mother's, stuck straight out in the centre of her back - surely more ornamental than practical, Aioffe thought, with a fleeting sense of superiority.

"Why am I surrounded by such incompetent workers? I will have names and you shall be docked!"

Aioffe's jaw jutted out, realising this was most likely Queen Illania. It could have been either of her daughters, neither of whom Spenser had many kind words to say about, but he had once joked about the vast quantities of cloth required to dress his Queen. She peeked sideways at him, seeking confirmation, but he was busy glaring at the worker fae and gesticulating where to fly. Guessing now was probably not the best time for an introduction anyway, Aioffe instead flew closer to the water and hoped not to be seen. Looking backwards to assess the placement of the vines, she dipped so low that her gown dragged into the river, unknowingly soaking the front of the skirt entirely before jerking up anew. The weight of the wet wool dragged, and Aioffe cursed under her breath.

"Where are you? I can hear your stunted wings, you pointless wasp-loving runts! You will rue the day you were ever pupated!"

The thought crossed Aioffe's mind that if she were a worker being thus abused, she'd be tempted to let the guide-vines slip and tip the Queen into the water. She had to restrain the giggle which threatened to burst out at the mental image of the golden blob flailing around in the shallows. That wouldn't do at all, she reprimanded herself. The threat to dock wings was a truly serious matter. No wonder the fae looked terrified as they carried out this unusual plan! That the helpers were complying with a complete stranger's orders at all was therefore a surprise; she could only assume it was because Spenser was there as well.

As she helped to guide the hoop at the back onto its target, Aioffe thought also that she could understand the Queen's thinly disguised terror. Concealed by greenery on all sides, Illania probably did not realise that the water beneath her, although churning and causing damage, was not actually very deep in this part of the river. One could probably quite easily stand up in it, assuming you could stand. The size and method of carriage for the Queen made Aioffe wonder whether walking, or wading, was an issue for the woman. Clearly, she was simply too large to fly with her own wings. As rotund as she appeared, there was always the option of rolling her out of the water, Aioffe supposed.

She clapped her hand over her mouth, horrified at her own childish thought process. Spenser's earlier silliness was definitely rubbing off on her. Or perhaps it was the liberation from her queenly responsibilities allowing her youthful sentiments to emerge. Either way, this was not the way a Queen ought to behave! But then, she reasoned after chiding herself, neither should a Queen threaten her own children.

By the time Aioffe regained control of herself, the workers had progressed to the second stage of her plan. The royal craft slowed in the water, and the team pulled in synchronisation to hold it steady. Spenser swooped down to cut the ties to the rafts behind it, enabling them to push past the lead boat and drift smoothly downriver.

Aioffe threw one end of the rope over her shoulder towards Spenser, and around the four guide ropes they flew. The creepers drew together mid air. Spenser and Aioffe crossed and passed each other, then tied the lash firmly. They parted slightly, Spenser to the front pair of ropes and Aioffe holding the rear pair an arm's length up from their binding. The weight was now balanced. "Up! Up!" Aioffe cried, rising so the vines tightened.

"What are you doing?"

Aioffe looked down to see a round, red face with a tiny rosebud mouth almost the same colour as her cheeks gawping up at her. Dark hair coiled from her crown to pool in the wet bottom of the boat all around her. The Queen was gross to the point of immobility. She shook a clenched fist up at the intrusion, "Get away, whomever you are!"

Aioffe's eyebrows raised and her mouth fell open; the venom in her voice shocking, and, as the workers had done before, she recoiled from sight. But the fae assumed that was their cue and the boat rose with her, majestically lifting free of the water. Aioffe's head snapped over to the riverbank, suddenly worried that Illania's weight could put additional strain on the hull. Her earlier silliness about dunking the Queen might become a reality if they didn't set her down soon. She pointed, "Over there!"

The Queen fell silent as her vessel swayed. Realising what was happening, her mouth set into an embarrassed pout. The airlift sedately traversed the river beneath, although keeping only a foot or so above the water. Spenser caught Aioffe's eye when the wood began to groan, then crack, and both their lips tightened. Without saying anything, the workers flapped quicker. Their reddened faces belied the effort and weight they bore as they advanced toward the river's edge. Aioffe didn't dare look down, her focus absolute on saving the Queen from further woe. When the entirety of the craft was suspended over a wide, pebbled shoreline, Aioffe gestured for the fae to lower it.

Once steady on the ground, Illania's cackle of laughter echoed around the valley, her tiny fat hands clapping together with delight. "Ambassador Spenser! My gallant saviour," she cried, then holding her chubby arms up as if to embrace him.

Spenser flushed as he hovered. "My most wondrous Queen," he said, holding his hand out to draw Aioffe closer. "I most graciously beg your forgiveness for my tardiness in returning to you, and confess, you are mistaken in your assumption that I had any part in your rescue. May I present, Queen Aioffe of Naturae."

Aioffe was close enough to see Illania's mouth drop open momentarily before she let out a short bark of laughter. Aioffe curtsied mid air, grateful that she was appropriately crowned but suddenly conscious that the front of her dress dripped onto the Queen. Worse, her hair floated wildly and she knew her face would be flushed by the exertion. She didn't trust herself to say anything at that moment.

"It was Queen Aioffe's talents which enabled your return to land, my Queen." Landing by Illania's shoulder, Spenser winked at Aioffe. But the Queen's shrewd eyes had already narrowed as they roamed over her dishevelled appearance.

"And yet," Queen Illania's lips pursed before she said slyly, "She is not talented enough to overcome the problems of her own realm. Or, she would not be here in the first place."

CHAPTER THIRTY

Acceptance

Naturae

When Joshua quietly conveyed his intention to leave Naturae to Thane before the Council meeting the next day, he looked bleak for a moment, then said, "Perhaps this is for the best." Thane's jaw jutted out as he turned away, doing little to change Joshua's mind.

Half-expecting at least an attempt to sway, or even delay, his plans, and more than a little hurt by the rejection, Joshua followed Thane into the High Hall without further comment. Perhaps this reaction was confirmation that Lyrus was correct after all. He was not needed here. Thane stalked in front of him, nodding to himself, mounting the steps to the dais with renewed vigour. Other Council members glanced past him to Joshua, their expressions seemed surprised. Joshua became aware that he was frowning. He ducked his head, forcing his forehead to relax as he sought to quash his own bemusement before taking his seat around the oval table.

Strangely few observers were present, only a few worker fae cleaning and keeping an ear out, and a solitary guard on the doors. In the relative quietness of the chamber, Joshua hardly had to raise his voice as he called the session to order, although most of the Elders watched him with tight blank faces rather than their usual side conversations. He opened by briefly and dispassionately presenting his plan for the spies to disperse into England. Thane politely supported the arrangements, acknowledging on behalf of the Council, their mutual hope that information would soon be forthcoming. Thane then steered the conversation to his proposals for the next phase of rebuilding instead.

The Captain seemed to give up his fight for the prioritisation of training grounds and Uffer was curiously silent throughout. The Elder responsible for the livestock complained about rapidly diminishing stock of the larger forest animals, deer, hogs and the like, but his diatribe was soon cut off by glares from the Captain and Thane. Another Elder, then alluded to the shortage being a short-term issue which would soon be resolved. Joshua wondered how, when the mating season of most of these creatures was past.

Rather than publicly declare his forthcoming departure from Naturae, Joshua's resolve wavered as an unusually civil discussion proceeded. Shifting his gaze around the table as people put forth their opinions, yet without the heated passion of earlier meetings, Joshua's disquiet grew. Ought he to go, he considered, as he sensed an undercurrent.

A knot began to grow in his stomach the more he contemplated the subdued nature of meeting. Perhaps it was the absence of Lyrus glowering from the sidelines, but today was by far the calmest Council session which had occurred in recent months. To Joshua, it certainly felt the least pressured, which was peculiar in itself given how conflicted he felt about leaving. Rather, Joshua sensed something unspoken distracted the strong characters - resulting in a hesitancy, rather than the previous urgency of defending their positions. Although nobody specifically referred to an event which was to occur, the speed at which Thane moved the discussion along, quashing any rambling or objections, left Joshua with the impression that something outside of the meeting was afoot.

Before Joshua could ask, Thane abruptly closed the meeting. No mention was made of Joshua's imminent departure. Council members rushed away as if they had better places to be, and the High Hall emptied with a flurry of feet and no lingering chit-chat. Frowning to himself, Joshua took his time rolling up his notes. The superfluous details of which spies were to be sent to which part of the country which he had laboured all night upon, no-one had cared to enquire about. As the Council had also ignored his (not confessed) oversight in assigning the individuals to a Noble, Joshua pushed aside the doubts in his mind and stood.

Perhaps, he reasoned to himself, it was merely that the Council had settled down to the business of running Naturae after Aioffe's abrupt and unannounced trip to Europe? Cooperative working was always the vision for how these meetings should run; Aioffe would no doubt be pleased that it was finally happening, albeit in her absence. In which case, he thought, his departure should cause even less ripples as the pond seemed to be smoothing out.

As Joshua walked away, still wondering what had changed since yesterday, he nearly collided with Uffer. "You are leaving," the elder fae stated, his expression neutral as if this were already a known fact.

"How did you know?"

Uffer shrugged. "The household staff saw your bags brought out, and packing begun."

Joshua studied Uffer's face, hoping to identify a reason to stay in his usually friendly expression. But it was carefully blank, as Thane's had been.

"I am, yes. The spies have been instructed this morning and they will leave shortly." He gazed over at the table, now emptied. "There seems little to keep me here."

"But this is your home. You are," he faltered, "our Prince. Your place is here."

Whilst the words should have comforted Joshua, the edge to Uffer's voice gave Joshua pause to wonder if he meant them, cared enough to ask him to stay, or was it just a polite placation?

Joshua's mouth turned down as he replied, "I am superfluous."

Uffer touched his arm, ostensibly reassuring, but his eyes darted over the empty chamber. "Queen Aioffe will come back soon, I am certain of it. Maybe then, all can return to how it once was." There was a wistful, worried tone to his voice.

"I don't see how you can be sure," Joshua said hollowly. "She may be gone all winter for all we know." He glanced around the High Hall, then lowered his voice. "I sense there is something different today. What has happened?"

Uffer's eyes shifted past Joshua's shoulder to the double doors behind them. Then, his chin set, he checked his own back before saying, "There have been gatherings occurring. Outside of the Council sessions."

Joshua raised his eyebrows. Uffer tightened his lips and stared directly at Joshua as if to impart significance to this statement. "Meetings with whom?" Joshua asked, slowly, although he suspected he knew the answer already.

"Lyrus."

"About what?" Joshua gritted his teeth in readiness.

"How things should be."

"And how is that?"

Uffer shuffled his feet. "He has said that only true-born fae should be able to make decisions on the Queen's behalf. As it was in the old days."

Joshua swallowed, then took a deep, slow breath in as Uffer whispered on.

"He puts forward the case that the discord between us is happening because there are those present here who are not fae."

Exhaling slowly, Joshua's mind resolved. The Elders around the table had avoided him; he realised it now. Initially, he wondered if it was because he had been less involved, contributed less because he had been focused on training the spies and missing Aioffe, but, as he reflected on Uffer's whispered confession, he now understood the majority of them had been deliberately ignoring him.

"And I suppose he includes me in this group?"

Uffer nodded apologetically.

Joshua thought back; the avoidance had been occurring for some weeks. Whilst his daily intention had been to keep his distance so as not to reveal his feelings about Aioffe leaving, it had been easier than he had supposed it would have been. During the usual course of a day, if he passed a worker or Elder, there had been nods of greeting, but no pausing to chat about matters, or cheerily biding him a good day, as there had been for many years previous. He could not remember the last time he had enjoyed a casual talk with Thane, certainly not since Aioffe left, now he thought about it.

"And what do you think?" Joshua asked.

Uffer appeared to find the floor compelling. Joshua noted that the hair on his head had thinned to the point of baldness, and the Elder was reed-thin. How had he not noticed how much Uffer had aged lately? He laid his hand on Uffer's shoulder, yet his heart sank. Naturae's most trusted advisor was reaching the end of his days.

"Please, I need to understand who I can trust. Who will look after my interests if I cannot?"

"My loyalty is, and always will be, to the Queen." Uffer mumbled. "But, I alone cannot protect who she loves in her absence." He looked at Joshua, who saw the sadness in his eyes. "Nor those she cares for who provoke such a sentiment."

Drawing a deep breath in, Joshua could not lay any blame on Uffer. The stalwart had always been uncomfortable with non-fae, yet he had loyally carried out his duties regardless. And now, he was the only one to tell him what else was occurring in Naturae, although Joshua realised he should have seen it earlier himself.

He also couldn't deny the hot tempers within the Council meetings had begun rising at roughly the same time as Fairfax had arrived as well. Both he and Aioffe had known the risk of chaos which the daemon implicitly brought with him, but it had gone too far now. Despite his own friendship with Fairfax, it had been challenging logistically to keep him separate from the fae who were, for some reason, drawn to him. And having two witches on the island, and indeed, a vampire, there was naturally more of a heightened awareness of their otherness. It was a sensation he knew intimately from a century of living amongst humans, and yet he had just ignored it because of his unique position among fae. Even if people couldn't identify why someone was different, their behaviour altered and the blame game started when a discrepancy arose.

He had made the mistake of assuming his friends would remain safe because of who he was. For the safety and smooth running of Naturae, it was right that he, and the oddities who he had invited into this sacred space, leave. Joshua squeezed Uffer's shoulder, resigned fully to what he must do.

*****

By the next morn, Nemis had gathered up her and Mark's belongings and Joshua stowed them away in their small, fae-powered boat. It hadn't taken much to convince her or time to decide that they all should leave together. The relief upon her face, as if it was a secret she already knew, when he had told of his concerns was palpable; she was as ready to flee their former sanctuary as he now was.

Joshua had only managed to form a vague plan, he warned - to seek the assistance of the only other fae he knew outside of Naturae. He hoped Lady Hanley in Beesworth would provide them with shelter. Joshua also envisaged she would also be familiar with the problems of living with a daemon, her late husband having been one he knew. Whether or not she would accept Mark into her accommodation was a chance they had little other choice but to take. The advantages of Hanley House outweighed the risk – Mary Hanley knew who and what he was, and lived in a large house which was familiar to Aioffe, and to which kestrels were known to visit.

He had dispatched a message via kestrel last night, quietly pleading with the biggest bird in the coop to find Aioffe and tell her that was where he was going, although he had been vague about quite why he was leaving their home. When writing the note, Joshua wasn't sure this was a permanent move, but his urge to leave had grown with every passing hour since the council meeting. Only her return could resolve the matter, he thought, and until then, neither he nor his friends were safe on the island. His run in with Lyrus had demonstrated his weakness; Joshua could no longer protect Nemis and Mark here. He no longer had the support of other fae he had once relied upon, like Thane. Now that he understood the impending danger of mutiny, which he was the cause of, the ache of Aioffe's absence grew. He had no heart for a fight without her by his side.

Everywhere he looked as he packed his bags, he felt her touch - the detail of her designs, the evidence of her abilities. Their chamber smelled so strongly of her unique scent, the want of her pained him all the more, until it became claustrophobic. As he fitfully attempted sleep, he began to yearn for the change in surroundings, to be away from these ever-present reminders of what they had accomplished together. For the opportunity to regather himself. Perhaps, recharged, he would find a way to bring them back together as a couple. That hope alone compelled him into full certainty - departing Naturae's shores was the right course of action to take.

By the time he strapped himself into the reins to pull the ship, Joshua had numbed himself to the sad prospect of leaving. Looking back served no purpose. At least this time it somehow did not feel as final as when he and Aioffe had so often fled for their lives in England. Although not quite at the stage of looking forward to the journey ahead, he checked his passengers once more before lifting up from the jetty.

Mark was still teary and had been since Nemis had told him of their plan. His reluctance to depart stemmed from friendship as well as fear of change. The boy had grown close to Fairfax, sensing a kindred soul perhaps, and loved his walks on the beach and through the forests of Naturae. When his behaviour last night had declined into heartbreaking sobs at the very mention of leaving, no matter how much they had tried to enthuse the child about an adventure ahead, Nemis had resorted to packing their belongings furtively overnight when the Mark finally collapsed into an exhausted rest. Only the prospect of more seal spotting as they skirted the islands had enticed the boy aboard this morning.

Jeffries stood on the beach, waving them off into the dawn light. Then, to Joshua's surprise, Fairfax and Henry emerged sleepy-headed and dressed only in nightshirts to cheer from the deck of their larger ship. They had both been keen to stay on the boat last night, after Joshua had suggested they also ought to leave sooner rather than later. He had not detailed his suspicions as to why. All hope of everyone sailing away overnight though was reluctantly delayed, to allow Jeffries to finish steeping a supply of tinctures for Nemis. Until the tide rose higher, the Wander was beached, but then Fairfax planned to drop off what remained of his cargo, and Jeffries, in the south. Their plans for afterwards had not been made known to Joshua, and frankly, he didn't like to ask.

"Still sails as well as she ever did then?" Fairfax shouted over the forecastle sides.

Joshua smiled, straining against the reins to bring the boat away from the pull of the waves against the shore. "A design like no other," he hollered back. In truth, the harness was already cutting into his shoulders and he experienced a moment of doubt that he could undertake the voyage across the channel without the wind picking up. He glanced back and down, expecting to see Nemis looking relieved at the growing distance from Naturae. Instead, her pale face was contorted with horror.

Joshua dipped, the reins slacking, and he realised that she was gazing, glassy-eyed, straight at Henry and Fairfax. Mark, who had been brought out of his funk by their shouts, was madly waving at the pair. The boat lagged as Joshua approached. Only then did Mark seem to notice something amiss with his mother. Shaking her arm with one hand and gesticulating furiously with the other, he said, "Look, Mama! That's Thomas's friend, he's come to say goodbye also!"

Joshua fluttered closer, shocked to see Nemis's eyes had turned a milky white, her mouth agape. She swayed into Mark, who was too little to hold her up. Joshua swooped down just in time to catch her arm before she tumbled overboard. Her body crumpled instead against the inside of the boat, cushioned only by their baggage. As he alighted onto the small vessel, Joshua lowered her, trembling from head to foot, between the benches. Mark screamed, "Mama!"

"What ails her?" Henry cried over the water.

"I know not," Joshua called back. "Jeffries?"

His shout went unheeded; Jeffries, not blessed with extraordinary hearing, plodded his way towards Fairfax's boat unaware. Joshua looked down at Nemis, pale and now shaking on the wood. Her lips trembled, and a hiss escaped. He bent over her, trying to catch whether she was saying anything.

"Leave. Now…"

There was no doubting the urgency in her voice, yet Joshua dithered. Her visions rarely made sense to him, and he was loath to travel whilst she was in the midst of one of her fits. Mark was of little help.

He heard splashing sounds approaching, and his vision narrowed on Fairfax and Henry. Both swimming, arms slicing through the water towards them. Momentarily, he was grateful for their kind intentions, if for no other reason than to quieten Mark's distressed wails. But, as they drew closer, Nemis's fit intensified.

Joshua crouched, holding her head so that she wouldn't bang it against the wood, yet she hissed again. "Go! Darkness c-c-c-comes! Leave!"

His head snapped out to sea. Henry had pulled in front of Fairfax. A shiver ran through him. 'A dark heir' Nemis had said in a previous episode. Could she possibly mean one of them? She knew Fairfax well and had previously no ill effects from being in his presence. Which meant… Henry.

He grabbed her shawl, wedging it as best he could between the deck and her head, then jumped back into the air.

"She'll be fine, but thank you!"

His shout caused Fairfax to stop swimming, but as he rose up, a grey shadow cast over Henry's face. Relentlessly he continued crawling towards their boat. Joshua beat his wings faster, hauling the reins until his shoulders burned in an effort to get the craft moving against the waves, relentlessly pushing them back to the shore. He didn't care which direction he was going, just that it was putting distance between his terrified cargo and Henry.

Every time the tiny boat hit a rising wave, the reins yanked on him, but Joshua ploughed on. He dared not risk Henry using vampire speed to swim, and thus giving away the only advantage a fae had. Joshua ignored the sinking feeling in the pit of his stomach, and ignored the pain in his shoulders, but his mind whirred. Dark heir. Dark heir.

Heir to what? And where?

CHAPTER THIRTY-ONE

Diplomacy be damned

Bavaria

As darkness fell, and the surrounding woodlands grew alive with rustles of night-time hunters creeping out into the twilight, a small group of fae patiently hid in silence. Aioffe sat on a branch overhanging the shoreline, awaiting she knew not what next, but enjoying for that moment the soothing babble of water over the pebbles. The solitude of her perch she found equally comforting, having turned away the two workers who, during the dying stretches of sunlight, offered her freshly caught trout. The plump fish were still wriggling in their nets, but she found she was not hungry, only anxious to find out where the vines had gone. Only the Queen, languishing in her broken boat, partook of the meal as the majority of workers continued down river with the bush rafts.

Spenser had disappeared with them, to prepare the encampment for the imminent arrival of two Queens, he had said, with a firm look which implied there should be no argument about his logic. Although this meant she was left stranded without his support with the now silent matriarch, Aioffe had been relieved when Illania dismissed her with a wave of her hand after Spenser departed, muttering that they would talk further when she had rested after her ordeal. The implicit blame was not lost on Aioffe, but she welcomed the release from her presence in favour of the opportunity to gather herself away from the Queen's piercing eyes. Having also sat still for some hours, the two worker fae lost interest in the new arrival and curled up to rest themselves.

A throbbing hum of wings brought Aioffe out of her meditative state; she leaned forward and peered downriver. Clustered together, a group dressed in mottled green tunics flew in tight octagonal formation towards their base. Each held a pole attached to a central golden tub. This tub sported a pair of large wooden wheels, resembling a chariot which could be pulled in any direction. Inside, plush purple cushions ensured its occupants' comfort. They flew straight past Aioffe's perch, and she noticed their distinctly swarthy appearance, with thickset, muscular limbs which would no doubt be necessary to convey the heavy-looking vehicle over land. Their dark blond, wavy hair bounced as they landed upon the riverbank, marching over in perfect synchrony to their Queen's stranded vessel. Without any verbal command that she could hear, the unit halted and laid the tub on the ground. They twisted the poles, then extracted them in a smooth pull to reveal spearheads, before marching themselves into two lines between the boat and their craft, facing outwards. With a thump of feet, the soldier-bearers stepped forwards on one leg, spears pointing out.

Only then did Aioffe see the bushy leaves twitch. The two worker fae who had remained behind to attend the Queen dashed up and over the line of soldiers, landing neatly in the centre of their row. They pulled the camouflage aside, tossing some of the branches clear over their heads to make an opening wide enough for Illania to step free of her cage. Aioffe held her breath and leaned forward, the curiosity too strong to refrain from what struck her afterwards as a moment in which the Queen might have preferred some privacy.

Illania's face peeked out from the barge, and immediately latched onto Aioffe's gaze. Her lips pursed together, then turned her head to stare stonily at the golden chariot. It was clearly going to require great effort to relocate her bulk from one place to another, so Aioffe decided instead to wait for her over the river. As she unfurled her own huge, luminescent wings, and took off from the branch, she heard Illania's sharp intake of breath. Aioffe averted her gaze, hoping that the Queen would not view her actions as rude, or deliberately flaunting her own fluidity of movement, but as the respectful granting of privacy which she intended.

Spenser's promised storm must have passed over them, Aioffe realised, as she waited alone over the river. Transfixed by the difference in the constellations, she suddenly felt very far from home. As she stared up at the carpet of stars glittering above, edged by the jagged outline of the steep mountains, the sight of them made her heart yearn to know if Joshua was studying the skies also, as they so often had done when lying in their bed. With her finger, she reached up and traced the patterns between the white dots. A faraway smile played on her face as she imagined Joshua's hand over hers, guiding her. Loving her.

"My Julius used to do that with me," Illania's voice drifted over, slightly breathy from her exertion. Aioffe looked across to see the eight bearer fae now airborne and approaching. Resplendent lying cocooned in her golden carriage, the Queen waved her hand at the twinkling lights above. "A bit before your time, I suppose, but the Romans did have a degree of accuracy with their charts back then. He was quite foolishly romantic about them - would only attack when the alignment was just so, or, worse, use them as a guide before becoming intimate with me. That was before he met that 'other queen', of course. The Egyptian one. The witch. She had a completely different set of guidelines for using the stars. Rarely did their portents concur." She sniffed, her mouth pouting again.

Aioffe flew to catch her up and for a while they coasted downriver in an awkward silence. It seemed rude to pry into what was clearly such personal history, and yet, Aioffe was not sure if the Queen was inviting her to ask further questions. Spenser had not coached her on this situation; the unexpected revealing of an emotional connection threw the usually very private Aioffe, and she knew nothing of the protocol which was expected of her.

"One should pay attention to differences, you know," Illania said. "I, myself, have never found *lasting* happiness with a mortal. Daemon or witch, their lives are so... short. They simply wouldn't be around to see the consequences of their actions." She sighed, then turned with narrowed eyes to look at Aioffe. "Does your Prince age, as mortals do or worker fae?"

"He does not," Aioffe replied. "He is as much a royal fae as you or

I."

The Queen snorted. "I cannot believe you would be so foolish as to think that he is fae, or royal. If you made him, as Spenser tells me you did, then he is your offspring, more than he is Fae. A mixture at best. Therefore, it is not unreasonable to expect that he would have only as limited a lifespan as any pupae you have created, or perhaps only as long as a mortal does." A chuckle followed. "You would be wise to assume the latter to be the case and enjoy what time you have together. He will not last. One day they are here, the next - poof - gone."

Watching the river below, Aioffe felt her ribs tighten, and she swallowed. There was an honesty in the venerable Queen's words which she would rather not have given consideration to at that moment. Not for the first time, she regretted leaving Joshua behind instead of asking him to journey here with her. In that instant, she hated herself for not defending him more. Yet the truth was, he had no precedent, so no-one knew how long he would live. Already, he was over a century old and had barely aged physically beyond his late teenage years. All signs suggested he would survive for eternity like her, but there were no guarantees of anything in this life.

"I would have liked to have met him. A fae-human." Illania nodded sagely to herself, as if Joshua were dead already. "You indeed possess some strange powers."

"Am I to understand that my ability to create is not... usual in royals?"

The Queen drew in a tight breath and looked out over the water. Quietly she said, "No. It is not usual. Yet each royal has their own unique abilities. It comes from the circumstances of their pupaetion. The influences. I have heard that your powers came into being before you ascended even." She peered at Aioffe through lowered eyelashes. "Perhaps you have peaked too early and have come for guidance on... something." Illania batted her eyes, and Aioffe imagined the calculations taking place behind them. "Now, what could a young Queen need, I wonder. Why would one so early in her reign, travel so far... What is it that you want from me?"

Aioffe baulked. She hadn't expected to be asked, in so direct a manner, the reason for her visit. From Spenser's diplomacy coaching, she had been led to expect lengthy tip-toeing around the subject, tentative questions to show interest, perhaps even negotiation. The

Queen's direct approach sent a shiver of fear through her.

"I… I wished to further my understanding of your glorious realm," she dithered, stumbling a little over the rehearsed phrase which Spenser had assured her would serve as a good opening gambit. "That I might learn from your ancient and prolific ways, for the benefit of my people."

Even as she said it, Queen Illania tipped her head back and laughed heartily. "I fear my dear friend Ambassador Spenser has filled your skull with wise words to placate me. There is no need for restraint between Queens. I guessed long ago that you would want to approach me about my daughters." A smug smile stretched through her cheeks. "They are much in demand - you would not be the first to seek to line them up for your realm."

Aioffe swallowed. Would it be rude to contradict her straight away, she wondered? The very last thing she wanted was to bring an older Princess into Naturae. She knew her mother had lived in fear of such an intervention. These were the same princesses born long before she, Aioffe, had even been pupaeted. By now, she guessed they would be fairly desperate for a Queendom of their own. Illania looked to be in the prime of her life, in full health if not as mobile. The prospect of bringing a foreign princess into Naturae in readiness was simply an invitation to be murdered, as Aioffe saw it.

"I have been waiting for your arrival to bargain for them for quite some time, my dear." The Queen tilted over the lip of her carriage and beckoned her to approach. Flying closer, Aioffe met Illania's eyes warily. "The question is," Illania smirked, "What do you offer me in return?" She winked at Aioffe. "A fae-human toy like yours would be amusing."

Aioffe's heart sank.

CHAPTER THIRTY-TWO

Back to Beesworth

Northumbria, 28th September 1553

The small vessel slipped up-river, silent bar the seagulls who wheeled around with curiosity about their guest in the dawn skies. High above the water and hidden by low cloud, Joshua had pulled them up the Tyne until the starry night gave way to an orange sunrise. Deep inland by the time the sun was about to crest, without waking the sleeping passengers, he landed lightly on the dewy deck. As quietly as he could, he stashed the reins and slid the patchwork sail up the mast. Ignoring curious looks from fishermen as they passed, he sent up a prayer of thanks that the wind had been in their favour for this last leg of the journey.

But the breeze did not hold far beyond Newcastle; by then Joshua was in too much pain from the overnight rubbing against the sores on his shoulders to row. When Nemis awoke, as was their habit now, she applied some pain relieving salve, which enabled him to rest easier as the low autumn sunlight beat down on the uncovered deck. After discussing their progress, she offered to try to paddle against the flow of the river with Mark, but all Joshua could think of by then was to sleep. Instead, mother and son dropped crab lines over the side and filled a bucket from the shallows while the boat languished.

When he next awoke, Joshua stared up at the clouds drifting

overhead for a moment. The blueness of the sky was the same shade as his wife's eyes. He ached to see them again. Even though Nemis and Mark murmured to each other near the rudder, he felt desperately on his own. The last time he had been in this part of the country, he had also felt adrift, albeit with Jeffries for company. That had been the start of his quest to find his kidnapped love, when his confidence in the status quo had been shaken and everything he thought he knew upended. Now, having found her, his faith in his place by Aioffe's side was uncertain. Once again, here he was, floating lonely on a boat, nauseous from hunger and heartache, and wavering in his decision-making ability. No wonder Aioffe had been so keen to leave him behind. He was weak... She didn't need to be dragged down by him...

"We need to land, and you need to feed. It has been nearly a week now since you have eaten, and you are no good to any of us if you are not strong."

Nemis interrupted his internal castigation. He knew she was right, sustenance would help his mood. They hadn't been able to land for a few days - since the winds had been favourable, Joshua had flown through the nights and Nemis supervised sailing through the day. The further they had travelled from Naturae, and Henry, the more at ease Nemis had become. Her anxiety about returning to human land was evident nevertheless in the way she fussed over both Mark and himself.

Rubbing his hand over his face and hair, he then stood, wobbling momentarily before finding his balance, and stripped his top off. After splashing some water over his chest, he grinned at Mark, who was staring at the raw wounds on Joshua's shoulders. "They will heal, do not fret," he said, then dropped his shirt back over himself, covering his wings. He picked up an oar and offered it to the boy.

"Let's go and make a fire and cook those crabs, before they climb back into the river."

Mark nodded, scrambling over the baggage to join Joshua on the middle bench. Nemis's lips lifted, and she tipped her head to feel the wind on her face as she took the steering pole. The river had narrowed, now too deep for non-swimmers to reach the riverside, edged by tall reeds. They rowed upriver until they found a shallow bulge in the waterway, where the grasses grew long. Their boat would be obscured enough from passing observers here and it was close enough to wade out. After dropping the stone anchor line, Joshua and Nemis loaded themselves with cooking utensils and splashed ashore. Time was wasted by an argument with Mark about leaving his collection of pebbles in the boat, resolved only by him filling his pockets with some of his favourites; the remaining treasures were safely bundled up in a cubbyhole in the prow to await his attentions later before he would he jump into the shallows and follow.

Stretching across the countryside, large fields enclosed by deep hedgerows lay empty. In the distance, Joshua could see yellowed spikes remaining after the harvest. Piles of straw and hay steamed, evidence of protracted days toiling against the weather for the local community. His sharp eyes caught a pair of hares streaking across the fields, long ears and light brown fur camouflaged but for their movement. Where there was industry, there would also be roads, such as they were in rural areas, which meant land travel would be slightly easier than rowing against the current.

Joshua's mouth watered - not from the crabs, boiling over the small camp fire Nemis had built, but from the scent of nearby deer. He caught Nemis's eyes sparkling as she smiled gently at him; his nose already raised high in the air, sniffing to determine the direction of the bouquet like a dog. "Go," she said. "We will be fine here for a while." Joshua set off towards a nearby copse at a jog and without a backward look.

*****

After two days of trudging in front of a rented mule carrying their belongings, Joshua began to recognise the landscape. He knew they were close to Beesworth, but, as he was likely still a wanted man and having not physically aged since he was last here, he chose to avoid the town. Instead, he led Nemis and Mark across the empty pastures below the mound atop which sat their destination.

Even though it was late afternoon, no lights were yet visible through the windows of the imposing three-storey Hanley Hall. Long shadows cast by the disappearing sun chilled the travellers as they plodded up a winding, overgrown pathway circling the steep hillock. As they reached the summit, rounding the thin, elongated building which rose from the ground like the swollen head of a pimple, Joshua peeked in through the dusty glass panes. He saw nothing but darkness inside. Passing the front door, the roses which clambered around the porch grew with wild abandon, obscuring the aperture with a sweet-smelling yet thorny tangle. Steeply below, where the stables were, he couldn't hear the rustling of horses, or the chatter of the succession of young boys which Lady Hanley took under her wing as messengers.

At the far end of the house, where the library overlooked the pastures below, he hoped to discover some signs of life, as this was Lady Hanley's most favoured room. But no smoke came from the chimney, nor could he pick out the rustling noise of movement inside. Joshua recalled sitting by the fireside, recuperating from injuries inflicted by Lyrus, being fed rabbits by Lady Hanley whilst Jeffries supped on warmed wine, and her one servant glowered over them. He also remembered his bewilderment as she told him about who Aioffe really was, of her abandoned heritage as the Princess of Naturae. Of how she, Lady Hanley, outcast and in a poorly thought-through plan to return to her homeland, had betrayed his wife by informing on her presence in Beesworth. No, Joshua was under no illusion that this visit would be a joyful reunion of friends.

Reaching the back kitchen door, he held out a hand to Nemis and Mark, sullen faced behind her. "Let me go first. Catch your breath and rest here. It looks empty inside, but there's no telling until we try."

He knocked and waited. After a minute or so, he tried the cobwebbed latch. The metal clicked, but the door stayed firmly closed. He remembered the large bolts from his brief first visit where he had waited for Aioffe in the kitchen, so he walked further down the building, checking windows for any loose or left on a latch. Finding nothing on the ground floor, he stripped off his shirt, tied it around his waist, and freed his wings.

Joshua circled over the roof to the front of the house, searching for the outside-locking window to the chamber he had slept in. The peculiar alteration was designed to imprison Lady Hanley's late husband in his madness - an unfortunate complication of elderly daemons - later re-purposed to keep Joshua from escaping. Finally, above and to the right of the front door, he found it.

He pushed his face against the dirty glass, peering inside, but the curtains were drawn. Nimble fingers shuttled the miniature iron bolts back before he dug his fingernails into the edges of the metal frame and pulled. With a scraping sound, the rusty hinges released a wrist-width opening and he poked his hand through, yanking again with more force. There was a certain bizarre satisfaction in breaking into a place which he had so desperately been trying to escape from, Joshua realised, all those years ago.

When the window was open wide enough for the breeze from his wings to waft the curtains, he swivelled and stuck his head through the curtains. As the sunlight was on the other side of the house and the shade of the roof allowed little of the natural light to enter by this time of day, the room lay in almost complete darkness. He immediately smelled decay. But not death? Inhaling so that he could identify what might be close to dying in such close proximity, his heart beat faster. Joshua dropped a leg through the window and levered himself inside.

The thick tester bed curtains were drawn all around, but the stench definitely arose from within. Joshua gritted his teeth and pulled back the red sash.

"Aaaaahh!"

Joshua jumped at the scream from the pitch black interior, dropping the curtain. Almost before he could draw breath, a skeletal hand reached out and clutched the edge of the drape.

"You!"

Joshua breathed out with relief. "Yes, your Ladyship. It is I, Joshua."

"What are you doing in my death chamber?"

He raised his eyebrows but said politely, "I apologise for the intrusion, your Ladyship, but I have need of your assistance." He pulled the other curtain back so he could see her. "But no-one answered the door."

The pale, thin face scowled back at him. "Why would they? There is only myself here. And I am trying to die."

"Why?"

"Well, why not? It's not as if anyone will miss me." Like a child, she swung her head away from him and he could have sworn he saw a pout.

Joshua's smirk got the better of him and a warmth of forgiveness spread through him. and he touched her Ladyship's hand. "I would." Then he lied for the sake of her feelings, "I did." He glanced down so that she would not see his nose wrinkling. Just how long she had been lying here?

Dark, deeply lined eyes turned towards him; the chink of light from the window allowing her to focus on his tall, shirtless frame.

"I would have thought you might dress appropriately for a visit," she snapped. "What happened to the fine breeches belonging to my husband which I lent you? I'll have those back if you've now got your own."

He laughed. "I am sorry, they are in my bags outside."

Grey eyebrows shot into her forehead, then she sniffed and turned aside. "Well, I have no rabbits for you any more, if that's what you came for. A quick bite and to run away again." She sniffed haughtily, and Joshua dropped the curtain.

Then he went to the windows and tied back the drapes; clouds of dust arose and caught in his throat. "It is still light enough outside, your Ladyship. If you were so inclined, we could find some together?"

A humph noise broke from the bed. He carried on, "Or, I could bring you back one or two, maybe?"

Leaving her to contemplate his offer, Joshua dragged the rich red surroundings of the bed to the posts and fastened them. From the corners of his eyes and being careful not to meet hers, he took in her slight frame, papery sunken skin and now completely grey hair. Having seen the last of her generation of spy fae age, he judged her to be approximately the same age, perhaps slightly older than Uffer but far younger than Issam, the last remaining older spy in Naturae. Compared to Issam, Lady Hanley had aged well, considering she had been able to partake of a better quality diet in her later years. The hollows in her skin would soon enough plump back out when she fed, and he did not buy the weak and feeble act she was feigning in the slightest. His suspicion was that she was deliberately starving herself in order to bring an unnaturally early end to the centuries of her life.

He sat on the corner of the bed and reached over to take her hand in both of his. "Your Ladyship, it pains me to see you thus. I am not alone in my return. My friends are outside, and I would dearly love to introduce you."

"Friends? You bring strangers to my house? Uninvited?"

Joshua nodded. "Once more, I have need of your sanctuary. Your Christian kindness. And they, well, they have even greater need of it than I."

"What on this earth makes you think that I would be inclined to help?"

Her haughty tone did not dissuade Joshua - rather, he guessed that above all else, especially now, the Lady Hanley was and always had been lonely since the death of her husband. There was no sign of her trusted manservant, Bray, who Joshua could usually identify by soured smell alone. No activity in the house at all. It looked as if she had simply boarded up the Hall and shut out the world. "What does Beesworth think about your disappearance?"

She sniffed. "As far as the town is concerned, this Hall stands empty. I travelled for a time then returned here, without being observed, to finish my days. But," she sighed. "That was many years ago." Her eyes flickered to his, and he saw a hint of the feisty old woman he knew before. "I am quite bored now."

Joshua beamed. "There is plenty left for you to experience; not least, you could return to Naturae now. Lana is dead, Aioffe has ascended. All past indiscretions are forgotten."

"You found your princess then?"

Joshua nodded. "She has built a wonderful Queendom now."

"Then she is still there? Why have you left, if life is so wondrous?"

He turned to gaze out of the window. "She is travelling herself, at the moment. In Europe." Then he squeezed her hand. "Which is why we have come to you for help. My companions are not fae, but witch and daemon." Might as well get the warning over with, he thought; Lady Hanley would sniff them out as different as soon as she saw them.

The old woman sank back into the pillows as if she had not heard, yet her lips tightened. Shaking her head as if to clear it of unpleasant thoughts, she said, "And what of *my* family? Do they remain in Naturae also?"

Shaking his head, Joshua said, "I fear not, I'm sorry. But, there are records there which might offer some clues? Elders who might know?"

She sighed, then contemplated this knowledge with a mournful expression. After a moment, Joshua stood. "Would it be acceptable for me to let my friends in? It turns cold and they will be wondering where I am."

"Keep them to the kitchen," she murmured. "Until you have brought me sustenance and I am presentable." Her eyes snapped to his. "I will require more than rabbits."

He squeezed her knobbly, cold fingers gently in parting and stood. "Thank you, I will bring you something large as soon as I can. And... fresh water and soap?"

As he strode to the door, hanging slightly open, she snapped, "No fire-lighting, mind. I do not want the town to know there is anyone here."

"A daemon child? Joshua, you did not say it was a child!" Lady Hanley stood in the kitchen doorway, resplendent in a green dress and an only slightly out of fashion French hood.

"This is Mark, your Ladyship." Joshua prodded the boy into standing, which he did, but kept his eyes on the large oak table when he had made himself comfortable tracing the lines in the wood. Lady Hanley sailed into the room, eyes fixed and gleaming on him. Too late, Joshua remembered her addiction to daemon Lifeforce. His jaw tensed, and just as he was about to warn her from getting too close to the boy, she was by Mark's side, inhaling.

At the sight of her ecstasy, Nemis's face fell and she rushed towards her son. Joshua grabbed Lady Hanley's upper arm and dragged her away from Mark's proximity. The child looked at his mother and let out a thin wail, his eyes wide open. Despite her dreamy expression, when Lady Hanley saw Nemis fold Mark into her protective embrace, she said, "I meant no harm. It's just been so long..."

"Will the boy be safe in your care, though?" Joshua asked.

She looked up at him with surprise. "Of course! Why, he is just enchanting! He will be perfectly safe around me. Do not fear." Her clear eyes caught Nemis's. "I would never harm a child. My family line has never been susceptible to their allure, but I myself am drawn to his kind as perhaps... a grandmother would be. Come now," she approached Mark cautiously. "Let us choose you a bedroom to sleep in. Does he bite?"

Nemis flinched at the question, but nodded once. "Only if frightened though."

Lady Hanley's pale face brightened. "Then we shall do our very best to ensure he is most comfortable and secure. I have just the room!"

"Not the bolted one," Joshua said. "He is not feral."

Her scornful expression reassured him. "Any fool can see that. What a special child such as this requires is a sanctuary. A space which will be his safe place. Tell me, does he like to collect things? Animals or books, or trinkets?"

Nemis nodded in amazement. "Stones."

"We have a great many here!" Lady Hanley exclaimed, clapping her hands together. "My late husband also collected pretty pebbles, some even have ancient animals inside." She bent down so she was Mark's height. "Would you like to see them?"

Mark's eyes widened. Taking his small hand in her own, Nemis said, "That would be very kind. I too would love to see these special stones."

Smiling tightly, Lady Hanley said, "Of course." She began to lead them out of the room, then turned to Joshua. "I think perhaps, a fire might be appropriate. Our guests would, I am sure, appreciate some warmth as the night draws in."

CHAPTER THIRTY-THREE
Kenninghall

Norfolk, 28th September 1553

"So this is where I, Duke of Richmond and Somerset, as was, ended up," Henry said conversationally to Fairfax. He squeezed palms, sweaty in the late summer heat. Henry had paused their travel to survey the flat, empty landscape. For miles around, it seemed they two were the only people occupying it and they felt secure enough to show their affection for each other. After a sip of bought blood from Fairfax's flask, Henry felt buoyed enough to confess, "This estate is where the Prioress told me my mortal body was supposedly delivered after my death. I was told my tomb in Framlingham Church is quite spectacular. Quite. Not very."

Fairfax looked ahead to the red-bricked manor house in the distance. Kenninghall, the imposing three-storey home belonging to the Duke of Norfolk, sprawled over the countryside like an angry pock on a quilt of brown and green. He squeezed Henry's hand again. "You don't have to go there if you don't want to?"

Henry's jaw set. "I must." He turned to Fairfax. "I cannot know where to start with my new life without finishing the old one properly, and that begins here. I thank you for accompanying me. I know it was out of your way."

Fairfax shrugged. "It wasn't that much of a diversion, and Norwich was where I planned to go anyway." His ship was moored at Kings Lynn; the barrels were on carts already under the care of his crew. Jeffries had left their company, to everyone's great relief, during a shore-break before they left the waters of Scotland. As Henry and Fairfax hadn't much time before Fairfax's business meeting to indulge Henry's request to visit one of his old homes, they had rented horses. After riding hard over the last day and a half to reach Kenninghall, Fairfax planned to return before joining the buyer in Norwich, hopefully just as the delivery of barrels would be made. Henry was conscious that Fairfax needed the income to pay his long-suffering crew after their lengthy distraction in Naturae. There was now scant time for dalliance.

They dropped hands and separated to trot down the track which led from the village towards the manor. Henry felt himself taller in the saddle as they approached the familiar walls running along the roadside which marked the inner gardens of the huge estate. He had visited the Duke's residence a few times in the past, with his son, Henry's best friend and first love, Henry Howard. With his new lover by his side, Henry felt at ease once more. As if he were completing a circle.

His mission had been prompted by a pamphlet left in an alehouse in Kings Lynn; Mary was to be crowned in a few day's time, and it was to be officiated by the recently released Duke himself. Thus, disguised in appropriate clothing provided by Fairfax Henry hoped to pass for a merchant, and leave a note at the gatehouse in the hope that it would end up in the hands of his godfather and benefactor, the Duke of Norfolk. Smoothing the pocket containing his hastily penned letter, politely enquiring after the Duke's health and requesting a visit, Henry's mind quietened with resolve. If his half sister Mary took the crown and the Duke was freed, then Henry knew he could achieve his aim. Given enough time and opportunity.

A clattering of hooves disturbed the silence of the afternoon. Henry and Fairfax pulled their horses into line, so there would be space for the approaching team to pass. A cart, pulled by a team of four, thundered towards them. Behind, a pair of men on smart bay's slumping in their saddles quick-trotted without rising in the stirrups. As they passed, Henry drew in his breath. He recognised the dark-grey woollen cape, bearing on the corners the three golden lions passant and blue and yellow chequery of the Norfolk heraldry, spread over the hindquarters of one of the horses. He dropped his head, but mumbled, "Good Afternoon, your Grace." As soon as he said it, Fairfax turned in his saddle, staring at Henry with raised eyebrows. "Careful," he mouthed, nudging his horse on.

Only twenty paces beyond, the Duke of Norfolk yanked on his reins and wheeled his mare around. Fairfax jogged on, but Henry couldn't help but glance back over his shoulder. Realising his godfather must have looked straight through his disguise, Henry pulled to a stop.

The two men stared at each other for a long moment.

"Fitz?"

Although the Duke had only muttered his name, to Henry's ears it was a shout. He nodded. The Duke, haggard and white haired, kicked his horse so hard he then almost fell backwards in the saddle with the lurch. Henry jumped down and waited for his godfather to reach him before he knelt.

"Can it be you, my boy?" Even though it had been but a few cantered steps, Thomas Howard's long, red drooping nose dripped from the chill. His austere, oval face beamed down at Henry. As he looked up to meet kindly eyes, Henry felt tears threaten to invade. As he stood up, they clasped each other's hands. Bathed in fatherly love once more, Henry was momentarily speechless.

All the recriminations he had imagined, the anger and the pain of deception and abandonment, fell away under the spell of the Duke's gaze. A man who knew very well what he was, and had been the instigator of his turning, then abandoned him. A man who could be the key to his ruling prospects. The other father-figure who had found a way to keep him on this earth so that he might one day fulfil his destiny.

Henry simply said, "Your Grace, I was trying to reach you," because the lump in his throat prevented him from more eloquence at that moment.

The Duke glanced up the road ahead, "Travel with me. I must know what... what brings you here." His eyebrows crossed. "Did you not know, I lost these lands to Mary when I was... detained. She lived here for a while after Edward passed. I am.... was... here only with her permission, collecting some memories, trinkets and the like. There are no guarantees she will return the house to my ownership." Seeing

Henry looking bewildered, he added in his gravelly voice, "But do not make my mistake. Do not look to the past, for it serves no purpose. Ride with me now, that we may discuss your future."

Henry glanced back at Fairfax, who had stopped in the middle of the track to watch on with an unreadable expression upon his face. "I will," he said to the Duke, and nodded just the once. "I will catch you up."

"I ride for London. Our Mary," the Duke said. "She has proclaimed herself Queen, and I am... officiating. But, it is not the result we intended." His lip wobbled as emotion threatened to overwhelm him. "Do you still hold the faith, my son?" The pressure of years of captivity applied themselves to Henry's fingers and he saw plainly how painfully the time had passed, how natural aging had been hastened. And, how strong his faith had kept him.

Henry's clear mind returned and he felt no deceit as he crossed himself. "I know. And I do, your Grace. A Catholic will sit on the throne again, and, with your help, this Catholic would, by God's grace and yours, support her as well."

The old man blinked his wet eyes then half retracted his hand, shaking Henry's fingers in unity. His lips pressed together as he swallowed, saying, "Find me then. I do not travel as fast as I ought to, or used to." He mounted, turned his horse's head towards the road, then peered down. A hint of the old Thomas Howard glinted in his eyes. "The disguise will work with some adjustment. No-one would question me arriving with a new servant." He laughed softly. "After all, I've only just been reappointed with an allowance for some."

Henry smiled without revealing his teeth. "I will catch up with you and we shall enter London together."

As the Duke trotted off, Henry led his horse towards Fairfax. His lover scanned his face and Henry's heart grew tight in his chest as they regarded each other.

"I must go with him," Henry said. "To London." The tingle which always ran through him when they were connected thus suddenly dulled as Fairfax's face fell.

"I cannot join you," Fairfax replied. Shaking his head, Fairfax's hair began to poke out from his cap. "I am needed in Norwich."

Henry's hand reached up to him. "And after?"

Fairfax looked away in the silence that followed. Then, his head tilted to one side. "You know," he said, "that I am usually to be discovered in the centre of any particular upset. Are you sure you want me to be in the same place as you, when the future you desire is so tenuously within your grasp?"

"Yes," breathed Henry. "My future must include you. Surely you know this by now?"

Fairfax grinned, then waggled his eyebrows. "Just checking."

Henry looked down at the ground. "I know it won't be easy though. Court life is… very public. We would need to be discreet."

"Or, very, very obvious," Fairfax argued; if it was possible, his beam grew wider and whiter. "What better disguise than to be flamboyant, extravagant even?"

"You have not met my half sister," Henry snorted. "She is not that sort of person, and wouldn't entertain those kind of characters in her court. She was always most properly behaved, with little laughter and joy about her. Flamboyance is not her style." He studied the verge, where Fairfax's horse nibbled on the daisies and dandelions littering the grass. The sense of excitement and opportunity which had carried him through the last few weeks travelling with Fairfax dulled as the prospect of entering the confinement of Mary's court loomed.

"Then, Tommy Fairfax will find you in due course." Fairfax slapped his shoulder in a half hearted boisterous manner. "And we shall make our own mischief behind the closed doors of the more dubious alehouses."

Henry grimaced. "I will try, but, my every movement will be watched as a newcomer. Even posing as a Howard servant, any improper behaviour would be noted."

"As a servant, you will run errands, messages, make deliveries. There is opportunity if you look for it. And, don't forget, we have winged friends who need our ongoing support and help, in exchange for their assistance of course."

Henry thought, tapping his lips. The small network of spy fae which he had helped to teach knew him, and he supposed there was no reason to assume that they would not help out carrying messages between himself and Fairfax. Opportunity indeed.

Fairfax glanced around then leant down to pull Henry's head towards him. His lips, warm and gentle, brought Henry a measure of reassurance before they parted. Together they cantered side by side to the village. At the crossroads, Henry's hands shook as they exchanged a last lingering glance before separating, he for the road to London, and Fairfax in the direction of Norwich. Then, Henry focused ahead and urged his horse on towards his future.

CHAPTER THIRTY-FOUR

Dilemma in Europe

Bavaria, October 1553

For her own protection, Aioffe had been told, a guard was posted, day and night, outside her quarters. Ever since her arrival at Illania's court just a few days earlier, when Spenser whisked her away into the isolation of her freshly constructed tent, Aioffe had heard nothing further from the Queen. His daily promises of an audience failed to materialise. And ever since her arrival, she felt like a caged bird - trapped under a cover and blind to what was occurring around her. On the first day, she had attempted to leave. Despite only wanting to explore, the armed and armoured soldier prevented her from taking flight by a firm shaking of his head and a piercing whistle, which drew further guards close. When they began pointing spears at her, Aioffe understood that roaming about was not an option. Before long, Aioffe grew frustrated by her captivity, and boredom set in.

Spenser was the only visitor thus far to her designated quarters - a simple treetop tent perched on a branch, barely roomy enough for her to lie down in. Erected far away from all other fae on the outskirts, where no-one would hear her scream. Perhaps that was why she was guarded, she justified. To protect the outsider from interference. During the shortening daylight hours she waited, listening through the rain for him, or for notification of an official audience with the Queen.

226

Every evening, he appeared to escort her away so that she could hunt and feed. He grew tight-lipped when she asked him why she was given so little freedom here, merely saying it was 'the way' his people got used to strangers in their midst. There was nothing he could do about it, he assured her. She believed him because she had no other court experience to compare her treatment with, except her own.

"Simply 'rude', is what I call it," Aioffe huffed. Hunger and entrapment did not make for good humour.

But, during these few hours of liberation as they flew away from the area where the fae were living and working, Aioffe scanned the woodland beneath her as surreptitiously as she could, searching for answers. More importantly, she searched for the distinctive vine leaves, but, thus far, had been unable to see where the barrels they had been planted in were relocated after their river trip. Spenser pleaded ignorance, of course; such matters were entirely out of his remit. As the days and nights passed, she grew ever-anxious as time ticked by with no progress on her mission.

"I feel quite sorry for them," she said to him, on their latest, and thankfully dry, excursion into the Tyrolean forest. Hanging on his arm as they returned to her dwelling, she considered whether it was the lack of permanent structures affecting how the community treated strangers. "To be constantly on the move is not an existence which I would choose. Even I like to have a home to return to now. Are they ashamed perhaps, to have nowhere to greet guests?"

"Their family is their home," Spenser solemnly replied. "They - we - have learned to take what we need only. Travel lightly and fast."

Aioffe looked over at him, dressed in one of apparently only two colourful jackets she had seen him wear of late. "Your usual wardrobe would suggest what is important to you is your attire. Is that all you packed?"

Her dry remark caused him to laugh. "I would agree with you there. My clothing is a part of who and what I am - it might even appear that is all that I am. My trade is information. How better to announce that I am informed than by flaunting the latest trends?" She frowned, then he shot her a wry glance. "Everything else which I do is held in here." Spenser tapped his head, then his chest. "And what is important is here. Nothing else really matters if it is not carried in one's heart in perpetuity. Besides, you were so desperate to get here I didn't like to stop off for a change of clothing."

Aioffe thought hard about carrying family in her heart. A yearning for Joshua's strength and courage to support her, which had abated during the distraction of their daily flight, sat heavy upon her. Much as though the distance between them was great, her need to find a solution to the problems of the future remained greater. She could not return to him, and Naturae, empty handed.

They flew slowly back as the sun set behind the mountain. In the dwindling light, Aioffe marvelled at the progress the fae had made in creating a new, temporary citadel for themselves. A variety of conical structures had appeared in the treetops, their mottled green fabric blending into the tall evergreens so well that, were a human to walk underneath and glance up, the tents would be concealed. Even from above, the teepees blended into the trees, making the forest appear denser than it really was.

In order to further reduce the chances of being seen, the workers, of which Aioffe guessed there were hundreds, possibly thousands, spaced out. The encampment stretched over a large area of the forest, some miles inland from the river. Housekeeping staff, crafts-folk, and hunters clustered together across several trees according to their designated purpose to complete their work and rest, zipping above and dipping into the treetop dwellings at speed to fulfil their daily chores.

From above the forest canopy, where Spenser and Aioffe hovered now, it was far more apparent that a community settled here. The air was where conversation and court occurred, rather than on the ground. Significantly more time was spent flying than Aioffe expected. During her lonely hours, questions about how their society functioned mulled in her mind. Such as, how did they raise pupae who could not yet fly? How did such a large population sustain itself for food? Questions which Spenser seemed curiously reluctant to answer, and she sensed again his divided loyalties now that he was in closer proximity to his people.

On their first flight away, Spenser had been more forthcoming, distracting her with descriptions about a ring of soldier fae, whose bases encircled the outer perimeter of the forest which the community claimed. At the approximate centre, with the courtiers' tents surrounding her, Illania ruled from her golden cup. A complex system of pulleys and ropes were used to haul her up, down and around the trunk of the largest tree in the area. By day, and if it was fine, Aioffe was told by Spenser the Queen would be hauled up, then flown, above the canopy. Kept in the air by a frequently rotated team of bearer fae, this was where she held court sessions.

The court, Aioffe soon realised, must have little privacy. It relied upon unspoken and invisible boundaries. Should a private discussion be required, the Queen would descend below the canopy and her tub placed on a branch-built platform. In relative seclusion, she could conduct her business under cover. Yet, with the fae's extraordinary hearing, it was more a matter of tuning a deaf ear to what was being said. Without walls to dull the sound of voices, only distance would provide privacy. She began to understand why her quarters were isolated so very far away from this central trunk. The realisation did nothing to improve her increasing sense of alienation.

When it rained, as it had done for the last few days, the Queen would simply stay in her tent. Diplomatic matters slowed as a result and still no-one arrived to instruct Aioffe. It was as if she, and her rescue of the Queen had been forgotten. Not that she wanted any fuss being made about her heroics - it was more the insult of being ignored ever since. But she did not dare disobey the instruction to remain in her abode except when in the company of Spenser or until called for, in case she missed her opportunity to speak with Queen Illania.

When they arrived back at her dwelling, however, a messenger hovered close by. He passed Aioffe a folded piece of paper and darted off without further interaction. Aioffe and Spenser went inside before opening it.

Aioffe, Queen of the far-realm known as Naturae, is formally invited to attend a celebration in her honour this night. There will follow a Presentation of the Princesses Caesaria and Tamara in the company of their most wondrous mother and ruler, the High Queen Illania, presiding over the five tribes of faekind, with dominion over the realms of Middle Europa, Southern Europa and Eastern Europa and all subjects within.

Aioffe turned to Spenser, shock upon her face. "Five tribes?" She whispered. "How many are there?"

He shrugged. "Perhaps only twenty?"

Eyes widening at the prospect, she said, "So if I can't gather what I need here, there are other options."

"It would require significant travel," Spenser said carefully. "Not accounting for the many years to track them down." He glanced away. "I am not well acquainted with other fae communities, although I knew some of their Ambassadors in passing."

"Over all these centuries, you only knew them 'in passing'? I thought you said Queen Illania was *the* Queen to meet?"

Turning aside from him, she reflected on the absence of other Ambassadors to Naturae's court, and realised that they had not returned since she had ruled. Even during her mother's reign, few had appeared with regularity, and none had stayed as often as Spenser. She had been so focused on rebuilding Naturae, other realms, other Queendoms, seemed irrelevant. Until now, when she needed them. How had she not considered this before? Had she simply missed the record of ambassadorial attendance?

When she span around to challenge him, Spenser glowered at her through lowered eyelids. "Queen Illania is, if I may be so bold, one of the last of her generation of Queens. From early in her reign, when she survived the Sation Wars, she is expected to live long into the future. Whatever that holds. Do not underestimate her. She is the strongest ruler, and her line of succession is already established. I am one of but a few Ambassadors left serving her. Illania alone remains the most likely to even acknowledge your position. That is only due to the geographical proximity of Naturae and my efforts to ensure that your achievements are known about here. She had been ready to add Naturae to her list of dominions by force, had you not returned."

His head bowed. "Forgive me, my Queen, but you fail to grasp how much our kind's numbers have dwindled. I have been trying to tell you of the threats. The most recent so-called witch hunts are simply the latest in a long history of persecution of creatures. From the East, the rise and spread of the Islamic faiths encourages extreme measures against those who do not follow their doctrines. Where once there was tolerance and passionate belief, I fear now many fae tribes live isolated, hidden and under threat. I have not seen Ambassadors from most of the other realms since, perhaps, the crusades ended. "

Aioffe was silent for a moment, then touched his fingers apologetically. "I should have asked you about this before. Listened better. I... I have only myself to blame for not giving these concerns sufficient attention."

"What good would it have done, my Queen? You alone cannot change what happens to faekind in the rest of the world." He sighed. "No one of us can."

Aioffe sat on the edge of the hammock which was her bed, rocking to and fro gently whilst she thought.

"Let us see how matters run here before deciding what to do next," she said. "What am I supposed to wear tonight?"

Spenser's easy smile returned. "I would suggest your finest robe, and it wouldn't hurt to embellish it as only you can."

"Do you have time to accompany me on a walk before this evening's entertainment, Ambassador? I would request some reminders on protocol, now that I have more of an understanding of how this community exists."

He took a step back and swept quickly into a deep bow so she could not see his expression. "I will return shortly. A change of attire for myself is also required. This ceremony will be very different from what you are used to." Leaving her to decide between the few dresses she had brought with her, Spenser flew away without further explanation.

CHAPTER THIRTY-FIVE
Coronation

London, October 1st 1553

Henry trailed behind the Duke of Norfolk, who was deep in discussion with Bishop Gardiner through the back corridors of Westminster Cathedral. The old men, stiff from standing throughout the long coronation service, shuffled along at a pace which frustrated a vampire. But, he drew no closer than propriety allowed, preferring to listen in on their whispered conversation.

"The Privy Council will never allow it," Howard insisted. "The very idea of a Spaniard so close to the throne, it's preposterous."

Henry heard the Bishop's slow intake of breath, before he said, "They are unlike to have much choice about the matter. And, as so many of us are indebted to her for our reprieve, she will hold our freedoms and seats on the Privy Council over our heads to achieve her desires."

"If our *friends* on the continent hadn't interfered, she would never have set eyes upon that painting of the half-mad nincompoops' son. Now, she passes over perfectly good Englishmen in favour of a ponce with fine legs. She may be the Queen, but she is as easily swayed as any other woman."

Henry's master had previously confided in him that he held grave concerns about how malleable Mary might be, given her female sensibilities. The Privy Council had already discussed the drafting of an Act to bestow the same powers on her as a male monarch would have, yet the Duke of Norfolk still wrestled with the actual idea of a woman leading the country in practise. Throwing an unknown foreigner into the equation gave him sleepless nights; Henry suspected the Bishop suffered the same pangs of conscience about the proposition.

Bishop Gardiner touched the Duke's arm lightly. "She must believe, rightly or wrongly, my Lord, that choosing King Philip will endear her to her cousin, his father the Emperor Henry, as t'was him who suggested the match. I do acknowledge, marrying Philip could bolster England's return to Rome. Not least in the eyes of the Catholic peoples which he ostensibly rules over. The same could not be said of our suggestions of Courtney or Pole."

Gardiner shrugged slightly, then scratched the bald skin beneath the black skull cap. "But," he sighed, "I placed that crown upon her head not two hours ago. I would not place it on another. Whether he will try and negotiate his way into being King of England as well as her heart is a matter which we, the Privy Council and Parliament, would have to agree upon."

He raised his eyebrows and the old men shared a glance of mutual agreement at how unlikely this was before he continued. "Perhaps she is wise to join with two most influential supporters of Rome after Edward so disparaged them. But, I fear she does not see how this marriage would reduce England to a mere offshoot of the Hapsburgs."

Henry hid his smirk, lest he be judged by the servant next to him, who was reverently holding the Bishops' mitre in outstretched arms even though the ceremony had long since finished. In the last few weeks since joining the Duke at St James's, Henry found himself acutely aware of how insular all levels of Mary's court was. How much gossip the change in monarch provoked amongst the serving class, and beyond. Already there were whispers about how she, a mere woman, planned to move into King Edward's rooms when she moved the court formally to Whitehall to be closer to the City.

They reached the hastily refreshed side chamber where the ceremonial robes were temporarily kept, and the two men waited for a priest to pass them before entering. Henry followed, assisting the Duke to remove his heavy, fur lined robe of state. A thoughtful soul had left a plate with some biscuits and wine on an ornately carved side table, which the Bishop headed straight for. After gulping down a full glass of thin-looking liquor, he poured himself another and nibbled on a snack whilst his assistant dressed him in his more usual frock.

"I dare say," the Bishop mumbled, crumbs falling from his mouth onto his long beard. "She will make some form of announcement within the next few days. I do not think though, after all this time waiting for her moment, that she would allow her history to be re-written with Philip as ruler instead of herself. No matter how unnatural it is. At least he is of the true faith."

He turned and addressed the unusually quiet Duke whilst studying Henry; his eyes wrinkling thoughtfully as they roamed. Although Henry kept his face lowered, there was little doubt the long-serving politician would know who he was, despite his rheumy vision. "Your new 'man' will need all the energy he has with the messages he will no doubt be dispatching. You've already been across the park several times, most likely, to the Spanish Ambassadors, eh?"

Henry nodded and looked at the floor as if guilty. In truth, the notes he bore enabled him to roam London freely to feed. He had mastered the art now, of enticement into dim alleys. The nearby roads were swamped with the faithful wishing to see their Queen. Henry had never been so satiated before.

"Well, it will be easier for the Spanish to slide in and out without being noticed so much when she moves to Whitehall." The Duke harrumphed, then glowered. "Already they are like beetles swarming around her. Come, we had better make haste for the carriages. It wouldn't surprise me if Ambassador Reynard was already in place behind her seat. He might as well keep his slippers there for all the time he spends whispering into her ear. Henry," the Duke lowered his voice to say, "I was unable to secure you a place in the processional. You'll have to meet us at Whitehall."

"Yes, your Grace," Henry replied. He hung the Duke's robe up and held the door for them. The pair shuffled only slightly faster back through the corridors of the Abbey. They were heading to the landing jetty, where Mary would doubtless be arranged in her splendour in readiness for the grand procession. Henry closed the room and left the building through a side exit.

He crossed the neat gardens outside the old Abbey buildings, noticing the reappearance of the Benedictine monks. A pair dallied in the lowering light, assessing the Abbey eaves. Rumour claimed Mary had already assured the order of reinstatement to their former home.

The many hundred witnesses to Mary's coronation, of which Henry had not been one, filtered slowly out of the Cathedral. Over the clamour of the waiting crowd, hungry and ready for the feast which had been promised, jolly music struck up from the band aboard one of the barges. A fleet bobbed in the river as far as the eye could see, to ferry those guests not granted a coveted position in the official procession through the city, to the continuation of the festivities.

Although he supposed he could tag along at the end of the boat queue or even blend into the hordes who would follow the carriages relatively unnoticed, Henry had no time to waste watching Mary's triumphant route out of Westminster to Whitehall. But, as he had not set his eyes on her at all since just before his 'death', it was entirely understandable that his gaze should wander down the line of guests to see who had been deemed worthy enough. Reaching the gateway by the landing stage, he drew in his breath sharply.

Elizabeth, his half sister, last seen by him as a toddling child who loved to laugh and pull at his hair, was now a woman. They must look about the same age now, Henry realised, as he absorbed her unmistakable, pale heart-shaped face, slim waist and the locks of red curly hair which blew loose around her headpiece. Her dress was, by Mary's ornate standards, plain. Maybe she was reluctant to completely concede her rumoured Protestant modesty, Henry wondered, although he remembered how even as a young girl she had adored revelry. She didn't seem to be much enjoying the pageantry of the day, though. Her white face downcast, and she clutched a prayer book in front of her penitently. As if suddenly aware she was being observed, her eyes swivelled and gazed straight towards him, through the crowd and low bushes of the gardens which separated them.

Henry quickly turned his head away, flipping the hood of his loose cape over his hat for further coverage. It would not do for his quick-minded sister to ask questions about court. Could she remember him after all this while, having been so young at his death? He had no concerns about Mary recognising him when they did eventually cross paths. Her eyesight was famously poor, and she did not allow many servants to loiter in her presence. But Elizabeth was another matter. He would have to avoid her entirely if he was to remain safe. As for Mary, there was time yet for him to find an opportunity to influence her. It was merely a question of which guise he should assume for his approach.

Yet, while his long legs carried him at a fair pace through the streets, a sadness fell over him. Not even the flags, pealing of the bells or laughter of people celebrating lifted his spirits as he mourned afresh the loss of his innocent younger sister. "My brightest, littlest star," he used to call her, when she had thrown her little arms around his legs and giggled to be picked up and tossed into the air by her big brother. He remembered the bright golden-pinky quality of her hair when the sun shone through it, always escaping the white cap when he had obliged with her desire to fly. The memory of those rare days when they played together in the gardens of St. James's seemed all the more bitter. Those had been his last days of innocence also, Henry thought, before the world had turned red with his own desire for blood, and power.

He reached the Gatehouse of Whitehall Palace - or 'between the walls', as the commoners called it - still in a reflective mood. Hundreds of Londoners still used Kings Road as a thoroughfare on a daily basis, even though it ran straight through the middle of the vast palace. Now fully constructed, his father had originally commissioned the building two decades earlier with the intention it would become the marital home he would share with Anne Boleyn. Although still being completed when Henry had died, the Queen's chambers being added on, the sheer scale of the expensive construction was awe-inspiring, even on this, his third visit this week.

He slowed as he walked between high brick walls to either side of him; terracotta roundels, each holding a bust of a Roman Emperor lined the tunnel, to inspire favourable comparison with England's kings. There had been no female rulers back then, he thought ruefully, as if they knew a woman could never have the strength to lead an empire. As he glanced to the rafters above, he wondered if his father's study and the long gallery which straddled the road above him, would be used by Mary, or if her soon to be announced husband would claim dominion.

"Credentials?" Asked the guard vetting the right side of the Palace, where the residential areas lay.

"Duke of Norfolk," Henry muttered, and rummaged inside his pockets for the papers detailing his patron. The sun had set during his amble across town, now the streets were filling with revellers who had partaken of too much ale. The steward disappeared with his documents into the small room, brightly lit with flickering, cheap candles against the gloom of the tunnel. Security around Mary was tight anyway, Henry reasoned, especially today.

Whilst he waited, he thought again of Elizabeth. Would she be in attendance at the feast tonight? Surely she could not avoid it. So ought he to attend also? Henry turned over his options in his mind as drunken shouts echoed through the underpass. He had been hoping to use the crowded court celebrations to slip closer to Mary's presence, but the risk of exposure had, without warning, increased. He decided that it was likely Elizabeth would be present. Even in disguise, he felt sure his younger sister would recognise him. Or, could he kill two birds with one arrow? Influence Elizabeth to get nearer to Mary?

After several minutes, the guard reappeared. Henry was just considering which of his disguises could best flummox Elizabeth and buy him some time, when his papers wafted in front of his eyes. He was grunted permission to enter. He smiled as he pushed open the heavy door and stepped inside. Tonight he would see the Queen, and he had no doubts about what he needed to do.

CHAPTER THIRTY-SIX
Blessings?

Bavaria, October 1st 1553

As regal as she could be with such a limited selection of attire, Aioffe had chosen her most elaborately embroidered gown of deep red to wear. She fashioned bracelets of tiny yellow alpine flowers and wove them around her arms and through her hair. Bright green new ivy leaves grown into a rustling cape hung between her wings, flaring out behind her as she climbed. With one hand on Spenser's arm and before they broke through the canopy, Aioffe checked her thin silver crown. Adjusted, presentable, she straightened her neck, breathing out slowly. Trying to calm her fluttering heartbeat, Aioffe mentally chided herself. This was the invitation she had been waiting for. Formality was just one part of being a Queen. Once they had stared at her for a while, she would be free of their curious glances, she hoped.

"You look glorious, Queen Aioffe of Naturae," Spenser whispered.

"Then why do I feel as if I am the poor cousin?" She muttered when she saw the court in all their finery before them. Her fingers tightened on his arm as they sailed through a majestic display, high above the treetops. The darkening sky twinkled with candles held aloft by hundreds of arms, flickering in the air from the beat of many wings. Columns of soldiers, resplendent in brilliant green and gold tunics, hovered in regimented blocks. Each wore a sash of emerald, slashed to display golden ruffles, crossed over their chests, a dead-set expression on their swarthy, identical faces. As Aioffe and Spenser approached the centre, the guard-lines curved, peeling away to reveal a trio of highly burnished, gold chariots.

Harking back to times when gods were believed to walk on the earth, Illania's enormous cup bore the telltale embellishments of Rome. Her bearers, gladiatorial in resplendent armour and not a lot else, carried flaming torches in their spare hands. Shimmering with their reflected glow, Queen Illania acknowledged Aioffe's presence with a slight incline of her head, a tightening of her full lips but not a welcoming smile.

Two smaller chariots on either side of her contained who, Aioffe presumed, were the Queen's daughters. They could not have been more different. Otherwise obscured by the curved rim, one did not register her in the slightest - all that could be seen was a high-pointed, glittering hairpiece. The taller of the pair stood with a stiff formality, long dark tresses piled on top of her head like a turban, narrowing her eyes as Aioffe approached. Aioffe's skin crawled as their judgement roamed over her. A sneer appeared, contorting her narrow face before she cast a superior side glance towards her sister.

The hum of wings grew louder as Spenser led the way towards them, looking dead ahead at the Queen. Aioffe refused to allow herself to be distracted by whispers from the crowd. Following his suit, she wrestled to maintain a neutral expression, as if this were a rite of passage she had done many times before. On Spenser's arm though, her fingers shook.

When they were a few feet away from the line of torch-bearers, Spenser pulled up. The other princess, slouching down almost below the rim of her golden cup-shaped vessel, pushed herself higher and peeped out at Aioffe's arrival. Aioffe caught the warning glare from her mother, after which she shuffled awkwardly to a stand. Meeting a dull, petulant expression, Aioffe softened. The girl looked as reluctant to be here as Aioffe felt. Short, squat and squeezed into a tight yellow dress, she was a miniature version of the Queen except with yellow curly tresses framing a cherubic face. Then, the chubby caterpillar stiltedly forced a smile. Aioffe gasped, as the red lips parted to show a mouthful of pointed teeth!

"Queen Aioffe of Naturae," Illania's deep voice boomed across the skies. "I bid you welcome to our realm."

Aioffe dipped into a curtsey as Spenser bowed.

"It is my great honour to visit you, most wondrous Queen. May our realms prosper in the spirit of friendship and kinship."

Illania's hand wafted to her right, where the thin fae stared again at Aioffe with barely concealed disdain. "I present my daughter, Princess Caesaria, pupaeted in the presence of Caesar the Great, Emperor of Rome."

It was rare that she took an instant dislike to anyone, but it was clear that the tight lipped and haughty Caesaria considered herself superior to Aioffe, and that alone made the hairs on the back of Aioffe's neck rise. Friendship and kinship appeared to be the last things which this princess was interested in promoting, thought Aioffe.

As Aioffe curtsied again, her mind resolved that she would not be intimidated.

"And my other daughter, Princess Tamara, pupaeted in the presence of Count Emicho of Flonheim, Last World Emperor and follower of Peter the Hermit."

Tamara's lips widened, revealing even more of her sharpened teeth. Aioffe wondered whether a vampire had influenced her creation. Had the Queen consorted with the Catholic Church? To hide her confusion, she curtsied deeply

The Queen clapped her hands together. Her tone, altogether more friendly now, lighter as she said, "There will be plenty of time for us to get to know each other, and conclude the joining of our realms as a result of our familial collaboration. Come, observe the spectacular beside me."

Eloquent though the Queen's Latin was, Aioffe wasn't sure she had interpreted what she said correctly. Aioffe glanced at Spenser, who dropped his arm and bowed once more to Illania and her daughters. Her silent, glanced plea for him to remain went unheeded, as he dipped his head to her hand and kissed it briefly before flying away. Her chest tightened as she joined the royal family.

Aioffe had little chance to digest or re-examine what she thought the Queen had commanded, as an unseen signal prompted a troop of soldiers to form a semi-circle behind them. Trapped and bewildered, she revolved to face the same direction as Illania. The crowd ahead fell silent and looked down; only the low throb of their wings could be heard.

On this cue, a group of fae spiralled up from the treetops. Spinning and twirling in front of them, colourful gauzy costumes floated around their frames as they swooshed through the air. Long trailing ribbons drifted outwards, tentacle-like as they spun close to the crowd, then into a rotating spiral. Aioffe was reminded of her own Blessing Ceremonies, of how the strands of belief danced towards her. Her fingers itched to feel the sensation again, but here she was only an observer of the balletic spectacle.

The performers, circling in widening loops, started to sing. An ancient, lilting and lyrical tune stirred Aioffe's soul. The familiarity of the fae song evoked her childhood. Aioffe closed her eyes; how long had it been since she last heard the lullaby? Without truly understanding why, she sensed herself swaying, her wings beating in a different way from usual. The hypnotic effect pulled her deeper into herself, and she yearned to go further.

Warm and comfortable. Effortlessly floating towards a remembrance of something joyful. Not her childhood, but a different memory she wanted to return to time and time again. To examine. To re-experience. Yet precisely what it was eluded her. Safety and warmth awaited her if only she could reach it... she could feel the tendrils of it already, making her want to burrow, wrap herself in its comfort. Stay there in the delicious ease the hazy image offered. At the end of the ache in her being, she would find it again...

Feeling a peculiar tug, Aioffe roused a little. Yanked awake by a flash of pain, then she felt herself pulled in again. The melody whispered encouragement in her ears.

Another tug, more delicate this time. Like an itch, distracting her from falling into the memory again... if she released it, perhaps it would allow her to fly into the warmth....

Aioffe resisted. It was as if the pull was trying to tear a piece of her very soul. Incessant. Distracting her from her goal to find what she sought. It wanted something intrinsic to her being.

Something which she could not give. Not now.

Something she innately knew would cause her far greater pain than the temptation which allured her.

Something dangerous.

Her eyes flew open. The sensation immediately stopped. With

blurry eyes, she saw the Queen's head snap back to face the performers.

Aioffe's eyes flared, forcing her to focus. She blinked again and again. The brightness from the yellow-flamed torches had been overshadowed by the glinting strands of Lifeforce emanating from the fae. Around the circle, the workers and soldiers were swaying in the sky, their heads tipped back. The troupe in the centre floated on the ribbons it seemed, rotating slowly like the centre of a spoke, drawing together the Lifeforce so it streamed towards the Queen in one long twist.

This vision would only be visible to a Queen, Aioffe knew. Indeed, from the corner of her eye, she noticed the princesses slumped in their chariots, boredom evident on their sullen faces. Aioffe peered over Illania's shoulder, unsurprised to see her chubby hands in her lap, twitching as the stream of Lifeforce entered them.

Here was the answer to the question which she was only partially aware she had been asking herself - how did this society continue to flourish without human interaction? Performance, evoking their mystical heritage. The Queen gathered her community's Lifeforce in the same way that she did.

Or did she? Had this community any choice in the matter?

The song had pulled them all into a trance of some kind. She had almost been sucked in herself.

Suddenly, Aioffe was swept on a wave of longing, back into a recent memory of her own ceremonies in Naturae. It had been months since she had last ingested Lifeforce of this kind. She desperately wanted a taste, although she hesitated, wary of intruding uninvited. But the idea itched, and she fluttered twitchily, trying to find the words to ask permission. This wasn't strictly her fae's Lifeforce, but Illania's.

A faint cry, audible as it jarred with the song, dragged her attention to the workers in the outer circle. On those faces nearest to her, she realised their expression winced. With the pleasure, there was a pain.

A fae dropped, plummeted down to the trees. If she hadn't been watching, Aioffe would probably have missed it. As the body fell, it disintegrated into ashes.

Another gasp of agony, not release. Another worker faltered in the sky, his face stricken with terror and his arms reached out. Then he too crumbled.

Illania was taking too much. Aioffe jolted - she had to stop this! Giving blessings, their Lifeforce, was a choice, not to be enforced. But the song had lulled the workers into thinking it was freely given.

These fae were being drained of their very essence - and with a pain which they were unable to resist. To prevent. This ceremony took... far more than it gave. Aioffe's mouth fell open. The spectacle, dressed up as a blessing ceremony, concealed an unwilling sacrifice. To take a life, any life let alone a fae one, like this was tantamount to murder. Was that why Spenser had disappeared?

Sensing her watching - realising - Illania slowly revolved her head around to meet Aioffe's eyes. Before Aioffe could do anything, trapped as she was with the soldiers behind her, Illania said, "I will taste your Lifeforce also, child. It is pointless to resist. And then, we shall have an accord." Although her voice held a dream-like quality familiar to Aioffe, there was no mistaking the threat.

Aioffe gasped, forcing her wings to pivot, then she dived away.

CHAPTER THIRTY-SEVEN

The wall of resistance

London

Trapped in the centre of the party, Henry grew irritated by the pomades. Not only did their cloying smells mask telltale signs he needed to size up his opposition, but the little boxes and balls were waved around in gleeful abandon without a care for who they might hit. Unusually for Mary, she had opened her meagre coffers sufficiently to lay out a lavish celebration of her coronation. In an effort to both show how popular she was and bolster support, invitations had been sent across the land. Insufficient attention had been paid to how many could fit into the, admittedly vast, Great Hall. The resulting squash of wide skirts and puffed shoulders made navigation about the room at any speed nearly impossible.

Dressed in a heavy yellow embroidered tunic with diamond quilted stitching borrowed from Fairfax, Henry assumed he looked the part of a low-ranking nobleman. Yet, surrounded by the finery of court, he felt nothing of the sort. Hidden beneath his fake beard, a wig and affecting a stoop which pained his back, he knew he ought to be pleased he was attracting no undue attention. Instead, it rankled. He ought to be known. He should be visible.

But, being recognised now would not serve his purpose, and so he hid. His nose twitched as he sifted through the markers of vampire, daemon and witch present amongst the overwhelming numbers of humans. As the night wore on, and the mortals ingested the freely flowing wine, Henry began to sense he was being watched by ever more creatures, stymieing his ability to creep closer to his goal.

Mary, who had barely moved from the throne at the top of the chamber, was entirely surrounded by courtiers fawning over her. Flanked by soldiers filling the tall bay window which framed her throne, she held court. Laughing and fanning herself, only able to focus on those immediately in front of her. By her side, like a treasured lap-dog, perched Elizabeth. As Henry manoeuvred himself into a gap closer to the royal party, the forced smile pasted upon her flushing face flagged. She kept glancing, longingly, behind her to the archway with stairs leading away from the pressure of the performance beside her, then back up to the ceilings as if to admire the gilded timber battens and rich panelling. The Queen, gaily chattering through the exhaustion evidenced by her middle-aged, sweating brow, ignored their sister.

Before he could sidle closer still, the exhausted Duke of Norfolk grabbed his arm.

"My boy," he said, and Henry understood the extent of his tiredness from the labouring of his breathing just to say two words. "I cannot leave until the Queen does, but you should."

"Why?"

"I have thrice been asked about you in the last hour alone." The Duke's grave eyes flicked to meet his. "And being noticed is not helpful to our cause."

"If I could only get nearer," Henry protested. "I'm sure I can plant the seed of doubt you need."

The Duke shook his head. "For some matters, there will only be a diplomatic recourse." He gestured to the corner where, on the black and white checked floor, an easel holding the painting of Philip of Spain had been prominently placed. It was perhaps the only corner of the hall which was not filled with people. Henry wondered if Mary knew this was out of fear, as opposed to respect, for either the artwork or the man?

"It could be," the Duke said in a low voice, "we will need to apply pressures in other ways. Via those surrounding her perhaps, rather than directly. Her announcement of intent to marry cannot be far off now, I am sure. She wants, nay needs, to produce an heir. If it is at all possible. By all the saints," he stopped to catch his breath in the hot room. "She will need our prayers for the Lord's intervention - she has precious little time to waste."

As he glanced nonchalantly around, Henry guarded his short temper lest it fray further. On the face of it, he was grateful to the old man for his continued support; indeed, he would not be here at all if it were not for his patronage. But the Duke appeared to forget why Henry was presently at court in the first place. Henry's purpose was not to go around influencing all and sundry with the aim of controlling them, but to get to the ear of Mary herself.

Mary must name him as her successor.

Only Mary needed to be influenced to do Henry's bidding, no matter other political point scoring he implied to his godfather. Henry realised that his intentions had not been discussed since their reunion at Kenninghall - too much time spent on how to establish his cover with the Duke's household and enjoying the delights of London humans maybe - but he had trusted that the Duke was still committed to their original cause. Perhaps that was an error?

Henry glanced down at the Duke, hearing his failing heartbeat. Time was running short for this human. And that meant time was short for Henry to take advantage of his patronage. "I will do what I can, of course, your Gràce. But, if you want my assistance, I must have access to her."

The Duke nodded. "I know. Be patient." He glanced around, his shoulders sagging. "And now I should continue to circulate." His greying eyebrow cocked, yet his face belied his reluctance to enter the throng. "You leave. It cannot happen tonight. There are too many who watch. And keep your head down."

Henry patted the Duke's forearm briefly, reassuring him with a sympathy he did not share. When he looked up, a vampire dressed in the serving livery stared straight at him over Norfolk's shoulder. The coldness of his deliberation tingled on Henry's skin - a warning.

Then, from behind, the sour scent of a witch reached his nose. Without wishing to have a sudden movement noticed, Henry turned casually towards the throne. One of Mary's ladies-in-waiting narrowed her eyes and he saw her lips move, silently muttering. Henry did not know her name, but he recognised her face.

The surrounding air seemed to thicken. The Duke's arm dropped heavily away, without Henry's assent, and his own arms felt as if they were being dragged backwards. His godfather's rheumy eyes missed nothing as Henry involuntarily recoiled. Muscles which tensed to resist the affliction felt powerless as, like a puppet being guided, his feet slid on the floor. Henry's mouth dropped as the invisible wall seemed to propel him back. Even his hands could not push against it; without warning, they were weak and floppy when he tried to raise them in defiance of the witch's spell. It was as if his speed and strength had been neutralised.

"As you can see, Mary is not without 'protection'," the Duke said. "Our task is not as easy as you perhaps thought it would be."

Henry blinked slowly, then, wrenching his body about, pushed himself away through the courtiers. His murmurs as he progressed out of the hall might have translated as apologies to some, but there was little sincerity behind them. Dissatisfaction and frustration grew in his mind as much as the repelling sensation faded, and the further he moved away from Mary. Finally, as he reached the hallway, the pervading fug of pomades reappeared.

His task was not going to be as simple as he had presumed. He had been naïve, yet again. Yet he would not give up. Could not give up.

CHAPTER THIRTY-EIGHT

No options

Bavaria

"Catch her!"

Illania's voice rang clear through the night. Aioffe's dive down into the forest sped up, although as soon as she heard the order, she realised the futility of it. She landed, feet snapping twigs underneath her with the force of impact. There was something comforting about being on the ground after having been airborne or in a treetop for so long. Her senses heightened. She was now the prey, rather than the hunter.

With a speed driven by fear, Aioffe ran. Crashing through the undergrowth in a most unladylike manner, not caring about the trail she left behind. Sensing this was her only moment to find what she sought, her nose sniffed constantly. Somewhere down there, they were keeping the barrels. She could very possibly not have another opportunity - she needed to find them. This evening. As she ran, Aioffe's head whirled as it sifted through the scents of the forest floor.

Half a mile later, her nostrils picked out a faint smell familiar to her. Before she could fully process which it was, her legs twisted her in its direction. Then her rational mind over-rode them and she flew up, not so far as to be visible through the russet of the turning leaves above, but skimming over the ground instead. Anything to buy her more time to follow the scent of pupae.

The bushes and ferns barely rustled as Aioffe swept past them, her eyes scanning for the camouflage she was sure she would find. Further she flew, past thin trunks reaching for the scant sunlight. Through thickets and clearings dripping with berries. The forest came alive with nocturnal sounds of crickets, tiny mice pattering their way to safety, and the deep rustle of wild pigs snuffling for groundnuts. The smell grew stronger, and she dashed towards it.

Just as the scent intensified, she heard them. A distinctive throb of wing-wind over armour. With a final burst of speed, she surged into a small open area where the pearly moonlight fell unimpeded by tree branches. Evenly spaced out across the moss and ferns which covered the woodland floor, the raft-bushes awaited. Her eyes focussed on a cocoon, wavering on its vine and almost ready to break free. This was the smell she had followed, even though she couldn't place it at the time. She glanced about - in Naturae, a nursemaid would be in attendance to catch the cocoon for its pupaetion. There seemed to be no-one here to witness its dropping, or care for the pupae.

Aioffe shook her head. Perhaps this was the way of these fae. Maybe they would perform a routine check, or perhaps the cocoon was awaiting the Queen to visit and bestow the blessings before it would finally breathe its first gasp of life. She hadn't the time to consider it further - this was not her realm, she told herself. Not her people. Not her offspring.

She poked around the bushes, hunting for the royal vine. Darting between the barrels, pushing aside the camouflage to examine each for the telltale signs of golden veins in the leaves, Aioffe's heart began to pound. It must be here, she told herself. It might be small, as surely no fae had grown on it for many a century.

The thrum of wings grew louder, circling close by. She pushed herself away from the barrels, aware that her rustling might have betrayed her location. Standing in the clearing, tears threatened whilst she considered her options. There were twelve bushes, and she thought she had searched each.

"The clarity you seek can only be found within the chaos of four."

Aioffe wheeled about. There was no-one there. And yet, she could have sworn the whispered suggestion appeared to have come from a gnarled trunk across the clearing. She stepped towards it.

"Do not approach!"

Aioffe froze. "What do you mean?" She hissed.

She stared hard at the tree, looking up and down, frowning.

"You must leave. I have work to do, and your presence is unwanted."

"I need to find a specific vine," Aioffe pleaded. "Perhaps you can help?"

A withered hand appeared from behind the trunk, making a shooing motion. Aioffe couldn't keep a small smile from her face. "Won't you even come out and meet me?" Maybe the owner of the voice was shy?

"No."

"Then you will forgive me, but I must keep looking." Aioffe turned aside from the trunk and began to search the closest barrel.

"You won't find what you want before they come."

Even though Aioffe had been half expecting an approach, the speed at which the wispy voice appeared next to her made her jump.

"And how do you know?" Aioffe said, and peered over her shoulder.

Standing about a yard away, a droopy-winged fae glowered at her. Long tassels of stringy grey hair, matted with leaves and possibly some twigs, reminded her of Nemis's dreadlocks. Her robe, such that it was, appeared to be coated in mud with bark tiles stuck to it, lending her the appearance of a stumpy tree. As she met Aioffe's eyes, her bottom lip jutted out petulantly and her frown deepened. "Clarity from the chaos of four, didn't you hear me?"

Before Aioffe could ask the fae's name or what riddles she was speaking of, leather boots, then familiar green soldier tunics dropped into her eye line.

"Do not run!" The command came from behind.

Aioffe wheeled around to see a further six guards descend, all pointing spears at her.

"Or fly!"

"Told you," said the stump.

******

"There is a wildness to you which I do find..." Queen Illania paused, as if searching for the right word. "Charming."

Aioffe looked down, avoiding her eyes as hard as arrowheads. She knew she looked like she had been dragged through a hedgerow backwards, and indeed, she supposed she had.

"And yet, if you had merely asked…"

"If I wasn't held as a prisoner," Aioffe began.

"A prisoner?" The Queen snapped. "Now, why would you think that?"

"The threatening guard posted outside my quarters?"

"A mere security precaution. We are in new grounds and do not yet know how clear of witches this area truly is."

"You did not allow me into your presence until you wanted to feed from me."

"I do not have to justify to you, of all people, how busy a Queen's regime is. I sought to introduce you to our ways."

The mild, impassive tone of Illania's responses to her accusations only infuriated Aioffe. "And when I do discover something of how your realm operates, you drag me away with a show of completely unnecessary force."

Illania folded her hands in her lap and sighed. "You could have been any intruder, to our most sacred of spaces. These soldiers have a responsibility to protect the vines at all cost, against all trespassers."

Gritting her teeth, Aioffe conceded were the situation reversed, she too would protect her vines with equal ferocity. And yet, the entire community knew who she was from the presentation ceremony just hours before. Aioffe glanced behind to the row of guards which blocked the entrance to the Queen's high ceilinged tent. Grey, impassive faces stared back at her, and Aioffe remembered the ceremony just hours before. The Queen was capable of far more than threats.

No, she resolved, she had come this far and been this close to getting what she wanted. Now was not the time to risk everything in an argument. Obviously, they held differing views on how a Queendom should be run. The power Illania wielded should not be underestimated.

She would have to grovel her way out of this.

"We come from different realms, with different ways," Aioffe said, stiffly. "I humbly beg your forgiveness for my curiosity." She looked at the throne although kept her head down with a humility she didn't quite feel. "As a young Queen, I have much to learn. I sought to find the answers to my questions prematurely and with poor judgement. Your grace is in the prime of her long life. I can only aspire to emulate your success."

The Queen raised an eyebrow and Aioffe steadied her breathing. Diplomacy - a new territory for Aioffe and she was on the back foot with nothing to offer. She wished Spenser was here, or Joshua, with their easy, charming manners to smooth matters. She studied the floor, feeling very alone and exposed. It occurred to her that she did not know this woman at all. Could not predict her, and had only scant advice from Spenser that she responded to flattery. The thin crown on her head slipped off kilter as she fought the tears which threatened. Automatically, she reached up to straighten it. Maybe, the action would highlight her inexperience rather than incompetence.

In the silence which followed as Illania preened at the flattery, Aioffe recovered herself. Why this fae made her feel so inadequate irritated her. She was just beginning to question why that should be, when Illania said, "All the more reason why you must make a decision about which of my daughters should succeed you."

Aioffe blinked.

"I have therefore sent for suitable human candidates for you to transform. As payment to secure our trade. I will forgive your indiscretion this one time, in the spirit of assuring our familial, regal connection. I assume your Prince does not age at the same rate as humans, but he ought at least to live as long as a worker." Illania waved her hand, beckoning Aioffe to draw closer. "Unless, you wish me to pluck the ability from you instead?"

If Aioffe's teeth were any more gritted, she thought, they would crumble. "No," she said. "But I believe you are mistaken. Joshua was created from love. I did not expect him to become fae. Just to heal."

The Queen's lips pursed. "But you can do it? I saw what you did with the creepers. It is merely an extension of that. You transform living matter to your will. I felt it within you."

Aioffe kept her head low, her eyes following the wooden boards, which, although roughly straight, did not quite meet each other. The underside she presumed still protruded branches so as to provide further disguise. It struck her how deceptive appearances could be.

How a simple creeper could also be a strong rope. When she had grown then woven the ivy, although she had done it before in Naturae, she had merely had the mental image of how they should end up. The vines had then arranged themselves into that shape, albeit guided by her hands as she thought about her desired end result.

The same could be said to have happened when she transformed Joshua. Overwhelming grief and a yearning to recapture that feeling of love again as he slipped into death had driven her pouring of her Lifeforce into him. To heal him. She had held foremost in her mind a mourning for the life which they envisaged leading together, which wouldn't have developed if he died. The end result had far surpassed her intention, or had it? Had she perhaps, without realising it at the time, wanted their lives to be more alike. Winged like her. A fae.

Aioffe gasped. "I did it," slipped out of her mouth before she clapped her hand over it. The Queen nodded slowly, as a teacher to a pupil.

"And that is why," Illania said, "You will do it again."

Aioffe frowned. "But it only happens when I want it to. When I will it."

"I cannot see any reason why you wouldn't wish for it to work," the Queen purred. "After all, you will not be able to return to Naturae until you have paid for your part of the deal." She shrugged and looked away, beckoning a servant towards her. "Fetch Ambassador Spenser, will you? I believe his other Queen might need some convincing."

"I'm sorry," Aioffe said. "It is not a matter of persuasion. You have not given me sufficient time to consider your request."

Illania tipped her head back and laughed. The deep chuckle had a sinister overtone, which did nothing to ease Aioffe's mind. When she finished, the Queen said with a smirk, "If you thought it was a request, my child, you were mistaken. You will take one of my daughters, and I will have a hybrid to replace them."

A shuffle by the entrance announced the arrival of Spenser. Aioffe turned and her mouth dropped in horror. Wrists and ankles shackled, his wings clamped, yet still with the wry twist to his lips of old, Spenser's eyes met hers.

"What have you done to him?" Aioffe cried out.

"'Tis nothing, my Queen." The gravelly tone of his voice worried her even more.

"Release him right now!"

Illania's eyes twinkled. "That would be very unwise of me. And I am nothing if not bestowed with the wisdom of nearly two thousand years of experience in these matters. No, your friend will not be leading you home until we have completed the deal." Her lips hardened. "So you see, you will want to create me a hybrid very shortly."

Aioffe could only watch with a sinking heart as Spenser was dragged closer to the Queen and deposited at the base of her tub. "No!" she cried out as Illania dropped her finger down and hooked a strand of Lifeforce from him as easily as breathing it in. Spenser's face greyed, his desperate eyes rolling towards Aioffe. She felt her fingertips tingle, and clenched them tightly into her palm. Illania's cheeks flushed with the ingestion and a smile played upon her cherubic lips. "He will keep me satisfied for a few weeks. Perhaps," she said.

CHAPTER THIRTY-NINE
Note from below

Aioffe had paced all night, for the fifth night in a row. Not only was she hungry, since Spenser had not been released to escort her to feed, but she was now exhausted. Since there was nothing else to do but wait, she flopped onto her bed and stared at the flapping roof. This was worse than being in the Beneath, she thought. At least then she had contact with people on a daily basis. A routine of Uffer dragging her into court to sit at her mother's feet. Here, she was alone. Meagre rations of a dead fish were occasionally pushed through the flap, but nothing else happened. Not for the first time, homesickness swept over her.

Whilst she resisted the temptation to dissolve into a ball of wet self-pity, wings buzzed closer, hovering underneath her tent. It couldn't be a guard, as they usually circled above or rested on branches close by so they had a view of her entrance at all times. As she stared at the rough wooden floor, she glimpsed something fluttering between the planks!

Grubby fingers poked a folded sheet of paper through the space, then, a tatty quill followed. The fingers felt along to find a slightly wider gap. Then, a small vial of dark liquid twisted its way up and wedged itself between the floorboards. The hum of wingbeats disappeared.

Aioffe flung herself off the low straw pile and grabbed the note. Her heartbeat quickened as she opened it.

'My name does not matter, but for **clarity**, my hand is yours. For Issam, I owe a message. Write it, and I will ensure it is received. There is One who has written but you will not hear it. One message, for a one love and my debt is repaid. I will collect it when chaos strikes once more.'

Her heart flew into her mouth and Aioffe gasped. A message could be sent - and one had been received! It could only be from Joshua. Only he and Nemis knew her purpose in travelling with Spenser. He must have used a kestrel, she realised, which had been intercepted. She smiled as relief swept through her. No other means of sending messages could be relied upon to find her, wherever she was. Someone, and some bird, knew where she was. Knew how lost she was.

Unexpectedly, an opportunity to seize control of her situation had been gifted to her. A way to reconnect with her world. A wetness formed behind her eyelids, spilling into a single tear. How she longed to read that note. His note. It had to be. To see once again his beautiful handwriting, perhaps smell the metallic perfume of his fingertips on the parchment. It almost didn't matter what his message said, only that he had written to her.

Then, re-reading the scrawl, the word 'clarity' struck her as odd. As if the quill had been very carefully leant upon when scribing it. The lettering sunk into the paper for emphasis. The only other person who had used it in her presence was that funny tree-fae in the vine clearing.

She read the sentence again. 'For clarity.' Which was what that fae said she needed to find. Who had that creature been, she wondered anew. Many times over the last few nights, Aioffe had replayed the incident over in her mind. The almost prophetic words which had been said. She had half convinced herself the fae was influenced by a witch. But, was she a spy, not a nursemaid as she had first assumed?

It didn't matter, not really. The important thing was to grasp the opportunity of getting word to Joshua of her predicament. Then he could find her, she had no doubt. He always did, and she loved him that much more for his dependability in that regard.

But then, the awful thought struck her. *Would* he? Or would he send someone else, who might take longer to get here, and stay in Naturae as she had asked him to?

Aioffe wrung her hands together, then took off her crown and twisted it around, hoping the cool, smooth silver would calm her. She should be happy to have this opportunity, but suddenly, the nerves began to gnaw. They had parted in such a horrible manner - so awkward and cold. Just supposing she did manage to reach Joshua, and he came, would he arrive in time? Should he come at all? Was she better off trying to do what the Queen asked, assuming a suitable person was brought to her, and saving Spenser?

What if the Queen discovered her message? Or, and her heart sped up, sent a message to Joshua herself, trapping him into coming here so that she might have him instead? The thought shot a chill through Aioffe, and she clutched the delicate crown in her arms.

She began to pace the small floor, anxiously aware of how frail a control she had right now on herself, and of how pressing time was to reach a decision. After a while, the walking routine both calmed and energised her. She needed to seize this opportunity. That much she knew. But what to say? The only piece of paper she had was the one this message had been written on. There was no room for error or drafts. And what could she convey to make it clear to Joshua that she hadn't seen the note intended for her?

What did she actually want Joshua to do? That was the first question Aioffe realised. He alone could not help both her and Spenser on his own - there were too many guards. She would be inviting him into a trap. But, if he bought support with him, her own soldiers from Naturae say, then that would take far too long. Guard-fae were not physically equipped for long-distance flying. Spenser, she suspected, hadn't much time. But how could she give both Joshua and Spenser more time? The Queen was most likely feeding from her friend daily, and that would deplete him.

The dilemma overwhelmed her. Aioffe collapsed onto the floor and put her head in her hands. Then she let out a scream of frustration.

"Are you well, Queen Aioffe?"

It was a guard outside. In her desperation, she had forgotten all about them. "No," she said. "I need to see the Queen, urgently. Please tell her…. I have considered her request and I have an answer."

It was worth a try.

Aioffe began to pull all of her dresses from her packs, her mind turning to practical matters. As she shook out one of the under-skirts, a small, tightly tied drawstring purse dropped on the floorboards with a dull thud. She bent down and frowned. She was sure she hadn't packed anything superfluous, so what was this? Her heart thudded as the scent of Joshua wafted up from the wrapping. Fingers shaking, she sat down on the bed to open it.

The knots were fiddly, especially as her hands shook trying to pick them apart, but finally the leather thong gave way. A miniature polished silver arrowhead! She picked it up, her fingertips sliding over the comforting warmth of the exquisite object, only the size of a fingernail. The sides of the arrowhead were dulled, just enough that it would not have cut the bindings or pouch, yet it was still sufficiently sharp to pierce. On one side, her lover had etched a tiny heart - much like the ones which she stitched into all of his clothing. It was, she remembered, exactly the same shape as the arrowhead which had pierced him a century ago. Old-fashioned by this age, yet a poignant and personal reminder of his turning.

Aioffe clenched it in her fist and brought it to her lips. She dared not reach out to him with her mind, she did not deserve to have his comfort. She had pushed him away from their partnership and tried to tackle their problems - her problems - on her own. And yet, he still wanted her to know he would protect her. Evermore. A sob escaped as she recalled the safety of his embrace. The togetherness.

But not now. She had chosen to leave him in pursuit of their future, and she was facing decisions alone.

Stroking the smooth metal, her mind resolved. The decision as to whether he still chose to protect and keep her after all this time ought to be his. She could only let him know where she was, and trust that he would make the right choice. She smiled, remembering Spenser's instrument which he would find a way to decipher, she was sure!

Satisfied, Aioffe looked again at the arrowhead, marvelling at its lightweight beauty, before wrapping it once more. She then tied it to the strings of her shift, so it laid close to her heart at all times. All else she could do was trust in him. In his love for her.

Even if she must betray him in the meantime…

*****

Spenser leant against the golden throne-tub when Aioffe was escorted in. He resembled one of those pet dogs she had seen in paintings, all floppy haired and dopey. His eyes brightened when he saw her though, but Aioffe waited until the Queen looked away whilst she shooed aside a fawning attendant, before winking at him. His expression cheered momentarily, then he faced down in mock subservience.

In her own time, Queen Illania finally swivelled her attention to Aioffe, jowls wobbling as she grumbled, "You have something you wish to say?"

Aioffe, dressed in her fullest skirt, curtseyed without bowing her head. She kept her eyes fixed on the old monarch so she would believe what she was about to answer. "Your most wondrous Majesty. I have been giving some thought to your 'request' for a hybrid companion."

"And?"

"And I think it might be possible - if I were to form a connection with them. As I did with Joshua."

The Queen's lips tightened. "I see."

"Joshua and I were in love," Aioffe said, keeping her gaze steady. "And I assume that is what made the difference when I tried to heal him. I think an emotional bond would be the only way I could achieve what you want. If I grew to care for them."

The thunderous frown on Illiana's face was accompanied by a grunt, which seemed to begin in her belly and get stuck in her throat.

"I was not suggesting you make another hybrid for your own satisfaction," Illania spat out. "What is the use in that?"

"Oh no, your Majesty. I did not mean for us to... fall in love. Only to grow to care about each other, as a brother would a sister."

Illania sniffed.

"That way, I would be emotionally entwined with him, which also serves to strengthen the familial ties between our two great realms." Aioffe continued, her eyes sliding towards Spenser and holding his, "This tiny world, just waiting beneath the moving stars which hold that message in their brightness, would seem less daunting as we face the future. We all need to be sure that it is always possible to navigate to each other, rely on the allegiances which wed us through kinship. It seems right that only those who truly know each other well can bring us together." Aioffe finished with an earnest smile at the Queen.

A chubby finger began to tap on the cherubic lips whilst Illania considered, or perhaps wondered at her odd choice of phrasing. Despite this, Aioffe hoped her message would be received. Her breath eased out as Spenser's mouth lifted a fraction. His approval of her strategy solidified when, seen from the corner of her eye, his hand surreptitiously slid into one of his jacket pockets.

Rather than give the Queen too much time to find a flaw in her plan, Aioffe pressed on. "I have also given consideration to your daughters."

Illania bristled. "Have you decided which to take back with you?"

Shaking her head, Aioffe said, "I have not. They are both so…. Unique. I would ask for your humble forgiveness in even making this request, but, it is an eternal commitment you are asking me to choose for. I must be sure that I pick the right Princess for Naturae. I must insist that I get to know each of your daughters better, as well as more about the ways they are accustomed to as well. To be sure we can live together in my Queendom until the moment comes when they are to ascend."

"I see." Illania's top lip turned into a sneer.

Aioffe suddenly realised that the Queen herself might have a preference as to which daughter she envisaged keeping as her replacement. "But, if you wanted me to prioritise one first and see how we get along, of course I'd be happy to spend some time with her… I can only imagine how difficult it must be for you to choose which of your children should live so far away. I wished only to make that dilemma easier for you by offering to determine between them so as to preserve your relationship with them both."

Illania waved her arm in the air, dismissing the notion. "Both Princesses would suit, and I did offer you the choice. I have trained them equally in the craft of ruling myself." She straightened herself in the tub before continuing graciously. "But you are right to try and ensure a good match for your smaller realm. Besides, their powers will not come fully into effect if they do not have a connection to the Queendom and its people upon your… passing."

Aioffe dropped her head, more to hide the slight smile which threatened, than out of deference. Then she stared directly at Illania with a straight face, then approached. "Your Majesty, how goes your decision on which human I am to…" She paused. "Work with?" Aioffe placed both hands on the side of the tub and crouched a little so she was of similar height to the Queen's head. This also meant the pocket of her voluminous skirt, chosen especially for this audience, would be close to Spenser's arm.

"I confess, it is not progressing as swiftly as I would like."

"Oh?"

"It seems there are fewer candidates than I thought." Illania sniffed. "It may require moving court to be closer to a larger selection of humans. None of them are, well, they are not Caesar." Her rosebud lips tightened as she lifted an eyebrow at Aioffe. "Physically, I mean. Humans these days…" She tailed off, lost in her memory.

Just as Aioffe felt the warmth of Spenser's metal astrolabe globe drop close to her thigh, the Queen shifted in her seat. Aioffe panicked for a moment - her plan hinged entirely on staying at these coordinates.

"Why, even Spenser here, was more how I envisioned a mate to be. That was before, of course." She bent her head down and a sneer appeared as her beady eyes roamed down his now gaunt legs. Too much feeding from him had caused his lanky physique to look decidedly wasted. The ashen tone of his skin made Aioffe worry he would not be able to manage a journey away from here.

"Perhaps if I were to see the ones you have already gathered?" Aioffe offered. "I might determine whether, through the change, I could… endow them?"

The Queen's face cheered. "You could do that?"

Aioffe blushed, "Well, Joshua didn't complain of that side effect… and neither did I." She let the suggestion linger with a slight arching of her eyebrow to Illania.

"I see." The Queen shrugged slightly. "In that case, I will review the options once again. There was nothing remiss about their companionship otherwise."

"Take your time, your Majesty. This is a lifetime commitment for you also," Aioffe suggested as she stood. As she backed away towards the entrance, her guards held the tent flap. Aioffe hesitated in the aperture, then said with wide eyed innocence. "Winter is setting in. Would it be possible for me to send word to Naturae that my return may be delayed? I thought perhaps they would have let me know how the last pupaetion went, is all. It surprises me not to have heard from my Council thus far."

Once again, the Queen's eyes narrowed. "A Queen does not need to explain herself, to anyone." Then she looked away. "The sooner you complete your side of the bargain, the sooner you can return to them."

Aioffe gritted her teeth but her hand slipped into her pocket. The polished knobbles of the astrolabe had cooled sufficient to calm the heat of the temper which threatened to rise. She returned to her quarters with a clearer mind. Pulling out the arrowhead, she dipped it into the tiny ink bottle and began to write.

CHAPTER FORTY

A treaty and a rebellion

London, 13th January 1554

An unusually bitter wind meant Henry's walk to the tavern would have chilled even the hardiest of vampires. It was barely past the supper hour, yet the mud underneath his feet crunched already with the evening frost. These back streets were busier by day, especially now advent had passed, yet he still checked no-one watched him before pushing the heavy door open. Once inside the only slightly warmer and lighter room, the bar-keep was quick to catch his eyes, which then slid to the narrow stairs at the back. Henry nodded and slipped him a few groats as he passed.

"I'll send up my finest," the whiskered lips muttered.

"Make sure you do," Henry replied. The blood here was barely passable but it didn't hurt to be polite. This particular inn, run by a former monk who awaited the reopening of the monasteries with mixed feelings, was one of Henry and Fairfax's regular meeting places. Henry preferred it only because of its proximity to the Duke's current quarters in Whitehall Palace. Fairfax liked it because he felt safe within. No vampire would dare to sup on a daemon, and Tommy Fairfax was known for adding gaiety and spice to the otherwise quite dull environment. Tonight though, the bar area was quiet. The usual clientele of vampires and their human prey, most often fallen women, enticed in from the cold streets thinking they would turn a trick later but leaving with a dazed look instead, were spaced out in the narrow stall seating areas. Queen Mary had encouraged conformity to the Christmas celebrations; thus, the underground churches where Catholics had secretly worshipped were once again busy with Masses. The underground blood business had slowed.

He did not need to knock on the door; Fairfax was expecting him and it had been left ajar. Henry secured the dilapidated room before approaching his lover. Gangly legs crossed, supine on the pallet-bed with an amused look upon his face, Fairfax greeted him with, "You're late. I thought we were to dine? I don't suppose you missed the slop this place served up. Or, have you feasted too much already?"

"Sorry," Henry replied. "I was held up. But I'm here now."

He crossed the room and kissed Fairfax as thoroughly as was practical on the narrow bed. Drawing apart, Henry stared into his eyes, enjoying the frisson which jumped between them as he held him. "It has been too long since I have seen your freckles. They have, I believe, faded in my absence."

"Then we must travel together again soon," Fairfax whispered. "For I have news which will interest you, and provide us with the opportunity."

"Really? And does that news involve some of your shady spirits, perchance?" Henry winked.

Fairfax shook his head. "Surprisingly, no. It concerns your area of expertise instead."

"Intriguing," Henry said, running his hand over Fairfax's curls. His fingertips brushed away the salty roughness still coating them.

"I have come from Rochester," Fairfax said. "It seemed to me that there was an unusual amount of activity there for a January." He raised his eyebrows.

"Why should that be of concern?"

"Then this morning, as I passed the Tower of London, I saw a friend of the Queen being 'escorted' in. Simon Reynard," he said, in a solemn tone. "The Papal Ambassador recently arrived from Spain."

Henry frowned. That made no sense. Kent, a Protestant stronghold county, far away from the reach of Spain, and Reynard, a staunch Catholic who whispered of Philip to Mary. How were the two connected?

"And then," Fairfax continued. "One of our fae friends gave me a copy of this letter, from Devon." He drew out a folded sheet. Henry opened it carefully, still confused.

No sign of the promised ships from France as yet, although I am told a formal announcement is imminent of the betrothal. Much as though I protest to our Lords here of the danger of the Inquisition's arrival, and, I believe many yeomen are behind our cause, I fear that moving the date closer will not persuade them that the time for action is upon us. I beg your forgiveness, but the pressures are too great and I have no other recourse but to retreat and gather support from the Low Countries. My position is compromised, but I wish you luck with the endeavour.

Yours in the true faith,
Carew

Henry's mind whirled. Although he held no liking for Simon Reynard, the Spaniard was highly influential with Mary. Did they mean to force the famed Spanish Inquisition into the country along with Philip? That would draw a greater presence of vampires into the court, and perhaps England. He glanced at Fairfax and saw the fear in his eyes. These priests were notoriously vigilant, rumoured to be suspicious about anyone who did not conform to their strict doctrine.

Henry knew Mary was concerned about bringing the faithful of England back to Rome, but this action, when the balance was already tenuous after Edward's reforms, was likely to be a step too far, too soon. The Duke of Norfolk had been urging caution to her during the Privy Council meetings. He'd grumbled to Henry as much.

"What was happening in Rochester?" Henry asked.

"I've been asked to supply weapons along with this letter.

Manpower and any arms I can lay my hands upon. For Wyatt himself. Come with me?"

"Do you think they plan to rise?"

Fairfax nodded. "Rise against Philip, yes. If Carew has been posting sentries to watch for ships from France, it could be they have asked the French to stall his arrival."

"The question is," Henry said thoughtfully, "How much of this does Reynard know?"

"That matter I will leave to you to find out. You could come with me and ask Wyatt himself?" Fairfax teased.

Henry shook his head. "I cannot. I am still sure I can get closer to Mary. I just need the Duke to convince her to grant me an audience."

"Then," Fairfax looked at Henry through veiled eyelashes as he snuck an arm around his waist. "The bigger question is..."

"Does Mary know?"

Fairfax grinned. "She will no doubt find out. No, the bigger question is... can we both fit in this bed?"

Henry tipped his head back and roared with laughter as Fairfax pulled him down. Politics could wait.

*****

"I can do no more," Norfolk protested. The quill he held quivered, blotting the papers on the desk in front of them. He kept his head low as he blotted the mess, saying, "Constantly, she argues against us in Council. Her mind is set. The marriage treaty is arranged. Despite Gardiner's best efforts to dissuade her, he cannot deny a direct order from our sovereign. Parliament will ratify the Spaniard's position as her husband, and we must all just learn to live with it."

The old advisor sounded defeated, Henry realised. "Letting the Spanish run riot over our shores?"

The elderly man bristled. "I don't think it will come to that. Mary has been quite clear in some regards. Even though the schism will be absolved, which Archbishop Pope will see to shortly, she does not wish for Philip to reign above herself and over her country as King. They will co-rule." His gaze dared Henry to argue.

Henry did not prevent his scepticism infiltrating his voice. "And we know how that will work. If you would only let me..." Holding the

Duke's eyes, Henry slowly blinked.

A rapid knock at the door; it pushed open before either of them could invite whomever it was to enter. Henry stepped back quickly and picked up a book from the desk. These constant interruptions whenever Henry tried to influence the Duke were getting tiresome. Right now, Henry had a suspicion that court matters were on the cusp of changing and he would lose his chance. More than ever, he needed to gain access to Mary, but his master was frustratingly adept at dodging his gaze and evading proximity.

"Your Grace!" The servant looked flustered; his hands opening and closing as hastily as his eyes darted between Henry and his master. "The Queen has recalled the Privy. You must come quickly. She awaits your presence."

Drawing in a deep breath, the Duke glanced at Henry before reaching into the desk drawer to replace his heavy seal of office about his neck. "I doubt I will be the last to arrive, fear not." Henry stepped forward and helped him arrange the links so the weight was properly distributed over the velvet robe.

The servant shook his head. "I cannot find Lord Ambassador Reynard. Do you know where he might have gone? Her Majesty seemed especially concerned to find him, and yet no-one has seen him since yesterday."

"Your Grace," Henry said. "Let me escort you down."

"You'll have to wait here," the Duke said. "You know how she feels about servants loitering in the halls. Tidy away these papers, and lay out some fresh in case I have need to write any messages after this... meeting."

The servant bowed, then dashed out. The Duke closed and straightened his robe; the corridors of the palace were cold and Henry suspected he felt the chill more as his age advanced and heart failed. After the Duke plodded out, Henry stayed, gazing out of the window with a tightened jaw. Rain began to fall; great lashes hammering the panes, and below, the grey and dark Thames twisted onward through the city.

*****

Dinner, a venison stew which Henry had procured, had congealed by the late hour when Norfolk returned to his chamber. Henry bustled around the old man, helping him disrobe and settling him into the chair by the fire. The Duke, so exhausted by the evening's proceedings, was only able to grunt his thanks before closing his eyes and napping against the high seat back. Henry sat in the silence, poking the flames occasionally and wondered if he ought instead to have assisted him to bed.

But, after a while, the Duke roused and pointed for some wine. Henry poured then sat back whilst the warmth soothed the Duke into talking.

"What was the urgency?" Henry asked after a few moments of staring into the embers.

The Duke's hand began to shake a little, then he spoke. "We must pack," his voice wavered. "And raise men to march."

"Where?"

"South, we think."

To Rochester, Henry wondered, but kept quiet.

"It seems," the Duke continued, "Ambassador Reynard, who has been so steadfastly negotiating for his Prince to marry the Queen, has been in receipt of information regarding an uprising before his master even sets foot on our soil."

He looked wearily at Henry, and the 80-year-old's jaw set. "And I am to quell it before it becomes a problem."

"Do you know who is behind it?"

"There are several, it would appear. Carew, and of course Grey, Lady Jane's father. My godson, Wyatt apparently, the young upstart. It's not very clear. There may be others. But," he sighed, "as the only one who could raise an army on such short notice, and at this time of year, I am to trek down and be ready to defend our Queen in the first instance."

"But…"

"There is no use arguing, Henry. I have a duty to defend the Queen, and that is what I must do. What they think it will achieve, I do not know. Fetch my letter desk. There's urgent messages to dispatch, with unusual haste, if you please. We shall muster the men at Leadenhall, then depart to Gravesend."

Henry stood and fetched the box. As he placed it on the Duke's legs, he said, "Am I to accompany you? Or should I stay here and…"

"You must," the Duke snapped. "A man cannot expect to go to war without his servant by his side. Without me here, you can do nothing to further our cause." He sighed again as his aging brow furrowed. "It's just the betrayal, Fitz. From Wyatt especially. I expected this of Northumberland; the Queen shouldn't have been so lenient on him, and with his daughter still in the Tower. But really..."

The Duke swigged his wine. Sadness seeped into his voice as he said, "I know he holds strong opinions about the Spanish - as do we all - but if he truly is marching against the Queen's marriage, then he risks his neck once again. Foolish boy. After Boulogne though, Wyatt is no great admirer of Reynard, and yet, it is the same Reynard who tells us of this plot. The fox which first negotiated against England for her father, then charms his way to bring Spain to our very shores. I can see how Wyatt would distrust the Ambassador."

"Perhaps it is personal?" Henry said. The diplomatic ups and downs of the last decade would be irrelevant if an immortal sat on the throne, he thought. "Forgive me, but ought a man of your years be travelling to battle? The Queen asks too much of you."

The Duke shrugged. "With the little time I have left on this earth, I would spend it in defence of her reign and faith. This, I have always believed in. This much will carry me into the arms of St Peter when I go. You cannot follow me there when it is my time, but you have no place here in London without me. If you want to keep this Queen on her throne, there is no choice but for you to assist me in this matter. And that's the end of it."

Henry shook his head. The man's conviction did him credit. He was correct; Henry could not stay at court without his patronage. The only chance he had to return with it was to stand by his side and ensure the Duke returned so he could commend him to Mary when it was over. To battle it was then.

But was she the right Queen to fight for, he wondered. Would Elizabeth be a better prospect?

CHAPTER FORTY-ONE
Turn tails

Kent, 29th January, 1554

Hastily pulled from their lands, the militia were equipped with as many arms as Norfolk had been able to borrow at short notice from the Tower. Given the short time-scale before departure, his hope wavered that they would actually be competent enough to use the hodgepodge of weaponry they carried as they limped through mud and rain. Training in the pistols and rudimentary flintlock rifles whilst marching was scant at best, and supplies limited. His own, better prepared, men were evenly dispersed inside the column of some one thousand 'soldiers' to provide support, but the Duke relied upon Henry to report back on progress as he was preoccupied with staying atop his steed and keeping his blankets securely bundled around his thin body.

After a few days of quick marching through the pouring rain, Henry and the Duke understood why this partially trained army was losing heart for the fight ahead. They would take any opportunity to rest, laying small fires by the roadside to ward against the harsh January weather. Mid afternoon and the men were already grumbling to break for the night, when the Duke and Henry encountered the first hint of what lay ahead of them.

The Duke himself, with Henry by his side, led the convoy towards Rochester, when a few men, weaving from drink, blocked their way. In the gloom of the rain, Henry pulled up his horse and stomped over to where they clustered in the middle of the track.

"Move aside," He shouted. "Or we will plough on and you'll end up in a ditch."

"Dah't bovver!" One of the cocky lads shot back as the other two dissolved into drunken laughter. "He's cummin' 'ter stop the Spanish bastard."

Henry heard the clatter of weary men-at-arms behind laying down said arms and offloading packs to the sodden ground. His gaze quickly took in the attire of the vagabonds, muddied and torn in places. One bore a bandage around his forearm though, and the scent of blood oozing from it piqued his interest.

"Who is coming?" Henry asked. "Who dares to stop her Majesty's men? You are a disgrace. Who is your master?"

The men fell about again. "Who's yer master? Well, I tell yer, it won't be the likes of Spain. No, sir." Then one of them punched another jokily, but the recipient had the grace to look down when he saw Henry's chain-mail and tunic with Norfolk's crest embroidered across his chest.

Henry approached the fellow and grabbed him by his collar, then stared into his eyes. "I would like you to tell me whom you serve," he breathed. As he blinked, Henry felt the soldier's body relax and hold his gaze.

"I serve... I served," he corrected himself, "Lord Abergavenny."

"And why are you no longer in his service?"

The man mouthed as if he could not find the right words to say what was truly in his heart, yet his face fell with shame. "I... I could not. I heard what Mr Wyatt said to his men."

"Sir Thomas Wyatt?"

"Yes, the same. And he spake the truth, sir. He did. We - England - we don't want no Spaniard here. There's what's right for them, the Inquisition and the like, but it's not how we do things here. It's not right, see? I can't fight for a Queen who would let that happen."

Henry swallowed. "And the rest of Abergavenny's troops?"

"All joined Wyatt, or fled," one of the other fellows said, and laughed.

"But not you?" Henry's dark eyes turned to examine the face of the militia, the one with the wound. "How did you come by your injury?"

"There was a tussle, to be sure. Many of us local's fell, but Wyatt's army is now bolstered by Lord Southwell's men and a goodly number of my Lord Abergavenny's too." He shook his head.

"Why did you not accompany them?" Henry wondered, having already overheard the grumbles of the troops behind him. He put his hand on the hilt of his sword.

"It wer' a simple enough decision fer us. I'll not fight for the Spanish, nor will I fight against the Queen." He stood taller as the rain lashed down on his shoulders. "I am no traitor, but he, Wyatt, has the whole of Kent's support, I believe. He'll make his point. And I will not lose my life, nor risk my family's livelihood in defence of the indefensible. It's just not worth the price."

"I should run you all through," Henry said, dropping the man from his thrall. The drunkard collapsed into the puddle behind him. Striding over to the Duke, Henry's face hardened.

"What's the hold up?" Norfolk had slumped in his saddle.

"Seems there has already been an attempt to slow Wyatt's progress. But he marches on - with the men previously sent to intercept him."

The Duke's dull expression barely changed. "Traitors."

Henry nodded, then whispered, "We must not let this lot know what has happened." He turned to the Captain behind them. "Give the orders to continue. We need to cover more ground before we camp for the night. I'll ride ahead and find somewhere suitable."

The Captain saluted and Henry climbed back on his mare. It felt good to command, even if the larger battle of minds and hearts lay ahead of them.

*****

Henry led his horse slowly through the array of low tents and temporary shelters which littered the field. A few small fires smouldered, barely alight under canopies under which men huddled against the driving rain. He passed hunched figures, furtively squelching through the shadows towards the roadside without comment. When he reached the largest tent, he grunted to the guard perched on a log nearby. Warily examined, Henry was granted acceptance of his entry.

Inside, the candles by the Duke's pallet flickered as he dropped the flap of the tent. The Duke was curled up beneath blankets, shivering still despite his slumber. Henry stared down at his ashen face and debated whether to wake him. His thin shoulders did not need the weight of the news Henry had learned just hours earlier, yet learn it he must.

"Your Grace," Henry said, touching the warmth of the wooden spread. "I have returned."

The Duke roused, his eyes blinking groggily. In an exhausted voice, he whispered, "What news?"

"I found them."

"Wyatt?"

"Yes. He has far greater numbers than we anticipated, surrounding Rochester."

"And?"

"It is a battle, I fear, we would struggle to win."

The Duke pushed himself upright with a groan, pulling his blanket around him. "This is not the weather, nor the place for men to be fighting." His lips tightened to prevent them from wobbling. "But, we are here now, and fight we must."

"There's more," Henry said.

The Duke mumbled, "There always is."

"On my return, I saw some of ours packing up. I think we will have lost more by morning. This is not a cause the men believe in, your Grace. You must rally them if they are to give their lives for the Queen."

"It is intolerably hard," the Duke said, "to give voice to a rousing speech when one doesn't even have the mind for it oneself." He glanced up at Henry, and raised his eyebrow. "I march at the Queen's behest, but I am no orator. If I spoke of duty and honour, explained again the purpose of this mission, they would see that I do not believe in this cause. Better they go to their graves with a clean conscience that the Queen has ordered this madness and so it must be."

"Wyatt has the advantage of you then." Henry straightened. The Duke nodded and leant back down.

"Perhaps, offer them more pay?"

The Duke shook his head against the thin pillow. "It will not work. Besides, I do not have it."

"Then we have come all this way to just give up? You are the leader of this company. I did not take you for a coward."

"You forget yourself, Fitz." Norfolk's tone turned harsh. "I have come to show I will take the Queen's orders. You have come to see more of how battles are fought. The men have marched as we ordered, but you will learn, it might be preferable that they do not lose their lives in a futile battle when the war is yet to come. It weighs heavy on me to demand that they lay their souls on the line when what Wyatt might achieve is to actually prevent that war."

Henry considered the old man's words. "Better they should defect then? Turn coat and run?"

The Duke closed his eyes. "Better for their consciences, and mine, if they show the Queen that the country does not want a foreign monarch. Now leave me to rest. You can attest to the fact that we came, ready to put up a show of arms in accordance with the Queen's wishes. But, with the love of the saints above, it may be the will of God which has driven men to follow their consciences in defiance of her desire." He mumbled, already half falling into sleep, "Does Matthew not say, and the Queen oft quote, 'But if you do not forgive others their sins, your father will not forgive your sins.'"

Henry stared at his master as the stealth of sleep crept across his wrinkles. A leader he clearly was not. A leader would not accept excuses, but demand loyalty. Inspire it against even the odds. That their sovereign, even a female one with the might of the Church of Rome supporting her, desired they fight in her name, should have been enough to preach upon. And yet, the old man seemed now to waver, on the very eve of the battle, and look to seek Mary's forgiveness rather than place his faith and energy in her divine sense of the righteous path.

The Duke was not a bad man, nor, he had thought, only a weak and elderly one. But now, the affliction of age and possibly disfavour with Mary would stall his usefulness to Henry. Whilst Norfolk might quote the Bible in the vain hope of forgiveness from the Queen for his failure, Henry wasn't sure he could forgive the Duke for failing to push him forward earlier.

He clenched his teeth together, resolving there was little purpose in him continuing to stay under the Howard wing when he returned to London. A new disguise was needed, a revised strategy, and maybe a new Queen. He sighed, suddenly missing Fairfax as a confidante, then quietly left the tent. After the night's exertions, Henry needed to feed in order to think of his next steps with clarity, and the guard outside was still awake. He would not flee in the face of a battle, and he would be at full strength.

*****

By mid-morning, the herald dispatched at dawn to read the Queen's proclamation at Rochester Bridge, had returned with word that the crowd assembled there denied doing anything wrong. The column of soldiers, several hundred men shorter than yesterday, trudged through Kentish villages outlying Rochester with a grim determination to catch up to Wyatt's army. Progress along the winding country lanes was slower than ever; their wagons carrying the four double cannons frequently required pushes out of the deepening mud by surly faced yeomen-at-arms.

The delays inspired Henry to suggest to the Duke that a smaller troop of mounted soldiers could slow down Wyatt's progress if they could be dispatched to pick off stragglers and his supply wagons from the rear. But Norfolk insisted on keeping his troops together. No matter the consequence, and seemingly oblivious to the fact that with each passing Inn, more and more of his men disappeared. It was close to evenfall when they rounded a bend in the hedge-lined road, when the Duke abruptly pulled his steed up at a gate. He raised a hand to stop the column, then rose in his stirrups. He pointed down at a field which fell to the left of them.

"I said there were greater numbers, your Grace," Henry said quietly, but even he was astonished at how many had joined the rebellion. Below, several thousand men sat in rough lines on the opposite rise. Their ranks had swelled; Henry realised hundreds must have been welcomed into neighbouring barns, housed in sympathetic manors perhaps, for their numbers were nearly double what he had estimated in the darkness of last night. With his keen eyesight, Henry could tell the army awaiting their arrival were armed and waiting only for the signal to attack. He could hear their casual laughter and quiet conversation whilst pikes and pitchforks were sharpened.

Behind the lines of foot soldiers, hundreds of mounted fighters let their horses graze. Well rested and dressed in a mishmash of livery, armour, or leather-wear, Henry's heart sank. Although he spotted few noblemen, most other levels of society had come together to join the cause against the Queen's marriage. Wyatt had picked his spot, and as an experienced soldier would, taken advantage of the cover of a wood behind them. Who knew how many more were hidden in there?

Henry and the Duke looked down the lane - bedraggled, dripping weariness shuffled as they waited, rippling like a brown eel in the mud. One or two took the opportunity to relieve themselves in the hedges. It struck Henry once again, there was little sense of a shared purpose about this bunch. He knew that were they to attack right now, even if they were matched in numbers instead of three-fold more with Wyatt, they would surely lose. Was the Duke correct? Was it better to save the fight for the inevitable war? Or was it better to tackle the threat in front of them and hope for a miracle?

Henry met the Duke's eyes. "We could lead them into this field," he said. "Now would be the time for you to invoke the great fighting spirit of my father and his father before him, if you cannot do it for Mary's sake alone. Tell them again why they fight. Of whom they fight for. If you have the guts for it, that is. Or you could continue down this road and head towards London behind them, and pray God she forgives your cowardice."

Norfolk looked down at his horse's mane, absently fiddling with the reins. "I do wonder at you sometimes, Henry. I thought, with the benefit of sacrificing your human life in order that you might better serve our faith and our country, you would retain some semblance of humanity. I wonder that instead you lost any compassion you may have had? Any sense of understanding that these men might surprise you. Be willing to give their lives in return for their immortal souls being granted passage to the afterlife, with a clear conscience that they may give it in service to the ordained sovereign. I believe they will, and that is enough for me to give the order that they should fight for the Queen. No speech should be necessary - if they believe in their sovereign and faith. Open the gate." He commanded Captain Bret, and pulled his horse to the side.

As the army picked up their packs and filed into the boggy meadow amongst the cows, Henry pulled his mare behind Norfolk's and seethed quietly. He kept his head down, as was his custom when playing the part of loyal servant, but his jaw soon ached from holding it so firmly shut.

Leaving the supply wagons to lumber through after them, Henry stayed behind the Duke as they trotted over to where their rag-tag army clustered in the field. Packs dropped, and weapons readied, but the prevailing sense of unease remained. The militia glanced amongst each other, silently spreading fear and discord. Norfolk, clutching onto the pommel of his saddle, slowly cantered up and down as a long row of soldiers arranged themselves.

Henry could only watch as the opposite side stood. A deadly row of pikes swung under the arms of the front line. The smell of piss wafted over towards him as he waited behind their men for Norfolk to give the command to attack. It was clear he had no intention of rousing the army. The Duke's face was pale with tension as he remained alert, not quite as straight in the saddle as he ought to be, but already with a sense of defeat. Henry glared at him, questioning how a leader - a commander - could send other men into battle without giving them hope that their cause was just. Was he right? Did these men believe enough to obey the Queen's orders without question? Did the Duke really believe that their sacrifice was guaranteed to allow them to enter the kingdom of heaven should they die? Could he be so naïve?

Wyatt's men began their advance. A raft of arrows, just an opening gambit, flew into the clods of earth. A few landed only metres shy of the stretch of militia. The Duke remained, his hand held in the air, holding the troops steady. Henry looked along the line, then back to Wyatt's men, who marched steadily towards them.

Captain Bret, the commander of the London militia in the centre of the front row, stepped forwards. Henry thought this might be the signal, for he drew out his sword. Then, the Captain wheeled his steed around and faced their army. Henry saw his face tighten with anger.

"Masters!" Bret cried, and Henry's heart gladdened. Here perhaps was a man willing to inspire the troops.

"We go about to fight against our native countrymen of England and our friends in a quarrel, unrightful and partly wicked. For *they*," and he pointed at the other side of the field, where Wyatt's troops had begun to shout obscenities across. "Consider the great and manifold miseries which are like to fall upon us *if* we shall be under the rule of the proud Spaniards or strangers. They are here assembled to make resistance of the coming in of him, or his favourers."

Henry's jaw dropped. He glanced at the Duke, whose head drooped and the hand he held up had lowered.

"And for that we know right well," the Captain continued, all attention now being paid to him. "That if we should be under their subjection, they would, as slaves and villains, spoil us of our goods and lands. Ravish our wives before our faces, and deflower our daughters in our presence!" Bret grimaced, then waved his sword. "For the avoidance of so great mischiefs and inconveniences likely to alight not only upon themselves, but on every one of us and the whole realm, they have taken upon themselves now - in time before his coming - this enterprise."

Henry started to urge his horse forward, of the singular intention to interrupt the dreaded words he felt sure were coming. But, before he could make an impression on the Captain, Bret's voice carried clear across the field. "I think no English heart ought to say, much less by fighting, withstand them. Wherefore, I, and these here will not spend our blood in the quarrel of this worthy officer - Mister Wyatt, and other gentlemen here assembled."

The men down the rows looked at each other, then a few voices cried out, "A Wyatt! A Wyatt!"

Without warning, a man dashed past Henry's horse, which reared slightly with surprise. "Stop!" Henry shouted. "Get back in line!"

But the man kept running. Then, more and more of their line dropped their weapons and ran - either back to the road behind, or, to join the army before them.

Henry stood in his stirrups, to better see the extent of the disaster as, like rampaging cattle, the army scattered along the field. He watched the Captain, sword now by his side, turn his horse, and kick it on down the slope towards Wyatt's troops. Henry turned around in his saddle and looked along the hedgerow. Desperate men pressed through the thickets, or straddled the top, helping each other to return to the lane behind.

The Duke sat motionless, his face blank whilst watching the army he had marched disintegrate. Arrows stopped raining down, the air filled instead with cries of "I surrender!" and "Shift your arse," as men pushed through the hedges and gate to escape. The chaotic sight bewildered Henry, who shook his head as the laughter from Wyatt's army reached his ears. Henry snorted in disgust.

A trumpet hooted, echoing above the shouts and scramble; Henry wheeled his horse back around to see what it signalled. A single horseman galloped through the troops towards the middle of the field then reined up. Henry didn't recognise him, yet he held himself tall in the saddle with the air of a commander. It had to be Wyatt himself.

"So many as will come and tarry with us shall be welcome. And so many as will depart - good leave have they," he said, beaming at the weary and still confused troops which had remained on Norfolks' side of the field.

Hearing Wyatt's acceptance of them into his number prompted hundreds of militia, dithering and yet to flee the field, to gather their weapons back up. Waving grubby handkerchiefs in the air, they staggered, without many glancing back in regret, towards the thousands on the other side.

Henry stared at the Duke, probably the only person on the field not currently moving. With a sigh, he turned and trotted towards him. He wondered if this was what the wise old man had intended all along? Few lives were lost, yet his loyalty to the Queen would have been proven by virtue of trying. More than half of their army were being welcomed into the ranks of Wyatt's men. Many more of the ones who had made it to the road would probably join them, Henry thought, especially after the persuasive argument made by Captain Bret.

"Are they traitors?" The Duke asked, glancing at Henry as he turned his horse to watch as well. "Or have they listened to the overriding pressure of their consciences?"

"You knew they would defect?"

The Duke's mouth twitched up. "It is the nature of man to follow the better, more persuasive leader. And today, that was Wyatt, and the Captain of course. This cause holds the promise of success, whereas my orders never really did. You can pay a man all the money you possess, but ultimately, it comes down to faith, my boy. If an army does not believe its cause is just and right, then it will not fight with its heart." He pulled on his reins and kicked his horse on. "And, I fear I also lose the heart for this never-ending battle."

"You are tired, your Grace. The Queen will surely be merciful."

Norfolk nodded, not meeting Henry's disappointment. "I will beg for her leave to retire to my estates. I have done what I can to prevent this marriage, but I can no longer put off tending to my soul. I must pray for its absolution."

Henry followed the Duke, determined to eke out as much information about Elizabeth as he could on the way back to London. It served him no purpose to withdraw to the country with the Duke when all influence was in the city.

CHAPTER FORTY-TWO

For it is wrytte: He shal geue his angels charge ouer thee, to kepe thee

Beesworth, 5th February 1554

Joshua was completing the most ordinary of household tasks, stacking the logs he had just chopped, when the day became extraordinary. First one kestrel, followed seconds later by another, landed on the fence enclosing the yard beneath the hillock. He approached, cautiously, for the birds had a tendency to nip the wrong recipient of their messages, and stretched out his gloved hand. The birds eyed him haughtily, and for a moment, Joshua thought perhaps he ought to wait for Lady Hanley instead, as they seemed to regard him with such disdain.

Eventually, after cocking its head and staring him up and down with black beady eyes, the larger of the pair hopped onto his glove. He was able to untie the wrapping from its leg only when the bird hopped onto his shoulder and peered at his back, nipping the tops of his wings as if it still wasn't certain it had found the correct recipient. Having duly passed muster, he then unrolled the note within the neatly cut thin leather. Joshua's heart sank. In rough and poorly written Latin, it read:

I intercepted this letter when it arrived but I was unable to access the carrier, so I believe it to be for you. In the hope that you can make sense of this, at least. From a realm which is much altered by your absences,

Issam

He moved his hand to the fence so that the bird could step onto its perch and be replaced by the other one, who repeated the same examination of his wings. The smaller kestrel felt curiously heavier than the first; the reason for which became apparent when he saw a small pouch nestling between its wings. First, he pulled off the wrapping around the bird's leg.

Aioffe's handwriting! He immediately brought the scrap of paper to his nose and inhaled. Closing his eyes, the image of her which was always clear in his mind, coloured as he smelled her unique scent. But there was something else - a piquant sense of fear - within the letter. Instinctively, he reached out with his mind, hoping as always for the touch of her to ease his own worry. A tendril of love, tinged with loneliness answered his heart's call.

Before even reading her words, Joshua's heart sped, acknowledging his surprise at the caress of her. So great a distance, and yet suddenly, and having tried many times over the last months before to reach her in this way yet sensing nothing, to feel that she was thinking about him too at that very moment filled him with hope. No less hope also surely lay in the contents of this message, he thought, uncurling it again to read.

My morning star, it is a revelation that five through to eleven of us suffer, although Luke brings forth the tenth only. No arrow can pierce us as before, and yet I must repeat the exercise. You are bid to stay away, for our friend is most gravely ill. The required medicine for our great matter is too difficult to find.

Annabella

Although written in English, the true message was oblique. Why would she need to hide what she said? Joshua frowned. Underneath the wording ran a succession of numbers and letters, were they also a code? That Aioffe referenced Bible quotes was not unusual in itself, for she knew he would recall the references, and her use of the name she last used in England would allude to that time, yet the figures beneath confused him. He would need to find a Bible to see if the sequence made any sense.

The bird shook its back, jolting Joshua into remembering the second parcel. Carefully, his fingers worked at the knots binding the tiny knapsack to its shoulders. Once freed, the kestrel stretched its wings. Joshua smiled as he fancied he heard the bird sigh with relief, and he thanked it with a gentle stroke along its back before lifting it up so it could reclaim freedom once more.

He sniffed the weighted pouch, hoping to smell his wife, but instead, Spenser's odour hit him in the nostrils. Sweat, salt and beechwood mingled with, again, notes of recent fear. Without tarrying, he ran up the hillside to find Nemis.

*****

"Spenser's astro-something!" Nemis said, as soon as she opened the pouch and saw the golden globe. Her eyes grew bright with tears as her fingers reached in and caressed its warm shine. Extracting it, the gift sat between them on the kitchen table and they stared at it longingly. "He uses it to find his way home and then back. To me. Why do you have it?" She looked wildly at him, panicking.

"I believe they are alive," Joshua was quick to reassure her. "I felt Aioffe, just now."

"Can you tell if she is with Spenser still? Are they safe?"

"No, and… I don't know." Joshua pushed forward the scrap with the cryptic message on, watching her with wide eyes as she read. When he saw her frown, he placed his hand over hers, saying, "We must find a Bible. I am sure there is more to this than first appears."

"Obviously it's a code," Nemis said, almost scornfully. "And I presume she alludes to you when she calls you 'morning star'?"

Joshua nodded. "She once claimed she made an angel, and well, it stuck. We used to pretend that's what we were if anyone ever saw us. The wings…"

Nemis's lips tightened. "I suppose, but why didn't Spenser write too?"

"I think that's who she means by 'our friend is most gravely ill'"

She paled, then put a trembling hand to her lips. Joshua squeezed her fingers. "She bids me not to come, so it cannot be too serious, I'm sure."

He could not tell her of how rejected he felt. Even in this testing time for her, she didn't need him. Didn't want him to come. To send a vague message like this - it was not like the Aioffe he knew. He swallowed, then said, "As for the rest of it, come with me to the Church, we can look in the Bible there. I'm sure she wouldn't have alluded to Revelations or Luke without context, and I want to be sure on the wording, rather than rely on memory."

Nemis nodded.

"Mark is with Mary still?" He asked. Lady Hanley was besotted with Nemis's child, which wasn't without its complications, but the boy's return of her affection had emboldened her to reclaim her position in the town.

"Yes, they were going into Beesworth. He was looking forward to the market and being her errand boy."

"Well then, if we pass them on the road we can tell them we are just going to market also."

"But won't you be recognised? It's not safe for you; we agreed." Nemis said, frowning. Apart from night-time hunting excursions, he had stayed safely within the grounds and house for the last few months. His previous foray into life in Beesworth had ended abruptly, and he could ill-afford questions about why he had not aged in two decades should he be noticed on roads or in shops or church. As there were no other staff at Hanley House, he had taken on all the manual labouring required to keep the household running, as well as to occupy his mind.

Joshua glanced down at his tatty shirt and loose trousers. "I could borrow some of Lord Hanley's clothes again. No-one would dare to question a gentleman." Nemis still appeared unsure, but before she could object, he pocketed the note and left her in the kitchen.

*****

The empty parish church in Beesworth had embraced the return of Catholic mass, it seemed to Joshua, with wide, welcoming arms. A new, rich green altar cloth awaited the chalice and other articles of the Eucharist mass. Whitewashed walls shone with a refracted rainbow as the sun streamed in through their freshly wiped panes, lending colour once again to the plain. The stained glass he had known before had been replaced during Dissolution, yet the rood screen remained - the dark, carved wood burnished by devotion, as if the labour of waxing and polishing would reaffirm the glory of the restoration of a cherished faith.

Joshua sighed as his soul, parched of the ornament and ritual, sang for the comforts of his church when he walked through the familiar doors. Inhaling deeply, remnants of the purifier's incense evoked memories of the last time he had been here. How he had denied himself, and dithered about the fate of his soul having turned fae, for so long. Then, during the trials of his quest to find Aioffe, he had circled back to belief. He was not sorry Queen Mary had brought about a reversal of the wave of plain Protestantism, but in that moment, and finding himself caught between faith systems, he fervently hoped that some sort of balance could be struck. One where all could practise their own manner of worship without fear of retribution.

Joshua circled, gazing upward to the vaulted wooden ceiling, and felt strangely as comfortable here as he did in silent worship or the noise of the blessing ceremony in Naturae. He smiled as he saw the new addition of subtle, carved and painted Tudor roses to the ends of the pews, and wondered how much the royals really understood their insistence on the divine right to rule, as much as he knew it to be for fae-kind. He had seen the power of belief in the actions of his Queen, and realised now how much evidence of communal faeth had reinforced his own multi-faceted faith.

Despite all the changes to simplify the service which Mary had ordered undone, chained to the pulpit still remained the official copy of the Coverable bible. That every man should have access to holy words in print was a great relief to Joshua, and he sent up a prayer of gratitude to King Edward for his decree in placing the English translation in every church across the land. Nemis followed suit as he knelt before the altar and crossed himself. With a bowed head, he gave thanks for the message from Aioffe and asked for guidance in deciphering his wife's intentions. Nemis remained deep in personal prayer when he finally approached the pulpit.

When open, the double pages barely filled a quarter of the resting ledge. Joshua skipped through to Revelation, then read the passages which he thought Aioffe was referring to. A shudder ran through him; the book of Revelation he had always found chilling. This section spoke of the book of seven seals, the Book of Judgement, which no man was worthy to open. Although he knew well that Revelation discussed terrifying portents, he tried not to think of the wider context, and focussed instead on the specific verses which she had referenced.

He read the verses, his eyes swimming when he reached the sentence about the lamb, which he knew in the Bible stood for Christ:

'And I behelde, & lo, in the myddes of the seate, and of ye foure beastes, and in the myddes of ye elders, stode a lambe as though he had bene kylled.'

A gasp escaped his lips. Who was the sacrificial lamb Aioffe meant? Herself or Spenser? Blood and sacrifice; Christ had given his life to redeem others. If Aioffe was the lamb, it didn't matter if she was worthy or not, she would still be dead. And, fae do not have an afterlife.

He read on, the passage growing more optimistic as the lamb proved worthy of opening the book, but then his heart skipped a beat.

'And I behelde, and I herd the voyce of many angilles aboute the trone, and aboute the beestes and ye elders, and I herde thousand thousandes,'

A thousand, thousand angels - or fae? Around a throne- it could only refer to the Queen of the Fae on the continent, for Naturae did not have thousands of people. And 'suffer' Aioffe said. No-one in Naturae suffered. If the angels were fae, did the European fae suffer?

He felt Nemis's presence at his side, and looked over to her, trying to quell his quickening heartbeat. He pointed to the passage and swallowed hard as she read in her head.

"And Luke?" She said, keeping her voice calm as if they were an ordinary couple, just browsing a Bible. She projected courage, and he admired her strength, for he felt himself already weaker. They flicked through the pages until his fingers found the relevant passage.

'For it is wrytte: He shal geue his angels charge ouer thee, to kepe thee.'

The section talked of the temptation of Christ, where the devil had kept him for forty days, challenging Jesus to prove he was the son of God by jumping from the pinnacle of a temple. The Devil's argument was that God would send his angels to guard him, lest he fall to his death. But Joshua read the passage with fresh eyes, as Aioffe had specified only that line. *To give his angels charge over thee, to keep thee.*

She was being kept.

Aioffe was being held as a prisoner.

"Thousands of fae, and she is being kept under guard. Do you agree?" His fingers found Nemis's cold ones resting on the text. She nodded, not taking her eyes from the pages.

"But Jesus didn't give in to temptation, did he?" She murmured, squeezing his hand back. "She is resisting, I think. But at what cost?"

Joshua pulled the note out and they sat on the pews, re-reading it in the silence.

"No arrow can pierce us as before and yet I must repeat the exercise," Joshua quoted. "That's definitely an allusion to my re-birth. I was dying from an arrow wound, and she and I shared blood. She is being asked to do it again? With someone else?"

"Who?"

Joshua shrugged. "We always believed the magic in my creation was down to love - love, tears and her blood. Do you think... she loves another?"

Nemis shook her head, "Absolutely not." She placed her hand on his knee. "Whatever troubles you have lately suffered, she has never stopped loving you. I know that, and I just wish you did."

Joshua's eyes flooded with the hopelessness he had tried for so many months to hold back. The very real possibility that he would never again see his wife, his one love, smacked him afresh. He deeply wished he had Nemis's faith in their union. All evidence seemed before to point to the contrary.

And yet, she had written to him, in her hour of need. Then, he read in his head, 'and yet I must repeat the exercise.' She 'must' create another fae like him? Was she intending to move on from their marriage in order to do that? Love another? Joshua's head swam, he felt his breath pull ragged.

"I do think," Nemis pulled his mind back to the message itself, "She means Spenser when she says 'our friend is most gravely ill' as we know of no other friends there. Wherever *there* is."

"What do you think the last line means?" Joshua asked, trying to focus.

"Great matter - isn't that what they called King Henry's attempts to rid himself of Queen Katherine? So that he could marry Anne Boleyn?"

Joshua's lips tightened. 'The required medicine for our great matter is too difficult to find,' he read aloud from the note.

"Medicine comes from plants, herbs and the like," Nemis said, trying to be helpful and ignoring his shaking hand. He looked at her with more cheerful eyes.

"She can't find the vines!"

Nemis's nose wrinkled. "I don't understand. Medicine from vines?"

Smiling now, Joshua said, "Her... *our*, great matter isn't a divorce. It's creating an heir. That was why Henry VIII wanted his freedom, so Anne Boleyn could bear him a successor. Aioffe needs a royal vine, she believes, to make an heir for Naturae. Required medicine – Aioffe means for the cure."

"But she can't find them?"

"That's what I think. That was her reason for going." Joshua nodded and stood. His head cleared when the pieces continued to fall into place. His heartbeat calmed as he made a decision. His own plan was needed.

"I think we have to look at each bit of this as a separate statement. Facts. A list, if you will. To update me, and ask for my help." He flapped the paper. "Firstly, there are lots of fae where she is - thousands upon thousands and I believe she is the sacrificial lamb here. Revelations. The book of judgement. She is the only one worthy, or capable, of saving everyone who believes, but, at the cost of her life. She has to be sacrificed. Second, she is under guard - Luke four, ten - he will command his angels to guard her, keep her. Though she is being tempted, as well as guarded, she is strong enough in her belief that it doesn't need testing. Then she, and this is the hardest part for me to talk of apart from the fact that she bids me to stay away, but she must produce another fae like me. Perhaps that is also why she is being kept?"

He paused, drawing in a deep breath and looked at Nemis with an earnest expression. Despite the danger he had inferred from Aioffe's news, in the church, he chose to focus on hope.

"'My morning star.' *My.* I will always be hers, and she knows that. She made me, I cannot be anyone else's, even if she wanted me to be. I am forever her original 'angel'. I do not want to, cannot even, believe that she would just write to tell me she wanted to marry another, or make another fae from a human." He chuckled and threw his hands up. "Who writes a letter like that? No, she wouldn't use code to tell me to leave her. She's far more honourable than that. She's also cleverer than that, but I always knew that of her. Brave and clever. She would, despite all of our problems, tell me to my face."

Nemis looked hesitant. "But, what about, 'You are bid to stay away'? Why doesn't she want you to come? Is she trying to protect you from whatever ails my husband? Why is she not ill also?"

He shook his head, pride and love shining from his eyes, alongside the conviction that he was finally back in the same mindset as Aioffe. "The thing of it is, I have never done her bidding and she knows that. Now I read it again, it is not her saying it, but perhaps someone else is? 'You are bid to stay away' doesn't mean that *she* doesn't want me to come, but that someone else doesn't want me to come to her. She's not saying, don't come." He smiled with relief; the rejection he felt earlier eased slightly.

"Leaving to one side the fact that my husband is apparently 'gravely ill,' I don't understand why this sentence is not coded like the others?"

"I agree, and I am sorry for the news, but maybe this is the clearest part of the message, so there can be no mistake made. No quibble about it's intent." He held open the door and ushered her through into the spring afternoon sunshine. Then he continued, the earlier momentum of his theory building. "There is no reason to put that sentence in code. Were the letter to fall into the wrong hands, it's simplicity binds the rest of the surface message together. It makes it perfectly explainable. Innocent. To a casual observer, the note looks like a letter updating a family member or friend about an illness, does it not?"

Nemis's head dipped, and he didn't want to see the tear flowing down her cheek, but there were people milling around the square still so he could do nothing to comfort her without drawing attention to themselves. Sideways glances as they crossed the cobbles confirmed - townsfolk were noticing them. Perhaps it was the oddity of a gentleman accompanying a pregnant and slightly dishevelled woman whose skin had paled to a worrying degree, but he distinctly sensed their curious eyes on them. Strangers. Unwelcome.

He walked by her side instead, as she pulled her cape around her as they turned out of the square and headed out of town. They ambled in silent contemplation, heads lowered to avoid their faces being glanced upon, until they reached the outskirts where the paved roads deteriorated into the muddy track.

Then, alone between the open spaces of the fields, Joshua asked, "But, if I go to her, despite whomever is bidding me not to, what to do when I am there? What if, she is trying to love again with this other? And, where *is* she?"

"She is not asking for your help, Joshua. That's not to say she doesn't need you, but she is not asking so much as giving you the information to make your own decision about whether to go. Of course she wants you to fight for her." She threw her hands in the air. "Men!"

Then Nemis stopped ambling along and crouched over, groaning. "Well, clearly I cannot travel anywhere, so I can't help with what you should do. Only get there and you'll think of something! I can barely walk up the stairs without puffing and panting, so there's no point arguing about me coming as well." Her hands rounded her belly, swollen with child after over half a year of pregnancy. "And you are no use to anyone here, moping around worrying. Go, find my husband and bring him back to his wife and child. Preferably before the next one arrives!"

"Have I been that awful?" Joshua said, "I didn't realise." He didn't feel rejected at all, liberated rather.

Nemis turned and sniffed as she walked onwards. The time for their evening meal drew close and all this exercise surely would make her hungry, Joshua realised. Worry, pregnancy and hunger doth a snippy witch make.

"As for where she is," she said, "I think you'll need a navigator's help. Those numbers at the bottom look like coordinates. I once saw

Fairfax jotting a similar formation down once before, when we were at sea."

Joshua half smiled. "And he might know how to use the astro-something."

"God alone knows where he is now though."

"I may have an answer to that," Joshua said. "It could take some time, but, better to know where they are, if those numbers are co-ordinates, before I set off blindly. I can then go on from meeting Fairfax, wherever he is, straight to where Aioffe and Spenser are." As soon as he spoke, he started worrying afresh. How much time did his wife and friend have, before it was too late? He didn't even know when she had sent the message, for that matter.

"As long as you avoid that vampire pal of his," Nemis grumbled, interrupting his rising panic with her own fears. "The further away we are from the dark heir, the better."

"Do you still believe he is the one you saw in your visions?"

"Aye," she said. "And the more time passes, the more certain I grow. He will be trouble. He is the darkness. But for which monarch, I cannot tell. As long as he's far away from me and mine, I don't rightly care."

Joshua watched a slight tremor spread through her back. Taking her arm in his, he propelled them forwards. However deserted this track currently was, it was still too great a risk for her should she be overcome by a fit. They were no longer safely in Naturae, and Joshua had just been reminded of how precarious it was to be 'different' in Beesworth.

CHAPTER FORTY-THREE

Falling blades

Naturae, 12th February, 1554

"I don't see the point in these meetings any more," Lyrus spat out, glaring at the seated Council. "If you aren't going to heed to what I have to say, then the solution is very clear. I am the most senior here, and the only royal you have left." He leant against the wood and heaved himself upright.

"Lord Lyrus..." Thane protested, but it would do no good, he knew. This same scene had played itself out every time he had tried to pull them around the table to discuss the state of Naturae, and each time, Lyrus poisoned the gathering with his contempt.

"I've heard enough. Captain, from this moment onwards, you will instruct the army to cease patrolling the outer edges of the island, but be visible and ready to intervene here, in the citadel. We should not fear invaders at this moment - we have the mist to keep us hidden, but our own people need to be kept in order. They must be fit for when the war comes."

Thane looked across the table at Uffer before facing Lyrus. "My Lord, that is not a course of action which will achieve anything but provoke further violence and unrest."

Lyrus's eyes narrowed. "That is precisely why I order this, but I shouldn't need to explain myself to you. I won't. The workers must know who is in charge now. They ought to be grateful that a true Prince of the royal line is stepping in to ensure their safety. They cannot do their jobs if they are constantly plotting between themselves. Don't think I can't see them, whispering away. The soldiers will make sure they are kept in line, doing what they should without being distracted."

Shaking his head, Thane nudged Uffer's feet under the table. Of all the times, he needed the old man to join him now in standing up to this bully who had asserted control of the Council after Aioffe and Joshua had disappeared. The fae workers no longer listened to him, ever since the food supply had dried up. Everyone had returned to the old days of scavenging in the seas, when they had time. The live animal supplies, carefully nurtured and bred, long since devoured by the army at Lyrus's suggestion.

Uffer only glanced at Thane from heavy brows. The set of his mouth downcast, greying like the rest of his features as he resumed studying the polished tabletop.

"Furthermore," Lyrus continued, "it is now a requirement for all fae workers, regardless of their main jobs, to attend daily fight practice sessions. Captain, I will organise a rota for weapons training which you will deliver. All workers must be readied to defend our shores and this will remind them of their duty. Every fae should be able to carry and use a weapon when the need arises." He spread his arms out as if calling them to his side. "After all, they should be proud to serve their realm, as all soldiers are."

Uffer said, under his breath, "First you want them to work, then to train. You want them to be peaceful, then you arm them." His voice grew in resolution, and he looked up at Lyrus. "You are a fool to think you can control hungry men and women. Even more so if you give them the weapons to fight with."

A sneer spread over Lyrus's face. "A fool? You dare to call me a fool?"

"You are a fool," Uffer said, louder now. "A fool who assumes that just because he says he is in command means he is. A fool who thinks so highly of himself that he does not see the problems at his feet." Uffer's face flushed, and he banged his fist on the table. "Our Queen would be horrified if she could hear you now. Her own brother, demanding respect when he has done nothing to deserve it." He pointed at Thane, then circled the table to the other worker fae representatives, squirming in their seats. "These people have kept this realm. Grown it. They know it better than anyone, and yet you assume that you know better. You are a fool!"

Red-faced, Lyrus beckoned with his crooked arm. "Guards, arrest *Lord* Anaxis. He dares to insult a royal. He dares to challenge my right to restore order to the realm." Lyrus drew in a deep breath and pulled himself upright. "This 'council' is a failure. My sister knew it, and left. Fled in the night like a coward. Even your beloved half-Prince Joshua dared not stay to fix your problem. Weakling." His lip curled. "You are all to blame for the state Naturae is in, and I will not allow it to disintegrate further. There will be no more pointless meetings. No more discussion. You will take instruction from me and me alone, from now on. Enough pretending that collaboration works. It doesn't. You will answer only to me."

He turned to face Uffer, who had been flanked by two stony faced guards. "An example is needed." Lyrus turned and walked towards the edge of the dais. Thane found he could not meet anyone's eyes as Lyrus announced, "Later, at high sun, I will proclaim my decision on what is to be done with you. I will not tolerate treachery."

*****

London

"Wyatt yielded voluntarily?" Henry could not keep the incredulity from his voice.

"Aye," Fairfax replied. "It was said he offered to yield only to a gentleman, who then could beg on his behalf to the Queen in the hopes of her mercy. I think the fight just went out of him."

Henry nodded. "There were so many of them, and feeding an army is hard enough work when you have adequate, organised supplies. He did well to get as far as he did without people giving up due to hunger."

"There was still a battle, but it sounds like more of a scuffle than a heart-felt fight." Fairfax leant over Henry's chest and picked up his wine glass. "At least you made it back in one piece."

Henry's lips tightened. "Not all will. The Duke has retired to

Kenninghall. I fear his heart will not last long. He was foolish to even take on the task at his age. And now, Wyatt will hang, and all those who supported him will never see their loved ones into old age."

"Ah, ageing. Dying. It will come to most of us. Perhaps it is better to die young and passionate about what you stand for? But in the meantime, let's live in the present and not think about those who will avoid age's deadly embrace!" Fairfax smiled, then bent down to kiss him. Henry squirmed away.

"You jest, but human lives are short. Even yours will be - you shouldn't be so flippant." He glanced into Fairfax's vivid eyes, reaching up his fingers to trace the freckles on his jawline. "And what will I do then? How could I watch that happen to you?"

Fairfax's cheeks and sides of his eyes creased. "All the more reason to enjoy the moment, I'd say."

Henry chuckled. These stolen times with Fairfax were what he lived for right now, but he knew it wasn't enough for him.

"I can't stay," Henry said, with great reluctance. "The watch on the Tower will change soon, and I need to learn what their routine is. My cousin, Lady Jane Grey, still lives there, and if I'm right, Mary will be persuaded that my sister Elizabeth is a part of Wyatt's plot, and may yet join her."

Avoiding Fairfax's disappointed look, Henry rolled himself up from the sheets and began to dress.

"Already you think like a statesman, working out the plots within plots." Fairfax said. "My carefree Henry doth leave..."

"I was never carefree," Henry said, glancing back at his lover. "You knew this. I am destined to rule, and that carries all the weight of responsibility I could wish for. It is a burden I will carry."

"Alone?" The faux mournfulness of Fairfax's voice warmed Henry to the core.

Henry crossed the room and grasped Fairfax's shoulder. "With you in my heart, I am never alone. I need never hide who I am." He sighed, then planted a kiss on his lips. "But, until I can rule, outwardly I am alone."

Exchanging smiles as he left, Henry worried this time, he had tarried too long. He urged speed into his long legs to carry him to the walls of the Tower within the hour.

*****

Outside the Tower's gateway, a crowd had gathered, to Henry's surprise. He dithered in their midst, if only for their gossip. As he listened to their muttering about the fate of Lady Jane, his brows furrowed.

"They say she's next," a washerwoman whispered to another close to her. "That cart were 'er husband. Left her with his head to look at when she goes!"

"Just awful, that poor girl."

"'Course, I fink she's right, but it is sad. A slip like her, all pious-like. You have to watch the quiet ones, don'cha? You can never be too sure, can ya, what they're plotting' next? Maybes she did encourage that Wyatt. No, Queen Mary has to be sure and get rid of her. That Tower, it's as leaky as my ol' tub!"

The women burst into peals of laughter. Henry moved away, towards the gate which was firmly bolted closed. His eyelids fell as he listened carefully within. Boards creaked, and he imagined a scaffold. He started when a bell tolled from the chapel inside. But it was not meting out the time, he knew now.

At the noise, the hordes fell silent. With them, Henry strained to hear what was going on inside the thick walls. A regular march of soldiers feet on cobbles rounded close by then petered out, their uniforms' clinking then stopped, weapons placed against shoulders with a slap. Heels snapped together, then a hush. Henry picked out the sorrowful sounds of women sobbing, lamenting he imagined, into laced handkerchiefs to stifle their wails. After a few moments, a shuffle of feet on roughened wood. Henry was probably alone in those outside the walls to hear the thin but clear voice speak across the green inside.

"Good people, I am come hither to die, and by law I am condemned to the same. The fact of my ascension against the Queen's highness was unlawful, and the consenting thereunto by myself. But touching the procurement and desire thereof by myself, or on my behalf, I do wash my hands of. In innocence. Before God and the face of you, good Christian people, this day."

There was a pause, and Henry glanced about the crowd. Many had their heads bowed, but on some, he noticed the glee on their faces shining through. He felt disgusted, shamed inside to be amongst those who would revel in death.

"I pray you all," Jane's voice grew with the conviction of her faith and she pleaded. "Good Christian people, to bear my witness that I die a true Christian woman, and that I look to be saved by none other means, but only by the mercy of God in the merits of the blood of his only son, Jesus Christ."

Henry turned away, unable to listen further to the begging for her soul which he knew was likely to follow. He pushed his way out, through the throng who barely registered him so rapt was their attention on the gruesome event taking place just metres away. Blinking away tears as the vision of his cousin, an innocent who he had never even met but who undoubtedly had been a pawn in the machinations by men of power, accepted her death with grace and honour.

Little Jane Grey was a nothing now, a mere footnote like himself in the histories which had been written already, but she should have been so much more. She was, however unexpectedly, in line to rule, as he was. Fate perhaps had twisted the hand she was dealt. At least she could face the afterlife with a clear conscience and soul. The difference between them was, Henry realised, she had never claimed to want that power. Never been led to believe it was her right. And thus, was it right and fair that the crown duly falling to her, had been manipulated away from her?

She had wasted her moment in power. He would not allow that to happen to him. Her weakness was not solely because she was a woman, she clearly lacked the fortitude to rule. Unlike him. The thought spurred him on and his jaw set firmly.

As he walked the streets away from the looming walls, his anger grew as he heard the cheer rise from the crowd he left behind. Around him, city life carried on as if this day were nothing extraordinary; people sauntered about their business, chatting and passing the time as if a Queen had not just died. Rather than being calmed by this continuation of normality, Henry searched his mind for possible reasons why Mary would have ordered this execution, an irreversible step, on a girl the same age as he was when he had died.

He found nothing, no logic to it at all. Lady Jane Grey probably had no knowledge even of Wyatt's protest against Mary's marriage to the Spaniard. She may well have witnessed the conspirators' deaths,

Henry wondered, but been a part of the plot? It made no sense to him, given the purity of her faith, which Jeffries had been so impressed by. Wyatt was a known catholic, Jane a devout Protestant. The piety and womanliness seemed correct to Henry, after hearing Jane's declaration of her innocence.

And, for a woman to have an intent to kill went against all that he thought he knew; it was unnatural. He could barely believe his sister had ordered this execution. Mary, malleable as a woman by nature is, he thought, must surely have been convinced beyond all doubt of her guilt. Of an urgent need to get rid herself of the one of two remaining threats to her throne. Convinced most likely by a man. Did she, by this order, truly understand the responsibility she bore? For that ultimate decision between life and death of her subjects? Henry doubted she was even there to witness their cousin's death. Her absence meant avoiding hearing Jane's calm entreaties of innocence, lest Mary should heed instead any doubts she may have had about the order to execute.

Only someone with a complete understanding of the power of that resolution to order an execution, a monarch's right, should take such decisions. Someone who could not be influenced to ignore what they knew in their heart to be the right choice to make. Someone who knew the balance between life and death intimately. Such as he did. His fists balled and his stride lengthened. His sister had probably merely signed a piece of paper without even reading it in her haste to get back to her prayers. That Mary was making extremely bad decisions within her reign frustrated him evermore. There had to be a change. Had to.

*****

Naturae

Thane propped himself against the Palace in a corner of the balcony, overlooking the clearing below. Clouds had gathered as the morning wore on, and rain now threatened. His jaw ached from clenching, and his head throbbed from the frown, which felt as if it had become etched onto his forehead like a tattoo. Below, guard drills followed by combat practice had finally ceased, although their disastrous results remained evident. Thane could not avoid the smell of fae blood splatter, still wet on the damp earth.

Only two had been wounded today, for which he was grateful. But they were the lucky ones. Worker fae were not bred to bear arms, of any kind, Thane knew. Their stubby wings just got in the way, insufficiently strong to whirl through the air. Arms which were made for scrubbing or crafting were not delicate enough to wield swords with any precision. Worse yet, the citadel held insufficient armour supplies, inadequate to protect all the trainees, as well as soldier fae endlessly patrolling, from harm - from friend or foe.

Thane forced himself to look over the railing, to the remains of the carnage below. As Lyrus had ordered, the entire community gathered and now shuffled in silence so they could all get a good view of the platform from the ground. Again, Thane lamented. Once proud fae, who could fill the sky so they were all able to see, now grounded and subdued. He thought of Joshua and Queen Aioffe, who lauded the freedoms of the fae to fly. Most especially today, he mourned the loss of Joshua and his metal mastery. The apprentices he had trained simply could not keep pace with the repair work, let alone create new pieces. In addition to which, Naturae had no thieves left, to steal the required ore, or, traders to barter for some, even if Naturae possessed any coins or goods to offer. The numbers shivering beneath the balcony had thinned again, and would continue to if a solution was not found.

Behind him, the doors opened and Thane glanced to the sky. Even though the sun was shrouded, he knew it was at its height for the time of year. He did not turn as Lyrus approached, followed by his guards, but stood straight in his corner, backed against the balustrade. Bitterness rose in Thane's throat as he forced himself to keep his head facing forward and not crumble beneath the daggers from Lyrus's stare.

His skin crawled; the crippled figure disgusted him. Not because of his physical deformities; indeed, Thane gave him credit for his recovery from those, but from his twisted behaviour since Queen Aioffe and Joshua had left. Thane was losing faith that they would ever return, and losing heart that he could fight their battles for them when none would listen to him any more.

He looked at the masses gathering below them in the clearing and sighed. No-one noticed. No-one noticed him on the edge of the balcony, watching over them. More than anything, he mourned the worker fae's lack of respect for him. He had failed them, and now felt as lowly as an outcast. Unwanted. Unheard. Not spoken of, or spoken to.

"I have decided, Fae of Naturae, that you need to learn the consequences of treachery." Lyrus's nasal voice rang over the clearing, strong and commanding. "Perhaps then," he sneered, "every fae will understand the seriousness of these actions. Discipline is at the heart of any defence. Rogue actions taken against the realm, whether taken as an individual or in company, will meet with the same result. Dissent will not be tolerated."

Lyrus paused for effect, and Thane could not resist glancing down. Pale, frightened faces focussed absolutely on their new leader. Some were standing tall, to attention, others sullenly watched through submissive eyes.

"Uffer, here, has abused his rank, of which he is now stripped. He incited rebellion amongst the council. Furthermore, he has insulted the crown." Lyrus beckoned behind so the guards would drag Uffer forward. Thane clenched his jaw, softening it only when he saw the dignity with which his old friend walked to the edge of the platform.

"He will pay for his dishonour." Lyrus drew out his sword. The rasp sent a shiver down Thane's spine.

"Kneel!"

Thane could not look, grasping the side of his jacket to prevent his hand from shaking as his eyes squeezed shut. Uffer's knees thumped as they hit the timber, a gentle bump which Thane felt as a goodbye through the soles of his feet. As his eyes closed, Thane heard the whistle of Lyrus's sword through the air, swooping down upon his friend. Uffer made no sound, yet vibrations echoing through the wood told Thane - punishment had been meted in a swift and brutal manner.

Beneath, the fae held their silence as the rain began again. Whilst it might rinse away the blood, it would not wash away the shame Thane felt at that moment.

CHAPTER FORTY-FOUR
Halfling Princess

London, April 1554

It had taken Henry and Fairfax much time observing and plotting after the news of Elizabeth's return to London reached them, but finally, they had identified a suitable candidate for Henry to disguise himself as. In a rented room overlooking the market outside the Tower of London, Henry pulled on stolen Warder's robes, then waited. He fidgeted with the bulky costume, glancing constantly through the window in anticipation. After months of failure to get close to Mary, hiding in plain sight at court using his old papers and excuses, he was ready to take any opportunity to further his destiny. Outside, Fairfax lurked underneath the casement, watching for the influenceable Mrs Astley, Princess Elizabeth's companion and servant.

When Henry heard Fairfax's whistling change to their code tune, he ran down the stairs and out into the bustling market. Affecting a more sedate walk, he followed the direction of his lover's gaze and found his target. At that point, Fairfax hollered, "Stop thief!" and took off across the marketplace. Upturning stalls, crates of lemons and apples, he tore through the square leaving chaos in his wake. For once, this was a planned incident; Henry had to catch himself from grinning.

"Why Mrs Astley," Henry said, bending to help her stand upright again. Fairfax had been sure to 'accidentally' shove her into the cheese stall as he ran past, waving like a lunatic. "I am so pleased to run into you here. What a dreadful commotion. Are you quite all right?" He held the woman's astonished gaze and blinked slowly. "I meant to ask you, how fares the Lady Elizabeth with her captivity?"

"She eats a little more now," Mrs Astley replied, almost mechanically. "Although it pains her to be held thus, of course."

Henry nodded sympathetically. "I, a Warder of the Tower who you have known for a long time and can vouch for, will kindly accompany you to your lodgings. Indeed, I would be honoured to carry that heavy basket on your behalf, to spare your back from further injury after your stumble just now..."

Mrs Astley's hand rubbed her lower back, then she hunched over to repack her purchases. "Oh, you are kind. What a kindness, yes..."

Taking her hand and placing it on his arm, Henry led his victim towards the gatehouse. He kept his head low, affecting to provide additional support to Mrs Astley as they waited whilst the young guard searched her basket for hidden messages. She duly gave Henry's explanation for his presence and the soldier took pity on her rather than leave his post. Once waved inside the daunting outer walls, Henry escorted her across the green. He barely paused as they passed the scaffold, still erected from Lady Jane Grey's execution two months earlier, as Mrs Astley hobbled through the entrance to the palace where Elizabeth was held prisoner. Henry handed her the basket and bade her farewell. He then walked calmly around to the locked gate to the small Queen's gardens in the shadow of the White Tower.

There, Henry stood as if guarding the opening, yet held his head low in case his face should be too closely examined. In the unusually inclement April sunshine, the short false beard Fairfax had glued on earlier in the day began to itch, but he dared not touch it for relief. He worried the thin layer of rouge paste on his face, providing a ruddiness to his pale skin, might sweat off if he had to wait much longer, but then, he heard the steady footsteps across the cobbles of a warder's approach. He snapped his head up to catch his prey's eye.

The guard frowned. "Who are you? Why are you here?"

Henry touched the warder's arm gently and tilted his hat back so his face was more apparent. As he pushed his will into the man's eyes, Henry couldn't help but feel grateful for the thorough planning which had brought this moment to bear. He knew the likeness, even his stance, was a duplicate of the fellow before him, even down to the slightly greyed side-burns poking out from their identical uniforms. Now he heard the depth of the man's voice, he could imitate it as well. Blinking slowly to ensure that man was completely under his influence, Henry then suggested that the Queen had elected to forgo her daily walk in the gardens.

Henry slid his hand down and pocketed the warders' gate key as smoothly as his voice purred his next instruction: the guard would take this brief respite from his duties to visit his children, and check they were not to interrupt the Lady Elizabeth, for this recent friendship was now forbidden. The veiled threat that he would be again reported to the Constable of the Tower, Sir John Gage, sent him quick-stepping away across the yard.

Henry returned to his guard of the gate and waited. The chapel bell chimed its passage of time and moments later, the door to the Palace lodgings opened. Beneath the brim of his hat, Henry smiled. The information provided by the susceptible Mrs Astley had been entirely correct thus far, and his sister was on time. He unlocked the gate, and stood just inside to allow her to enter without glancing up, then locked the gate behind them.

Although the gardens could be overlooked, Henry doubted very much whether Lord Dudley, also a prisoner in the Tower with a view over the grounds, or anyone else who watched from above, would think anything suspicious about the warder walking in the company of the Lady Elizabeth now. Sir John had stipulated she must at all times in the garden be in the presence of an armed guard, after all, and it was only proper that would include a degree of proximity. He hurried to catch up with her, as she wandered the neat pathways between box-row hedges. The warmth of the day brought a brightness to the spring flowers which gladdened his heart, yet her head remained bowed in contemplation.

Elizabeth turned at the crunch of his feet upon the gravel. "Is something the matter?" Her voice held a catch in it, and Henry lifted his face to meet her cool look. Between them ran a frisson of energy. Assessing each other for the first time in eighteen years, Henry's body flushed with coldness. It was not only like looking into his father's eyes, but also his own. As they stood silently facing each other amidst the blossoming trees after two decades apart, Henry felt his brain swim under her frizzling gaze.

Henry blinked, trying regardless of the shock of the unfamiliar energy, but something prevented him from forcing his will into her. After a second slow blink, he realised.

Elizabeth was a daemon. Perhaps only a halfling, but a daemon nonetheless.

Henry staggered, breaking their connection. He stared into the flowerbed. How could this be? How had he not known this before?

Boleyn. It had to be her. The calculating bitch of her mother. For he was damned sure it wasn't his father who tainted Elizabeth with the chaos.

Like Fairfax, like most other creatures, she could not be influenced.

He had failed. Again.

He bit his lip and glanced up at Elizabeth again. Intelligent crystal-blue eyes studied him intently; he could tell her mind whirred with implications as well.

His lips tightened as her thin ones rose slightly at the corner.

"I see you," she said. Her statement was light, almost playful, before it turned serious. "I knew you."

"Brightest, littlest star," Henry croaked out. She had not run away.

Elizabeth smiled, little white teeth flashing, and for a moment Henry was taken back. He wanted to crumple, overwhelmed by grief for the innocence that was. This slight, austerely dressed young woman who remembered him, and fondly it would appear, was marred. Did she even know it, he wondered?

She leaned in and placed her slim hand on his arm, saying hesitantly, "How fares my brother now?"

Her earnest question brought him to recover his senses. Henry stiffened. "I… am not as you knew me, but you must know that to even ask."

Elizabeth's white capped head tilted towards the chapel. "What happened to you was only recently told to me." She looked back to Henry, where he saw desperation and fear in her eyes. "A priest…"

Henry's eyes flared. "Who? Did he hurt you?"

The horror of what had transpired flashed across her fine features. Henry grasped her arm. "Did he hurt you?"

She shook her head, shocked now at his instinctive, protective response. Henry relaxed his grip.

"But he frightened me. He said you were… a revenant. Dead yet alive, and without a soul. He said, you chose this, to live on, to serve the Catholic faith evermore. But I cannot see how?" She looked down.

When Henry said nothing, for the last thing he wished to do to this sweet girl was detail the tortuous process by which he had been made a vampire, she continued in a small voice which tore at his heart. "I am warned, that if I displease Mary, she would order this terrible affliction upon myself as well." Her words came out as a whisper. "And for the sake of my neck, I am forced to go to Mass and see him, the revenant who made you thus, daily. To be reminded of my misery and yours. I carry your secret with me as a warning."

Henry's irritation at Mary's poor decision making flared again. "And no doubt Mary has ordered this threat. To subjugate you. Does she also know of my fate?"

Elizabeth shrugged, then her jawline firmed as she swallowed. "I will not take the sacrament, for it is a falsehood and now, I believe it is a reminder of the evil by which the Church has defiled so many."

Like other daemons he knew, the lightning fast change of subject not only avoided answering the question, but also betrayed their nature. Looking again though, Henry shared her pride in her defiance over Mary's wishes which he saw growing and evident in her stature.

"You are brave," he said gently. "And strong. Do not waver in your beliefs, sister. It may provide you comfort in these darkest of days."

Together, they started to walk again around the garden.

"She wants to implicate me, you know. In the rebellion."

"It does not surprise me."

"Me, her own sister."

Henry sniffed. "She knows you are a threat to her. That is why she is so desperate to be wedded, bedded and with child."

"And you?" Elizabeth smiled sweetly at him, but the sudden chill in her tone belied she already suspected the answer. "Would you threaten me? Or her?"

Henry pulled himself away from her side. This very question had lurked since he had begun planning this introduction. When his target had been Mary, the strategy seemed simpler, almost pre-ordained. But, having failed to reach her inner council, guarded even closer due to the imminent arrival of King Philip, the option of persuading Elizabeth had appeared an easier target. Despite the challenges of her imprisonment in the Tower under suspicion of treason, more humans surrounded her than Mary.

But now he was here, with the discovery of a half sister who was not susceptible, his resolve wavered. He even felt sorry for her - that a priest, no doubt under instruction from someone higher up who knew of his condition, should be ordered to keep Elizabeth subservient by telling her of his existence. Threaten her with the same fate. Although he now understood what it was to live without a soul, to lose one's humanity, and despite his own survival in this condition, he could not wish it upon her. As it turned out, from personal experience, he recognised it wouldn't be possible anyway. Daemon and vampire blood cannot mix, not without deadly consequences. Whether she knew that or not, he did not know, but it was information he decided to withhold for now.

He laughed, making his best efforts to make it sound genuine. "Of course not."

Elizabeth turned her face away. "Then I have only Mary to fear, along with the might of Rome who influence her decisions."

"You should fear nothing, sister, for as long as your conscience is clear, there is no doubt your soul would be received into heaven." Henry had absolutely no idea if this was true or not, but it seemed to placate her.

"You should escort me out now," she said, glancing at the clock on the White Tower. "I wish… I wish we had longer to talk, but, I am to dine with the Constable of the Tower tonight and questions would be asked if we walk together much more. I'm only lately afforded the luxury of fresh air."

"As you wish," Henry said, pulling the key from his pocket.

"Will I see you again? I should like to be in each other's company as freely as we did before." She flicked her eyes to his.

"I cannot promise anything, sister."

"Your protection perhaps?"

Henry looked down, fiddling with the gate lock whilst he considered. She could not know how difficult a question this was for him to answer. He pushed sentiment aside. "If I am able - always," he said. 'Perhaps', his lack of conscience mentally corrected.

CHAPTER FORTY-FIVE

Labours

Beesworth, May 1554

Mary Hanley did not usually run. In fact, her cumbersome skirts and advancing age as she lumbered down the steep pathway to the stables brought to Joshua's mind a marionette doll.

"It's started!" The screech to her voice suggested her panic.

Mark, lining up his precious stones along the top of a stall to make a bobbly snake, stared at her with equal alarm.

"Nemis's baby comes?" Joshua said, forcing a stalwart expression. It was imperative he remained calm for the sake of the boy.

"And Jeffries has not yet arrived!" She wrung her hands together, then darted towards Mark. Gathering him in her arms, she buried his head in her chest as if he would not hear her hiss, "The labour pains come thick and fast. Already her waters are all over the kitchen floor!"

Joshua placed the broom against the stall. "I'll go, fret not. Is she in the bedroom yet?"

"Tis no place for a man! Childbirth should have a cunning woman in attendance at the very least." Lady Hanley said primly, then released Mark and bent down to instruct him. "Now, you run into the village and find Mistress Amy."

"No," Joshua said. "No cunning woman. This may not be an ordinary birth."

"But…" Mary Hanley's mouth gaped trout-like. "She must have someone with her, to assist."

There was no other time but now to deliver the unorthodox plan which Nemis had agreed with Joshua. They had both acknowledged that it would likely meet with resistance from the protocol-conscious woman, but, Nemis insisted it was her right to have an order of preference when it came to companions in her birthing chamber.

"I will be with her. Nemis has delivered enough babies herself to be able to instruct me on what is needed. Mark can stay as a lookout on the path for Jeffries, can't you? It's time for you to get ready to meet your new brother or sister."

Mark nodded solemnly, then his questions tumbled out. "Mama said it might hurt and take a long time. Will it hurt her very much? Will the baby hurt too?"

Joshua and Lady Hanley exchanged a look, then he took the boy's hand. "With the pain of it comes the joy. Do not fear, your mother has done this before, remember? You didn't get hurt, did you? And look how much joy you bring to her. Do you think she feels pain when she looks at you, or, her happiness and love?"

Mark blinked. "She says she loves me to the edges of the skies and I soar her all around the world, like Papa."

"Well, there you are then. That doesn't sound like pain to me, it sounds wonderful." He squeezed Mark's little hands, enjoying the simple and easily given emotion of comforting the youngster in what was a fearful time. "Would you like Lady Hanley to sit with you while you wait?"

The boy nodded. Mary's lips pinched together, then softened as she understood how best she could help this awkward situation. Joshua shot her a grateful look, although in the back of his mind, he knew it was what she undoubtedly wanted to do anyway. Nemis's impending birth held no interest to the old fae, with its completely alien and messy human hazards.

After jogging up the hill, Joshua paused to wash his hands in the empty kitchen. Conscious of his lack of skills with childbirth, now the moment was upon him, he mentally reviewed the tasks he had been set. His hand shook as he filled the kettle and hung it to boil, then gathered the wrapped bundle of clothes and equipment which Nemis had prepared. Ignoring, for now, the splash of amniotic fluid underneath the table, he headed upstairs to find Nemis.

She and he had already discussed their contingency strategy for if the babe should make an early arrival, and whilst he had little practical experience to offer, she had spent hours trying to impart upon him what could happen, listing out the equipment and materials which she used when birthing other women. What she really had been imparting, as much as her own experience of midwifery, was her need for a calm presence with her. Someone who would not flap or panic mawkishly if the birth did not proceed according to usual. Someone who would not be afeared of what may be pushed out. And, most importantly, given the likelihood of a winged babe getting stuck, someone who had precise and steady hands, should surgical intervention be needed. Debating this potential instruction terrified Joshua the most, but he had sharpened a slim knife and pre-threaded a needle with sheep-gut in readiness.

When he reached her room, all he could hear were the low moans of agony within. He knocked, to delay his entry more than anything else. He was the second choice of companion, in Jeffries' absence, and would have to suffice.

"Gahh…"

Joshua took the increase in volume of the cry as his invitation to enter. Nemis was bent over, clutching a windowsill. Heavy curtains blocked out the daylight, in the hope that the darkness and warmth would provide security and protection to mother and babe. Except Nemis, presumably craving the freedoms of the outside, had opened a chink to peer through. She turned her head aside from her view, glancing towards him as he approached. Bracing herself on one hand, she flung out an arm to reach for him.

"No word from Jeffries?" She panted out, then bent double again as a contraction rippled through her. Joshua wondered how she even had the strength to stand; her back visibly contorting from the pain. He took her proffered forearm, which she bore down upon immediately, rubbing her shoulders until the groan abated.

"Shouldn't you be on the bed?" He placed his hands under her arms and tried to lead her away from the window.

Nemis's expression of desperation mixed with scorn made him rethink his approach. He remembered her telling him only a few days ago, 'Let the woman, in this case me, decide where she is most comfortable - be it walking, leaning, lying or sitting.'

"... Or here, if that is best for you," he hastily added, waving his hand in the general direction of the window. "Here's fine as well."

Her body seemed to beat out heat as she panted for breath in between the labour pains. Joshua drew out his clean handkerchief and dabbed her brow.

Even though she was curling into another contraction, he saw he was forgiven in the smile which she forced onto her face. "Hoping for a miracle .... to fly through the window," she said through gritted teeth. "And, it's moving so fast .... I didn't have time to pull back the covers."

"Thick and quick by the looks of it. I'd better start praying for St Margaret's help," he half-joked. He'd actually been praying for her guidance long into the night for some weeks now, ever since it became apparent that Nemis would not let him leave her side without a suitable stand-in. "Are you feeling the urge to push yet?"

She shook her head, and he remembered then that he was supposed to tie away her dreadlocks so that long strands wouldn't get in the way. He pulled away from her and placed the bundle on the table close to the fire. After unwrapping it, he took the ribbon, then gently pulled the hair back, plaiting and tying it as neatly as he could. The thick, dark blond braid hanging against the white of her shift reminded him of rigging, and he wondered again where Fairfax had got to. There had been no reply to his urgent appeal for help in understanding the workings of the astrolabe two months ago, and he knew Nemis was giving up hope of him ever being able to leave to find Aioffe and Spenser. They had both been praying daily for a miracle to occur and their spouses to return without Joshua having to leave her at all. Protection promises had been made, after all.

"Do I have time then to fetch hot water?"

"Ruuun!" Another moan began to fill the warm room.

*****

Bavaria

Aioffe gazed deeply into the young man's eyes, searching her own soul as she did so for the warm sensation she hoped to find there, which would speak of the love she needed. He smiled, but there was little intimacy in the gesture. The lack of a meaningful connection, on this of all days, bothered her. The vampire had been well paid to ensure that Durant seemed to participate in this venture willingly, but there was an emptiness to his soul regardless. She sought to find a resemblance to Joshua, but this man, swarthy, shorter and dark-haired, was the antithesis of him in almost every way. Sighing, she took his enormous, somewhat sweaty hand and clasped it in her own cool, slim one. They walked onwards, down the path to the site which she had chosen to be his pupation ground.

As she stepped, the ominous task ahead of her dragged her every foot-fall. Despite having spent the last weeks getting to know Durant, so that she might engender some sort of brotherly feeling towards him, she still considered this day to have come too soon. But, Queen Illania insisted, and Spenser grew ever weaker, so there was no point in delaying it further. Who knew where her note to Joshua had ended up? Even if he were to come, not enough time had passed for even the fastest of travel. She did not expect an intervention soon.

Trying to distract herself, Aioffe studied the canopy of leaves above. Optimistic sunlight peeked through, but instead of lifting her mood, her heart thudded, oppressive with anxious fear. What if she couldn't do it? The worry pressed upon her. Not even when the gallant Durant plucked a pretty bloom from the path side, could she shift the sensation of imminent failure from her mind. She smiled courteously, of course, but she thought he surely must be aware of the insincerity behind it, as much as she understood the time-worn actions he was attempting to play out for her benefit. Not for the first time, Aioffe questioned Queen Illania's choice of eternal mate. She herself couldn't escape the conclusion that for all of his physical perfection, good manners, and ready small talk, there was no getting around the fact that she found his company unimaginative. Dull even, once you looked past the obvious. Dull Durant.

This was going to be a long shot, she knew already. And a very long day.

*****

Beesworth

When Joshua returned, Nemis had planted herself into the birthing stool which Joshua had carved to her specifications. She was doing some sort of timed, long panting - to what end wasn't immediately clear to him. If anything, she looked to be more tense than before. He set the jug of hot water and bowl down next to the equipment.

"Close?" He failed to keep the anxiety from his voice.

She nodded, groaning. Her hands gripped the chair's arms so hard, her knuckles were white.

"Should I put the towel down and be ready to catch?"

She nodded again, then the tone of her moan changed. His heart skipped a beat as he watched her slump forward, over the bulge of her stomach.

"Nemis?" He rushed over, and knelt in front of her. "Nemis!" Joshua shook her shoulder, sensing his presence was no longer of reach to her. From one second to the next, the entire motions of labour had shifted to a still.

The shaking had no effect; her body suddenly limp, held in place purely by the position she had collapsed in upon the seat. "Oh no!" He recognised this frailty. Casting his eyes around, as if there was someone else to advise him nearby, Joshua swallowed.

They had discussed this very possibility. Yet Joshua was frozen, unable to act on their plan. His mind blanked in panic. What was he supposed to do if she had a fit during labour?

Joshua tried to breathe in and out, hoping the calming technique would release his memory. Again. And again. His lip wobbled and he felt tears threaten behind his eyes. This was not supposed to happen - he was expected to know what to do. They had a plan. Many plans. What was the plan for if this happened?

St Margaret! The saint for childbirth. He should think of her... He conjured up the prayers he had said, the earnest begging for her support, her guidance in this dangerous time. He thought of the good Lord and asked him to watch over them. But the desired sense of purpose didn't materialise.

Nemis had paled. Joshua's toes, trapped by the boots he wore and by kneeling, tingled. What to do? Why couldn't he remember? Oh Lord, Nemis was going to die! The babe would die!

He closed his eyes and reached out for Aioffe, just to feel her would help, he thought. To know he was not alone.

*****

Bavaria

Aioffe stared at Durant's blood seeping from his arm. A large pool formed from the initial spurt sank quickly into the dry earth, sucked in as if the dust had an insatiable thirst and leaving only a dark stain the size of a palm behind. The torrent had slowed yet his overall paleness suggested most of him was nourishing roots deep below.

He looked at her with clouded, trusting eyes, then nodded towards the knife she still held. Aioffe's hand trembled as she inserted the point of it into her wrist and slashed down. Everything about this farce of a ceremony felt wrong. Despite planning it herself, explaining in vague terms to Durant what to expect, she remained sceptical that the pupaetion process would work. It seemed too sacrificial somehow, to bring forth a new life by the very planning of it. Durant was too willing, too suppliant.

And that, she realised as she lifted her arm to hold it above his, was likely to be the biggest problem. For all the Lifeforce which she had gathered last night to fortify herself, from all manner of beasts and humans who attended the contrived gathering in a nearby village, it wouldn't be enough. She did not truly believe it would work.

Her wound began to throb, pulsing out her own rich red blood and wanting to close itself. Feeling curiously absent from the flow of herself, Aioffe studied it. Her life-force, visible now to her eyes, bubbled from the cut in an almost stately manner. It ran over his wound, then in a globulous blob, slipped on top of his on the earth. Not at all like when she had mingled blood at Joshua's creation. Without meaning to draw an allusion to his re-birth as she was trying hard to focus on her feelings towards Durant, the hopes and expectations which this process would consummate, Aioffe thought of Joshua. How her heart had beaten so rapidly then. Of the threat of his loss - more - the deep seated fear that he might die and leave her alone to face the world added urgency to her desperate attempt to heal him.

A jolt coursed through her, and she closed her eyes quickly. He was reaching for her! Now, of all times! Her first instinct was a rush of gratitude. She was not alone, and never would be. The guilt and deception which she had been avoiding facing within herself then flushed hot in her cheeks. The urge intruding into her warmth bade her get up! Leave! Avoid the confrontation. Break the connection somehow, as if movement would sever it.

She opened her eyes instead. Durant, another man and not her husband, gazed up at her. There was no guile about what he was doing, which was the opposite of how Aioffe felt. She gritted her teeth. If Joshua could only understand why she did this - to escape back to him and him only - perhaps he would forgive her infidelity.

But the shame could not leave. It lingered between herself and this body on the floor. Aioffe tried to push Joshua from her mind. Close that doorway. Yet, an insistent tingle kept their connection wedged open. Aioffe shook her head. Now was not the time for delay. For any sort of comfort. Durant was bleeding copiously on the branches beneath him.

Aioffe flared her eyes. She must stay focussed on the task ahead. There would be a time for recrimination, explanation, but not now. Not here. With a mental shove, Aioffe slammed the connection closed. Part of her began to weep inside - a sensation she clutched close to herself, for what was grief but an expression of love? She turned back to the still Durant and began rubbing her wound against his.

CHAPTER FORTY-SIX
Birthing

Nemis was lost. She knew this because her mind had wandered far away from the pain, still lingering in her extremities perhaps, but veiled nonetheless. She was walking, her feet landing lightly as if cushioned, yet the pathway was unclear. There were no tracks meandering into the distance, only the wide open space of somewhere else. Somewhere hazy and blurred. Her walk seemed purposeful though, but to what end or destination currently eluded her.

A cramp shot through her, causing her to stumble; her entire torso enveloped in the pain she thought she had left behind. In the chill, walking became impossible, the effort too great. She looked down at her feet, somewhat surprised to see them. It was like looking at strangers' toes. Lifting her head, a light ahead beckoned her. Its brightness drew her attention, and without thinking about it, she no longer needed her stubborn feet. She could fly... drift towards the enticing warmth which the light promised.

The arid, cold landscape beneath her disappeared as she reached the source of the glow. She turned her head away, shielding her eyes against the white heat which pulsated gently. After a second, she dared to glance sideways back at it, determined to understand what it was. Forcing herself to focus, despite the pain which grew when she gazed upon it, Nemis leaned in.

The 'thing' was not large, perhaps the size of a bucket, only shaped more like an egg. It was covered with a glistening, nearly translucent membrane, through which the glowing light emitted. Criss-crossing the entire surface ran thin, sparkling lines which reminded Nemis of ribbons. They danced across the surface, each with a pathway of their own forming beautiful, ever-changing swirls. A spectrum of reds, bright greens, buttercup yellow and vivid blues drew her into the strange egg, fluttering in intensity.

Watching it with awe, the 'thing' overwhelmed her senses and, as she absorbed its beauty, grew within her a sense of hope. A promise, which had attracted her towards the 'thing' in the first place. Peace spread through her being, a calmness which held at bay the questions and quandaries which her mind tried to answer without knowing what precisely they were. They fell away into the kaleidoscope. They did not matter, when she was close to this... promise. Intuitively, Nemis understood that this bewitching, light-filled promise held a destiny. A part to play in something wider than this moment.

As she watched, the blob moved! A lump poked out of the ovoid, and she felt a nudge to her own stomach. Nemis's heart surged with joy - a baby! Her hand dropped to cradle the bulge of her own, but found it flat.

This child was not hers! Or was it?

Fascinated still by it, Nemis reached her arm out, desperate to touch the alluring covering. Was the membrane a caul? It felt like one - slippery and smooth. Did it need breaking so the child could live? She hesitated, for something about it reminded her - this was not her baby. Not hers to hold. *Not* hers, but destined for someone else. Something else.

But then, there was no-one else here to save it?

Did it need saving?

Nemis frowned. Of course it needed the caul breaking; how else could it live and breathe? How else could it fulfil its promise? But there was a risk in breaking the membrane - exposing it to this harsh, barren and frozen world, where it might not survive. There was no alternative though, for the child to live, truly live, it had to be exposed or the promise would die.

She gazed around, understanding in that instant that this was a bargain. For the child to fulfil its promise, there was a cost.

But, just as she rationalised this to herself, the hopeful joy which had grown in her heart rose up, circling around her neck. Tightening, a silvery rope pulled, choking her. She noticed her heart beat twice, quite slowly but firmly. Then Spenser flashed into her consciousness. He gazed at her tenderly, inviting her to join him with his hand stretched out. A searing pain bolted through her neck, encompassing her head, her ears, her vision… and he was gone, dragging her with him. As quickly as it had risen, the light blinked out, and she floated in darkness with Spenser. All felt right with the world again.

*****

Beesworth

Joshua breathed out sharply, almost painfully. His chest had tightened so much when he felt Aioffe, that the sudden loss of her in his mind then wounded his heart. He glanced down at his arms, half expecting to see blood flowing from them because they ached that much. Eyelids fluttering, Joshua tried to unscramble a logical thought from the jumble of threads which tugged his mind.

Distinctly, he understood that he had been altered by his silent, mental encounter with his wife - comforted in one way, yet he was also burdened. The question he had sought had been answered - he was not alone. Aioffe was with him, or had been at least. But his heart filled with a query he had not expected. He glanced at Nemis's huddled form. The burden was guilt. He recognised the weight of it.

But why?

Guilt because he was sat at the feet of a labouring friend, when he had no right even to be in the room?

Guilt because his wife was in pain perhaps, at the very least preoccupied, with something which he could not know of. Did not know of?

Or, guilt because he was doing nothing to help anyone with the problem at hand?

His mind shifted and he clamped his lips together. No - this was not his guilt to bear. It must be something Aioffe was going through. His head cleared as it resolved. There was nothing he could do to help Aioffe right now; perhaps that was why she had severed the connection between them so abruptly. He refused to let his mind wander off into self loathing, repetitive thoughts about why she didn't need him any longer. That could wait. Here and now, he could help. He would solve the problem before him. He knew what to do.

Standing up, he then bent over and plucked Nemis from the stool. Her head lolled against his shoulder and she groaned as he straightened. Her body was curiously cold to touch, so he cuddled her into his chest to warm her skin. As he staggered to the bed, he noticed her body ripple again with a contraction. Although his heart thumped with fear for her, he reminded himself that he knew the next step. Their plans would work. He would assist. Joshua believed he could. To his mindset, that made all the difference.

*****

Bavaria

Against rising desperation, Aioffe nearly drained herself of blood. She grew ever weaker. She had rubbed and rubbed their wounds together, muttering any prayers which had come into her mind as she did so. She had already given Durant enough of her essence, pausing in the rubbing to drip the flow into his parted lips as she had done to Joshua. Now, her cut was healing of its own accord and she could not bear to re-open it. She would not sacrifice herself without making things right with her own love. Could not.

And yet, witnessed by only the trees and fauna around, her own blood-loss was reaching a critical stage and her head swam. Water sprang to her eyes as she panicked that her efforts hadn't been enough, and she blinked, letting her tears fall onto Durant in the hope that they too would change what she suspected was going to happen. Then, she laid down beside him and waited for the haze to clear.

He lay completely still. Aioffe felt and heard his heartbeat slow. Even the woodland fell silent as she listened for the next one. She lifted his arm to her mouth and kissed his wound. A blanket of hopelessness dropped over her, trapping her in this moment with a dead human; its weight suffocating all her hopes of freedom with him.

Nothing. No heartbeat came.

Barely breathing herself, she rolled away. Then, pulling from within, she reached out her hand to draw the greenery close by to them.

Whether it was due to her own weakness, or her possible failure to heal him adequately, but the leaves and bindings she had prepared took an eternity to bend to her will. Using the last of her energy, she visualised the cocoon she wanted them to create and wove her hands in the air to form it around him.

For now, the hoping for his successful pupaetion would have to be Queen Illania's task. She closed her eyes, her hand creeping to close on the arrowhead bundle in her pocket, and slept.

*****

Beesworth

"Nemis!" Joshua squeezed her pale hand, lying his head on the pillow next to her. "You must return, please." The pungent smell of the dregs of Jeffries' 'fitting' medicine lingered on her lips. He whispered, "I do not want to have to do this on my own. Please, dear friend, your child needs you to awaken."

After a few heartbeats more, but no other response, he sat up, twisting to examine her swollen belly. Ever since he had administered the concoction, which was a risk in itself as neither he nor Nemis were entirely sure of the herbs which went into its creation, he hadn't seen the ripple-tightening of a contraction. After rinsing his hands quickly, he placed a hand beneath and slightly to the side of the bump, pushing firmly against her skin. Then he leant closer so his ear pressed against her shift. Eyes closed, he concentrated on feeling for any movement, listening for the babe's heartbeat.

Nemis had allowed him to hear the heartbeat before, and it had surprised him with the strength and rapidity of it. She'd joked that its little heart must have been racing because a prince was near. But now, although faint, the definite pulsing he heard was far slower. Joshua moved his fingertips around the bulge. He had placed his hand initially on the tiny bobbles of a spine, and now he sought to determine where its head lay.

Sighing with relief as he figured out the baby's position was correct for a birth, he curved his palm around where his poking had suggested the ball of its shoulder, ushering some gentle comfort to the child within. He muttered a prayer to St Margaret again, asking forgiveness for what he was about to do.

Nemis was still not responding to anything, his touch nor his rasping voice when he begged her again to return. She remained breathing so shallowly; despite everything, she was still not in this world, and, in all likelihood, would not survive. Were this to happen, his instructions from her had been clear.

Joshua stood and considered bidding her farewell. For, what he had agreed to do next was by far the hardest task he had ever - or probably would ever - undertake. But these were her wishes, no matter how much he dreaded having to carry them out. The chances of Nemis's survival dropped significantly from this point onward. Blinking back the tears which filled his eyes, he checked once more the implements gathered on the unwrapped cloth. As he dragged the entire table to the foot of the bed, his heart slowed with dread.

Then, he pushed up the hem of her shift and laid a thick towel over her pale legs.

The knife handle was fashioned from a doe antler, he realised, as he picked it up. Briefly, he wondered why he hadn't particularly noticed it before when sharpening the blade. It seemed appropriate that a rarer, female bone would guide him in his onerous task. A deer had so many special, magical qualities for witches. As Nemis had directed him, the incision needed to start above the pubic area. His hands shook slightly as he held them against her skin.

The fire popped loudly behind him, and the knife slipped. In his shock, Joshua managed to slide the knife-edge away from her belly, cutting his own index finger in the process.

No matter, he thought as his blood immediately swelled up, a nick of me will heal, but the baby must come out quickly or it will be lost as well as its mother. Carefully, Joshua held the taut skin between his splayed fingers and prepared to insert the blade. Now that he was focusing, his heart steadied once again. He knew to cut shallow at first. The knife slid easily into her stomach, making a tiny incision.

Nemis let out a moan, which halted him from dragging the wound further.

"Nemis? Should I do this?" He asked, pulling the knife away.

The answering groan was unclear but her head swept from side to side. Joshua straightened, but kept his index finger pressed to the wound to stem her blood. Relief swept through him as he watched for further signs of her return, but as he waited, he sensed the pulse of his blood seep into hers. It was too intimate a connection - despite the inviting, tingling sensation as her magic mixed with his Lifeforce. Perhaps his essence was imparting some strength to her, he told himself. As soon as he perceived his nick had woven back together, he pulled his finger away from her body. She groaned, muttering something under her breath which he could not decipher.

Joshua felt his face flush, and, just for a moment, was perplexed as to why? He had done nothing against her wishes, and although his recollection of their plan was slightly delayed, he had tried to objectively diagnose the problem and solve it. His head swam; for a time his vision clouded with hazy, shiny threads wriggling across his vision. Grabbing the bedpost, he forced his eyelids to blink and focus. All the while, knowing time was short and he could ill-afford to be anything less than fully cognisant right now. He swallowed, glancing at her exposed belly - just as the muscles in her tightened!

"Aaaaah..." The tone of this grunt was different. As soon as the contraction was over, Nemis was alert.

Joshua sighed heavily, "Oh thank the Lord!" His vision snapped into focus.

But the ordeal was not yet over.

"Help me sit me up," she said, then started panting. "I need to kneel."

He ran up the bed, to the pillows, and lugged her upright. They shared a glance, and then both burst into soft laughter at the ungainly nature of manoeuvring a heavily pregnant woman around a bed. Nemis's laughing turned into pants as soon as she was on all fours. Joshua grabbed the towel and re-laid it out between her legs.

She strained, knees bending as she bore down. Joshua rubbed her back, wishing he could take away the pain stretching red across her cheeks. When the next contraction eased, Nemis felt down her stomach, between her legs. She looked up at him and frowned.

Unsure of what she was asking him to do - verify something or... Joshua's lips tightened together as another wave of agony abruptly swept over her. "Breathe," he commanded, suddenly remembering what he was supposed to remind her to do at this point. He panted himself, quickly puffing out his air in short, sharp bursts by way of encouragement. The action cleared his head also, and with renewed vigour and focus, he rubbed her back again. He paused as he saw her knees bend and the evidence of her exertion began to drip onto the towel.

She gave a few more long, groaning pushes. Standing by her side, Joshua grinned as he heard the slop of something, hitting the wet towel. "Well done!" he said, as proudly as if he had done the hard work himself.

"Look at it," she said, nerves in her voice.

Joshua sidestepped and glanced down, unsure if the ordeal was over. Encased from head to toe in a grey, slightly glossy membrane, there lay a baby! Joshua widened his eyes, knowing from his own experience of being re-born as fae, the cloying sensation of the sac.

"It's still in the caul," he cried. "A blessed babe! A miracle!"

"Tear it!" Nemis ordered, her own breaths coming easier now. "She needs to breathe!"

Joshua leant around her legs and picked up the warm, slippery bundle. With the cord hanging over his forearm, he bent over the bed, cradling the baby in the nook of his elbow. Just holding her nearly overwhelmed him - this new life, so precious, so precarious. With his fingernails, he pinched at the membrane closest to her mouth. Her tiny lips were pursed and a terrifying blue. As he worked his fingers through the stretchy sac, widening the hole, he blew across her lips.

When the gap was wide enough for her head to slip through, he peeled the stickiness away from her face. He caressed her cheek with this thumb, and muttered a brief prayer of gratitude up. As he pulled her body gently out of the sac, her delicate limbs stayed limp, her skull unmoving in his cupped palm.

"Put her chest on your hand and rub her back," Nemis said through gritted teeth. He heard her moan as she pushed out the last of her pregnancy.

The baby's body looked grey and slack. Too slack he thought. Yet the position he held her in, fluttering heart to his palm, reassured him that there was life there still. It was not too late. If only she would take in air!

He firmly pressed his hand to the tiny back, his fingers splaying between the wing joints between her shoulder blades. As he rubbed up and down her spine, he studied her wings - red and limp, falling around his hand. She didn't look that different from other newly pupated fae, Joshua thought. Perfectly formed, and yet unique. It was peculiar to frown and smile at the same time, but hope and worry battled across his face nonetheless.

Without warning, the baby gasped, then spluttered. A reedy wail and her body flushed, pinking within seconds. He kept rubbing as his grin broadened. Her cries grew stronger, legs and arms juddering as they stretched in the warm air, until he felt that perhaps it was time to look at her. With cheeks aching from the stretch of his smile, Joshua grabbed the edge of the towel and flipped her gently back into the crook of his arm, so he could wipe away the white, waxy substance mottling her skin.

It was then that he noticed the other side of her beautiful face. Red and angry, her cheek was not blushing from being upside down. A deep stain rose, shaped like a long leaf, curving along her jawline and up to the edge of her eye with its tip almost meeting her faint eyebrows. It reminded Joshua of an elegant branch sweeping towards the sky, or, as he studied it, perhaps reminiscent of the dramatic curve of a supporting arch in a church, holding up a pitched roof. There was little doubt in his mind that this was a unique child, special and blessed. Destined to support great weight. As if sensing his assessment, the babe's eyes, framed with long, blonde eyelashes, opened and immediately fixed on him.

He could not lift his eyes from her bright blue-grey ones, even as his fingers fumbled to wipe away the remnants of her former prison. This little angel would be able to fly freely now, Joshua thought as he smiled down at her. As he wiped her tiny palms, she grabbed his thumb with a grip so fierce he wondered that she had just moments earlier lain so weak and lifeless. Oh, but she was amazing!

"Is she quite ready yet?" Nemis interrupted. Joshua realised he had been standing right next to her, completely oblivious to Nemis's movement on the bed. He glanced down - she was kneeling up, arms out and ready to receive her child.

He wanted to say something to take the edge from her voice, to reassure her that her babe was perfect. About to be placed in her waiting arms. He wanted to. And he didn't. The lump in his throat swelled painfully. Then he looked at Nemis's face. Expectant but guarded.

With joints that dragged, he bent over and settled the baby into her embrace, but he could not take his gaze away. Already his heart yearned to once again hold her; she completed a part of him which he never knew was empty.

As Nemis peered down into her daughter's face, he wheeled on his heel, not willing to see the look of disappointment he thought might cross it. He crossed the room, collecting the peg and string for the cord, jars of salt, honey and filling the basin with warm water. Wearing a fresh cloth over his shoulder, he put the washing equipment on the bedside table and avoided looking at them both.

His eye fell on the grey mass of the caul which he'd dropped onto the bed when it was removed. The babe was still connected with the grey rope from its stomach. Joshua knew to count four finger-lengths up, tie it off and cut it. This much he did with steady hands that he had no conscious control over. Setting out a clean cloth on the bed, he then pulled the chilled caul, so it was opened out, stretched to dry as fully and as wrinkle free as possible. The rare sac was much coveted; he would need to ask Nemis what she wanted to do with it later. Sailors prized them in the belief that they would prevent drowning, but he thought it likely that witches also used them in their craft as well.

Still avoiding looking at mother and child, he busied himself with removing the other evidence of the birth, wrapping them in a towel and placing them in a wide rimmed bowl.

"Would you like to sit by the fire so I can change the sheets?" Joshua called over his shoulder.

"Will you hold her?"

The sadness in Nemis's voice made Joshua wheel around to the bed and stare. She was still kneeling, tenderly gazing at the baby in her arms, but tears streaked down her face. Joshua rushed over. "What's wrong?"

Nemis shook her head, clamping her lips.

"Is she ill? Are you ill?"

He watched her swallow, then she looked at him finally. "Everything is perfect. But she is not mine."

Joshua frowned. Nemis had just given birth to the baby - what on earth was she talking about? "She is. She even has your eyes, and I just watched you give birth to her! And look, you were right - she has wings!"

"She's the perfect hybrid," Nemis said, still too sadly for Joshua's liking. Nemis clutched the babe closer to her chest. "But, she isn't destined for me." She looked up at Joshua, her light blue eyes clear and dry. "She's meant to be for you and Aioffe. You are her parents."

"What?"

"She is the heir." Nemis shrugged. "It's just who she is. Yours."

CHAPTER FORTY-SEVEN

After the rain, a rainbow

Beesworth, June 23rd
St John's Night & Midsummer's eve 1554

With the exception of Jeffries, who arrived a day after the birth and left the next day satisfied everything was well, the household had done their utmost to avoid visitors with great success. Jeffries reported no sightings of Fairfax since they had parted, and Joshua had received no messages following his kestrels months ago. The chances were, Joshua told himself each time a bird returned, Fairfax was busy darting around the country and dodging trouble as he always had, never staying still for long enough for a bird to find him. Although increasingly frustrating, the household's new arrival provided plenty of distraction from his near-constant worrying about Aioffe.

Since their arrival at Hanley House, everyone had kept a low profile, especially Joshua. Whilst the locals had seen Lady Hanley was back in residence, sometimes to be spotted accompanied by a 'stable boy', no-one had dared to visit the house itself. It suited to let everyone think that Lady Hanley's return was due to recurring ill health; gossip would have it, she now had a live-in nurse. Since the birth, however, Nemis had quietly cultivated a reputation as a cunning woman, with her simple healing draughts and uncanny ability to find things. But, she took care to discourage visits to the Hall and kept the baby swaddled and close when running errands, avoiding questions by hiding behind a 'widowed' status as much as possible. Nobody knew of Joshua's return, as far as they could tell.

More bewildering, he had felt nothing further from Aioffe, although his mind constantly reached out to her. Especially in the darkest hours before dawn, when the loneliness and longing grew unbearable. With so much work to do about the home, and no idea about where to begin looking for his wife, Joshua kept putting off leaving. Yet his frustration grew daily, evidenced only by the incessant jiggling of his knee when he sat, or the snappiness of his replies when asked a simple question when he was trying to numb his mind with menial tasks.

As no-one was thus expected, the sound of the front door knocker jarred. Sitting cosily about the fireplace in the library room, which Lady Hanley preferred, the rat-a-tat-tat jolted them out of their soporific yet companionable silence. Joshua and Nemis lowered their books, Lady Hanley put down her quill, then they all glanced uneasily at one another.

"I'll check," Joshua said, standing. His mouth softened at the sight of the child he thought of as his own, asleep on her birth mother's shoulder after a feed.

Lady Hanley replied, "You can't. Besides, one should never answer one's own front door at this time of night. Especially in this filthy weather. It could be any old vagrant come begging for shelter." She sniffed and picked up her quill again, although it wavered slightly as she pretended to continue with her diary.

Nemis's drowsy eyes widened. "Who would come calling here at this hour, anyway?" She nuzzled the sleeping child higher up her chest. "Most people should be a-bed by now."

Joshua crossed to the window and peeked out through the drapes. He smiled, then pulled on his jacket and cap, saying, "It'll be fine, it's just a friend." He winked at Nemis before hurrying out.

Insistent banging of the door knocker loudly, again echoed through the empty corridor. "I'm coming, I'm coming," Joshua muttered under his breath. It took a few minutes to rummage for the key in the drawers next to the door. His heart clamoured; finally, he could hope for a change to his current predicament. A direction. That was all he needed and he would be able to find Aioffe. As he fumbled with the rusted lock, he tried to reach her with his mind, but was distracted by shouting.

"This porch is pointless. You need to fix the roof!" Fairfax's voice reached through the rain via the keyhole. "I'm getting absolutely soaked here!"

Joshua chuckled, then threw his arms as wide as the door as soon as he opened it. Fairfax stepped inside - a grinning, sodden scarecrow.

"Finally! I sent kestrel after kestrel trying to find you. I would have come to you," Joshua said. "All you had to do was say where."

Fairfax snorted. "I'm never in one place for long enough. It seemed easier to come and find you."

"Well, I'm very glad you have. At last. You cannot possibly use the rain as an excuse for your tardiness when you travel mainly by ship."

Fairfax hugged Joshua fiercely, soaking his clothes in the process, then pulled back from the embrace with a twinkle to his eye. "I wasn't aware I was on a deadline, old friend. But I am here now. Could you have chosen a more out of the way place to hide from the world?"

"Hardly hiding away," Joshua said, his eyes sliding into the hallway. "Beesworth is a respectable town, I'll have you know. So it's probably better you don't stay too long there."

Fairfax laughed. "True enough."

"Are you alone?" Joshua glanced into the darkness of the night behind his guest.

Fairfax shrugged. "I left the crew on board; I'll have to be back to them tomorrow as we've a delivery which cannot be late. Again."

"I meant your pale friend."

"Oh Henry, he's... he's..."

"Otherwise occupied?"

Fairfax tilted his head, before saying, "He's busy, you know. Court life."

"Court life?"

Rainwater dripped from the rim of Fairfax's flamboyant hat as he studied the floor. "Yes, quite the courtier he's pretending to be. Although Queen Mary is, as yet, unreachable for what I think he has in mind. She's too consumed with excitement about her impending nuptials to the Spaniard with the fine legs." Fairfax's voice turned decidedly grumpy. "I wish that he'd just hurry up and arrive, then we can all decide the measure of him, then Henry can stop... stop being so uncomfortable. Stop borrowing my clothes all the time." Fairfax sighed, his eyes flicking to Joshua's. "He thinks it's necessary though, to get what he wants."

"You taught the art of disguise too well," Joshua said wryly. He helped Fairfax with his cape, leading the way to the kitchen to hang it to dry. "Speaking of which, have you heard whether our spies are settled? I, ah, hear nothing from them." He looked hopefully at Fairfax, trying to conceal his desperation.

"You don't?" Fairfax frowned, then collapsed into a seat at the end of the kitchen table. He stuck his boots close to the fire and began to pull the dripping laces. "I thought you would be co-ordinating their efforts? Thought that was why you called me here, in fact."

Joshua shook his head. "My departure from Naturae wasn't.... planned, as you know. Rather hurried. I've heard nothing since leaving."

The daemon's eyes narrowed. "Where's Aioffe? Back from Europe I hope?"

"That's why I called you here." Joshua went over to the cupboard in the corner, where he kept clothes and cleaning items. He rummaged behind them and pulled out the golden astrolabe globe. "Nemis says this is Spenser's. He uses it to navigate."

Fairfax held out his hand, eyes immediately curious as Joshua dropped the tiny instrument into his palm. "We hoped," Joshua said quietly, "That you would be able to show us how to use it. She and Spenser are still there but, without figuring out this, we won't know precisely where they are."

Holding it closer to the fire to examine the faint markings, Fairfax then fanned out the elegant spokes and gasped. "I've never seen an astrolabe like this before." He looked up at Joshua, who was relieved to see recognition in his bright eyes. "Given a little time, I can probably work out how to operate it."

Joshua recognised by the way Fairfax stroked the sheen of the metal that his daemon friend coveted the globe. "I know, it's a pretty thing, Fairfax, but it belongs to Nemis in the absence of Spenser," he reminded.

"What are these markings?" Fairfax said, pointing to the faelore swirls. "I don't recognise them."

Joshua said, "Faelore, the fae language. Lady Hanley can translate."

"Who?"

"Mistress of this house. Be warned, she has a liking for daemons. A little too much liking if you ask me."

"Is that so?" The subject's voice intruded upon the calm of the kitchen. "And yet you saw fit to bring *another* one into my home?"

Joshua had the grace to blush. "I apologise, your Ladyship. This is my friend, Thomas Fairfax. I invited him here. Some months ago, but still. He's here now." Fairfax stood, smoothly pocketed the astrolabe and approached her with a broad smile and outstretched hand. She ignored the hand and her eyes narrowed.

"Mister Meadows," she snapped. "It is exceedingly rude, not to mention dishonest, to fail to inform the lady of the house when there is a guest, expected or not. Even a sodden one."

Joshua looked down at the floor, expecting the chastisement and not caring a jot. He was under no obligation to tell Mary everything. Indeed, it was pertinent in this instance that she should not yet fully understand the reasons for the visit. After many months of sheltering himself and his charges, Joshua did not wish to cause her distress or create an unpleasant atmosphere for Nemis with their anticipated departure. But, as soon as he had the knowledge which he hoped Fairfax could provide, he intended to leave. Also, the quicker his daemon friend was away from the Hall, the less chance of her getting attached to the alluring taste of Fairfax.

"Your Ladyship," Fairfax bowed. "It is I who should apologise. My arrival is unannounced, tardy and... well, I wasn't sure I had the right place."

"How many other Hanley Houses are there?" Lady Hanley looked down her nose, then was distracted by a small hand clutching at her skirt, then pushing past her.

"Mark!" Fairfax cried. "How wonderful to see you!"

The boy, still dressed in his night-shirt, rushed forwards and flung himself into Fairfax's arms. Lady Hanley's hackles rose. "Mark! That is not how we greet a guest to this house." She frowned, then sniffed. "Even one you clearly are fond of."

Joshua's lips twitched. "Perhaps we should take some wine to warm, and Fairfax can dry out by the fire?" He said, "Nemis will want to catch up with our friend, I am sure."

Assuming a familiarity which he had no right to, Fairfax proffered his arm to Lady Hanley. "My good Lady, would you do me the honour of escorting me? I am sorely in need of some warmth, and would prevail upon your generosity."

Lady Hanley straightened, sized him up, then glanced down at the puddle forming on the flagstones. She swivelled and walked haughtily ahead into the corridor. "Joshua, bring the man a towel to sit upon. I will not have my seats ruined."

*****

By the next morning, Fairfax's infectious energy had pervaded the house, entirely lifting it from the pall of gloomy isolation under which the household usually lived. It had been a cold and damp summer thus far; the weather more like autumn, so his cheer was as welcome as sunshine for them all. All except Joshua, the daemon's surprise arrival had overnight re-awakened an agony of indecision. Easy smiles passed around the table as warmly as the bread which Nemis had risen early to bake. A familial glow lit Mark's face as he begged Fairfax to take him into town for the Midsummer festivities. Lady Hanley's brows pinched for just a moment, before, under Nemis's glare, she forced then to relax. Even the littlest one, cuddled on Joshua's lap mouthing on a crust, watched the new visitor with rapt eyes.

"Maybe we could all go then?" Mark's plaintive tone weighed on Joshua's heart. Treats were few and far between for the child, who had come out of his shell better than anyone could ever have anticipated now they were settled into a routine. Perhaps it was the attentiveness of Lady Hanley which had layered him with a blanket of security, or her total acceptance of his peculiarities, but Mark, today emboldened by the company of Fairfax, was far more garrulous than Joshua had ever heard him to be.

Joshua leant over the table towards him and said sadly, "I cannot, I'm afraid, but perhaps your Mama can go with you if you would like? Fairfax could join you later, for the fire wheel." As soon as the words tripped from his lips, Joshua regretted his suggestion - fire and Fairfax was a combination destined to lead to trouble.

"I do have some remedies I need to deliver, and Mark would enjoy the Marching Watch parade," Nemis said, smiling warily at Joshua. "I don't think I will be of much use here if you have some 'business' to discuss with Fairfax?"

Lady Hanley delicately put a handkerchief to her nose. "I will not be able to join you in town. This weather, it is too much. I would catch a fever or cough from the bonfires. I've seen it all before anyway, many times. No, I shall stay."

Joshua glanced at Fairfax, then to Lady Hanley. "There is something I would ask your opinion about, actually."

She nodded, standing then before peering down her nose at them both. "I will be at my desk."

After Nemis and Mark had also departed, Fairfax brought out the astrolabe and Joshua the message from Aioffe. The pair sat around the table, discussing Joshua's interpretation of the note, then examining the instrument in the only slightly brighter light of day. "These seem like they ought to be coordinates," Fairfax concurred. "But not like I have seen before."

"Could they be star positions?" Joshua asked, for he had been considering this for some while.

"I still need to understand how the 'faelore' fits into the picture; if it tells us anything about how to use it." Fairfax said, absorbed in twirling the globe around his fingertips. "I'm assuming you haven't brought this up before because Lady Hanley doesn't know about the message?"

Joshua shrugged. "There was no need to tell her until we knew more, and had worked out a plan. Nemis thought I should go as soon as, well, as soon as we could work out where to go. But that was before the baby arrived. And now, even though travelling together would take longer, I can't see how I can leave them behind." He glanced at Fairfax, who avoided looking at him by studying the globe intently, before voicing what had become foremost in his heart. "I can't leave the baby behind. Nemis says... she says the baby is destined to be ours. Mine and Aioffe's."

He shook his head. "It makes no sense, but I cannot deny that being a father to her comes so naturally. I already love her so much, I can't see how Nemis could ever give her up."

His eyes filled just at the thought of separation from the child he adored. After a moment to gather himself, during which Fairfax thankfully kept quiet, Joshua's voice turned gruff. "Besides, it would upset Lady Hanley greatly if we were all to leave to find Aioffe and Spenser, even if we knew where to find them. We thought, Nemis and

I, that if she knew we intended to go, she would throw us out in a temper, before we had a starting point. With a newborn, and Mark as he is, that didn't seem like a sensible course of action. So I've just had to wait until we could find that starting point. Hence my messages to you."

Joshua gazed into the fireplace, grateful for the opportunity his friend was giving him to unburden. "I've sent out every kestrel I've found to the continent, hoping for anything which might reassure us, or give us a clue to a location. But they return with the letters intact. Even the birds don't know where to find my wife." His voice broke and he swallowed. Much as though he liked Fairfax, the pressure of voicing his fears caught up with him.

Fairfax paused in his examination, and uncharacteristically placed his hand on Joshua's shoulder. "I'm sure she's fine," he said. "I would have heard something by now if she'd been discovered by humans. Even if your interpretation is correct, fae do not kill fae. As far as I know, anyway."

"What do you mean?" Joshua's heart thumped.

Fairfax tipped his head to one side. His eyes grew serious. "Amongst other things, I trade in information about creatures. I'd hear if one with wings had come up at a trial."

"A witch trial?"

Fairfax nodded. "There's been a spate of them - mostly silliness about licking toads and suchlike, but I saw Mother Shipton a few weeks ago, and it was enough to concern her." His expression took on an owl-like pomposity. "Her prophecies are coming truer with every passing year."

"What does she say will happen? Did she mention anything about fae?"

Shifting in his seat whilst playing with the globe, Fairfax's manner was almost off hand as he said, "She'd have mentioned if she heard anything about a witch being discovered with wings, I'm sure. I'm sure."

Joshua watched the prominent knob on his long neck dip as he swallowed. For all Fairfax's mastery of disguise, to those who knew him, he was easy to read. The daemon hid far more than he was saying right now. Joshua couldn't help but wonder whether Fairfax had begun placing much too much reliance on prophecies than he previously had. Stomach sinking, Joshua realised Fairfax had barely reacted at all when told about Nemis's baby being destined for Aioffe and himself.

CHAPTER FORTY-EIGHT

Durant

Bavaria
June 24th - Midsummer's Day 1554

Steadying her hand, Aioffe hesitated momentarily before bringing the knife down with a surety she did not feel. Durant's pupaetion had to end; it was time to see what she had wrought. The blade slipped through the crusty outer cocoon, which crumbled under the metal intrusion. She sawed down the length of his prison; her face screwed with concentration as the stench - not crisp and freshly baked but mouldy - released its assault. In response, her pulse fluttered with dim expectation. After coughing away the cloud, she re-focused, dragging the knife down to his feet.

"Mind you do not mar him," Queen Illania said, in a quieter, tight tone that Aioffe thought she deserved. The Queen's snappy impatience had brought them to the pupaetion clearing sooner than Aioffe would have liked. Delaying the dreaded inevitable to give Joshua time to decide versus saving Spensers' life.

But the timing was fortuitous - Midsummer. The Queen had demanded that her new Prince's pupaetion should take place on this ancient and blessed date.

The vine barrels had been moved, and were now arranged in a circle around the raised earth bed which Durant, in his cocoon, lay upon.

Illania insisted that he should begin his new life as all fae do, as much as it was practical for a fully grown man anyway.

Being amongst the vines was bittersweet for Aioffe. Appropriate, she could not deny, but irksome as a reminder of her failure thus far. Their glistening white cocoons, dangling in the sunlight, witnessed her shame. Her infertility. These plants were the reason she had travelled here, and yet, she had been unable to locate the royal vine to solve her problem. Even today, when they arrived, Aioffe had tarried too long glancing around the circle to check if it had appeared, resulting in a glare. A poke from a spear by the Queen's Guard suggested that her question about where the royal vine was kept, if not with the others here, would not be welcomed without a successful pupaetion.

As her knife reached the foot end of the cocoon, Aioffe glanced back. By this time, Joshua had begun wriggling, pushing against the inner membrane which enclosed him. Durant was still. She listened for his heartbeat, hoping that some kind of miracle would have occurred in her absence.

There was nothing. Only the rustle of the leaves blowing in the gentle breeze. She felt the soldier's eyes on her, assessing her every movement with curiosity.

"Well?" Illania said. "Should he be moving by now?"

Aioffe nodded without looking at her. She reached into the shell and touched Durant's feet. Her fingers stretched around, feeling for the soles. A scrap of the cocoon broke off with a quiet crack. It lay, bark-like, by her knees. As she rubbed, she realised that the cocoon's inside was riddled with red threads. A remnant perhaps of the blood they shared? She began to hope, and pressed the sensitive arches harder, massaging the skin beneath the cold membrane.

Still no response. No heartbeat or wriggle.

The warmth of his foot seemed so far to be entirely transferred from herself to him. Aioffe thought quickly. Something more was needed to awaken him, maybe?

She slipped one hand out and delved its fingertips into the earth next to her. Then, as her fingernails scraped beneath the soil, she found the tiny roots of the trees all about and pulled. Her eyes closed as she envisaged the Lifeforce within the forest surrounding them. Green and brown - she tasted it and tugged harder. Musty, like mushrooms, but potent. Aioffe forced the strands down, out into the hand clutching

Durant's foot. The essence of the earth - all the wriggling creatures buried deep inside, succulent roots and juicy bulbs, even the decay from life-giving compost, she channeled through her arms, her body, and tried to conduct it into him.

This man must live! Like a mantra, she repeated it in her head, not realising that she was mouthing the words as well.

Her eyes flew open - there was another! Another Lifeforce present in the earth… no, it was next to her!

She glanced over her shoulder to see Queen Illania behind. Her chubby face was set as she concentrated also, white eyed and unfocussed. But, she was pulling the Lifeforce from her guards! Aioffe gasped, watching the strands flow into Illania's outstretched arms.

The soldiers crumpled as one, dropping to the ground with a clatter of armour and spears. Their bodies shrivelled and greyed for just a moment, then crumbled into ash.

"Oh!" Aioffe gasped, horrified, as chest plates, no longer filled, collapsed onto the grass. Empty.

Then, with eyes turned a vivid green, Illania rose up from her tub. Thin wings rippled with energy as she flapped them in a blur. Her chubby arms were outstretched in front of her, as if she were carrying a tray laden with full mugs.

Aioffe froze, unsure of her intentions. She could feel the earth-energy twisting through her, trying to escape into Durant's body.

But death does not accept.

Death has no flow; it is an end.

Aioffe looked back at Durant's grey carcass, still encased in the slimy sac which was supposed to preserve his life. She smelled the decay, and suddenly understood then that trying to push her earthy Lifeforce into him would be futile. She pulled her hand away from his feet and retracted her fingers from the soil.

A dark shadow, Illania, hovered above the body. Aioffe dared not look up at her, fearful of her retribution.

All of that power which the Queen had drawn in - it had to go somewhere.

Chubby hands grabbed hers, and instantly the searing heat made Aioffe want to pull away. But, Illania kept a-hold of them and pulled them both closer to Durant. Aioffe could not tear her eyes from Durant's chest. Illania pushed both of their hands down, onto the sac and splayed her fingers over the back of Aioffe's hands.

Aioffe exhaled, a long and loaded breath. In that instant, Illania released the Lifeforce she had gathered, and Aioffe felt the blessings coursing through her palms and into the body beneath. The threads jolted out, lightning rippling, scorching from her hands. Aioffe's breath clouded, brown and murky green, billowing over Durant.

"Again," Illania commanded.

Aioffe pulled from her toes, embedded without realising it, into the dirt beneath. The Lifeforce flowed through her limbs, a sensation which she recognised from the first time she had ever blessed in Naturae, when her faes' belief in her had been so strong, so trusting. Her fingers flexed, and she bent forwards, sliding her hands away from Illania's to embrace Durant. Lifting his chest towards hers, Illania shoved her final burst of energy into him and Aioffe felt his body jerk.

The sudden spasm kicked his legs, bursting them from the cocoon. Aioffe kept clasping him, believing that she would hear that blessed heartbeat against hers. Tears filled her eyes, her mouth contorted, twisting with hope as she breathed out the last vapours of the forest Lifeforce.

Then, sensing Illania had retreated, Aioffe pulled back from the tepid, one-sided embrace. Durant's arm moved! Beneath the sac, she noticed a slight twitch! She reached up and tore a hole in the head. Surely he would need a breath…

Her fingers widened the gap. More arm wriggles, encouraging her. Gently, she laid him back onto the ground, so she could use both hands to pull the stretchy membrane aside.

But, as she unwrapped him, she saw. Saw the horror. Saw the decay. And saw her failure.

Durant opened his eyes. Black, blank ovals in a face of mottled grey. His lips, a darker shade of grey, mouthed at her, but did not draw breath.

She touched his chest, and the tears which had gathered slipped down her cheek as she stared into his eyes. There was no heartbeat. No soul in the dark pools of his eyes.

Her own warm, alive, heart thumped. Had she just created the Dark Heir? She panicked, eyes shooting over him as the terror took hold. The one which Nemis had foretold? Fear tingled around her core. A cold which drained the warmth from the earth's Lifeforce sapped her, and she sagged.

"What have you done?" Queen Illania screeched.

Aioffe's head snapped around. "I do not know." Her tear dropped onto Durant. "What have we done?"

Illania dropped to the other side of Durant, whose grotesque face rotated to look at her. Aioffe gasped as his arm pulled free of the membrane and reached for the Queen. His naked body, she saw now, had no marks on it at all. No scars from the wound she had inflicted at his creation. Yet the skin, which ought to be pinking surely by now, remained a pale blotchy grey.

Queen Illania turned her head, retreating from the slimy arm approaching her person. She shrank back, repulsed. Durant's dark eyes fixated upon her, his lips moving, mouthing something soundlessly.

Aioffe's bewildered gaze rose, meeting the Queen's. She saw her fear, and knew there would be recriminations later.

"He cannot be," Aioffe said. "He is not alive. Not in the sense that we are."

"He is not dead either!" Illania replied, still retreating. She turned herself over, breaking the eye-contact and began to crawl away.

"We cannot leave him like this," Aioffe said. She looked down at Durant. "We cannot." She pushed herself up to standing. Whilst staring at Durant with a curious fascination which she couldn't help but feel, Aioffe dusted her gown off. Her mouth set and she straightened her crown. Only then did she have the courage.

"We have to do something to release him," Aioffe said. She stepped deliberately back from the cocoon, wondering if he understood what they said. Under her breath, she hissed, "He is wrong. Un-dead."

Illania turned, a furious red flushing across her cheeks. "Well, he certainly isn't alive." Her cherubic lips pursed. "You'll have to try again."

"What?" Aioffe's mouth fell open. "You can't mean that. I cannot do it."

"What choice do you have, dear?" Illania's eyes tightened. "We had an agreement."

Aioffe glanced back at Durant, her heart sinking. Although he was still lying down, he had begun to experiment with movement. His limbs jerked and twitched, as if trying to rid themselves of the constriction but not knowing how to.

"Deal with that 'thing'. No-one can see the mess you have made of him," the Queen commanded, and attempted to stand. Her little feet scrabbled as her rotund form flailed, arms not strong enough to propel her upright over her fat belly. Aioffe found she could not move, so dumbstruck by the implications of her order.

"What do you mean, 'deal with'?" Aioffe felt the burn of anger rise inside.

Illania's hand waved in a small circle. "Deal with it. Kill it. Whatever. Just remove it from my sight."

"I can't just kill him," Aioffe said. Whilst Durant, as he was now, horrified her, the thought of taking another's life having given so much to create it was too much to even entertain thinking about.

"No," she said, "I will not. We made this - *him*. And now, we must face the consequences. Together. There will not be another whilst this one 'lives'. Until we figure out what happened. I cannot. I will not."

"Fine," Illania said grumpily. With an enormous groan, she heaved herself up to standing. Wobbling as she adjusted to her new upright position, Illania waddled across to Durant.

Aioffe turned, calming now the Queen seemed to agree. "I don't understand what went wrong?" She shook her head, not expecting an immediate answer from her counterpart. She began wondering how to phrase the question of what they were going to do with him. How would they explain him? He obviously wasn't going to suit being a Prince. They hadn't even seen if he had wings underneath him or not, so was he even a fae? What if he was the Dark Heir?

Illania waddled at speed, straight past Durant, to where the dust of the fae guard lay. Picking up a sword from the ground, the Queen coughed under her breath as she straightened. Aioffe rushed towards him. "No!" she cried out. "Not like this!"

"Not like what?" The sword was almost as long as Illania was tall. She lumbered towards Aioffe and Durant, brandishing the blade in their direction. A cruel smile threatened on one side of her lips.

Aioffe's mouth dropped. The tip of the sword pointed directly at her! She didn't deserve this - it wasn't her fault, she thought. She flung herself over Durant's jerking torso.

Oh Joshua... where are you now? What have I done?

The squelch of the blade slicing through Durant's neck, followed by the crunch of bone as it hit his vertebrae, was the most awful noise Aioffe had heard in many a year. She squeezed her eyes shut, wishing she could hold her arrowhead just one more time. Tried desperately not to think of how the cold steel might feel slicing through her own neck - which was surely next.

"Fae do not kill fae." Illania's cold voice broke through her terror. "And a Queen should never kill a Queen."

Aioffe lifted her head. "They killed my grandmother."

Illania's eyes narrowed. After a heartbeat of staring at each other, Illania said, "You will try again, though. Or I will re-write the rules and thus the terms of our deal. And then you will have two deaths on your conscience. Spenser won't last forever."

Aioffe closed her eyes, sinking on top of Durant's torso. The fact that he had not crumbled into ashes beneath her as fae did served only to reaffirm her failure to convert him. No blood seeped from his neck, his head had barely moved after his execution. The one consolation was that he probably would have felt no pain by Illania's swift and merciful actions. She doubted she could have so unremorsefully killed him, however much of a salvation it was. Now she had to live forever with the knowledge of her part in his death.

Her hand reached into her pocket and fingers closed around the leather bundle. As she listened to the Queen's footsteps crunch away, she wept. For poor, innocent Durant. For her failure. For Joshua, whom she should never have betrayed. Never have pushed aside.

CHAPTER FORTY-NINE

Sacrifice

Beesworth
24th June - Midsummer's Night 1554

Obscured by the clouds of smoke, Joshua hovered. Fires had been lit on the windward side of the crops so that cleansing power of the vapours would drive away disease. Its damp musty scent caught in his throat as the plumes drifted across the town, but he remained hidden, watching. Below him, the common land and marketplace square in Beesworth thrummed with music, whistles, and whoops as the traditional 'threading the needle' dance signalled the closing of the summer solstice festivities. Joshua's hope-filled heart sang along, although, as he watched Nemis lurking in a doorway rather than joining the line of dancers, he knew their imminent parting would be difficult. Fairfax whirled gaily amidst the train of people bobbing and weaving with the line as if he had always been a part of the tight-knit community. Joshua smiled at his carefree nature, knowing he was intoxicated also by their earlier achievements in deciphering Aioffe's location.

He briefly considered dropping down to join them. Perhaps he could rearrange his clothing to hide his wings in a back alley, pull a cap low, so he might mingle once again with humanity. It would be a welcome infusion of their Lifeforce. But then, a group of shouting women caught his eye. They pushed their way through the crowd, stumbling towards the corner of the square where Nemis quietly stood.

Squinting against the smoke, he realised one of them had Mark in her grasp! The boy's whimpering reached his sharp ears through the noise of the celebrations. Sensing an upset about to occur, Joshua dipped down. His eyes darted around for a suitable place to land. He settled for dropping onto the familiar thatched cottage next to the forge, knowing the billowing fire there would still give him a measure of security. It was close enough that he could better hear, maybe even see, what was happening.

"Is this Lady Hanley's boy? You work for 'er. Well, is it?" One of the women screeched. Nemis shrank into a doorway but her arm stretched out to grab at Mark.

The woman holding him didn't let go, but thrust him forward so he fell, kneeling into the mud.

"He's the one!" His captor snarled. "Helpin' his'self to my trinkets. Yer should be ashamed o'yerself." She glared between them both and carried on scolding. "Lettin' him out without accompanyin' him. To stare at us. He's not right in the 'ed."

"Turn out 'is pockets, let's see what he took!"

"'E's touched by the Devil, that one. A child has no right to stare peculiar at 'is betters like that. Much less be pinching' things."

"Lady Hanley won't take kindly to her lads bein' priggers!"

Onlookers clustered around Mark and the ladies; a thief caught in action was always of interest. Joshua could only imagine the accusers pulling at the poor boy's clothing, as his view became obscured with legs and skirts. Craning his neck, Joshua glimpsed the muddied hem of Nemis's skirt as she jostled out of the doorway, pushing the women aside to reach her son.

"No! Get off him. He's done nothing wrong!" Nemis screeched.

"Look! My sacred amulet!" One of the women cried out victoriously. "Ow! He hit me!"

The onlookers gasped, then began muttering amongst themselves. The sound of clothes being ripped told Joshua the searching continued, despite Mark's wrestling against their intrusive fingers. Then the child screamed. It was a noise fit to put anyone on edge, piercing and filled with terror. Gritting his teeth, Joshua pulled himself higher on the roof, and inched as silently as he could towards the side to see better. He cursed under his breath, regretting not landing earlier so that he might intervene.

"And another!" A fist shot up holding a polished stone. Glinting brightly in the flickers of the torchlight, heads started shaking, tut-tutting when they saw the token.

Mark's scream escalated. Joshua's heart dropped into his boots - when it came to pretty pebbles, Mark had little care for whose property it was.

"Oh, this little prig is fair loaded with our things! He's been watchin' us. Waitin' ''til we was distracted so's he could take 'em."

"Well, I saw him starin' at my cow, and now she's no milk... Now this!"

"No," Nemis cried again. "It's not his fault!"

"Not his fault? The proof is on him, right here!" The woman who had dragged Mark across the square shouted, shaking the stone at Nemis. "He took it 'right enuf!"

Nemis had pushed forwards enough that Joshua could see her standing, arms stretched out in front of Mark. "He does not mean any harm." She had to shout to be heard over his deafening scream.

The lad was held splayed by three people, at his wrists and collar, and pulled up from the mud. His skinny legs kicked out in all directions. Nemis jerked into the fray as if she might catch him. The baby's head, falling clear of the shawl strapping which held her close to Nemis's chest, nearly collided with Mark's airborne feet. Nemis ducked her bundle clear of flailing limbs, but she kept trying to reach for her son, her feet dancing a muddy jig in the street. The threesome shuffled backwards and yanked him from side to side, desperate to keep their grip on the wriggling thief.

Joshua felt helpless as the women holding Mark snarled at Nemis in a most impolite manner. Mostly, all Joshua could see between the heads jiggling into his eyeline was their heavy-set faces, frowning against the protective ferocity Joshua suspected was on Nemis's face.

"'Ow do you know he means no 'arm?"

"Yeah, who's he to you?"

Nemis looked desperately around the faces surrounding her; Joshua knew she was searching for help, but he could do nothing from his perch without making a bad situation worse. He stared intently at her, but she did not spot him.

"He's my son," she pleaded. Anguish stretched across her features. "And he means no harm. He's just... Mark!"

"Mama!" His piercing scream did nothing to help his situation. After the loud wail cut off abruptly, he collapsed, dangling between his captors' arms. The weight in Joshua's chest doubled. It took a few moments for the onlookers to adjust to the difference in noise level, then a silence fell as everyone stared at the limp child.

Joshua's pulse raced as a voice piped up, "Look at her baby!"

Before Nemis could raise a hand to cover the red scarring across the baby's face, the woman who held Mark's collar screeched, "Touched! Touched by the dev'l his'self!" She flung her arms in the air as if she had touched a hot pan.

Mark fell to the floor as the women retracted their grasp, immediately wringing their hands on their skirts as if the taint of the Devil would cleanse by wiping. The accusers wailed, a pitiful, self absorbed and frightened cloud of sound which spread through the superstitious crowd like the flames had earlier licked the crops. With mounting horror, people began to step backwards, menfolk pulling their wives away from the source of terror yet reluctant to flee from what was turning out to be the exposure of the decade.

A witch in their midst! Her children marked by Satan himself!

Nemis rushed forward and dropped to Mark's side. Joshua, knowing all eyes were on his friends right now, rolled off the roof and landed, crouched, but on his feet. There was no other choice. He had to get them out of this situation. Being exposed had become irrelevant.

He peered up - then breathed a sigh of relief.

Fairfax's cape flared out as he loped towards the crowd.

"Good people!" Fairfax shouted. "These children are not touched!" Heads turned towards him as he confidently announced, "Why, I saw them blessed in Christ's name myself. Just the other day."

Joshua stood, keeping to the darkness of the overhanging forge roof. Frowns formed on the sea of faces in the square. He held his breath, hoping Fairfax would manage to produce something more substantive to save his friends.

"They are innocents. Baptised in my chapel and by my own revered chaplain of Denton Hall. I can vouch for them."

Joshua recoiled inwardly at his lie - the baby had not yet been baptised because Nemis insisted Aioffe was to choose her daughter's name. It pained Joshua she was not truly accepted into his faith, but Nemis would not hear of it. The baby was known as 'Little One' at Hanley House.

"But what about her?" Another woman in the crowd called out, pointing at Nemis. "She sold us a draught, but my husband took it, then died not five days later!"

Joshua winced - recognising only then the voice of his old friend, Margaret Tunn. His vision focussed on the once friendly woman he knew; now she looked haggard and greyed. He closed his eyes and thought how very sad it was that William Tunn, whose forge he had recently alighted upon, was no longer of this world. A loving and kind man, he left behind a large family who had already suffered at the hands of fae-kind. Lyrus had killed their youngest daughter Alice when he had kidnapped Aioffe nearly two decades ago. This was the very reason why Joshua had been forced to hide his return to Beesworth ever since, for he was still implicated in the mystery of her gruesome death.

Fairfax raised his hands, "That can happen, not even the best potions and prayers can save some I'm afraid."

"It was naught but something to soothe his pain, Mistress Tunn," Nemis said. "There was nothing anybody could do for him. I warned you of that."

"Witch!"

Joshua's heart leapt into his mouth. Margaret had always held firmly Catholic convictions about what was right and wrong with the world, and grief can cause even the most level headed of people to lash out for someone to blame. Her husband had been passionately Protestant, which had caused many arguments when Joshua and Aioffe were last here.

"Witch," another voice spat. "Witch witch witch!"

Fairfax looked behind him, as if he sensed Joshua was watching. "Ridiculous!" He said as he turned back to the crowd. "Do you all wish to ruin this perfectly pleasant evening on such a note? Good people of Beesworth, let us take a moment to reconsider. You have no proof of this accusation."

"Witch!"

Joshua didn't think - his feet had a mind of their own as he walked towards the throng.

"Lock her up! She's brought nothing but sorrow." Margaret wailed. "My poor William... he walks with the Devil for sure now. Her son," she pointed at Mark, white-faced and still inert in Nemis's arms. "Was watching us an' all, the day he died. He's the one told the Devil t'was time to collect." Margaret burst into melodramatic sobs; Joshua heard vague placations as someone dragged her away.

Joshua froze. Having just come from the forge himself, she would pass him on the road. There was no doubt Margaret would remember the face of the man accused of her daughter's murder. Then, he jutted his chin forwards. Discovery was less important than protecting Nemis and his family right now. But he ducked his head all the same, inwardly praying Margaret would not look up.

"I have done nothing!" Nemis protested.

"Maybes, maybes not," a strident yet slightly slurring voice called over the rising clamour. "But you'll have to tell it to the Assize. All of you. 'Tis not for you to rule upon here and now. This woman and her," and he paused to emphasise, "children, will face the judgement of your betters. Now, move along, so they can be removed to the gaol."

Joshua reached the perimeter of the crowd, just as Nemis dropped to her knees. "Not my children, no...."

"I vouch for her - as well as the children," Fairfax blustered, stepping towards the portly man who seemed to have assumed authority. "She can leave now, with me, and nothing more need be said."

"The accusation has been levied." The man waved a hand across to Nemis and the still pale and limp Mark. "And as Assistant to the Sheriff of this county, I am obliged to take the matter to be heard and investigated. Now," he shook his head, looking back to Fairfax, "I don't know who you are, Sir, but you have no standing hereabouts to be making such claims about a woman of this town without announcing on whose authority you can claim to vouch for her."

"I am Sir Thomas Fairfax, of Denton Hall." Fairfax bowed slightly, then straightened his jacket as if that alone would persuade the crowd of his status. Joshua wanted to nudge his way closer as everyone was now paying attention to their official. But his wings... he had to remain in the shadows. The risk was too great.

"Well then, Sir Fairfax, are you laying claim to the responsibility for this woman? Is she a member of your household, perhaps?"

Fairfax looked flustered. "Err... no. But I know her. Know her well enough to vouch that she is no witch."

"Let him take my children at least," Nemis begged. "Take me. Try me. But for the love of God, my children are innocent."

The portly man's lips pursed, then he twitched, realising that the accused had been very careful with her wording. His eyes narrowed and he leaned towards her. Joshua smelt the hops on his breath as his gaze studied first Nemis, then the baby beneath her.

"You have touched your child with your evil, so great it has left a scar," he muttered, passing judgement even though he had no right to, yet the conviction in his tone told of his awareness of the support of the crowd around him in his assertion. He drew in a long breath, thrust his hips forward and shuffled his legs to stand with some pomposity. "But," he held up a finger and ruled. "The babe can be cleansed. Baptised again, back into the graces of the Lord God himself. It speaks not yet, so cannot have knowingly consented to this blasphemy." He glanced over to Fairfax. "Can you promise to baptise her again? Immediately?"

"Absolutely." Fairfax said, his eyes wide. "And the boy too; he's a fool and does not know what he might have said." Joshua's teeth grit together as Fairfax babbled on. "I can take them all with me. Take them far away from you so you aren't exposed any more. I was on my way home anyway. Only passing through your fair town..."

Mark's accuser shouted out, "She's been here for months! The boy stole from me, and she encouraged it!"

"Er... Yes. I know I've only just arrived, but... she's a good woman, a kind one. I've known her for years." Fairfax said. "I..." He spread his hands convivially as he reached for words which would persuade. Placate rather than infuriate.

But then, to Joshua's dismay, the townsfolk rounded on Fairfax as if he were entirely responsible for Nemis's behaviour. "Did she always refuse to join in, then? Back where you came from? Is that why she moved away?"

"She didn't dance, or sing at all!" Another chirped up, "I saw her, she didn't even join you in the threading line..."

All about the crowd began muttering again, nodding confirmation between each other. The new cunning woman, still an outsider, had chosen to stay on the edges of the celebrations, as if she didn't want to give thanks like everyone else did. Only so many excuses could be made for her behaviour. Joshua caught the glee in their voices as they said, now she's exposed as a witch! Well, this just confirmed what we thought all along…

"It was me," Nemis interrupted. "I am the one you want. Only me. I… took their innocence. I made them behave like this, I confess it! I thought to bring them to the Devil, but I knew it was wrong. For their safety, I beg you. They have a higher destiny than I sought to give them. The babe must go to her father," Nemis said, her eyes rolling up to the skies. To where she presumably thought Joshua was. "Take them, Thomas. Sir Fairfax, I beg you. For the love of God, let my lord here take them both. Take the baby to her father, so that she may meet her true mother."

Joshua's heart thudded so loudly he was surprised no-one turned at the beat. He could only stare as Nemis unwound the shawl holding the baby. She shoved the child into Fairfax's arms and hung her head low.

With eyes which threatened to spill over, Joshua stepped back, silently sneaking away from the judgemental townsfolk and wishing she could as well. But it was not possible for Nemis. No amount of prayers or gallant intervention would help her now. The Sheriffs Assistant had already been passed a length of rope, which he was untangling in readiness.

Hopelessness swept through him. Nemis… gentle, noble, and wise Nemis. How to extract her from this predicament? To barge in now would only make matters worse for her. He was a marked man, and his unhidden wings would cause even more fear. The longer this spectacle continued, the greater the charges which would be levied against his friend. He glanced up - the cover of smoke had thinned, so no aerial escape was practical, and there were too many people gathered to barge his way in and grab her. A tightness constricted his chest, a vice of fear he knew too well from having been hounded out of many a town before under threat of exposure.

"Mark, come here, let's go," he heard Fairfax say. Joshua glanced back to see Nemis shoving Mark, groggy and bewildered, into Fairfax's outstretched arm. The other held his daughter, clamped under his elbow. A bundled parcel who had no idea she was being ripped away from her mother with slim prospects of seeing her again.

The only small mercy was that Mark didn't realise this either. The lad looked up at Fairfax, his friend, and Joshua saw his lip wobble briefly before Fairfax pulled him away.

"Now disperse, please." The Assistant to the Sherrif decreed. "This woman shall remain under my watch, fear not good people."

Joshua's heart broke with Nemis's sob, yet he dared not linger in plain sight. He would be no good to any of them if another hullabaloo arose, which it would should he be recognised now. The town did not need reminding of the murder of a beloved child to re-ignite their fury. Slipping through the shadows until he was a safe distance away, he then paused, slumping against the corner of a house like a drunkard. Head lowered, he waited until Fairfax approached, the baby pinned under his arm, his hand clutching Mark's. Thomas's gaze met his, seeing him yet not acknowledging him. As they passed, Joshua glanced back up over to the square. Nemis's head turned and he caught the flash of her eyes as she was pushed away.

"I will keep her safe." He whispered the promise, as if she could hear him across the distance. "And I will find Spenser and Aioffe."

"And Lord help us all then," Fairfax said crossly under his breath. "For her sacrifice cannot be made in vain and I would not wish the fury of the Fae upon anyone."

CHAPTER FIFTY
Rags and a response

The chaos Joshua arrived back at Hanley House to find was, for once, nothing to do with Fairfax. Having left him handling a screaming and rigid Mark on the track out of town and flown back through the darkness of night, Joshua was still feeling guilty when he landed outside the kitchen with his daughter in his arms. The door was slightly ajar; he heard fevered whispers inside the kitchen. He paused, glancing down at the sleeping baby, and hesitated, wondering if he ought instead to simply fly up to his room to begin packing without interruption. But, curiosity overtook him, and he pushed the wood open further and peeked his head around.

"He cannot stay here!" Mary Hanley's urgent whisper drew his eyes to the tall heap of rags on a chair in the fireside corner.

"But I don't have anywhere else to take him," a familiar, creaky voice insisted.

Joshua stepped inside. "Issam! What are you doing here?" At that moment, the change in temperature caused the baby to fully awaken, with a lusty bawl. He jiggled her in his arms and closed the door behind them.

"My Prince!" Issam exclaimed and walked unsteadily around the table. The old fae looked exhausted, a greyness to his wrinkled face darker still by the light of the tallow candles. His spare hand shot out to grab Issam's when he stumbled on the uneven kitchen flagstones. A hooded figure, wearer of the tatty rags on the chair, turned towards the noise. The baby's cry increased in volume. Lady Hanley winced as Issam retracted his arm in horror.

"She needs food," Joshua said. "I think."

Ignoring for a moment his friend and the hunched over guest, who seemed to shrink further into a ball in the corner with his arrival, Joshua grabbed the jug on the table. Pouring into a warming saucepan with only one cold, shaking hand, the milk spilt. Lady Hanley tut-tutted. The baby's angry cries grew louder than he thought possible, making conversation impractical. For a long moment, and aware that all eyes were watching him whispering entreaties and jiggling her on his hip, Joshua swilled the milk around. Something, anything, to fill the void in them both. He knew he had to focus on her, calm her somehow, but he couldn't keep a straight thought in his head, especially when she shrieked with renewed gusto. Joshua glanced about to the stony faces staring at him and decided the better of asking for help.

"Where's Nemis?" Lady Hanley demanded.

There was no sense in hiding the truth - the consequences would become apparent come morning. It would not be long before the townsfolk would ask questions about her relationship to Nemis. Aware that he was about to further disrupt Lady Hanley's life, yet again, Joshua said, "She was taken for a witch. The women of the town." He sighed and shook his head. "They rounded on Mark for taking a stone, so she defended him. Then, the babe's birth mark was exposed." He bit his lip, the fright of what happened threatening to overwhelm him. "Thomas..."

"What did that devil do? I'll tear him limb from limb..."

"No, no, no," Joshua interjected, holding his hand up to calm her. "He intervened! Promised to have the children re-baptised, take them all away to safety." He looked down at the baby, whose bright blue eyes fixated upon his as she took a breath in, before she screwed up her face and bawled again. "Without him, Mark and this little one would be holed up in gaol as well as Nemis."

Lady Hanley sniffed, and just then, Mark's screaming drifted into their earshot. "So he's bringing the boy back then?"

"Sounds like it," Joshua said. Lady Hanley collapsed into the nearest chair, put her head in her hands and sighed. From the corner of his eye, Joshua noticed the hooded figure straighten. Joshua turned in his crouch over the fire, so that he might study him better. The boots, poking out slightly from beneath the shroud, looked familiar. Fae-made.

Before he could ask for an introduction, he heard Fairfax shouting. "It's only a little further Mark, come on now. There's no need to resist any longer."

Biting his lip, for Fairfax was very good with the difficult boy yet obviously the daemon's frustration was mounting, Joshua asked, "Mary, could you watch over Mark for Nemis? He will need your help, and," he glanced down at the baby, then back at Lady Hanley. "I cannot be sure what will happen next for his mother."

Through her fingertips, she met his eyes, then nodded. Joshua poured the lukewarm milk into a cup and tried to tip some into Little One's mouth.

"Issam, why are you here? And, who have you brought?" Joshua asked.

The old spy shot Joshua a look of desperation. "My Prince," his voice faltered. "I do not know where to begin."

"I got your note, and I thank you for it," Joshua said. The babe caught onto the drip drip of the milk and was rolling the warmth about in her mouth. Her lips scrunched up and she frowned. Joshua took the moment of silence to prompt, "What has happened?"

Issam sighed. "I cannot go back. And neither can Uffer."

Joshua's head snapped around. "Uffer? Is that you?" The bundle of rags shrank further into the chair. His legs pulled up until he was a ball. Joshua stood. "What has happened, old friend?" Uffer froze.

Tipping a little more milk into the baby's mouth, Joshua placed the cup on the hearth and crossed to him. As he put his hand on Uffer's shoulder, he felt the tremors underneath. "Why do you not greet me?" Joshua frowned briefly, then raised his eyebrow at Issam.

"He is outcast," Issam explained.

Mary stared at the floor, her hands dropping in a clutch to her lap.

"Who did this?" Joshua demanded. "By what right?"

"Lyrus," Issam replied.

"Is he hurt? Uffer, tell me, did he hurt you?" Joshua knelt by his friend's side and cast his eyes over the rags. Now that he was closer, by the light of the fire, he could see the dark bloodstains dried on

Uffer's rags. Uffer's head, still covered, pushed deeper between his knees.

"You are not outcast here," Joshua said gently. "And whatever he has done to you matters not to us. You are safe here." He squeezed Uffer's arm, understanding the shame which the very phrase 'outcast' implied to the once proud fae. "You could never be outcast to me, you know this."

Lady Hanley's voice was stiff as she concurred. "Nor I." He caught the glance between herself and Issam. She too had been outcast from Naturae, almost a century ago, for failing to catch Aioffe and falling in love with a daemon. Aioffe also had considered herself outcast - it was the very worst punishment for a fae and had been quietly outlawed since Aioffe had taken the throne.

Still, Uffer did not move. Without thinking about it, Joshua's fingers moved to his jacket, to stroke the heart he had sewn there to remind him of Aioffe.

"Why did Lyrus do this?" Joshua's question caused Issam to look away, not meet his eyes.

"Because he stood up for the Council. For Aioffe. "

Joshua's face darkened. "Why did he need to?"

Issam shrugged. "Naturae has changed, my Prince. Lyrus has taken his royal lineage too far and now thinks he rules in place of Aioffe. Lyrus called him a traitor."

Exhaling, Joshua's head dropped. He suspected this might happen. And by leaving, he had allowed it to. "And what did he do to Uffer?"

"He docked his wings. Publicly," Issam's voice broke. "To make an example of him."

Lady Hanley gasped. She also had suffered the same shame under Queen Lana's rule and had not returned to Naturae since.

The door squeaked open, interrupting their shock. Issam stood, his chair clattering to the floor in his haste to make ready to run again. Before he could move any further away though, Fairfax chattered to Mark. "Go along now. We're home. Let's go in and get warm."

"Come in, Mark," Joshua's voice sounded hollow as he automatically tried to help bring the terror-stricken child inside. "Lady Hanley is here as well. We've been waiting for you."

Mark stumbled across the threshold, pushed by an as yet unseen hand. Fairfax followed, his hair wild as he glanced around. Then, a broad grin spread over his face as he recognised Issam. His delight was not reciprocated; Issam shrank away, his eyes frantically darting between Joshua and Lady Hanley.

Joshua sighed and said, "Issam, sit down. Thomas will not betray you and I'm sure you can stand to be in the same room as a few daemons for a minute while we sort out what to do." Lady Hanley went over to Mark and knelt down in front of him.

The boy's white face stared straight ahead, his eyes blank. Joshua feared he might begin screaming once again, but, she took his hands in hers and said calmly, "Now young man, I hear you have had quite a night of it."

Mark ignored her, tremors running through his whole body. Yet she carried on soothing, stroking the backs of his hands and waited for her touch to reach him. "We won't let anything happen to your Mama. She will be home to you soon. Let me get you some warm milk and tuck you up in your bed so you can rest until she gets here. You must be so tired after that long walk." She paused and gazed daggers at Fairfax, as if the child's state was his doing.

Wisely, Fairfax said nothing.

The babe broke the expectant silence, letting out a belch, then a contented gurgle. With amazement, Joshua watched as Mark's head swivelled to his sister, widened eyes seeking confirmation that she was safe. Holding the baby up so Mark could see, Joshua nodded encouragement. "Little One thinks so too, Mark."

When Mark looked back towards Fairfax, Thomas ruffled his hair and said, "Bed sounds good," and almost instantly, the shaking ceased. Fairfax grinned, winking at Lady Hanley. He then had the wit to pour some warmed milk into Mark's favourite cup. Mark stayed silent throughout, his gaze moving between the known and the unknown, before his eyes lowered and he turned towards Lady Hanley. She led him out of the room, glaring at both Joshua and Fairfax on her way.

Joshua moved Little One to his shoulder and rubbed her shoulders and spine while he thought. The action calmed both of them. Fairfax collapsed into the fireside chair and warmed his hands. With his back turned to the visitors, Joshua gazed into the fire, watching the dancing vapours twirl around. The small, persistent flames would keep burning until the wood underneath was blackened, turning eventually grey and spent. And so it was with his love.

Nothing else must distract him from being like the flames; no amount of smoke should mist his path, or diversions from added fuel. He saw then the way which matters must unfold. Although his heart felt heavy with what was happening with Nemis and Naturae, they would eventually be suffocated if he did not address the foremost issue. Aioffe.

She was the air which breathed into his fire. Without her, he was only smouldering. Ineffective.

It was merely a question of putting matters in motion, he thought, as he watched Issam sidle towards Uffer. A plan took shape. "I must pack," Joshua said, turning to them both. "And Thomas, I think it's best you leave as well."

"What of us?" Issam said. "Where are you going?"

Uffer's head, still concealed by the cape, bobbed up from his knees.

"I have a job for you both to do," Joshua said, turning to Issam as he gently gripped Uffer's shoulder. "One which, while you wait for our return, might give your lives back it's meaning and purpose. Both of you."

Fairfax raised an eyebrow. "Definitely time for me to go!"

Joshua chuckled. "Yes, those two words aren't ones which I felt carried much weight with you. Although," he smiled, "I am already in your debt enough as it is, but we still require your assistance."

He turned to Uffer and pulled back his hood. Uffer's greying head remained lowered, yet the dips and folds of skin to the sides of his neck showed how malnourished he was. "Lord Anaxis, I will ask Lady Hanley if you could assist her with the running of this small but important household in my absence. I must find Aioffe, and I cannot take Nemis's son with me. Lady Hanley must look after him, but she will need your help as he takes much attention. She will require your gentle guiding hand in the absence of his mother. I believe she cares for him in a manner which is proper for a fae to feel for a daemon, but you, I trust, will be able to sense if that changes and tell me."

He then looked at Issam. "Old friend, I must ask that you also support Lady Hanley. I need her to resume her old spy duties from here, and keep me apprised of what happens with Nemis. I also need you to continue to run the network. Show her how we have set it up and share the responsibility for the spies. You do not need to return to

Naturae. You can co-ordinate it from here in Beesworth."

"And Thomas," Joshua said, spinning to Fairfax and smiling his encouragement. "If anyone can finagle a plan to free Nemis, it would be you." He adopted a stern look. "At the very least you can write to the Assize and swear blind that Nemis is no witch."

"I may have some sway I can conjure up," Fairfax said. "And if not, I'll think of an audacious plan to spirit her away, fear not. Have you told Lady Hanley of her new responsibilities?"

"Not yet," Joshua grimaced. "I will though."

"Rather you than me," Fairfax grinned. "Perhaps I'd better not be around when you do." Little One snorted, the long snort of one who has cried for a protracted time and finally relaxed into near sleep. Waggling his eyebrows, Fairfax then said, "Well, before she wakes and starts up again, I will take my leave of you good folks." He peeked out of the window. "I can be sailing for reinforcements by morning. Say goodbye to Mark for me." He clasped Joshua by his free shoulder.

"Godspeed and farewell," Joshua said. "And next time, send a kestrel back?"

"I might be able to lay my hands on a pigeon. Or perhaps a seagull?" Fairfax joked as he shut the back door behind him.

With his departure, the earlier tension eased; the kitchen fell silent as everyone absorbed Joshua's requests. "There is one more thing, Issam," Joshua said. "I know you to be men of honour, both of you. Bringing Uffer to me, Issam, risking your life for another loyal to the crown, you are one of the bravest men I know. I am grateful to you, and I know Aioffe would be as well. That is why, though, you should be careful about what information you send to Naturae." His eyebrow lifted. "But, I must ask you - to please ensure that all relevant knowledge you gather is also sent to me. I will be with the Queen shortly, and above all, she needs to know what is happening both in Naturae and in her wider realm."

Issam's dark eyes lingered on Joshua's, then he nodded curtly. "I report to you and her Majesty then, not Lyrus?"

Joshua's lip twitched up. "Report enough to him that he trusts you still, and in what the spies say. To remove their information completely might give rise to his suspicions. His paranoia. And, Thane will be able to tell you what is developing there, perhaps?"

Issam nodded. "We need to know what Lyrus plans. Although

Thane is not held in high regard any more by Lyrus or his workers, he can tell us. I have been teaching him, and Uffer, how to write. I thought, with my age, more fae should know."

"You have our gratitude, Issam, a very sensible precaution, and I know Aioffe intended to share that knowledge. You have given Naturae a fighting chance for the future by teaching its leaders." Joshua took Issam's initiative as a sign that Aioffe's philosophy was working - by trusting people with the power to shape their own future, they contribute to the common good.

"I'm sure I don't need to say this, but to be clear," Joshua dropped his voice and glanced at the doorway, half-expecting Lady Hanley to be there. Seeing the empty arch, he continued, "I trust you both to keep silent about where the Queen, myself and everyone you have seen at this house are located. Issam, you trained Mary well all those years ago, and she is an expert at imparting only what is appropriate back to Naturae. I ask you both, be careful what you send. Just until I can tell of your Queen's safe return. And then, you will all be welcome back to Naturae."

Issam smiled and gracefully lowered his head. Joshua watched his features relax as Uffer shifted in his seat and, although he still could not look at Joshua, he stretched his legs.

The babe began to issue rather unladylike snores, and Joshua smiled. He took a chair at the table and casually glanced around the room. A sense of optimism returned to Joshua as he silently bid goodbye to the kitchen where he had experienced some of the most pivotal moments of his life as a fae. Here, now, with new hope on his shoulder, he was ready to take action. In this moment, he basked in the warmth of the fire, and the joy of finding a path through the chaos. He had a plan to reach Aioffe; the next morning, he and Little One would leave, and he would find his wife again. He had to, not least for the baby, who needed a mother now. Nemis's sacrifice tonight could not be in vain - he owed it to her to fulfil the prophecy by which she had entrusted him with Little One's care.

He traced a heart upon the baby's back, moulding his fingers around the curve of her wing joints and down the edges of her tiny wings. A flame needed air to survive, or it would be snuffed out, he mused as the redness of her appendages blazed bright through the holes of the shawl. But fire is powerful, consuming all that blocks its way - as long as it has sufficient air and fuel.

The baby's wings fluttered; a dream no doubt, Joshua thought. But, if air was blowing another way, it needed redirecting towards the flames to make them grow. Then he frowned, not certain as to why it hadn't been clearer to him before. Perhaps he had been so concerned with the other fires that he had not tended to his own, but everything served a purpose, he believed. It was all in God's plan for them all, wasn't that what the Bible told?

Little One could well be the solution, he realised.

Indeed, that was what Nemis had been saying since her birth. Was she not also, then, the answer to his? What was more intimate than raising a child together? A shared and personal goal - to love and cherish a Little One into adulthood.

Into her destiny.

CHAPTER FIFTY-ONE

An unequal pairing

**Winchester Cathedral, Hampshire, 25th July, 1554.
Wedding of Queen Mary I.**

Henry settled himself within a cluster of anxious men, none of whom he knew or wanted to. He ignored attempts at conversation. Perhaps they took him for a Spaniard, perhaps just rude, but he was, at this moment, happy not to be known. Not interested in their youthful and pathetic jokes about wedding nights or how many maidens they planned to dance with later, when their twittering grew so loud it threatened calling attention to the group, he 'suggested' to one or two that they ought to be quieter and watch the proceedings with a dignity they did not yet possess. After which, they shuffled as they stood around him, eventually falling quiet. Henry understood their nervousness building as the appointed hour for the marriage ceremony drew close. To be here at all was an honour. Everyone knew the English Court was required to present a united, welcoming front to the Spanish King. Henry's own invitation had been 'lost' but the humans checking them at the entrance to the building were very susceptible to his influence; several attendees before him had clearly done a better job of opening their minds to unfamiliar faces.

They were grouped underneath a lavishly adorned archway, close to the open double doors. In the heat of the day, wilting blossoms dropped pollen onto golden cloth swagged between columns and pews, their sweet scent losing the battle against the smell of sweat as the congregation waited for the wedding parties to arrive. Behind Henry hung one of many Flemish arras, further insulating the stone walls, boasting needlework so fine they could have been paintings. Yet Henry had long since ceased being impressed by the expensive decor. After standing motionless for so long with feet pinched into too-narrow shoes, his mind wandered. He fought the urge to lean against the hanging, slip his shoes off and wriggle his toes. His gaze missed nothing however.

From this position, the view of the altar was as good as could be expected, given the ornately decorated rood screen obscured most of it. However, being in proximity to the entrance would grant him the best opportunity to assess Philip and Mary from relative safety. The hated Spaniard's retinue had already filled the pews, continuously whispering snide comments assuming they couldn't be understood. Henry's skin crawled - the vast space held an array of highly placed vampires, from both England and Spain, daemons and the occasional witch in the immediate vicinity. Too many creatures to differentiate one from another within the crowd; for once, Henry knew he blended in perfectly.

Just as Henry was debating whether his own proposed marriage to Mary would have been so lavish - a brief suggestion which had been made whilst he was in his early teens and dismissed just as quickly after a word with his father - trumpets from the square outside heralded the arrival of Philip. Henry shouldered his way through to get a better view..

Philip looked like a king, Henry determined, as he watched him stride through the doors then stop once over the threshold of the church. No matter what the marriage contract said, his proud bearing suggested he thought this was a merger of unequals. As the tall, ginger haired man with an oval face and neat beard paused, posing in the entrance as if waiting for applause, he struck Henry as pompous. Dark eyes, framed by high arching eyebrows, stared ahead, not even flicking over the decorations, the pageantry of the occasion or the amassed congregation. Perhaps the elaborateness of the arrangements was simply what he duly expected, Henry wondered. Philip's face transformed into a determined expression when he looked down the aisle, at the cross on the altar. Looking down his long nose, he seemed to sigh as he walked towards it. Henry held his breath as Philip walked past, oblivious to the tracking eyes of a mere courtier.

But Henry knew then.

The proximity of the man told him by the prickles that rose on his neck. As his eyes bore into Philip's back, this entire morning, his entire plan, to be exact, was doomed to failure.

Philip was daemon as well. Maybe not entirely, as Elizabeth also wasn't. Henry glanced around, sensing the unease of other vampires, similarly meeting a block. Maybe the Spaniard had been enhanced by a spell of some kind? Either way, Philip reached the steps before the rood screen and turned. A victorious smile, a raised eyebrow. Philip knew there was no persuading him into anything he didn't wish to do, and the congregation now also knew it.

Henry sagged, retreated backwards through the human chests behind him.

CHAPTER FIFTY-TWO

The Pyre

Norfolk, 1554

Bidding his last father-figure goodbye at his bedside, Henry gritted his teeth as he shut the door. The Duke had been so weak he could not stand, so breathless he was unable to converse, and filled with a fear which Henry remembered all too well. In a rare moment of faithlessness - or as Henry saw it - weakness, he had begged Henry to turn him. The very thought of it repulsed both of them, once the coughing fit had passed and reflection and reason returned.

An older vampire would find the process too hard, Henry had said, easing him back to the pillows; he could not, in godly faith, put his mentor through that agony nor deprive him of his soul. Out of respect, he chose not to mention that the Duke's influence had waned and he was of little use to him now. The old man didn't have long, Henry knew. Better to leave him with the comfort of his religion than an endearing curse or reminder of his failures. The courtesy visit left him on edge as he quick-ran away through the darkness of Kenninghall.

He reached the route into Norwich before dawn, slowing his pace to a sedate walk as he joined the outlying road. It took a few miles before he realised that there was an unusually great number of people heading into the second largest city in England. The majority hurried past the harvesting fields in silence, their heads bowed. Smelling the anticipation or anxiety which emanated from the steady stream of travellers urged him towards the Maid's Head, to where Fairfax would most likely be.

His route took him along the river, meandering to the centre of the town to where the inn hid behind the Cathedral, and across which he could identify his lover's ship. Smiling as he passed Bishops Bridge, Henry glanced over to Lollard's Pit, outside the city walls. He paused, eyes narrowing as he listened to the early-rising crowd shuffling over the busy waterway.

In the pit, the site of so many executions, they were again building a pyre. Furtive whispers, stained with fear and dismay, reached his ears.

The faggots laid at the base, blessed by Queen Mary herself they say...

A husband and his wife accused of heresy, who else is next?

Only the other day I saw them, they'd sworn they were Catholics once more...

So quick of the Queen, to get rid of poisonous dissent...

They're a pox on good society, the Queen makes a bold move for Rome...

Curse Kett, and curses on Wyatt. It's all that Spanish influence, I told you, King Philip was bent on bringing honest men before his Inquisition...

Rumours he'd heard before swirled around his grieving mind. Henry staggered, his hand falling to the cold stone of the bridge. His sister was making good on her threat to purge England of Protestants. And in Lollard's Pit of all places, where so many heretics, both Catholic and Protestant, had been purged of their sinful beliefs before.

"Did you choose wisely, Master Fitzroy?"

Henry's head whipped around. Jeffries stood a few feet away, a middle aged man with a wispy beard beside him. "Which side to ally with, I mean?" Jeffries said, advancing. A sadness punctuated his tone and his shoulders slumped with the weight of the knowledge of what was about to happen.

Henry looked at the dank mud beneath his boots. "I did not choose," he said slowly. It was so much more complex than he cared to share with the former monk. "I could not."

"Then, you may join us," Jeffries said. "Perhaps the sight of a family dying for what they believe in will persuade you of something. Maybe then, you will understand that this royally sanctioned act is the loss of a freedom. Of choice. By choice. The only truth you are left with is in what you believe." He shrugged. "As my friend John Foxe would have said, were he here to intervene for these poor innocents, 'Those whom the fates don't lead, they finally drag,' and that is a question for your conscience to answer."

"Do you always speak in riddles?" Henry growled.

"They would not be riddles if you had a clear vision."

Henry's hand clenched atop the stone. Sharing a steady gaze with the witch, he was compelled to break eye contact after only a few seconds. He had no desire to see their sacrifice. Worse, and, annoyingly, Jeffries was correct. He had lost his focus. Lost his truth, and been left vacillating between the two religions, and too many rival monarchs, trying to recapture what had been promised to him.

He strode away without a second glance at the former monk. The reality of it all was, Henry Fitzroy did not want to *have* to choose. He didn't care enough for either ecclesiastical argument. To use religious righteousness to drive him towards the power he truly wanted. And he was tired of hiding that indecision. Tired of hiding who he was. He had allowed himself to become distracted by uncertainty. That stopped today.

As the screams of the man, agonising as the flames no doubt licked his feet, echoed over the walls, Henry paused. In the middle of the street, he closed his eyelids to the stares and smiles of the pathetic humans. Anger simmered still within him, but by this action he could control himself. He drew in several deep breaths before opening his eyes again.

There was no point in venting it on the mortals. They could not see what he could. Were blind to the waste of their limited lifespan which this fervent obsession about the right way to embrace God had led them to. His lips sneered. Their short-sightedness was a symptom of their humanity, their frailty. They had no real concept of what afterlife entailed. There was no proof, and Henry was, if nothing else, proof that living forever was, despite the agony, vastly preferable to dying. If humans could know what vampires did, they would surely want to live.

Henry glanced at the sun, knowing that the warmth of its rays would never penetrate his cold skin as it once had. Never again fill him with the optimism of a bright new day. Smoke from the fire reached his nose, acrid with burnt flesh distinguishing it from all the other fires around town. Those martyrs to their faith - if they knew what the flames teased, then consumed, would they be so welcoming of its heated fate? If this was what conviction of their doctrines led to, then both the Church of Rome and the wave of Protestantism challenging each other for dominance were guilty of murder. For that was what this execution was. Whichever way you preached, or however you died, the end result would be the same. Their illusions of an afterlife were flawed.

Afterlife was a worse option - for it was a void. The only thing a human truly possessed was a soul, which cannot survive death. He had sacrificed his, and knew without requiring further evidence that it was gone.

Absolutely gone. There was no heaven, no hell. A soul, and a life lived, simply disappeared as smoke joins the sky.

He had accepted that, Henry realised. Faced mortality head on and chosen to live longer, regardless. The realisation brought his anger finally under control and with it, humility. Giving his soul did not make him a martyr. It released him from the constraints of humanity. He now knew more than mortals did.

Across the street, he watched the hustle and bustle with fresh eyes. Ordinary people continued their daily business, ignoring what was happening just outside the walls. A few had paused at the front of the Cathedral, no doubt to give thanks for it not being them on the pyre this time. But tomorrow it could be, and all because they believed in something different from the monarch of the country. It could be any country, of course, Henry rationalised, for the conflict was not contained to England. But, even a King, with the power over life and death, should not enforce their choice of religion upon their subjects to this degree, for they, as humans, knew no better. No-one should die because of something so intangible as a religion. It was a fabrication, a structure to live by, not a proven reality. To die for it seemed a waste of life and of a soul to Henry.

Dying in defence of a realm, a nation or a person, that was acceptable, honourable even. But this? He shook his head violently, in a vain hope that his disgust would shake off. There was no escaping it. Every land he knew of was blighted by the same problem. Except...

There was only one place he knew of where belief actually produced something tangible... the one place where his lack of faith set him above others, rather than being vilified for it. A paradise where he could be King. Where he would not have to live amongst the blindness of religion, but control it for all time. Where he would be free to live without falsehood.

It was as if a bolt of lightning had struck him, so strong was the realisation. Energised, Henry walked as swiftly as was reasonable to the Maid's Head. He banged on the door to Fairfax's usual room, tapping his feet as he lingered outside. Receiving no response to repeated knocks, he clattered down the stairs and ordered a draught of blood from the bar. Henry slugged it back, beckoning for another as soon as he'd slapped the wooden cup down. Then, he sat in the corner and watched the door - plans churning through his mind whilst he awaited the one person who could assist. The one person he could not trust with his intentions, but who loved him enough not to question the requisitioning his ship for an undisclosed plan. A man who lived for adventure, who loved without restraint. He sipped the blood, rolling it around his tongue with relish.

With glittering eyes some minutes later, Henry swallowed the last drops and sealed his choice. He had never felt more powerful than at this moment. He looked over the bar area, absorbing the braying laughter, the porky bellies and the feathered caps; his fangs lengthened. He wanted more blood. His thirst was greater than these humans could possibly comprehend. They were food to the likes of him, no more than cattle. Just as foolish and easily led. Just as weak. If he struck now, would they scatter like a herd, he wondered, or freeze while accepting their fate?

But he turned his head towards the fire and withdrew his threat. A king has control, he reminded himself. There was no need for bloodshed; it served no purpose. He did not *need* their blood. A ruler rises above pettiness, ordinariness - as his father had known - and sits at the head of it. He is the one who ordains what people believe in. He, Henry, was also the only vampire who knew how weak Naturae was. The only one who already had influence over their Prince of Naturae.

Henry smiled. He had been right to influence Joshua, for the half-human was all that had stood in his way of that throne before, and he had left Naturae as well. With that witch and her spawn. His lips twisted and Henry laughed quietly to himself. Queen Aioffe was long gone; Naturae would be in a state of chaos.

This wasn't just a choice for today, or even the next decades, it was for eternity. It was right that he had taken his time to realise where his destiny lay. The fae would not be able to resist Henry Fitzroy. They needed him to bring order to their mess.

He would be king, and there would be no petty squabbles over religion evermore.

CHAPTER FIFTY-THREE
Disguises and Assizes

Bavaria, early autumn 1554

In the weeks following her failed attempt at pupaetion, Aioffe had lain listless on her pallet. Weak and apathetic, she knew she ought to feed. She was clearly out of favour with the Queen still; the guards poked plates of silt-clogged catfish through the flaps of her tent rather than allowing her out. She could not bring herself to get up though. Staring at the billowing fabric above, she recalled the last time she had been in such a dark place in her mind. In the Beneath on Naturae. Also, it was the last occasion she had been forced to eat repulsive dead fish. Where she had wrestled with the prospect of living without Joshua. A prison so hopeless, she had considered starving herself into oblivion just to escape.

She hadn't been given a choice then - Uffer, under orders from Queen Lana, her mother, had dragged her kicking and screaming into Court on a daily basis. Forced her to face her new reality until she saw the truth of Naturae for herself. In turn, the surrounding misery of her people had motivated her to take care of herself, to build up the physical strength to perform the changes which were necessary. She had been forced to take the throne then, after the demise of her mother.

What would Lana say if could see her now, Aioffe wondered? A forlorn tear dripped from the corner of her closed eyes. Her mother probably would have scorned her decisions, and derided her past choices. Even at her end, and despite their reconciliation, Aioffe suspected the Queen would have given anything to have kept her lover alive. Her delusions that he had returned led to her accidental death.

She clutched Joshua's arrow head, listening to the wind rustle the leaves outside. Aioffe had knowingly left her lover behind. Her palm tingled; the wound reopened from the repeated action. As tears welled in her eyes again, she wondered if she held the love token into the cut, whether it might seal itself with the arrow embedded. What that might feel like, a permanent reminder of what she had lost. Aioffe blinked away the burning wetness and stared again at the mottled fabric. What use was the arrowhead, if all it did was remind her of her mistakes? Yet, she could not let it go.

She couldn't release Joshua, or forgive herself, without telling him how sorry she was. How much she regretted leaving him in pursuit of an heir. How she had realised living in the present was just as important, more so in fact, as securing the future. She had wasted too much time already, delaying hundreds of miles away in the hope of a solution presenting itself. She now had no choice. If she wanted to get back to Naturae, to Joshua, she needed to be free of her debt to Illania. She would have to choose between Illania's daughters. Accept that one of them was the likely heir of Naturae. And try harder to fulfil her side of Illania's bargain.

The 'how' of that still eluded her though. Desperation wouldn't be enough. If only she could make peace with Joshua, tell him what she was doing and why, perhaps that would make it easier. If she could only have his blessing to love another, she thought that might make a transformation work. She was convinced that emotion was intrinsically bound with the turning; it had to be. Sighing at her own weakness, she reached out and opened her mind to Joshua.

A strong sensation of wind rushed over her, prickling her skin. She blinked, and reached further. The immediacy of their connection shocked her momentarily. Then she felt his warmth flood into her. A relief. A purpose. His love. Without thinking about it, she stretched out her hand to him, yearning as if he was there with her. She licked her lips and swallowed, a fresh taste of fir in her mouth.

He was airborne! And, she smiled, close by.

Despite her warning message, he had come for her, as he always promised he would, and no matter how they had left things. He was coming! Their connection - the strength of it - told her so. The arrowhead burned in her palm, so she sat up. Casting her eyes up at where the fabric tent gathered at the top, Aioffe stood.

Her love was coming.

If he was close, he would need to know in which dwelling to find her! With a thumping heart, she took the arrowhead between her fingertips and began to cut the fabric above her head. The stiffness of the canvas was no obstacle for the sharp, tiny blade and her practised seamstress fingers, and, within minutes, she had cut out a small heart shape. The edges tinged with her blood from the blade, which he would know and be drawn to, or so she hoped.

Was that enough, Aioffe wondered? The way her heart felt right at this moment, the shape ought to be bigger, but that would be noticed. Better be sure. On the opposite side of the tent, she then cut out the shape of the arrowhead. Two windows. Two symbols which only he would know the significance of. To make it easier for Joshua to see them in the night sky though, she lit one of the candles which had been left for her.

Aioffe smiled to herself, lighter in her being than she had been in months. No-one circling above would think her peculiar - only that she gazed at the stars - she rationalised, as she sat directly underneath the holes watching. Her hand reached over the floor to the plate of fish and she ate in the company of the twinkling night sky.

*****

Norwich

"Have you lost your mind?" Fairfax shook his head, the ginger waves sticking straight out from his scalp in a frizz. "When all I can think of is how to save Nemis, you want to come on a business trip with me?"

Henry nodded. "I realised today that I am tired of being alone. Grow ever-weary of being in disguise every day, hiding who we are. What we are. Life for mortals - for you - is too short. I don't want to waste what time we have together denying ourselves. The only place we can be free is at sea." He shrugged, then, as Fairfax continued gazing out of the dusty window, Henry placed his hand on his shoulder. He spoke with utter sincerity when he said, "You know as well as I do that once these people have set their minds to it, no-one can save a witch - a true one or not. I am sorry for your friend, but there is nothing you can do about it here."

Henry sighed, although he barely knew the woman, Fairfax cared about her deeply and he did not want to give him false hope when the English justice system was so intertwined with religious doctrine. Nemis would be kept in gaol until the arrival of the travelling magistrates. Her punishment, most likely her life, would depend entirely on this periodic, seasonal court's decision. She would doubtless become the scapegoat for all manner of inexplicable but highly personal disasters from the folk of Beesworth. Henry knew her chances of escape were slim at best, but Fairfax had been tasked to rescue her, which seemed unreasonable to Henry.

"I have already made matters difficult enough; you know what happens when I'm around." Thomas turned to Henry, "There's something you can do though." He held Henry's gaze, blinking slowly, deliberately, until realisation dawned.

"That is your price?" Henry couldn't help but admire his lover's most obvious of solutions. "If I influence the judges at the Assize, you will take me north?"

"I was thinking you could be a judge, covering for someone else who would have another urgent matter to attend to. With a little legal training, you should be able to get close enough to ensure that we cover all eventualities." Fairfax grinned, his eyes sparkling with energy. "I can take you to the Inns of Court; find a barrister to teach you the basics. A smart, well-educated man such as yourself should pick it up in no time."

The effect of his intense enthusiasm jolted Henry into weakening. He groaned, "Another costume?"

"A very flattering robe and wig. And some eloquent, persuasive words."

"When is the trial?"

"I would be surprised if they came late autumn as the travelling conditions get so poor, so possibly early spring next year. She could be months away from a reprieve," Fairfax said. "Maybe Joshua will be back by then as well, with Aioffe. We can ferry them all to Naturae afterwards."

Henry smiled broadly. Now taking Naturae for himself would be even easier than he thought. Reaching his arm down Fairfax's chest, he pulled Fairfax's back towards his heart and clutched him. He whispered, "I was rather hoping to spend some time with you before then. Where's Joshua gone?"

"He's found where Aioffe is. I've helped him work out their location from a code Aioffe sent. He's on his way with a kind of astrolabe for guidance. It's a long way, and frankly, I don't think he knows quite what he'll find when he gets there. God only knows what's happened to Nemis's husband." His head shook slightly. "It didn't sound like he was in a good way."

Henry had to rein in his grin before Fairfax turned and noticed. "Sounds like they will be absent for a while then." Henry said, kissing the back of Fairfax's neck. "The sooner we leave, the sooner we can be back with money for Nemis. Just in case Spenser doesn't return, she'll need it. I don't suppose you have funds to support her in gaol right now, anyway?"

Fairfax leant into Henry's caress, sighing. "I never knew you to be so considerate - of my finances!"

"Our finances. I'm a changed vampire, I told you. Life is too short for mortals. You should live and love while you can." Henry snaked his other arm around Fairfax and whispered in his ear, "I'm sure your spies can let us know when a date has been set in Beesworth. There's plenty of time for both business and pleasure."

"Tomorrow we shall sail then..." Thomas twisted, pushing Henry back onto the pallet bed with wolfish glee.

Henry's eyes glittered, and not just with lust. "When the son will rise."

*****

Bavaria

Morning sun warmth beamed down through the holes Aioffe had cut above, but it was the ripping back of the tent flaps which jolted her from her meditation.

"You are required by the Queen," a guard called. "Quickly."

"What's the hurry?" She asked.

"Just get ready. We will be waiting outside."

Aioffe stood, pocketing the arrowhead before straightening her gown. Something in the soldier's voice warned her to be prepared, and, knowing Joshua was on his way to her, she slipped her slim crown into the other pocket. There was nothing else she travelled with which she could not leave behind, if it came to it.

An entire troop circled her as Aioffe took off from the wooden ledge. She glanced at them from the sides of her eyes, as the show of force seemed a little excessive. They flew in a diamond formation about her like birds, ensuring that she could not fall back or escape. Below, streams feeding the river meandered through the dense woodland; their persistent trickling reminded her that time moved relentlessly onward. Unease grew within her. She slowed her pace, looking around the skies and ground for any sign of Joshua and finding only the bright blue stretching clear to the horizon and a patchwork of greens, golden yellows and brown below. Aioffe reached out with her mind as she flew - but there was nothing there. The chill of the air reached her fingers and she touched the arrowhead through her pocket, hoping for its earlier warmth to return.

Dipping down, the retinue skirted the tops of the tallest pine trees before a clearing came into view just next to the riverside. Aioffe spotted the three golden tubs with their royal occupants, awaiting her arrival. The troops landed, but Aioffe paused, hovering above the forest for as long as possible in case Joshua should arrive.

"If you wish to speak with your friend for the last time," Queen Illania snapped, "then you will need to land."

Aioffe looked down, seeing then what she had not been able to spot from her approach. Spenser, barely recognisable so thin and grey was he, dully stared up at her. Lying behind the largest cup, his hands were bound above his head with the chain attached to a ring. His clothing darkened with mud and dust, and peppered golden-brown with leaves from the early autumn fall. Immediately, Aioffe dived to his side.

Before she could speak, Spenser shook his head. "Don't," he croaked through dry lips. "This is a choice you have to live with forever." His eyes cautioned her that he was ready to make the sacrifice.

"I must," Aioffe said simply, squeezing his arm with a gentle resolution. His life was not a sacrifice she was prepared to have on her conscience, not after all this time. Not when there was still hope, even if she didn't believe she could make another fae from a human. But she could not tell him Joshua was coming.

She stood up, stepping backwards from him slowly so as not to cause alarm, then turned to face the two smaller tubs. The Princesses stared back at her with guarded eyes.

"Choose your heir," Illania said. Her cherubic lips tilted upwards, but her eyes remained a flinty cool. "And then, you must decide who to transform to complete the bargain." Her arm swept out to a line of men, their faces covered by hoods, lurking by the treeline, before returning to jerk her thumb at Spenser. "He has little time left, so if I were you, I'd make your mind up quickly."

"If I choose," Aioffe said, "then you have to release Spenser. Now."

"And give up my leverage?" Illania laughed.

"If he dies, you have no leverage anyway."

"And you will have no heir."

The guards must have been warned this confrontation was about to happen, Aioffe realised, when they took to the air and encircled her. Weapons aimed down so she could not fly up or away. As one, the soldiers then shrank the dome of points. There was no escape.

"Who is to say you return at all?" Illania said. "One way or another, Naturae will come into my realm."

Aioffe shook her head. "There is no need for aggression. Our bargain stands, Illania." Examining the two princesses, her eyes roamed over them as if she were merely deciding between two loaves of bread at a market. The pair had not spoken to her at all over the last few months except in the presence of Illania, and now did not meet her stare. Instead, they kept peeking at each other, as if they were in competition - which Aioffe supposed they were - or perhaps shared some secret between them.

Aioffe gritted her teeth, then chided herself as her mind moved on to judging their clothing - as if how they looked had any bearing on how they would rule her realm! But, her options for information about them was now reduced to the superficial. Even though she innately understood that the choice and the design of what was worn showed the persona which they wished to present, it was not an accurate or true reflection of what an individual was. A queen-in-waiting which she would have to live with, not to mention fear, on an everyday basis.

She had to get this choice right. Her heart hammered as, after a clearing of Illania's throat, she found herself on the receiving end of their impatient glares.

Aioffe glanced again at Spenser, worrying afresh about how to stretch out this decision, whether to play for more time when there was obviously little left for him?

Realising she was no longer the object of Aioffe's attention, Caesaria's thin lips tightened as she rolled her shoulders back and glared at Illania. "She doesn't know how to choose. Too... new."

Aioffe's head snapped back to stare at the slim princess. Astute she may be, but the long, black pointed cuffs she wore to her dress unsettled her. The triangular tips served to highlight Caesaria's elongated arms and spindly fingers, now reminding her of Illania's charged hands in the clearing before. How much Lifeforce could she channel through them, Aioffe wondered, barely suppressing a shudder. The disdainful fae struck her as cruel, uncaring, and the last thing which Aioffe would do for her Queendom was subject her people to the machinations of a Queen who did not care for them.

She looked again at Tamara, who had struck a disinterested pose in her tub. Given how squat she was, the choice of an orange dress which clung to her rotund form was a mistake, lending her the appearance of a pumpkin.

"Oh, put your claws away, Caesaria," Tamara said, her voice whined. Aioffe heard the little stamp of a foot. "You're showing your age."

"Age has nothing to do with it," Caesaria sneered. "It doesn't take millennia to learn how to make a simple decision."

Tamara rolled her eyes, then her lips pulled back as she picked at something on her finger, revealing the pointed teeth which had so alarmed Aioffe the first time they met. No. She could not risk her Queendom to one who was so clearly affiliated with vampires.

Aioffe met Illania's eyes. "Both of your daughters are worthy successors," she lied. "As you would know them best, which would you choose?"

The Queen's eyes narrowed. "You ask *me* which of my two girls you would take away from me?" She tried to dodge Aioffe's steady look by glancing away, but her eyes darted between the two princesses. "As you said, both are worthy and able to rule. I remind you of how generous I am being in offering them to you in the first place."

"I understand how difficult it would be, being so blessed with two heirs." Aioffe suspected that whichever she chose would lead to the other moving against their mother, and Illania knew it. Even though Caesaria was older, and possibly more fed up of waiting for her time to rule, Tamara's petulance and temper were not to be underestimated.

"Perhaps," Aioffe said, advancing on Illania's tub, "it would be prudent to select a companion for you first and get that under way. It would allow me more time to get to know your daughters whilst he pupaetes?"

Caesaria and Tamara huffed. The Queen shook her head. "I grow tired of you constantly delaying. You will choose an heir, choose a companion to turn, and start tonight. There is no requirement for you to be here as he pupaetes." Her head lowered as she looked steadily at Aioffe. "You will get it right this time. I have no need to tell you that your Queendom suffers from your absence."

Aioffe sighed, then turned to look at the four men who leant against the trees behind her. Their faces were obscured by hoods, their feet shuffling with uncertainty. They barely registered her approach, but, as the Queen's golden cup rose behind her, the guards stood next to each man poked them until they straightened.

As she walked across the clearing, distracted by wondering how she was going to wrangle delaying the inevitable this time, she heard the snap. Twigs in the undergrowth? Aioffe slowed, her eyes darting into the depths of the forest.

CHAPTER FIFTY-FOUR

Anarchy

Naturae

"I can still taste the rainbow," Fairfax laughed as he bounded up the steps of the forecastle. "You'd think I'd be used to it, but somehow the colours infuse into my soul every time I pass through this mist." He turned to Henry, stiffly faced straight ahead on the bow of their ship. "Why so silent? It was you that steered our course towards Naturae. I thought you might be happier?"

Henry's dark eyes slid across the deck to his lover's. A smile played on his lips as he said, "I am happy. You have made me very happy." He turned back. "But I do not feel the same sensations as you when I travel through the grey wall."

Fairfax approached and touched his arm. "Henry, why *did* you want to come back? You weren't very welcome the last time."

"I will doubtless be more welcome after this day, although, not at first, I am sure."

Frowning, Fairfax dropped his hand, not noticing the other side of Henry's face, where the smile widened. Henry reached into his pocket and pulled out a rolled scrap of paper that he had prepared whilst Fairfax slept last night. With a voice laden with sorrow, he held it out. "A kestrel found us this morning."

Unrolling the missive, Fairfax reeled, then his wide eyes glanced at

Henry, seeking confirmation. "Is this true? No wonder you changed course overnight. I have made a sailor of you."

Henry nodded. "And, a bearer of bad news of us."

Thomas's head bowed, his shoulders slumped. Henry patted his arm but said nothing more. The mist was thinning, and already he could make out ahead the twinkling of silver armour in the low sunlight. He leant into the prow, fingers gripping the wood as he counted them. A patrol of four fae, armed and flying in formation up and down the beach. Henry rolled his shoulders back, unperturbed. The autumn winds had carried them swiftly here, and would now propel him onto his destiny. Henry strode over to the centre mast and hauled the mainsail away, enjoying the strength he felt coursing through his biceps.

"Our welcome approaches," Fairfax called over.

"Entirely to be expected," Henry replied. He tied off the line and stood by Fairfax, who had moved to the stern to guide the rudder. Within moments, the clump of boots landed on the deck and spears pointed at them. Fairfax sheepishly raised his hands; Henry chose not to react at all.

"Turn around and go back!" One of the fae soldiers barked.

"We mean no harm," Henry said, turning his palms face up to the troop. "Perhaps if we could dock, we can explain?"

"Explain now or leave. Vampires are not allowed on these shores."

Henry nodded. "I understand, however, we bring news which your Council will want to hear."

The soldier who had been issuing the orders raised a pale eyebrow. "Tell us and we will inform our superiors. Then leave."

Fairfax stepped forward. "I am Thomas Fairfax, and I can vouch for this vampire. We have both been here before; Thane will attest to it."

"Just because you think you know us doesn't give you the right to step onto our shores. Thane has no standing here any more. Leave!"

At a nod from their commanding fae, two of the guards took to the air and wheeled around, heading back inland.

"All we ask is to speak to Thane, or any member of the Council," Fairfax pleaded, stepping closer to the lead soldier. The fae's nose twitched, and he licked his lips. Henry could tell that Fairfax was winning the battle of daemon allure when the guards' spear dipped. "We will stay on the beach if that makes you more comfortable,"

Fairfax continued. "But you should know, if any harm comes to us, you will be responsible for other vampires coming."

"I'm sure you wouldn't want to provoke a 'treaty incident'," Henry smoothly suggested. "Here is an opportunity for us all to behave responsibly. And once your Council has heard what we have to say, you will be commended, I'm sure, for keeping a calm head in the face of a potential threat. We are happy to be escorted by you; there is no need for bloodshed. I'm certain you know the dangers of shedding daemon blood…"

The two remaining fae shared a hungry but begrudging glance, and Henry knew he had won this battle. On to the next, he thought, as he dropped the anchor stone.

*****

Henry and Fairfax rowed towards the island in silence, the pair of guards hovering above. Fairfax's nerves became more evident by the way his hair rose higher, spiking wildly the closer to the shore they got. By the time they pulled the boat onto the sands, the beach had filled with fae. Henry glanced along the line, which marched forwards as soon as his foot hit the sand. The army circled the intruders. He frowned; only a quarter of the few hundred assembled wore metal armour and carried proper weaponry. The rest, a mixture of worker fae and youngsters, wore thick leather panels, tied awkwardly around thin frames and cumbersome with stiffness. Their expressions were uniformly anxious, but determined. The mass of eyes on them were unfocussed, uncertain, which struck Henry as odd. Ignoring the peculiar array of make-shift weapons pointed at them, Henry caught Fairfax's eye.

"Not so welcome. Yet," Fairfax muttered, flashing him a tiny grin.

Before Henry could reassure him, a cluster of fae flew forward and began to wrap them in thin silver chains. Their brown wings fluttered around his face as they awkwardly bound his arms and legs together, flummoxed by knotting the unwieldy lengths until an older soldier stepped forwards and pushed them aside to fix the problem. Henry fought to keep his mirth at their incompetence under control, for he could see his lover was surprised by this entirely understandable imprisonment. The bindings would be no match for his vampire strength, but the same could not be said for Fairfax. "Trust me," Henry called over to him. "We will be welcome soon enough."

Shooting Henry a scowl, Fairfax yelped as the chains tightened around his body and they were lifted into the air. Henry's eyes glittered. Beneath them, the trees receded into a green blur. The buzz of wings behind him roared, causing Henry's unbeating heart to swell with pride. These would be his people, his realm, and these marvellous creatures, his subjects. It would not be long before they swarmed behind him as their leader. Their King.

Drop-landing on the balcony outside the huge outer palace doors, Henry looked back, hearing the swarm noise diminish into the citadel. They were allowed to disperse presumably, once their mission to show their force had been completed. Underneath, on the ground, he could hear laboured breathing as the toll from the exertion of flying hit. Surprised, confused even, about the change to these once healthy people, Henry's eyes cast around the platform seeking sight of Fairfax. Last seen close-by whilst in the air; now, he had disappeared! Only an armoured company of soldiers, flanking Henry three-deep on all sides, accompanied him through into the glass ceilinged atrium, towards the High Hall.

He stopped shuffling. "Where's Fairfax? Why have you separated us?"

The soldiers prodded him onwards, their faces set ahead.

"No, stop! I demand to know where he has been taken!"

Once again, a soldier behind him poked his spear at Henry's back. Henry's eyes narrowed, but he shuffled through the doors.

There was a stillness to the High Hall which he had not expected. It wasn't a calm, but a lack of anything at all happening. The last time he had been here, the vast room had echoed with life, with business, friendship and the warmth of family. Even fractured and dissenting, there had been a vibrancy to the fae community, especially in this central gathering point. Today though, the cool, still air spoke of emptiness. The chairs had been pulled to the sides, exposing the large map laid into the floor, which Henry had never noticed before. Muddied and forgotten about, the fine marquetry was barely visible, further reinforcing Henry's suspicion there was something deeply amiss in Naturae. Could it be as simple as the absence of Queen Aioffe, he wondered?

He looked over to the vast oval table on the dais and noticed there were fewer chairs around it than previously. The silver gilded throne had been moved away from the table and placed at the edge of the steps, not unlike the prominence at a court he was more familiar with. The guards' pricking pokes began to annoy Henry through his dark tunic as they urged him through the Hall. Then, the march stopped at the foot of the platform and they turned, spears pointed towards him in a deadly spiked circle. Their silent expression of fear raised further questions to Henry.

The wait for something to happen, or someone, gave Henry time to consider his options. Thus far, his entry into Naturae had been entirely as he had anticipated. There had been no point in resisting capture - and no purpose in demonstrating his power at this moment. And yet, Naturae itself was not as he had expected to find it. Malnourished and diminished fae, pretending to be soldiers? Where was the Council? The only show of fae unity - for it would be a stretch to call it pride - was distinctly lacklustre, which gave him greater cause for concern. The entire response to his arrival, the danger he could bring, felt deflated. Subdued.

This was beyond the chaos he had anticipated, for that had it's own energy and here there was none. The apathy fuelled his own desire - for what kind of leadership would pay such poor attention to the needs of the many?

Before he could turn his mind to more personal concerns and give consideration to Fairfax's separation from him, the soldiers stiffened. Then two feet landed with a bang on the table top. Henry's gaze shot up. In front of him stood that strange fae which Joshua had nearly killed, but let get away. This, he now knew, was Aioffe's brother, the cripple. The blond haired man stood, legs apart and hands on his hips in a pose which proclaimed his authority. His wings hung limp behind him as two fae darted backwards, then hovered like angelic bodyguards. Thin blackened lips tightened on the emaciated face as his eyes bore into Henry.

Henry's hackles rose; understanding dawned. This fae was responsible. Lyrus was the one hurting his own kin. He may not have been wearing a crown, but perhaps there was no need for a symbol if the force of your own belief in your power is sufficient.

"Vampire." Lyrus sneered. "I thought it had been made clear to you that your kind, and all bastards and half-breeds like you, are unwelcome here. Yes, I know who you are. Or, *were*. And yet, you have once again set foot on my shores."

Henry met his eyes - sharp and steady as only one who would truly challenge him could. "I have. And I do not like what I find here."

Lyrus's laugh barked, then abruptly stopped as Henry continued. "You have failed your sister. The people of Naturae suffer as a result."

The narrowing of Lyrus's eyes warned Henry of the strike about to occur. With one leap, the fae jumped, airborne like a cat, his arms outstretched with clawed hands. Henry dived, rolling with vampire speed straight towards the dais steps. Such was the force of his roll, the soldiers toppled like pins. By the time Lyrus had landed in the space Henry had just vacated, the line of guards lay prone on their backs, weapons scattered across the floor.

Henry pushed against his bindings, bursting through them to freedom. The clink as they fell in silvery coils on the wood satisfied him. Lyrus quickly spun about to find him as he rose from his crouch. Between them, still struggling to find their footing, his soldiers wasted precious seconds to understand what had happened. In no hurry, Henry waited, watching as his foe's face twisted in disbelief. It occurred to him that perhaps the guards were in such poor physical shape they couldn't put up much of a fight. Or maybe they hadn't the heart for it? Lyrus must not be as well regarded as he thinks, Henry realised.

"Perhaps you were mistaken to think there would be no consequences to your actions?" Henry asked calmly. His hands unclenched, then he sprang forward. The speed at which he moved, grabbing two spears from the still standing guards to his right, swooping his feet under theirs so they fell also, meant that Lyrus had barely any time to realise what Henry's intention was. Henry ended up back in the centre of the circle in front of Lyrus - both spears crossed with their long knife-tips on either side of the fae's neck. The entire exercise had taken less than a heartbeat for Henry to achieve. Staying on the ground was a miscalculation when it came to vampires, and now the fae knew it. Strange then, that they did not immediately use their one advantage, Henry thought.

Before Lyrus could react to his swift capture, Henry hissed, "Where is Fairfax?"

Finding himself at a disadvantage, unable to move lest his head be severed, Lyrus's eyes bulged as he swallowed. Henry knew the fae would have squirmed but the sharp edges of the spearheads at his neck prevented any movement.

"Where!" Henry roared into his pale face. When the fae's mouth looked like it was about to twist into a sneer, Henry's arms tightened the blades edges until he could hear the rasp of his breath.

Lyrus's eyes darted to the side wildly.

No-one moved.

With an audible squelch, Henry drew back his lips, baring his fangs for emphasis. With a deliberate slowness and not taking his eyes from the enticing throb underneath the skin, he tipped his head closer to the fae's bulging artery.

"He... he... is..."

Henry loosened the blades a fraction.

"Is... food."

Henry lifted the spears; Lyrus was pinned aloft by his skull, his feet dangling like his useless wings. As a knife slides through butter, Henry uncrossed his wrists. Scissoring the spearheads, the thin skin and fragile bone slashed apart.

Now headless, the puny body dropped to the ground briefly before collapsing into ash.

Henry stood over the dregs, watching as the skull fell off the blades and rolled away. There was a silence touched with disbelief as the severed head finally stopped tumbling on the north east of England. Then, the skeletal features, grey and horrified in its death mask, crumbled and disappeared.

So that was what happened to fae when they die, Henry thought. At least it was tidier than having to bury a corpse.

CHAPTER FIFTY-FIVE

Hoods

Bavaria

Aioffe's eyes widened as Illania's tub drew to her side after a few paces across the clearing. Spenser had been dragged behind her and groaned when he saw her. "Start at the right," the Queen said in a conciliatory tone, wafting her hand towards the line of men. "Make your decision. I've vetted all four, and physically they are in good shape." Her lips pursed. "All with suitable credentials and promise. I would not be disappointed with any of them, but, I think you would be wise to sense by touch, then visualise how they could be. They will not talk in case you get distracted from the feel of them. I believe that is the key - how they could be. Make sure you have the perfect connection to make it work this time."

Aioffe nodded, her palms suddenly sweaty. "I'll try. Can't I see their faces?" She caught Spenser's dull eyes and wished she could reassure him that help was on its way.

"Does it matter what they look like? You are not the one spending eternity with them. I am. You have this one chance left, I will not tolerate another failure."

Swallowing, Aioffe walked across to the hooded men. Disloyal thoughts lurched into her mind, but, after a glare from the Queen, she forced herself to look at the man. Up close, she noticed the outline of his powerful biceps and bulging thighs bursting through expensive hose. An athlete, she thought. Shrugging off her reluctance, she touched the arrowhead in her pocket for reassurance and then took the man's hands in hers.

Aioffe closed her eyes and tried to reach into his being. Without thinking too much about it, her mouth opened as she inhaled, tasting his Lifeforce. Immediately feeling a muggy tasting chill, she dropped his fingertips as quickly as if they were embracing ice and walked to the next. She shook her head, glancing over at Spenser. He nodded in weary reply. There was no point in dragging this particular process out, she sensed he was telling her, but this man in front of her felt wrong. Within every fibre of herself she knew it, which surprised as well as repelled. Perhaps she could spend more time delaying with one who appealed more.

Taller, thinner and distinctly smellier, with the second she tried again to see if there was some sort of connection. He wore a finely embroidered coat in a flattering shade of light green, a colour which had always suited her. As she held his fingers with one hand and wrapped her palm around his wrist, he flinched at her inquisitive touch. His skin was cool, insipid like his Lifeforce. She didn't even bother to try with her mind with this one.

The next two were almost identical in height and physique. Less swarthy than poor Durant had been, a sort of happy medium between the lanky one and the muscled one. One wore a human soldier's uniform; she didn't recognise which country he represented, but, she supposed it didn't matter. The other dressed in the clothes of a commoner, a simple spun shirt and leather trousers. Surprising choices, Aioffe thought, given Illania's previous pupaetion partners.

When she took their hands in hers, even though they were warmer and responded to her touch, she failed to feel anything at all. It was as if she were being introduced to corpses. Not even a hint of Lifeforce touched her. Was it her own reluctance blocking her ability to sense them? With a heavy heart, she dropped the soldier's hand and dragged her eyes along the undergrowth to her last hopeful.

His shoes were battered, but well stitched. Her eyes travelled up lean legs, past an old fashioned jerkin, and to a bundle strapped to his front. The bulge against his chest wriggled, and she noticed the outline of a head, then an elbow. A tiny fist was visible at the side of the swaddling - a child!

Aioffe frowned. Was this some kind of trick Illania was playing upon her? A demonstration of virility? She glanced over her shoulder - Illania was conferring with a soldier from a distance away, with a frown upon her face.

Aioffe grabbed the man's hand and immediately pushed her mind into his with every intention of understanding what the joke was before Illania could humiliate her further. The rush of warmth and love which swept through her was akin to a surge of the richest Lifeforce - Joshua!

"Stop!" Illania's voice rang out, ending in a screech.

Without dropping his hand, Aioffe said, "I choose! I choose this man." She wheeled around to face Illania.

"Who is he? There were four I selected, and then five here. Who has infiltrated my private gathering?" Illania rose in her tub, glaring at the soldiers. "Unhood them all, now!"

CHAPTER FIFTY-SIX

A pickle and jam

Naturae

Henry spun slowly around, absorbing the collective shocked stares of the soldiers who had just witnessed his power. The ashes which had been Lyrus scattered away with the slight gust of his tunic edge flaring. A clatter of weapons hit the wooden floor, then a thump of knees as they knelt and bent their heads. Looking down at the fae, Henry realised the majority were shaking beneath their polished armour plates.

He sighed. Although there was no doubt in his mind that the fae army was a formidable force in an aerial battle, his attack had been ground based, and he was but one vampire. Henry knew he *could* have slit every one of their throats if he had chosen to, with a speed they would not have comprehended. That wasn't because he was a superior being, or a royal, he was just a vampire. The subservience, a lack of will, grated against the flush of victory he should be feeling. He could smell their fear, and it irked him. Why did they not see that en masse, they had the advantage of him? If they so chose, their retaliation could be swift and his quest would be over. If they were only organised enough to react as one. Or better led.

Today, now, their inexperience and fear held them back, rather than respect for him or his kind.

He chided himself internally - respect was earned. They did not yet know of his destiny to rule. His lips rolled over his teeth, and he gestured with his hand. "Arise." Repeating the motion as faces warily peeked up at him, then to each other for reassurance, Henry smiled his encouragement. "My quarrel was never with you, so please, stand and be thankful it was not you. Today."

A whimper from somewhere at the back of the crowd, but still no-one moved

"Perhaps someone could enlighten me as to where my companion was taken?" Henry asked. The troop shuffled uncomfortably. Most diligently studied the floor to avoid meeting his glower. "Anyone?"

Raising an eyebrow, Henry softened his expression as he glanced around the circle. They all looked the same, he thought. How was he supposed to pick one to make an example of? With a start, he realised the trap which he had almost fallen into. This was how Lyrus had operated, he guessed. To win their respect and hearts, he must not repeat the mistake of punishing an individual to scare the whole into doing his bidding.

"What is your name, soldier?"

The guard in front of him flinched as if he had been struck, yet Henry had deliberately kept his tone mild.

"How about you?" Henry touched the shoulder of the next one. "Mine is Henry. And yes, I am a vampire. But no, I won't eat you or harm you. I'd rather work with you." He turned on his heels and spread his arms wide so that they could all see his unarmed status. "If you are worried his fate will be yours, then use your god-given gifts and fly." He smiled. "I cannot catch you in the air."

Three fae immediately rose up and retreated to the rafters high above. "At least you are honest," Henry said, smiling. "And I would take honesty from any man in preference to deceit or cowardice." He turned back to the troops remaining on the ground, just as the double doors banged open.

The Captain strode through, thunder on his face. "Are you implying that Fae or our soldiers are cowards?"

The soldier's heads whipped around, then they straightened. Several had the sense to retrieve their spears and point them once again at Henry, but most looked like rabbits mesmerised by an approaching lamp.

"Why has this prisoner been brought here and not kept with the other?" The Captain advanced, shouting. The soldiers parted like a wave, dipping down to reclaim weapons and resume their original defensive stance.

A voice from Henry's side piped up, "Lyrus's orders, Captain."

"We just did what he instructed," another chimed in.

"And what of the orders *I* issued?"

Henry refrained from commenting on the Captain's clear dilemma over who had the higher authority.

"Where is Lord Lyrus now?" The Captain demanded.

The soldiers unanimously stared at Henry. Guilt streaked across their faces; Henry held his head high.

"You?" The Captain frowned. "We had a report of intruders. I sent a platoon to repel, not capture and bring back. And then I hear we have taken prisoners instead."

"Is Fairfax still alive?" Henry tried to prevent the catch in his voice, but failed to entirely.

"Barely." The Captain sniffed. "Where is Lyrus?"

Henry licked his lips before saying, "There was a conflict of interests."

Seeing the old man's eyebrow rise, Henry seized the opportunity to win his trust. "As in, I decided his interest was not in Naturae's best interest. Or yours."

"You *decided*?"

Henry nodded. "I would like to meet with the Council."

The Captain snorted. "I don't know who you think you are, vampire, but you have no authority here." The old man did his best to wheel around on his heel and turn his back on Henry, but he was not fast enough.

"Then I will take the authority," Henry said, having darted forward to grab his neck. "You would be wise to listen to me."

Choking, the Captain wheezed, "So, you have killed one bully and now we are faced with another? Never."

"Never is a very long time," Henry said, lifting the Captain up as easily as a toast of wine. "And you will find I am far more amenable than he was."

The Captain's wings and legs waggled, but there was no escaping Henry's grasp.

Henry's lips twisted into a smile. "You can all either work with me or," Henry glanced around at the soldiers staring at him, "you will all starve to death." He brought the Captain down, waiting until he had his feet planted on the floor before he said, "I would not wish that painful and meaningless end for you. For any of you."

Henry looked deep into the Captain's eyes. Even though he knew there was no influencing him as he could a human, Henry only needed to convey his sincerity. "Only I can protect you from what is coming. For they will come eventually."

The Captain's jowls flickered with fear. "That is what Lyrus said also, that we needed to be prepared."

Henry pulled the Captain's arm, leading him towards the doors. "He did a poor job of it though. No people can defend themselves if they have hunger. No-one fights if they don't have a home or an ideal to protect. It seems to me that Lyrus, in the absence of Queen Aioffe, forgot this." The soldiers watched in silence as they left the room. Relaxing his grip on the old fae, Henry watched the Captain nod wearily in agreement. Henry sensed the soldiers were warming to his ideas. It was time to get the respect of the rest of Naturae.

As they approached the stairs down from the landing platform, Henry paused and glanced over the citadel spread around them. "Look at your home, neglected and tired. Naturae shouldn't be like this." He turned to the Captain. "A realm needs decisive leaders. Your Council has failed, Lyrus has failed. You can see things must change."

"But... Queen Aioffe. She will return and all will be well."

Henry's eyes darkened. "She left you. Abandoned you. Have you even heard from her? I would not leave you all to descend into anarchy like this."

Shaking his head, the Captain said, "You don't understand. Naturae needs belief. We need our Queen. Not a vampire."

From below, Thane's voice drifted up, pleading. "Don't do this. His blood is the path to destruction, I tell you. I know this daemon, and he is not to be harmed. Your Queen would not want this for you."

Your King doesn't either, Henry thought. "Take me to Fairfax," Henry said, nudging the Captain towards the stairs.

It took every fibre of his control not to rush ahead; Henry knew he had to be patient this once. That didn't stop his relief - Thane would not be asking for restraint if his love were already dead or drained.

Also, the final piece in his plan needed to be delivered by Fairfax. Someone the fae knew was allied with Aioffe and Joshua. Someone who was fractionally more trustworthy than a vampire who had just killed their leader. He grabbed the Captain and propelled him towards the fae clustered by a tree as soon as they reached the ground.

"Let us through," Henry said, forcing the Captain ahead of him to part the crowd. Thane met his eyes. Standing in front of Fairfax, he alone seemed to be defending Thomas against the advancing hordes. A ball formed in Henry's stomach as he glanced quickly over his lover, who laid quiet and motionless on the ground, alive but only barely.

"I know you are hungry," Henry said, turning to address them but keeping hold of the Captain's arm. "But Thane is right. If you drank from him you would just crave more. Believe me, I know these things." He bared his fangs. "It's bad enough wanting human blood, but daemon…" Henry laughed softly. Dangerously. "You would not want to live with the effects when there is no more."

The Captain looked at him with surprise.

"Go and find food. Proper food, that nourishes you," Henry said to the fae, putting his fangs away and smiling convivially. "There will be no repercussions, I promise. Stand down, fae of Naturae, I will defend the realm in the meantime."

The officer glanced at him, and saw that Henry believed he could. Then he confirmed the order and chose his side. "Go. Feed yourselves and your families. There will be no training, no need to patrol." Glaring from underneath his whiskered eyebrows, he barked at the group. "Tell the others. This order comes from the top."

The fae shuffled, glancing to one another for encouragement, still wary of the telling even though it had come from a respected figure of authority. Thane nodded likewise, clearly suspicious himself at the switch of loyalty yet wise enough to play along. Henry saw a compassionate expression spread over his noble features as he endorsed the Captain. "Go - we are all hungry. The sea awaits."

Eventually, the fae began flying away, shooting uncertain, disbelieving glances back as they dispersed.

As soon as most had gone, Henry knelt by Fairfax, unable to resist stroking the dear curve of his face. Eyebrows knitting together, he wondered at Thomas's freckles - peppering his cheeks vividly orange against such pale skin. His fingers gentle in their caress, relieved by the familiar warmth underneath them. Fairfax's eyelids fluttered at his touch, then slowly opened.

"Jam," Fairfax whispered, as his green eyes focussed on Henry and the fizzle between them spluttered.

Henry grinned, then looked up at Thane. "Thank you for defending him. I will return."

CHAPTER FIFTY-SEVEN

Castle takes Queen

Bavaria

Joshua squeezed Aioffe's hand. "I choose you too, my love," he whispered. *"We* choose you. Always."

Aioffe wheeled about, standing in front of them, holding out her other hand as if that would ward away the approaching soldiers. The warmth of the baby he held strapped to his chest radiated into her back. She felt Joshua drop his hand from hers, then heard the slap and creak of leather straps being released.

She crouched into a defensive stance, with her arms out. Her fingers tingled in readiness. "I have decided," she called again, looking at Illania. "This man." Her wings rose behind her, shielding whatever he was doing from being seen by the soldiers who advanced. Aioffe's heartbeat pounded against her chest and she tried to relax the worry from her face. Just pretend he's a normal man, Aioffe repeated over and over in her mind, just a human like any other here.

The Queen's tub, dragging Spenser along, set down before her. Illania's gathered eyebrows gave no clue to her intentions. "I see," the Queen said in a cold voice. Behind her, Caesaria and Tamara had left their transports and flanked their mother. The pair stared at Aioffe, floating just a foot from the ground. Illania ordered her guard, "Take off his hood first," without taking her eyes from Aioffe.

Spenser was looking at Aioffe and Joshua with a curious expression. "My Queen," he croaked. "You have what you wanted, Queen Aioffe has made her choice." He rattled his chain. "Set me free."

Distracted by him, Illania swivelled in her tub. "Not until the turning begins. The human must become Fae."

Aioffe felt the wind of wings on the back of her neck and looked up. Joshua hovered above her, the baby in his arms. With his long black wings, dark clothing and striking blond hair, it was hard to believe he had passed himself off as a mere man; to Aioffe, he glowed with energy and Lifeforce. A proud smile crept onto her face.

"I am already Fae," he said, pulling off the hood and dropping it to the ground. "And you will no longer require my wife to betray me for an heir." He turned and lifted the baby, freed from the sling on his chest, and offered her down to Aioffe. Her wings fluttered as she accepted the bundle into her arms without drawing her eyes from her lover.

"Free Spenser now," Joshua commanded, as he flew above his wife and child defensively. "And we will leave your realm."

Queen Illania's gaping mouth clamped shut; her eyes narrowed as they roamed over them. "No, you will stay. She can go." Her beady eyes stared at Joshua and a subtle shift of her body suggested her attraction to him.

"No! You cannot deny me!" Caesaria screeched. Without warning, she dived at Aioffe and the baby, talon-like fingers outstretched. "Not this time!"

Joshua met her head on, his black wings a blur as they propelled Caesaria to the ground. He landed on top of her, cutting off her charge before it even got close. The baby whimpered as Aioffe's clasp tightened at the threat. As soon as Joshua's stance settled and she sensed he had control over the princess, Aioffe looked quickly around. Guards had taken to the air and were closing in on them rapidly.

Worse, Illania's face flushed red as her hands reached out...

Thinking quickly, Aioffe planted her toes into the soil and drew. She imagined the vortex of Naturae, the swirling mass of fae believing in her. Pulling from the roots of the trees, those tiny veins filled with Lifeforce of their own kind, reaching up at her command. She thought about castles. Fortresses raised from the earth - strong, barricaded. Impregnable.

The tubers pushed up, twisting around, knotting together in a lattice wall of wood. Dried earth flew into the air, breaking into a cloud of dust swept up by the movement of the embedded defences.

As larger roots tore up through the clearing and heeded her call, they toppled those on the ground in their quake. Spenser cried out in pain, but Aioffe could not now see what had happened to him. Her body began to quiver with the natural forces which she channelled and controlled. Aioffe gazed up, reaching for the branches to provide cover from above. They answered with a rustle.

But it wasn't enough. The guards could fly over or through her defences. And Spenser and Joshua were still outside them.

"Joshua," Aioffe cried out. "I need you!"

His head whipped around, and with one swift motion he left Caesaria grovelling on the ground, flew over the top of her woven wall, and was by her side. He grabbed her hand - and she pulled from him as well.

But then, she felt it - a difference in his Lifeforce.

A peculiarity. She looked down at the earth, wondering what was happening.

"The wood," he said, encouraging her with panted breaths. "It's growing, hardening!"

Aioffe's palm burned where he held it, hot like the arrowhead she had clutched so often before. She turned to meet Joshua's suddenly panicked eyes.

"My legs," and he looked down. "My legs..." His voice was filled with wonder, and she looked. The dirt dispersed by the roots growth from the earth had drawn itself to his legs and blackened. As they both watched, it smoothed like clay, and wrapped itself like armour around him. The dark brown dirt suit then stretched up, rolling out as a wave across the shore - up and over his entire body!

Suddenly, she knew what was different - his Lifeforce had been altered! It felt... magical. Powerful. The armour reached his fingers, and she dropped her hand for fear it would sweep over her also. "Joshua!" she cried, as he shook his leg.

The dirt-defence flexed, then rippled, pulsing across him. He held out his hand, flexing it, and the armour pulsed again, allowing the movement like clothing. Joshua frowned, tapping his forearm with his finger. A faintly metallic thunk replied. Iron, silver and other metallic ores infused with earth magic, Aioffe wondered?

But then, as she studied it further, it made sense to her - Joshua was a master of metals, a creator of shields. A protector. And she - a controller of the Lifeforce of nature. Together they had instinctively created something new - something purposeful. Aioffe beamed at him, as everything seemed possible in that moment.

Laying the baby she held gently down to the ground, they ignored the encroaching army. She reached into her pocket for the arrowhead. "Try this," she said. "Focus on what it is for." He flexed his hand - still not quite used to the armour protection - then plucked the tiny metal blade from her fingers. He grinned as he took her hand once again.

Between them, she felt a jolt and she pushed her Lifeforce and the earth's into him. The roots wavered in their growth, but then resumed their rise of their defences as if the power supply was inexhaustible. Aioffe glanced sideways at Joshua - who had closed his eyes and seemed to be muttering something. Around the walls, she heard the approaching wings throbbing as they darted around the wooden cage.

Joshua pinched his fingertips and held the blade like a quill. Bending down, he traced the shape of a bow in the dust at his feet, then laid the arrowhead into the centre where the grip would be. Then, next to the bow, he marked a series of straight lines, each with a pointed tip. He knelt then, glancing at her and asking. He pushed his fist into the earth, closing his fingers around the arrowhead. Aioffe felt the pull as he took what he needed from her powers to create something entirely his own.

Aioffe breathed out as she willingly released the Lifeforce. Then, as it flowed, from the corner of her eye, she saw the baby flip. It rolled over onto its front! The movement reminded her that she had to protect it. With a renewed focus, she resumed controlling the wood. Guards began sawing, jabbing at the roots with their spear tips. Imagining again - the tunnels of the Beneath, how the earth and roots had moulded into their maze through which she could escape, more roots began poking through the earth.

With one eye watching the baby, released from its wrappings and now rocking as it tried to manoeuvre itself, she tried to visualise instead where she had last seen Spenser rather than worry about the troops which were battering their way through to them all. That was the direction she needed to guide the tunnel-trees towards.

But the baby... she shook her head and pushed her mind back to her plan, understanding in a heartbeat that the best way to protect it was to protect them all.

Joshua tugged at her, pulling his hand away from her fingers. A whistle of an arrow and she knew he had succeeded with his designs. With a cry, the soldier he hit fell to the ground. Aioffe took a tentative step forward, her fingers wriggling in front of her to guide the roots to part. Another soldier fell, tangling himself in the spiky wood still growing and waving around their protective cage.

"It's only wood," they heard Illania screech at her army. "Break it down or I'll break you down to ashes!"

"Spenser," Aioffe said. "We cannot leave without him."

"I know," replied Joshua. "Nemis would never forgive us. Let me go ahead of you both, for what is the point in armour if not to protect?"

"The how of it you can tell me another time," she said, then groaned. "It's always about time, isn't it? Never enough of it." She dared not pull her feet up too quickly from the earth - her connection to the underground Lifeforce too tenuous. The baby cooed as Aioffe slowly lifted her foot to place it in another step. Her heart melted at the innocent sound, and she turned, determined to protect it from this situation it had never asked to be in. Yet she dared not pay her more attention than simply keeping her safe. No spare hands to hold her.

The baby's face beamed up at her. Aioffe could not help but twist her body towards it, yearning as if that would comfort the child enough. To her astonishment, from behind its loosened swaddling, red wings unfurled! Aioffe's mouth dropped open. The wings then flapped once, twice and then rapidly. The baby cooed again, its little rosebud lips pursing with surprise.

"Joshua," Aioffe gasped. "The baby!"

"Our baby."

With seemingly little effort, the red wings blurred and the pupae lifted off from the ground. "She's flying," Aioffe said, a lump rising in her throat. Chubby little arms reached out for hers and the baby lumbered, falteringly, towards her. As it covered the few feet between them, its flight grew steadier. Aioffe was amazed at how quickly the little thing had mastered direction - it was almost like her own innate ability to fly!

And, it was choosing to fly to her!

"She's ours? Really ours?" Aioffe said as the babe flew right up to her chest then wrapped its arms around her neck. Aioffe's hand automatically rose to support the thin little back, its wings flopped down over her wrist.

Joshua thwacked another arrow into his bow and let it loose. "That's what Nemis prophesied when she gave her to me. To us."

"But, I don't understand. Whose baby is she?"

He let fly another arrow, then turned to face her, holding out his hand. "I believe she was created from love, and will be protected by love - all of our love," he said. A twinkle in his eye told her he believed his next statement to be true. "She is the heir. Our heir."

Aioffe glanced down at the baby she clutched, nestled to her collarbone as if she was at peace there. Wide, bright blue eyes like her own beamed back at her. In wonder, she stroked the downy hair on her head, a bright ginger reminding her of Fairfax. Then, her fingers traced the blood red veins staining her tiny wings. The baby softened in her arms, stretching languorously into her, but Aioffe's heart thudded a warning.

Aioffe's lips parted and she breathed in the child's Lifeforce. Layer upon layer of strands rolled around her tongue. Aioffe gasped, "Witch... daemon.." Then she rubbed her tongue against the roof of her mouth to release the danger she knew within. "And vampire?"

"What?" Joshua frowned. "How can that be?"

"But fae also," Aioffe confirmed, frowning. "I don't know how, but they are all in her Lifeforce."

They spun around as, behind them, the roots echoed an almighty crack. Joshua raised his bow and slapped an arrow in. Aioffe turned back to the tunnel and peered. "Go!" Joshua urged. "Get to Spenser."

Aioffe pulled her sunken foot from the earth, dropping Joshua's hand so that she could hold the baby better in one arm and control the wood with the other. Crouching, wings fluttering, they ran between the lattice walls which Aioffe had created, towards where Spenser had been lying next to Queen Illania's vessel.

A cackle from outside the walls stopped them in their tracks.

Illania then tittered. "There is nowhere to run now."

Through the cracks in the roots, silvery ashes - just the remnants of the soldiers - blew into their castle.

CHAPTER FIFTY-EIGHT

King takes knight

Naturae

Henry ran as fast as a vampire could, then rowed, then leapt onto Fairfax's ship. Tossing the food chest open, he grabbed a stale loaf and, most important of all to Fairfax, his treasured honey-strawberry jam. Then, as swiftly as he had arrived, he left, and was back by his lover's side.

Thane and the Captain stood a safe distance away from Thomas. Henry paid no heed to them as he ripped a crust of bread and dunked it in the jam. Fairfax had not moved, yet he roused when Henry held the dripping sweetness to his lips. His vivid green eyes flew open and his lips opened to receive.

"Gather the Council," Henry ordered over his shoulder as he fed scraps into Fairfax. "I will take their questions as soon as they are assembled."

"What about him?" Thane asked.

Henry glanced over Fairfax's body - there seemed remarkably few cuts and bruises. The scrappy daemon had obviously put up a fight before Thane must have intervened. "Fairfax will recover soon enough." The more jam he ingested, the stronger Henry heard his lover's heart beating.

The Captain wheeled away, but Thane stayed. "I have dealt with overbearing rulers before," Thane said. "It ended in ash. Fae do not kill fae, however. This daemon did kill once, long ago. Liberating us by his chaotic but accidental deed. And now you are back, and once again, there could be chaos. Anarchy where there was order, of a sort. Are you here to liberate us or dominate, I wonder?"

Henry nodded slowly. "I believe I have done Naturae a service by dispensing with Lyrus." He looked steadily at Thane. Fairfax had told him of Thane's wary kindness when he first visited Naturae as a teenager, of when he had accidentally killed Aioffe's mother, and of the respect the fae workers had for their informal leader. Henry considered, from when he had last been here, the man's authority had since been pushed aside. "I believe a ruler should listen to trusted views before making a decision for the good of the realm. I think you would be one to trust, am I right?"

Thane's head tilted but his bearing grew taller. Henry stood and looked around the clearing. "I would respect your opinion," he said. "If you were to respect mine."

Before Thane could answer, they were interrupted. "Is it true?" One of the fae approaching called to Thane, who swivelled and gave a curt nod. Within moments, ten or so fae, most advancing in age and looking exhausted by their short and hurried flight, landed. They kept their distance from Henry, but he could see relief on their faces.

"I have grave news," Henry started, just as the Captain arrived and shushed them.

"He killed Lyrus," the elderly soldier snapped. "And has in return, demanded we hear him out."

"And, although as he is vampire, he has not technically broken fae laws by doing so," Thane interrupted, "he has broken the Treaty between our kind and his." His expression was neutral, but his words were intended to pave the way to condemnation of Henry. But, Henry had already considered that his actions on Naturae would put him at odds with his own kind and had made peace with this possibility on the voyage here. He now saw the opportunity which his isolation from the Church, and the vampires who ran it, presented him with.

"I did so only to restore order to your realm and defend myself. The sad fact is, it was all too easy for a vampire to defeat him." Henry drew himself up. "The treaty is irrelevant; it was broken as soon as Aioffe allowed Fairfax and I to set foot on these shores. She knew that. She put Naturae in danger as a result. But," he feigned a sigh, "We bring worse news." He nudged Fairfax. "News which has come from your most trusted sources - the spies which this daemon helped to train on your behalf."

With a groan, Fairfax pushed himself up to sitting. He looked around the Elders who were staring down at him. His face white, he faltered over his words. "They sent word, received last night... came as quickly as we could." Rummaging in his jacket, Fairfax held up the slip of paper Henry had forged earlier. "It says, 'Queen Aioffe has died. I pray for us all. Joshua.'"

Fairfax flapped the scrap as proof, forgetting that most fae standing around them couldn't read. "I'm sorry to have to tell you, but... we thought you should know." He collapsed back to the ground and reached for another piece of bread and jam.

Henry's head bowed, listening to the gasps of dismay from the Council.

After a moment, he said quietly, "You need a King, not a Prince. A royal for eternity, beholden to no faith but fae. Joshua will not return. You need a vampire who will defend Naturae against his own kind. Teach you how to resist their coming, for they will. Who among you could offer the same?"

He deliberately did not look at the elderly Captain, the only one who he suspected would have experienced fighting with vampires. With growing conviction despite their bewilderment, Henry proclaimed, "No-one. No fae." He drew in a deep breath, as if this was a sacrifice on his part, and offered, "I will be your King now. Naturae is weakened and I will make you strong. Your Queen is dead, you have no other, and the time for a change is now. If vampires find out that the fae have broken the Treaty - several times - then you need me to bridge that breach. They will not take revenge when one of their own is King here."

He gazed silently and solemnly at their shocked faces. "My first order will be to restore this Council of advisers. As Queen Aioffe intended, you will all be heard. But, make no mistake, I will be making the final decisions needed to strengthen this realm and its people, back to full prosperity. I will bear the mantle of responsibility for this realm. You have seen how I pass judgement on those who would threaten Naturae's future. Do not be one of those, or you will come to the same fate."

His dark eyes waited for them to acknowledge his threat. The Council members glanced at each other, nobody daring to voice a concern. Not one challenged his assertions, which pleased him. He had expected Thane to stand against him, or the Captain, but it appeared that they were too weak. Henry was grateful that he did not have to enforce his will, realising now the usefulness of their support. Understanding that there would always be politics, yet knowing that he held the ultimate advantage over them. He was immortal, they were not.

Then, Henry knelt and faced up at them as he made his final promise. "I will protect you. Feed you. Enable you. I will show you how to arm yourselves against those who would take what you have on Naturae. I give you my loyalty, my protection. In return, I ask that you give me your fealty." Henry's fist clenched. "Forever."

One by one, the Council nodded. Fairfax gazed at him, his mouth hung slightly open. As their eyes met, Fairfax shoved another piece of bread into his mouth and chewed it thoughtfully. His eyebrow raised just a fraction and Henry's mouth tipped up just a little. Thomas swallowed, then lowered his head to Henry, the King.

CHAPTER FIFTY-NINE

Loyalty

Bavaria

Aioffe clutched the baby's head and guided her face into the pit of her shoulder. The ashes from the guards Illania had killed swirled around them in the tunnel. Choking as the dust storm entered their throats, Joshua pivoted to shield his family with his body.

"Stop this!" Aioffe cried out, "Illania, please!"

"I warned you," the Queen screeched. "Hand over my fae."

"He is mine," Aioffe croaked, then coughed.

Joshua turned his head; the root walls were being forced apart, spears used as levers to make a hole in Aioffe's defences. "I am Prince Joshua of Naturae," he said. "I belong to no other Queen but Aioffe."

"Then you will die alongside her," Illania cackled. "And Naturae will be mine." But then, Joshua heard the clink of a chain and a strangled yelp.

The gritty ashes suddenly seemed to stop their dance mid air, and floated gently down. Joshua rushed forward, hands grabbing the roots and widening the gap to see.

Spenser, ashen-faced and airborne, was pulling with all his might on the chain attached still to his arms. Caught with a loop around her neck, Illania's chubby arms flailed trying to free herself.

Aioffe wedged herself next to Joshua in the hole, then shouted,

"Don't Spenser!"

Spenser's head shot up, eyes dark with passion.

"Fae do not kill fae," Aioffe cried. "If you do this, then you are no better than she is."

Joshua clambered out through the gap, taking to the air as soon as his wings were freed.

"Let her down," Aioffe pleaded. Illania's face looked like it was about to burst!

Reaching Spenser, Joshua put one arm around his friend's torso and propelled him in, towards Illania. The chain loosened around the Queen's neck.

Spenser glared at him. "She does not deserve to live."

"That may be so, dear friend, but Aioffe is right. Fae do not kill fae."

As the two men stared, battling wills and wings, into each other's eyes, Aioffe cried out, "No!"

Tamara had thrown herself onto her mother's breast. The choking chain wrenched from Illania's neck and tossed over her head. Joshua's eyes widened, his wings scrubbing to counter the sudden release of Spenser's weight. But he could not react quickly enough to prevent Tamara's mouth from burying itself in Illania's neck. The smell of rich, thick blood sprang into his nostrils as they watched Tamara drink directly from her red faced mother.

Half dropping Spenser to the ground on his way, Joshua dived down, yanking on the fat princess's hair to pull her free and out of the gorge. His nose wrinkled when he saw her tiny, pointed fangs, dripping with the ancient blood, fury in her eyes. Tamara hissed at him, wriggling like a wild cat caught stealing yet pinned by the scruff of its neck. Behind him, Spenser collapsed on the earth, spent.

"It has to be one of us," Caesaria's voice floated weakly up from the side of the clearing. Joshua pulled up, dragging Tamara with him. She yelped as she dangled from his hair-bun clutch. "It was always meant to be," Caesaria said. Slowly, brokenly, she staggered towards them. "One to rule here, and the other Naturae."

Illania wheezed, her fingers reaching to the holes in her neck and feet scrabbling against the sides of the vessel. Her reddened face now white with fear. All her remaining guards had been depleted. Only Joshua and Aioffe stood in her defence.

Joshua nearly lost his grip on Tamara's hair as she wriggled with more vigour. "Me!" She exclaimed. "It is my time to take over. A new generation of fae needs to be pupaeted," she squeaked. "She's taken too much from this realm to have control over another."

Tamara's arms grabbed towards Illania and her wings began to beat furiously, yanking them both down with the strength of her conviction and desperation. Joshua pulled against her querulous fight, dragging her further away. Aioffe, holding a hand over the baby's head, stepped through the tunnel walls and dashed to Illania's side.

"Family should be loyal," she said sadly, her eyes flicking between Spenser, Tamara and Caesaria. "And what are we, if not family? We are Fae."

Illania lay still, shocked into submission, then let out a raspy cough.

Spenser smiled weakly as Aioffe nestled the baby against his ribs, then used the tiny arrowhead to snap his chain. Joshua's heart flopped over in his chest as he watched his wife gaze lovingly down upon the baby as soon after she had freed their friend, then pick her up again as if she could not bear to be parted with her for even a moment.

As her hand reached up to stroke her soft red hair, Aioffe glared at Tamara and then Caesaria. "Your royal services are no longer needed for Naturae." Both princesses' lips curled.

But Illania had roused and pushed herself to stand in the tub. "Neither of you shall take me down. You disloyal brats! How dare you presume that your moment had come?"

Her croaky chastisement had an immediate effect. Caesaria froze, only a few feet from Aioffe, the baby and Illania. Her face blazed with fury yet she obeyed her mother's implicit command. Joshua's wings faltered as Tamara sagged. He flapped, taking them both higher even though the effort of carrying the heavy weight ached.

"You, on the other hand," Illania said, looking straight up at Joshua, "have proved your loyalty. To both your Queen and I."

He blinked. All the sincerity in her voice could not disperse his wariness. This Queen shifted like the wind. He remained on his guard.

The Queen smiled. "Aioffe has chosen a worthy mate for herself." Then Illania sniffed. "I would have chosen you also, for loyalty should stem from love." Her lips pinched and she glared at her daughters. "I would have thought as much anyway. Fae should not kill fae. Especially royals."

Aioffe shook her head, Joshua could see she was struggling to contain her own temper at the Queen's hypocrisy. She flew up to Joshua, her eyes darkened, wordlessly telling him to release Tamara. The princess dropped to the earth with a thump.

Without looking down, Aioffe asked, "I need you to help our family, all of them." Then she glanced at Spenser.

Joshua smiled and dipped down. He slung his bow over his shoulder. Spenser's pale, gaunt face turned to him as Joshua gathered his lanky frame in his arms. He weighed barely more than a child.

"Thank you, my friend, for stopping me from making a hypocrite out of myself also," Spenser said.

"And thank you for protecting my wife as you promised," Joshua replied. "I wouldn't have found you both without your astrolabe and help from Nemis. Now, let us help return you to her."

Without even a glance at Illania, Joshua and Spenser rose to join Aioffe and the babe. Below, the Queen gathered her energy and began shouting reprimands to her daughters. This was not their fight now, Joshua thought, as relief energised him once more. The armour he wore dissipated into a cloud of dust behind their wings - no longer needed, he freed it to return to the earth. By some notion, he kept the bow solid, its shaft comfortably held pinned to his shoulder by Spenser's body.

As they flew away toward the reddening horizon, Spenser asked, "What's our daughter's name?"

"Hope," Aioffe replied, beaming at Joshua. "It has to be Hope."

"For us all," Joshua said.

"Hope," Spenser repeated. "A worthy name for an heir," he mumbled, before passing out in Joshua's arms.

Aioffe and Joshua flew as closely together as wing-spans allowed. The forests beneath them an endless tapestry, framed by grey and white Alps, but they only had eyes for one another and their child.

"Who shall you be today, my love? Prince and Papa?" Aioffe said, after some miles. She giggled at the name-game they used to play with every fresh start.

His face split into a grin. "Queen Mama sounds too old though," he joked. "We'll need to think about a suitable new title for you."

Aioffe laughed, agreeing. "I don't feel old when I'm holding this little one." Then she asked, "Can we go home now?"

"Not yet," Joshua's face looked grim as he remembered who he had left behind in England. Spenser had roused in his arms and Joshua began to feel concerned. "He needs to get better quickly," Joshua said. "Nemis has been accused of witchcraft in Beesworth. I've had to rely on Fairfax to save Nemis from the stake." He shot Aioffe a wry look.

"He's family too," Aioffe said and shrugged. "To her, to us. To Hope."

"And that's what worries me," Joshua said. "I'm not sure he knows the meaning of loyalty. Not when he is still so influenced by Henry."

"He'll try his best, surely? And, I think Henry might be Hope's family as well. Somehow," Aioffe said. "So, Nemis first, then we can go home with our heir."

Joshua smiled - she was positively glowing. Motherhood suited her. "Then we can go home with all of our family," he said.

HISTORICAL NOTES

Wyatt's Rebellion

In writing the chapters where Henry Fitzroy accompanies the Duke of Norfolk to the ill-fated encounter in Kent, and his visit to the Tower to see Princess Elizabeth, I have relied upon the diary entries and first hand witness accounts to draw a picture of what occurred and the locations. I find it fascinating, I confess, to read the actual words of Captain Bret and Thomas Wyatt used to incite men to turn against their Queen's direct orders. His speech in this book is only slightly altered to modernise the language for the contemporary reader, and I beg forgiveness for the slight plagiarism in this instance.

Biblical passages

I have cited the Great Bible of 1539, which is largely based on Coverdale's bible translation used at the time.

Whitehall Palace and Kenninghall - great buildings lost to time.

My descriptions of these locations is based upon contemporary research, for sadly, some of these places no longer exist. You can get a sense of them though from re-discovered architects plans, materials lists, and where chroniclers have noted various features or rooms where things took place. One such place is the King's secret study in Whitehall where Henry VIII married Anne Boleyn, in the very palace he built during their long courtship, and where he planned to make his marital home with her. I love the idea that commoners could literally walk under the heart of power on their daily business, as the study (later known as the Jewel House) was in the bridge which crossed above King Street (as it was then, now we call it Whitehall) bisecting the two halves of the palatial grounds.

Lollard's Pit

For the purposes of the storyline I have brought forward the date when Mary ordered the burnings of Protestants in that well known chalk pit in Norwich. 50 people would meet their death here during her reign. Having revised the Heresy laws in 1555, Mary began a campaign of burning people for openly practising Protestantism. In 1557 (not 1554 as I have used), pewterers wife Elizabeth Cooper and Simon Miller, of Kings Lynn, were the first to be executed having interrupted a church service by retracting their earlier recantation of their Protestant faith. It is estimated that 300 people were thus executed - earning Mary the nickname, Bloody Mary.

Useful resources if you would like to learn more:

The Chronicle of Queen Jane and of Two Years of Queen Mary: and especially of the Rebellion of Sir Thomas Wyat. Published by RenaissanceAlive.com.

Houses of Power, by Simon Hurley. Published by Black Swan.

The Lady Elizabeth, by Alison Weir. Published by Arrow Books.

ACKNOWLEDGEMENTS

As always, I owe a debt of gratitude to my family and my wonderful beta readers CM, JC, MW, CF and AM who delight in pointing out plot holes and typos in the most encouraging way. I, and my readers, thank you for your diligence and support.

Dear Reader,

A Polite Request:
I am an independently published author and as such, reviews are critical to successfully reaching new readers. It would mean the world to me if you could leave a review on Amazon or Goodreads about this book so that others can find it!

If you have enjoyed this book, why not visit www.escapeintoatale.com to find out more about Jan Foster and the Naturae Book series?

A Prequel to the Naturae Series - Risking Destiny is available to purchase at
https://www.books2read.com/riskingdestiny

This prequel is also available as a free gift to you if you would like to stay in touch via my monthly newsletter. Sign up at
www.escapeintoatale.com/subscribe

Book 1 – Disrupting Destiny is available to purchase from all good book resellers. Read on for the first two chapters in Aioffe and Joshua's journey. **www.books2read.com/disruptingdestiny**

DISRUPTING DESTINY

Book 1 of the Naturae Series

1427AD - SOUTH WEST ENGLAND

The growing pains were excruciating. Tearing his skin, continually stretching as new cells formed, split and formed again. In his conscious moments his body railed against the constraints of the cocoon, ripples of agony searing through his gangly limbs, straining for release yet finding none. He had no concept of how long he had endured the pain, only that it was ever present, peaking until he could bear it no more.

Gradually, he became more lucid as the pain diminished. In those brief moments, he was aware of light filtering through the thin membrane, and a shadow hovering over it. This time, consciousness arrived and with it, a realisation that the agony had gone. His nails unclenched from his palms, leaving bloody half-moons. Working his hands up past his naked chest to his face, his fingers sought instinctively to remove the source of the suffocation. The shadow darkened, and he heard it say a muffled, "My love..."

The yearning to join the voice, to be free, drove his panic. A guttural sound came from his throat as he clawed frantically at the suffocating veil. With a squelch, his nails snagged a hole and he pulled, straining with his entire being to enlarge it. Taking a huge gasp of breath, he realised that tender hands were smoothing limp membrane away from his face.

"Open your eyes," she said, that gentle yet somehow familiar voice again, as her touch wiped mucus from his nostrils. The panic subsided in him and, for a moment, he was aware only of his heart thumping uncomfortably in his chest, beginning to slow as the breaths came easier. He forced open his eyelids, turning his head in her direction.

Focus blurred before clearing, then began to blink from the light streaming through the window behind the shape.

Part of him expected the pain to return when he moved his limbs, yet instead the joints felt lubricated, smooth. Stretching out, he became aware again of the cool, wet membrane, now slipping from his naked body. Feeling it with his toes and hands, it suddenly revolted him. He instinctively jerked away from it, falling towards her.

His knee hit the earthen floor hard as he fell, and the jolt sent a quick wave of pain through his leg. To his surprise, it wasn't the same kind of agony as he had so recently endured - quite dull by comparison. A pale hand clasped his arm, supporting him as he straightened to look up at her properly.

"My love..." she repeated, and his eyes finally came into focus on her mouth. Small white teeth peeked through smiling red lips, framed by long silver-blonde hair. He knew her... he knew that voice and he recognised her smell. Lavender, witch-hazel and fir - all mingled to provide a scent that was uniquely hers. His arm reached up to touch her face, still not daring to speak, and in one smooth movement, he stood to his full height, instinctively yearning to be nearer. As he breathed in, her arms joined his and they clasped each other. Their eyes locked together, searching for confirmation that their very souls were still intact.

From the edge of his vision, he glimpsed iridescent wings unfurling from behind her. He was mesmerised by the light from the window aperture which shone through them like the finest of stained glass, illuminating and shimmering. He felt his shoulder blades quiver and, turning his head, saw his own newly formed appendages rise up, silvery translucent grey yet with the radiance of hers catching the sunshine. In wonder, she reached out and stroked the edges of his wings; it tickled as rain falling on cold skin.

His senses exploded at her touch and the immediate surroundings rushed at him, overwhelming him. Almost involuntarily, his toes scrunched away from the vibrations of the worms wriggling through the earth beneath his bare feet. The distant call of a lone seagull circling high above briefly deafened, piercing his ears to the point of painful before fading as it glided away. His heart pounded as the volume of the next noise washed over him. As his gaze darted to the window, he frowned, before his drowsy mind identified the ominous rustling sounds - fir trees creaking in the breeze accompanied by the crackle of pine cones flexing to share their seed.

He turned back to her, wide-eyed and seeking reassurance. His newly sharp focus met a gentle, knowing smile and his grip tightened. Opening his mouth to try to speak, all he could taste was the burnt ashes emitting the last of their woody tang, chalky and spent as they lay in the hearth. Instead, he gulped sour air with a tinge of iron lingering on its edges. He swallowed to clear the mustiness from his throat, hoping the other smells and sounds would stop their assault as well.

Drawing in a deep breath, feeling his chest expand without the anticipated stab of pain, he recalled - he'd needed something, anything, to take away the pain from the injury.

The blood. Running his tongue around his mouth with the lingering iron taste, he remembered the blood. But not just his own. Mingling, warm and salty, rich, red. He had absorbed the long history of her Lifeforce, and she his - a much shorter, human life. He jerked away from her gaze; something akin to shame caused him to study the ground beneath him as he searched his foggy mind for clarification.

Her blood held the only promise she could make him at the time, and neither of them had understood the consequences. But, he would have done whatever it took to stay with her.

Then, the change had begun. Numbing his senses as she had bundled him tightly, suffocatingly. Somehow, she must have known he needed to be wrapped - she hadn't mentioned it in their frantic discussion before they shared blood, he was sure. He looked up at her in horror, reeling from the invasion of the memory. Stepping back, his face formed the question before he could speak it.

"I didn't know..." she tailed off, her hand clasping his arm with a wobble in her voice. "I... I'm sorry. I'm sorry for the pain. I've never done this before," she said. "The wings are... unexpected. I thought it would be as it is for animals, you'd just heal. But you were in so much distress, I felt I needed to cocoon you, like a pupae. When I saw the lumps form, I hoped the wrapping would make it easier."

She blinked, but her eyes still pleaded for understanding. Forgiveness even.

Drawing a ragged breath, he took a moment to reply. Should he tell her that it had been unbearable? That he had changed his mind? Was

414

that the truth, or just a remnant of the hurt talking? A childish plea to return to his former self?

He contemplated how best to respond to her unspoken request, searching the depths of her pale eyes as he tried to calm his breathing. The familiarity of her shapes, her colours and scent reassured him. And with that comfort, he remembered he had been enthralled by her. That, from the minute he had unclothed her and revealed the truth of her, there had been no other thought in his mind but to join her. The knot in his ribcage eased as clarity returned. How could he ever have thought to pull away from her when all he wanted to do was be with her? And, if possible, be more like her? Love itself had infused their ribbons of blood, binding their destiny together, for what would now be an eternal lifetime.

He felt a waft of cooler air soothe his neck, rhythmical as a heartbeat. His lips lifted and he felt a rush of unexpected giddiness as he acknowledged her unintended gift. His own wings, beating without effort, as if they had always been there.

He had chosen this. Chosen of his own human free will. He knew what had been done could never be undone.

"No longer Tarl, the smithy's son," he whispered as he stroked her pale face. "Change is upon me." He pulled her closer and searched her luminous blue eyes in wonder and forgiveness.

He did not know, nor could have known, that she had truly changed her own destiny; he only knew the future she now had was with him by her side. "And I, I relinquish Aioffe... She was alone, and now is not," she said, with conviction and hope in her voice.

He had a sense of responsibility for her happiness falling silently from her shoulders onto his, as she took his hand, whispering, "Together, we can be truly free." She tilted her head to one side, eyes flaring as she absorbed the noises outside. "But, we need to go now - before we are discovered!"

CHAPTER 1 – SEPTEMBER 1534

Tendrils of smoke filled the young man's sensitive nostrils with the lingering scent of waxy paper, apples, sea salt and lichen-covered bark, evoking happier memories of the last five years. Tasting the essence of their temporary home as if that would commit it to the past only, he had to subdue the cough tightening his throat. No matter how many times they ran, the thought of starting over again sat on his heart, heavy and full of dread and sorrow. He swallowed down the bitterness, resolving to look to the future. He tried looking up at the clear skies, but the canopy of stars through the array of amber leaves blurred as his eyes welled. Shaking his long blond fringe away, he jabbed at the embers. Bright sparks gracefully leapt into the air and twinkled before vanishing with a quiet pop.

The snap of a branch behind him made him spin around, but his face quickly lifted into a smile as he saw her. Pale in the moonlight, her skin always glowed clearest at night, lighting the shadows with its luminescent tone. She smiled gently at him and held out a slim hand. "Ready?" She said softly.

"Soon," he answered, taking her chilled fingers in his and leading her to the warm log at the fires' edge. In the still, dark forest where they were most comfortable, they sat companionably, slowly pushing in their paper identities nearer the glowing core. The moment of sadness he felt earlier lifted in her company; she was, and always would be, his partner in their long journey to survive. Together they would carve out another future, in another town. It never got any easier, no matter how many times they resettled.

He replayed memories through his minds' eye - the lowered gazes from the once welcoming shop-keepers, a lull in conversation amongst the previously courteous ladies after church when they approached. Then, inevitably, the anger. Always under a veil of suspicion, the striking young couple were ultimately people with no verifiable roots who never truly fitted in.

Often, it started innocently enough with the women noticing a peculiarity about the newcomers - even after years of living in the community. Talking, gossiping about why they weren't quite 'right'. Then the menfolk joined their wives, voicing their anger, their sense of injustice. Before long, something would happen which wasn't 'usual', and, having nothing more than guesswork and gossip to interpret, sometimes the mob mentality would begin. Despite their efforts to lie low, the couple would find themselves hounded out of town, if they missed the warning signs and delayed.

Here, the apples had tasted so juicy, the surroundings so beautiful, they had almost left it too late to move away. Life here had been unexpectedly rich and varied, with its frequent visits from travelling performers and community rituals celebrated with gusto and wine. A temperate southern climate made it harder to resist the temptation to feed from them, especially her - she was trickier to keep sated. The people in this seaside township were generally so happy and full of Lifeforce, it was hard to leave. Some he had counted as friends. Stranger still to have no time to say goodbye or make their excuses for leaving.

The sunlight was just starting to pick through the forests when he heard the voices, faintly at first, then growing closer. Then, the crash of dogs bounding through the drying undergrowth. Picking their way nearer to their hideout, he knew they would have discovered their empty rented house by now and come looking for them in the nearby copse. Maybe even the bodies of the animals they feasted on, desiccated and hastily buried in the dead of night, had been found.

He rubbed her shoulders in his lap, gently whispering, "It's time, my love, we need to go. They are close." She opened her eyes and sat up quickly, blinking in the pinkish light of dawn, her ears suddenly picking up on the sounds as they got closer. The dying embers of the fire would give their location away, and she hurried to pick up the heavy leather sacks she had brought with her earlier.

Without warning, a large, shaggy-looking dog bounded into the clearing. Pulling up and planting its feet wide, it glared at them, judging as it sniffed. Then, it lifted its head and started barking loudly. The clipped yaps ensured that other canines arrived, circling them and noisily declaring their hunting success. Salivating jaws anticipated the reward awaiting them from the men not far behind.

The hounds didn't advance on them, instinct warning them they were not top of the food chain in this instance. But they wouldn't betray their masters and back away. Dark pairs of eyes fixed on the couple, unblinking. Hunter versus hunter. Beast versus beast.

The fae were trapped. He stepped towards one, making to shoo it away, but the dog growled, digging in with its haunches and baring yellowed teeth in a snarl. Fetid breath puffed in the crisp dawn light, surrounding them with a foul-stenched net.

"We will be seen if we leave from here," she murmured, barely audible to most ears over the noise of the barks and snarls. She hurriedly fixed straps behind her, the bag altering her slim silhouette, making her look strangely unbalanced with a protruding pot-belly where it hung.

"Probably, but it's a risk I think we need to take," he said. "I'm willing if you are?" Despite his long cloak, now draped over his chest, he also appeared cumbersome with his front-strapped sack on.

"Over 'ere!" Shouts, sounding close, followed by dull snapping branches as boots crashed their path through the undergrowth.

She nodded and pulled the bonnet from her head to free her hair. Shimmering wings unfurled, the morning light bouncing off them as it streamed through the tree leaves. "Straight up!" he said as he bent his knees to lift off, his darker wings already freed and waving slowly.

They shot up through the canopy and into the bright sunlight. Shrinking below, the fields were dotted with sheep and horses, mottled green and brown hedgerows marking their boundaries. Small thatched dwellings laid low to the ground, their stone chimneys spouting thin wisps of smoke as early morning fires were stoked. Higher they flew, out of the range of the voices shouting, cussing as the enraged and frightened humans found the still-warm ashes of the fire. Higher, to where the birds circled, swirling in formation around them.

Looking up through the trees, one of the men saw their odd-shaped silhouettes, out of reach of arrows, disappearing into the clouds. Shaking his head, the notion that he had witnessed something not of his world was forced from his mind. It did no good to stir up further talk of the devil amongst them. A man would only have to spend yet more time in the confessional and at prayer if he had seen anything sinister, after all. Best not to mention it.

"Who shall you be today, my love?" she called over the clouds. "I like the name Joshua!" He smiled and shook his head, grinning at her. "You like Joshua because you liked the boy, not because you like the name, I think."

"He had the sweetest tasting Lifeforce I have had in a long time," she said, remembering, "but I nearly got carried away. I caused this relocation, and for that, I'm sorry."

"You are insatiable, in more ways than one," he called back, moving closer to grasp her hand mid-air. They slowed, joined hands, then fluttered to face each other. In the brilliant sunlight, they gazed at each other, searching, studying and reconnecting. Together they hovered, hands clasped around the bulky sacks filled with their only belongings, two halves of a lumpy, bejewelled butterfly. In the unfiltered light, high above the clouds, their love glowed through in its intensity. It would be absurd to think that they had ever blended in - no human would have mistaken them for mortals were they to glimpse them now. Fair skin, ash-white hair almost translucent as the sunshine poured through it, and wings rippled with rainbow tones, fluttering as they lingered in the moment.

"I can't promise more boys like him," he said, looking at her lips as he leaned in for a kiss. "And we must try to blend in more next town, and not risk losing control with a human, however much we become lost in their energy. We can survive without them, you know!" He reproached, but still with love in his tone. "We could have stayed longer if only we had been more careful. I think the lad will recover with some rest. The young usually do, then attribute their lack of get up and go to overdoing it, or some sort of malady."

She smiled and nodded, but nevertheless felt remorseful. Her need for sustenance from the unseen joy humans emitted was compulsive, necessary even. The Lifeforce fae-kind gained from its root source in blood was enough for him, but satisfying her needs was more dangerous and required crowds of people. Keeping control of herself during these times was always a challenge. A moment or two longer in her thrall, and it would have been too late for that poor boy. She sometimes forgot herself in those heady inhalations, but had so far never broken her own rule of not killing a child in the heat of the inhale. But youth, they were so free, so deliciously innocent. Their Lifeforce had no filter and its purity was sublime.

"I just want to build a home with you, where we can live in peace. I don't think that's too much to ask?" Joshua's begging broke through her guilt-laden reminiscing.

She pulled back from the embrace and stroked his face, feeling the boyish stubble along his jawline. "I know, I wish for that also," she said wistfully. "Maybe this next time..."

"You always say that..."

"I know."

"Never satisfied," he teased.

He flapped his dark wings and spun her around and around. She leaned her head back and relaxed, allowing him to take the lead in a dizzying spin. They both laughed at the release of the exhilarating action. As he slowed, he lowered his face to embrace her again.

"My head!" she said, breaking off the kiss. "It's still spinny... if this is what death feels like, I could die right now, happy. It's like a little death."

"Believe me, this is not what dying feels like," he said, nuzzling her ear. "I could remind you what a 'little death' feels like if you want though?"

Her grin broadened, "You'll have to catch me first!" She darted upwards, playing. Like dancing dragonflies, they dashed around the skies, giggling and whirling.

"I won't lose you again, minx!" He caught her slender ankle, "I will follow you, find you, hound you down like we are hunted now, even if there were an arrow still jutting from my side!" He paused, hovering up to look her fully in the face earnestly.

Stroking away loose strands of hair from his cheeks, she whispered, "Never, I'll never truly run from you. Nothing will ever part us." They embraced again, and he gave her bottom a squeeze through her skirts. Squealing in mock outrage, she pushed away from him and dashed off. He followed, of course, and they continued their journey north together.

*****

They slowed after a few hours and dipped down through the cloud blanket, to where it was raining and grey. Flying lower, yet still out of sight, they scanned the ground with hawk-like eyesight for a group of houses - a town, not just a village. The occasional straight Roman road cut gash-like through the landscape. He pointed northeast, and together they gracefully swung around and headed for a small wooded area they noticed, close to a sizable cluster of dwellings. Rough tracks weaving their brown trails around the countryside meandered through fields less enclosed by hedges than they had been in the south. Through the drizzle, the patchwork of leaves turning golden amber enticed them for the cover it could afford.

They landed by the side of the woods and pushed aside undergrowth to enter the forest. Hidden by branches, the couple dropped their packs and loosened their garments, secreting their wings close to skin. Helping each other, they straightened their attire, pushed hair back into caps and tucked smock edges neatly into jerkin and kirtle. A last check before hoisting their belongings onto their backs, a brief kiss for luck, and their windy and unusual travel method was obscured.

Returning to the muddy track, they picked their way through the puddles left by carts and carriages, and headed towards a cluster of buildings ahead.

"How about Annabella? For me. Mistress Annabella Meadows," she said, as they approached an inn nestled on the crossroads of the road into town.

"I'm flattered you remember my little treats," he said, glancing down and smiling at her. "And a fitting way to honour her charms. I plan to demonstrate how stimulating I found her Lifeforce, just as soon as we find our next abode." Giggling, they pushed open the faded oak door and entered, hoping to buy a room for the night where they could rest. It was getting dark, and experience had taught them it was best to view a new possible home in daylight. The smell of damp leather and stale ale assaulted their noses as they crossed the threshold, but there was comfort in the humanity within and a warm hearth.

THE NATURAE SERIES

RISKING DESTINY

Order your copy now www.books2read.com/riskingdestiny

DISRUPTING DESTINY

Order your copy now at www.books2read.com/disruptingdestiny

ANARCHIC DESTINY

Order your copy now at www.books2read.com/anarchicdestiny